THE AETHER CHRONICLES

REBELLIUM

AJ WOLFE

Pluviam Press

To my family and the warrior, Nataliya.
And to those at The Heart.

"It's said that when we die, the four elements—earth, air, fire and water— dissolve one by one, each into the other, and finally just dissolve into space. But while we're living, we share the energy that makes everything, from a blade of grass to an elephant, grow and live and then inevitably wear out and die. This energy, this life force, creates the whole world."

—Pema Chödrön

VALG
THE ICELANDS
THE VAESIRIAN ISLES
THE VAESIRIAN RUINS
BROSA TERRITORY
EITRI CATHEDRAL RUINS
THE ELDINGAR LINE
THE DARK PLAINS
VINDUR TERRITORY
RUINED LANDS
THE SECTORS
1   2   3   4
REBELS' CAMP
ARAEDIA
North
THE AETHERIAN ISLES
THE AETHERIAN RUINS

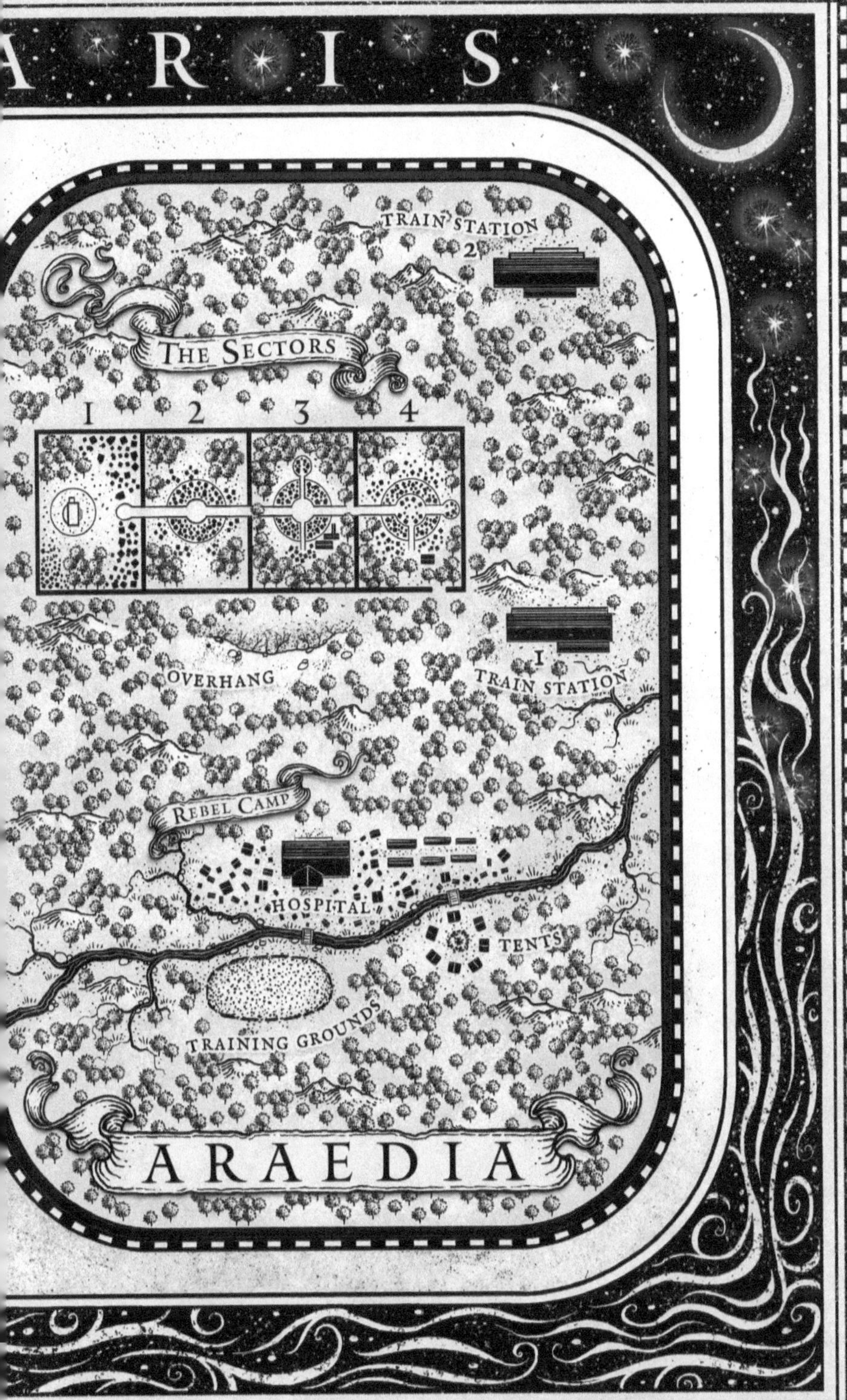

A R I S
TRAIN STATION
2
THE SECTORS
1   2   3   4
OVERHANG
TRAIN STATION
1
REBEL CAMP
HOSPITAL
TENTS
TRAINING GROUNDS
A R A E D I A

CHAPTER ONE

RUN

"You're not sorry."

Natalia smiled as she studied the old woman in front of her. Her tan face was wrinkled, and her hair was as white as freshly fallen snow through the dim lighting of the dining hall. There was a mischievous gleam in her green eyes. She was right. Natalia wasn't sorry, but she loved asking the woman so many questions.

"If you don't hush up..." Vale threw Natalia a conspirator's grin before elbowing her playfully. "...we'll never finish the story."

"All right, all right," Natalia said, holding her hands up in mock innocence. "I promise I won't interrupt any more. Continue the lesson, *please*!"

The old woman shook her head, but Natalia didn't miss how the corners of her wrinkled mouth twitched up. Natalia leaned against the back of the wooden bench in the dining hall of the orphanage that sat on the outskirts of Sector Four. The hall was large and empty, and several long tables—identical to the one their company now occupied—were scattered throughout the room. Seven people gathered at their table. The old woman taught from the head as she always did while Vale and Natalia listened from the bench running down the length of the wood. One of the orphanage's cooks and three fellow orphans sat along the bench opposite them.

Vale Ashlocke, her sixteen-year-old brother in everything but blood, sat to her left, his hands behind his messy, pitch-black hair. He was three years Natalia's senior, and they could easily pass for siblings, regardless of their unknown parentage. In fact, most of the time, Natalia and Vale didn't even bother explaining to others that they weren't related. They were always together, and both had black hair and fair skin. They both had blue eyes, too, though Vale's were darker than the deepest ocean while Natalia's were a blue-gray.

To Natalia, Vale was the whole world. From as far back as she could remember, he'd been there, taking care of her. He'd been the one to teach her how to tie her shoes—to throw a punch without breaking her thumb. He'd taught her how to survive on the dirty streets and alleyways of Sector Four. Vale had even learned how to braid hair from one of the older girls in the orphanage, so he could teach Natalia how to do it. He was her guiding light—the only constant that kept her anchored to the world around them.

"Last week," the woman said softly as she glanced out one of the many windows in the dining hall. Rain pounded against the glass, and lightning shattered across the night sky. "We talked about the construction of the walls surrounding the four sectors of Araedia. This week, I will teach you more of our forbidden history, and I will teach you the prophecy of the ultimate Elemental."

Vale turned to Natalia and wiggled his brows. She grinned. *Elementals.* Natalia was infatuated with every history lesson the woman taught, but her lessons on the Elementals were fascinating. They never failed to bring her to the edge of her seat. Unfortunately, the old woman's knowledge only went so far, and that was because of the president of the four sectors, Vayne Averie. President Vayne had been a common, displeasurable topic in their lessons over the past few weeks. Natalia recalled the day she and Vale had stumbled into her first lesson in one of the back alleys of Sector Four. She had been speaking to two children before their mother had anxiously called them away. Overhearing their conversation, Vale had asked her to continue, and she had. The colorful words the woman had cursed Vayne with had been music to her and Vale's ears. After that, Vale had practically begged the woman to teach her lessons once a week at the orphanage to whoever was brave enough to listen.

Not only had President Vayne destroyed all of Araedia's history and declared speaking of it and Elementals a crime punishable by death, but the old, cruel brute had been the cause of the walls that had separated the sectors from each other and the outside world for *decades.* The danger of the lessons and conversations they had in this hall was insurmountable. Everyone at the table had been sworn to secrecy. They couldn't let the guards find out what they were doing—or even worse, the matron of the orphanage.

The old woman turned to Vale. "Why don't you remind us what the four elements are, Vale."

"Air, water, earth, and fire," he said, wiggling his dark brows at Natalia. She giggled. Whenever they'd played when they were younger, Natalia and Vale had always imagined themselves as Elementals. Vale had always been an earth Elemental, and she had always been a water Elemental.

"Yes, and Elementals possess the ability to wield one of the four elements. Does anyone know why our *president...*" She spat the title. "...subjects all our children to testings at the ages of fourteen, sixteen, and eighteen?"

"It's rumored he's looking for Elementals within the sectors," the orphanage cook, a stout older woman with graying brown hair, answered.

"He's not looking for just *any* Elemental." The old woman's voice grew quiet. "He's looking for the ultimate Elemental who can wield all four elements. Vayne is looking for *the Aether...* Are any of you familiar with the term?"

"I heard a drunk man use it once." Natalia shrugged. "I never knew what it was until now, though. I always thought of it as some old legend."

Natalia had heard the term other times too—when the matron of the orphanage tripped over a wooden toy and shouted *By the Aether!*, and when some kids were whispering about the legend behind their hands. She'd always thought it was just a myth, another old legend to give false hope to an oppressed people.

The old woman chuckled. "Oh, no, darling. The Aether is very real. The prophecy states that the Aether will be born in one of the four sectors of Araedia, and they will be the one to save us. Vayne searches by testing the blood of all our children. That's why you have to attend those pesky mandatory testings."

"Is that why some don't come back from the testings?" Vale asked. "Is it because they're Elementals?"

Natalia's face blanched. Every two months, children of the proper ages were chosen to be tested. Vale's second testing would be in two weeks... She remembered the tremors of fear that had wracked her body when his name had been announced over the projector that every household was forced to keep—no matter how rich or poor—at the age of fourteen. She hadn't been able to sit down until he'd returned safe and sound. Every time she'd asked him what had transpired at the testing center, Vale would simply scratch his head and claim he didn't remember much. A huge, armored truck had transported him to the testing center, some guards had asked him a few questions, he'd filled out some paperwork about his life, had a little bit of blood drawn and run through a machine, then he'd simply been returned to the orphanage. It was the same story that every other returning participant repeated; however, it didn't stop the looming terror that filled the sectors during the testings.

"It's my belief that, yes, if Vayne tests a child and the test is positive, they are taken to a lab out beyond the walls and brainwashed and trained for his army," the woman answered.

"Why are there multiple tests at different ages?" an older, red-haired boy with freckles questioned from across the bench. He fiddled with his pale fingers nervously.

"The Elemental gene is different with everyone who possesses it, but if it's carried, it usually makes its appearance during those years before adulthood."

The boy nodded as Vale leaned forward. "How common is the gene?"

"When was the last time you heard of a child not returning from the testings?" the woman asked.

"I don't remember." Vale shook his head. "It doesn't happen that often."

She smiled. "There is your answer."

Natalia found herself staring out into the stormy night. She couldn't see the towering, thirty-foot concrete walls that surrounded the sectors through the dark, but she knew they were there. To her dismay, they always were. Yet again, Natalia wished she could see the world beyond them and escape the prison that was her life. She wished those outside the walls—the rebels, oh, how she adored them—would come and tear them down for good. She'd never forget the first time she'd heard whispers of the rebels. Natalia and Vale had been scouring the alleyways for food when they'd overheard several adults murmuring that the rebels, who were rumored to have been formed by those who'd escaped the testings after positive tests, were attempting to sneak over the walls and spread their desperate want for a rebellion against Vayne. Natalia had thought the rumors were too good to be true, but then Vayne had positioned guards atop the walls in Four...

Ever since then, Natalia had tried and tried to convince Vale to find a way to escape the walls so that they could find the rebels and join them and their cause out in the woods of Araedia. They could fight against Vayne together and end their people's oppression.

Natalia tore her eyes from the window to find the old woman staring at her.

"Speak your mind, young one," she said.

Natalia bit the inside of her cheek and glanced at Vale. He merely nodded encouragingly. She faced the old woman once more. "The sectors can't be the only civilization with Elementals...Where are the others?"

"Like the rebels, the other civilizations and Elementals lie beyond the walls. Some Araedians will tell you I'm just a crazy old hag filling your head with nonsense, but those who say such are scared, young one. They allow Vayne to hide the truth from them. They convince themselves that the other civilizations have been destroyed as he says, but they have not." She lifted her hand to her heart. "Never let them take your curiosity—your desire to learn and your ability to think for yourself. It's what makes you strong. It's what makes you *brave*. You must always fight for it. *Protect it.*"

Natalia turned to Vale. He flashed her a warm smile. It was an echo of the woman's words—of the promise they'd made to each other years ago. They would *always* protect each other. They'd protect each other until their dying breaths.

The red-haired boy lifted his head. "Tell us more—"

The wooden door to the dining hall shattered apart with an ear-piercing *crash*. Splinters of wood and sparks of electricity rained through the air as soldiers from Vayne's army clad in the darkest black armor piled into the room. In their gloved hands sat guns and spears of crackling blue-purple electricity. Sparks glittered up and down the spears, reflecting against the soldiers' smothering black helmets. There were dozens of them.

For a few moments, the entire world seemed to still. Natalia could hear her thunderous heart pounding rapidly in her ears. She wondered if the others could hear it too. She slowly turned to Vale, who now stood in front of her. Natalia didn't even remember standing herself. She then glanced at her companions around the table. The Aether save them. They'd all be killed for this. Natalia's eyes locked with the old woman's. They weren't filled with fear as Natalia had expected. In fact, they seemed to glow with energy as the woman whispered one word: *Run.*

Within seconds, Natalia and Vale were through the side door of the dining hall and sprinting through the pelting rain. The tall grass clawed at their legs as they ran. Behind them, shouting and bolts of electricity from the soldiers and their guns filled the air. Lights flicked on in the second-story windows of the orphanage, illuminating the two large shadows and three tiny ones fleeing through the side door. Dozens of bulky, armored shadows followed after them. Natalia looked over her shoulder to watch as a bolt of electricity fired from a gun and collided with one of the tiny shadows. A horrid, gut-wrenching scream filled the air. Vale's hand immediately found hers, pulling her farther—faster.

"Don't look, Talia!" he screamed over the howling wind and rain lashing at their faces. They neared the dirt road that connected the heart of Sector Four to the lonely clusters of one-roomed wooden shacks surrounding the outskirts. "Just keep running!"

"But Vale!" Natalia exclaimed, throwing one last look behind them. The dozens of shadows had split in two, the majority following the five—now four—fleeing from the orphanage. The other half of the soldiers, which had to be twelve at least, raced after Natalia and Vale. "The soldiers! They're following us!"

"I know!" Vale's voice broke. "Just run!"

The rain stung Natalia's skin as she pumped her arms and legs as fast as she could. The sharp air that filled her aching lungs was blindingly painful, and vicious thunder shook the earth beneath them. No matter what, she had to keep running. Even though all she felt was fear and adrenaline spreading through her veins, *she had to keep running.*

The cluster of wooden houses and shops that made up the heart of Four quickly faded behind them, and they soon found themselves sprinting between the small clusters of shacks that fanned out across the rest of the sector. The soldiers continued to race after them, and the dirt path disappeared beneath their feet. Still, Natalia and Vale ran. They ran through one of the many forests that spread over the rolling hills of the sector, not once looking back. Natalia squinted through the rain and the break in the trees ahead to see one of the towering walls looming before them. What was Vale doing? Once they reached the wall, they'd have nowhere to go—nowhere to hide. Natalia didn't even know if she could make it to the wall.

"Just a little farther, Talia!" Vale called as they burst through the tree line, the world opening up to rolling hills and tall grass again. They passed an old, abandoned shack before disappearing down a large slope leading to the base of the wall. Soldiers' shouts echoed after them.

Vale came to a halt before a large tree at the foot of the wall and let go of Natalia's hand. She simply stood there, watching as he hurriedly circled the tree. Lights flashed across the shack atop the slope as the soldiers' shadowed forms peeked inside the shattered windows. This was it. There was nowhere left to run. This was where they'd die. Fear rooted Natalia to the spot. She couldn't protect Vale, and he couldn't protect her. Tonight, they would die, but at least they would die together. Natalia was thankful for the years she'd had with her older brother. She wouldn't have traded them for the world... But it didn't stop her from wishing that they'd had more.

Suddenly, Vale knelt before her, grabbing her shoulders. His dark blue eyes were wide and full of panic, surely mirroring her own. "You have to listen to me, Talia, okay?"

Natalia nodded, covering his hands with hers. She squeezed them tight.

"I'm going to ask you to do something for me, and no matter what happens, you have to do what I say." He stood, leading her over to a cluster of roots sticking out of the ground near the wall. Natalia's brows rose. Parts of the roots—no, the tree—had grown into the wall... He shoved her toward the roots. "Talia, you have to crawl.

Crawl in as far as you can, and no matter what, do *not* come out until you know for a fact that the soldiers are gone. Don't turn back."

Behind them, the soldiers' shouts grew louder. They'd finally crested the slope.

Natalia whirled around to face her brother. "What about you?"

He smiled his conspirator's grin, but it didn't quite reach his eyes. "I'm right behind you." He ruffled her wet hair. "I'm always right behind you... You'll never be alone, I promise... Now crawl."

So, she did. Natalia crawled under the uprooted stem into the mud and darkness. The mix of mud and rain was freezing, and she had to clamp her teeth together to keep them from chattering. She continued to pull herself forward as the sound of shouts and armored feet rushing down the sloping hill filled the air. The rain began to fall even harder, and thunder boomed, drowning out all sound. Natalia reached out her hand and paused as it met with cool concrete. She'd reached the wall. She went to drag her hand across the rough cement but nearly face-planted into the mud as her fingers met the cool night's air. Her brows narrowed in confusion. Natalia slid forward a few more feet and found herself encased between two slabs of concrete.

No. It was impossible. She kept crawling, and a few pulls of her arms later, rain began to pound against her body once more. Natalia lifted her head to the night sky—to the opposite side of the wall and the forest that waited beyond. There was a crack in the wall. And she'd crawled through it. Her heart beat rapidly in her chest. Natalia shook her head, trying to calm her thoughts and racing pulse. She needed to get out of the way for Vale.

Natalia pulled herself forward one last time before clearing the wall entirely and pushing herself off the ground. She turned and waited, staring into the darkness of the crack. Several long seconds passed.

"Vale?" she whispered, kneeling in the grass. "Vale, come on."

Maybe he couldn't hear her over the rain... Or maybe he was waiting to make sure the soldiers hadn't seen them and followed. She could crawl back in and see, but the space was too narrow for her to turn around in after she'd found him. She'd have to crawl out backward, which would take a while, and what if the soldiers had called the wall patrol to search from above? What if they were too slow to get out from under the wall because of her, and they were caught? Natalia jumped as lightning struck nearby, causing the earth to shake.

She'd wait for Vale in the tree line. If any soldiers passed overhead, they wouldn't be able to see them. It'd give Vale all the room he needed to make sure they weren't followed, and he could make a quick escape. It was perfect. Natalia turned and darted for the trees and brush.

She looked around, unable to believe what she was seeing. She was outside the wall. Natalia grinned through the rain as she knelt beside the large trunk of a tree, hidden from sight. Once Vale got out, they could search the forest for the rebels and join them. They'd be safe from Vayne's wrath, and they could finally fight back for their freedom—for all of Araedia's freedom.

Any minute now. Vale would be out any minute...

Natalia leaned her head against the tree trunk, her wet hair catching on the rough bark. Rain trickled down her face while she waited. The minute turned to minutes, and the minutes turned to an hour...

But Vale never came out.

CHAPTER TWO

BEYOND THE WALLS

Morning sunlight peeked through the canopy of branches above, and dew clung to Natalia's clothes, hair, and skin as her eyes fluttered open. She sat up, rubbing the sleep from her eyes and inadvertently smearing dirt across her face. She glanced around to find nothing but the vibrant green forest and the towering walls of Sector Four through the tree line. Wind wound through the trees, rustling the leaves and causing her to shiver. Her clothes and hair were still damp from the dew and rain. The events of last night flashed and replayed through her mind. Vale never came out, and she was alone now. Natalia couldn't stop the tears from welling in her eyes.

You'll never be alone... His words echoed through her head.

He'd broken the very first promise he'd ever made to her—the same promise she'd made to him when they'd decided they were in this life together.

Suddenly, voices filled the air, shouting back and forth to each other. Natalia jumped up and crouched behind a large tree trunk, breathing rapidly. She peeked around the side and through the high tree branches to look up at the top of the wall. Her eyes widened at the sight of half a dozen soldiers clad in solid black walking the edges. They were searching for something... Or *someone*. Had Vale somehow evaded capture? Did they know she'd escaped beyond the wall? She bit the inside of her cheek. She couldn't go back to search for him now. There were too many guards, and they'd easily spot her trying to slip back through the crack in the wall. She'd have to wait until the soldiers left or the sky fell dark.

Additional voices filled the air, and Natalia looked to the right to find another six guards walking out to meet the others. Fear spread through her veins like a ravenous poison. She sprung to her feet and turned, sprinting deeper into the forest and away from the vulnerable tree line. She couldn't wait for Vale any longer. Bushes and branches tore at her skin and clothes as she ran, leaving behind small scrapes and tiny trickles of blood. Natalia batted at them uselessly, trampling through the brush.

A second set of footfalls crashed after her, and she felt her heart speed up. Had the soldiers seen or heard her? How had they gotten off the wall so quickly? Natalia pumped her arms harder, drove her legs into the ground faster. She *had* to outrun them. If they caught her, she'd be put to death or worse... Taken into Vayne's custody. She would not let them catch her. She refused. Vale had sacrificed himself so that she could be safe, and she wouldn't just throw his sacrifice away. But she was alone and running. Again. How long would she last by herself? Could she survive outside the walls long enough to find the rebels? She didn't even know where to begin to search for them... But she had to keep running. What other choice did she have?

Natalia veered to her right, leaping over a fallen, rotting log and ascending the gradual slope that had begun to take over the ground. The footfalls grew louder and louder. She risked a glance back over her shoulder. Nothing. There was nothing. No soldiers, no—

Natalia huffed as the air was knocked from her lungs, and the sound of skin and bones colliding filled the forest. She slammed against the forest floor, viciously rolling through the last few feet of brush into a clearing. She clutched at her stomach with a wince, desperately gasping to try and reclaim the breath that had been stolen from her lungs. Tears welled in her eyes once more, and for a moment, she was completely lost in the pain. But hearing someone else gasp and pant dragged her out of it, and Natalia lifted her head to meet a set of angry, hazel eyes and dark narrowed eyebrows. A boy, who appeared to be around her age, scowled at her, strands of his messy, dark-brown hair falling over his forehead.

Natalia and the boy popped up from the ground, facing each other like wild animals trapped in a cage. She scanned him with a frown. He wore all brown—the mandatory color assigned to citizens of Sector Three. She watched as he scanned her mandatory gray clothes in return. Each of the four sectors had their assigned colors. Sector One's citizens wore white, while those from Two wore beiges and creams. How had this boy from Sector Three ended up outside the walls?

"Who are you?" Natalia asked, adrenaline pumping through her veins.

The boy's scowl deepened. "Why should I tell you?"

"Because you just clobbered me!"

"*I clobbered you?*" The boy scoffed. "By the Aether, is everyone from Four as stupid as you? You ran into me!"

"What?" Natalia exclaimed, anger rising. Who did this boy think he was? She eyed him up and down once more. He was a few inches taller than her, but she was stronger. His arms and legs were too skinny—almost as if he were on the verge of being malnourished—causing his clothes to hang loosely.

He rolled his eyes. "Clearly you can't hear either."

Every emotion Natalia had felt within the last six hours came crashing to the surface, overwhelming her with a consuming wave of fury. Enraged, she launched forward, tackling the boy to the ground. He grunted as they hit and rolled several feet further into the clearing. Natalia gripped his arms, trying to pin him down, but the boy bucked up and they rolled once more. Suddenly, he flipped over on top of her. Natalia immediately tucked her knees to her chest before sending them up and kicking him in the stomach. He flew backward, rolling to a wobbly stop as she rose. Natalia's eyes widened at the sudden drop behind him. She had been too distracted to notice before, but the clearing led into an overhang with a daunting—possibly lethal—drop. The boy had no idea of the lack of land behind him as he took a half step back to steady himself.

Natalia cried out in panic and lunged toward him, barely grabbing his hand as he tipped backward. She tightened her grip and threw herself back, tugging him with her. They collapsed on solid ground a few feet from the edge of the overhang. Natalia lifted her head to meet his hazel eyes, which were full of fear and adrenaline, surely matching her own. They both panted hard, merely staring at each other in shock.

And then Natalia laughed, a grin lighting her face as the wind blew her hair to the side. If only Vale could see her now. He would've been livid at her for being so careless and... Well, *stupid.* But in a way, the boy reminded her of Vale—a very angry Vale—because of the way the air around him stilled as if the entire earth was revolving around him. He captured everyone and everything's attention, ensnaring them in an aura of curiosity and... Just the right amount of recklessness. Natalia rose and extended her hand to him.

"My name's Natalia Rhys."

He took her hand with a smirk, and she helped him to his feet. "Damien Mendax."

"How'd you end up out here?" she asked, studying him closely as he dusted off his brown pants and ran a hand through his hair.

"I met this old woman in my sector...," Damien said, meeting her gaze with furrowed brows. He shrugged. "At first I thought she was just crazy, but then she started talking about rebels, the walls, Elementals, and—"

"The Aether," Natalia breathed.

Damien nodded. "Yeah."

"An old woman told me the same thing...," she muttered. "What did she look like?"

"Wrinkles, white hair... Green eyes, I think." Damien frowned "Yeah, they were green."

Natalia shook her head. It wasn't possible. Vayne didn't allow travel or any form of communication between the sectors. They were all confined to their own mini civilizations and ruled by him. Any attempt at outside communication was considered an act of treason and was punishable by death.

"Did she tell you her name?" Natalia questioned eagerly.

"No, but by the look on your face, I'm guessing you know exactly who I'm talking about."

"But it's not possible! There's no way that—"

"That the same old woman told both of us the exact same story and prophecy?" He smirked. "Sounds pretty possible to me."

Natalia rolled her eyes before shaking her head. Only then, did her eyes catch the scenery around them, which she'd previously neglected. She turned in a slow circle, her breath catching in her throat.

"What are you...?" Damien's brows rose as he, too, turned. "*Oh...*"

The clearing they stood in was fairly large and full of tall grass and scattered patches of wildflowers that waved in the wind. The trees guarding the edge stood tall with large branches and tons of swaying leaves, and the overhang... She could see for miles at the crest of the overhang. The rolling hills and forest seemed to stretch on forever, an endless sea of vibrant green. Natalia spun around toward the sectors, and her jaw dropped. Her eyelids fluttered, attempting to blink away the mixture of awe and fear coursing through her. She could see all four of the sectors, and her imaginings of them hadn't done them any justice. They were terrifyingly beautiful. Furthest to her left was the luxurious Sector One, home to President Vayne Averie, the majority of his army, and the citizens lucky enough to be born there. They could actually afford three meals a day *and dessert.* The population of One amounted to over three thousand—the largest of all the sectors. Natalia huffed in amazement. She could see up to the tops of some of the city's stark-white buildings and even a few tall trees within the walls.

Sector Two sat to the right of One. Nothing was visible within its plain concrete walls. Two shared the same population as Three, which was over two thousand. Those in Two had enough to buy food for every day, but they were nowhere near as wealthy as Sector One. The top of Three, however, was teeming with treetops. They stretched as far as Natalia could see. She glanced at Damien, who stared at the sectors in awe beside her. She wondered what his home was like. Was it true that Sector Three was like Sector Four? That they couldn't always afford to buy food for their families either?

Finally, Natalia's eyes wandered to Four, and a hole seemed to dig deep down into her heart. She loved the landscape of her sector—the thousands of trees and rolling hills—but without Vale... Everything in it looked lonely... Four was the poorest and least populated sector, barely amounting to 1,800. Vale had always seen that as a good thing. According to him, it kept Vayne and the bulk of his soldiers from influencing their people too heavily. If rebellion were ever to start in one of the four sectors of Araedia, it'd be Four. They'd be crushed immediately, but... Her mouth snapped shut to form a thin line. She feared the rebels would never be able to spread their rebellion within the walls. Because no matter how hard they tried, regardless of the status and financial differences, there *was* one thing each of the four sectors had in common. They all bowed and obeyed the orders of their oppressive president.

"I've always wondered what the other sectors looked like...," Damien whispered.

"Me, too." Natalia glanced at him, finding his eyes still transfixed on the towering walls. "How long have you been coming out here? How'd you escape the walls?"

Damien faced her. "I first came out a few days ago. My family was starving, and I couldn't afford any food in Three's market." He took a deep breath, turning to gaze out over the hills and forest that stretched beneath the overhang. "I met the old woman in an alley on my way back to my house after work. She told me about a world beyond the walls, rebels, a prophecy... I never really bought into what she was saying, because how could I know if it was true or not? But I knew the rebels were real, and if they could survive out here, then that meant there was food... As you can see, Three is covered in trees, so I picked the tallest one near the walls, climbed it, and jumped across."

"You sound like a squirrel," Natalia said with a small laugh.

Damien's lips formed a thin line, but she could see the humor shining in his eyes. The hole in her heart dug a little deeper. Yes, he was indeed like a very angry Vale.

"What about you?" he asked.

Natalia felt her chest tighten as she told Damien about meeting the old woman and how Vayne's soldiers invaded the orphanage. "Vale and I managed to get to the wall. He found this hole under this tree, and..." Natalia choked back the tears filling her eyes. "..he said he'd be right behind me, but he never followed me out. I fell asleep waiting for him and awoke to guards atop the walls, so I ran. And then...I found you."

"Do you think your brother's dead?"

Natalia bit the inside of her cheek, wiping at the tear that had escaped from the corner of her eye. No, Vale wasn't dead... Right? He was just captured, and when night fell and she could sneak back into Four, she'd look for him. He wasn't dead.

"He can't be." Natalia shook her head. "He's alive, I know he is."

A small smile of pity lifted Damien's lips as if he thought she was lying to herself. "For what it's worth," he said, meeting her gaze, "I'm sorry."

"I am, too," she whispered.

Silence enveloped the clearing, and for a few long moments, they simply stared out over the landscape together. There was no sign of the rebels within sight. How far away were they? Would she be able to find them if she tried? Without Vale... She wouldn't last long. And no matter how brave Natalia wanted to be, she couldn't help the fear that wormed its way into her heart. She couldn't leave. Not yet... Not without Vale.

"What will you do now?" Damien questioned. Natalia could feel his stare boring into the side of her face, but she kept her head straight.

"I'm going to go home and look for my brother. If I can't find him... Then I want to try to find the rebels, but I'll die if I leave by myself." She finally faced him. "What about you? Will you come back here?"

"Probably." Damien smirked with a shrug. "I wouldn't mind doing some rebel searching of my own. I hear they have good food, but who knows? Maybe you and I could help each other out—get stronger together, so that when we find them, we'll be useful."

Warmth spread throughout Natalia's chest as she nodded with a smile. A friend. She'd made a friend, and he was willing to help her search for the rebels and train. And if she failed in finding Vale, maybe that hole in her chest wouldn't feel so empty after a while... Maybe Damien could help her fill it. But she had to admit that no matter how brave she wanted to be, she wasn't brave enough to leave just yet. Not alone.

"Meet me here tomorrow at noon?" she asked.

A small smile lifted the corners of Damien's lips. "Tomorrow at noon."

CHAPTER THREE

A NEW FAMILY

The summer day was hot. Sweat dripped from Damien's forehead and sawdust itched at his skin as he threw a log of wood across his shoulders and began to walk through the dense forest within the walls of Sector Three. Several men and women accompanied him, logs across their backs and shoulders as well. Together, they all trudged through the brush and trees. Damien could see Vayne's soldiers' large, black armored trucks through the tree line in the distance, looming like vultures to take them back to the heart of Three. Every day, Vayne's soldiers supervised their work at the mills.

The sound of a whip cracking and connecting against skin a few yards behind him set his blood ablaze with anger. He cursed Vayne, his mother, the old woman who'd told him to escape, the rebels, Sector Three—hell, he cursed all of Araedia. How could the civilians of his sector be content to live under this oppression? How could *anyone* be content to live like this? However, there was one person he didn't curse—one person who, like him, wasn't content. Damien's mind wandered to her... Natalia... She was fascinating and intriguing, and unlike everyone else, she wasn't going to give up. She wasn't going to give up on her brother, the rebels, herself... Maybe she wouldn't give up on him, either. Everyone had given up on him except for his father.

A throb of pain shot throughout Damien's chest. His father... Damien glanced to his right where his father had always walked beside him, two logs strung across his broad shoulders. But he wasn't there now, and he'd never be there again because he was dead.

Damien gritted his teeth, shifting the log on his burning shoulders. His father would've liked Natalia. He would've told Damien that he'd finally found a true friend—a friend who would stay. Damien had to bite his tongue to keep from scoffing, turning back in the direction of the trucks they trudged toward. No one had ever done anything as selfless as staying for *him*. Not since his father's death. His father had stayed regardless of the fact that he'd known he'd lose his life if he did. After all, it hadn't been his father who'd stolen the bread...

"Hurry up!" a tall guard with a deep voice snapped angrily, marching through the tree line to snarl in Damien's face. "You know the drill! Load the logs in the back!"

Damien met the man's glare with a scowl and glanced between him and the break in the trees. He only had to deal with Vayne's dogs for a few more yards, then he could disappear back into the woods he knew better than anyone—the woods of Three that his father had taught him how to survive in every day after their shifts at the mills ended. He only had a few more hours until noon... He could make it. This didn't have to get messy.

Damien went to march past the man with his chin held high when a hand suddenly grabbed his arm, knocking the log off his shoulders. The soldier spun him around and snatched the collar of his brown shirt. Damien curled his fists as his entire body went rigid with anger.

"Answer me when I address you, *vermin*," the soldier spat, spittle flying from his mouth.

Damien didn't flinch as the soldier's spit splattered across his face. He remained silent, sealing his mouth shut and simply staring past the soldier into the woods behind him with every ounce of defiance he could muster. He would bow to Vayne and his pigs no longer.

"I said answer me!" The man reared back, slapping Damien across his left cheek and knocking him to the ground.

The entire forest fell silent as everyone paused to watch the exchange. Damien cursed the tears of anger and pain he couldn't stop from welling in his eyes. He quickly pushed himself up from the foliage, ignoring his stinging cheek and giving into the blinding rage that threatened to consume him before sending an uppercut into the soldier's chin. The man's head snapped up as his helmet flew from his face and bounced to the floor, revealing a mess of graying blond hair and pale skin. He teetered backward, tripping and falling over the upturned root of a tree. The entire world seemed to slow as every head—Araedians and soldiers alike—turned to Damien with expressions of shock, anger, and disbelief. However, a few of the fellow mill workers' faces, who Damien recognized as friends of his father, were alight with glee and rebellion. His father had known them for years, and they had always been kind to him during the two years Damien had worked at the mill. But then the world came crashing back down, and the soldier stood on wobbly legs and glared at Damien. Adrenaline and fear shot through his veins. If looks could kill, he'd be dead three times over.

"Run!" a feminine voice yelled from within the crowd of gathered mill workers, and just a moment later, Damien was sprinting through the forest toward the wall. He pumped his arms and legs as fast as he could, desperately trying to outrun the footfalls, shouting, and curses that raged after him. Fear pushed Damien to the point where he felt like his legs would fall off. He knew there would be consequences for his actions today. Extra labor was far too kind. He was facing twenty lashes... Maybe even fifty, but Damien didn't care, and he didn't regret any of it. He wouldn't be able to return to the mill after today... He'd have to find work in one of the others scattered around the sector, but unless the soldiers were willing to search every house and mill in Three, they'd never find him or his mother and brothers to carry out those consequences.

Damien swerved in and out of the large trees, sprinting into the denser half of the forest—the half that flanked the wall. The crashing footfalls behind him had grown to a mere whisper on the leaves as he launched himself at the tallest and largest tree in sight. He quickly scaled the branches, the rough bark biting into his fingers with a familiar and comforting pain until he was invisible from the ground below and level with the smooth concrete surface of the top of the wall. Here, he paused and leaned his head against the tree. Fighting to supply his lungs with air, Damien scanned the guards clad in black stationed every ten feet. He was directly between the two nearest guards—with the perfect gap sitting right before him.

Natalia's face suddenly flashed across his mind, and he imagined her waiting for him on the other side of the concrete cage. A new, brighter determination set him alight, and the next thing Damien knew, he was running along the thick branch and jumping. He landed in the gap between the soldiers with a soft crunch, immediately flinging himself at a large branch on the opposite side of the wall. Before the soldiers could turn to find the source of the noise, he was already gone and safely hidden within the trees. He quickly scrambled down, dropping from one of the lower branches onto the soft grass below and sprinting into the forest toward the clearing.

The trees flew past in blurs of dark green and brown, and Damien's lungs were beginning to burn, but he continued on. He could rest while he waited for Natalia, and he didn't want to give the soldiers a chance to realize where he'd gone. He slowed as he began to ascend the slope before breaking out into the clearing full of wildflowers and flowing grass. He hesitated slightly. Damien walked to the edge of the overhang, gazing over the rolling hills and trees. He took a deep breath.

The rebels were out there... Somewhere... His conversation with Natalia yesterday replayed in his head. If he could, he'd run away to search for the rebels, but like Natalia, he had a brother—*two younger* brothers. He couldn't leave them with his mother, but he couldn't exactly take them with him, either. They were too weak. Even with his help, they'd never last... And he wouldn't abandon them. It was his responsibility as the man of the house to take care of them and his mother, despite her best efforts to turn his brothers against him because of her hatred. She still blamed Damien for his father's death as he sometimes did himself, but his obligation to his family didn't mean he couldn't help Natalia try to find the rebels. Besides... Maybe one day when his brothers were older and could stand up to their mother's abusiveness and provide for themselves, he could join her...

Damien sighed, turning his back to the overhang and wandering to the left toward the largest tree bordering the clearing. The shadows of the branches stretched out like vicious claws reaching for his feet. He plopped down into the soft grass and laid back against the rough bark. It was oddly comforting as he closed his eyes. Suddenly, overwhelming fear and helplessness overcame Damien, and he remembered standing in the crowded market of Three while his father knelt before the executioner's block. He'd taken the blame for the loaf of bread six-year-old Damien had stolen... He remembered the murmurs and whispers drifting through the crowd, the utter silence and anger on his father's friends' faces, and the way he'd screamed when the ax had fallen. After his father's head had rolled along the ground, Damien had run and disappeared into the forest of Sector Three and cried for hours against a large tree like this one. He'd cried until he'd puked. Twice.

Damien shot up, eyes flying open and scanning his surroundings. He wasn't there any more. He was outside the walls, and away from all of that—his mother, his brothers, Vayne... It was just him and the forest. Suddenly, a cool breeze drifted through the trees, weaving the grass together like waves and ruffling his hair. He took another deep breath and laid back against the bark once more. He couldn't think about all this now. It would tear him apart, so he resorted to his newest and best distraction. Natalia.

Damien had been so entranced with her when they'd collided yesterday. She was beautiful with her black hair and large, blue-gray eyes. He liked to imagine they were the exact color of the rising and falling waves of a stormy sea. He'd always wanted to see the sea... But one of the most beautiful things about her was the way she studied the world around her as if every minute detail was vitally important. It was mesmerizing and comforting to know that someone else appreciated nature like he did—like his father had, too. She was intriguing, and like Damien himself, she didn't want to be alone. It had been written all over her face—how scared she was without her brother...

But she wasn't alone, and now Damien wasn't either. Yes, he had his brothers, but his mother wouldn't allow him near them for more than five minutes. She was too busy trying to convince them that it had been Damien who'd swung the ax to chop off his father's head, but there was so much more to that story that she didn't even know... No matter how alone he felt, he convinced himself that he wasn't. Natalia would be there soon. He wasn't alone. He wasn't alone... Damien sighed, closing his eyes and allowing sleep to take him as he waited.

~

The noon sun was high in the sky, and not a single cloud was in sight as Natalia trudged through the forest. Though the day was bright and happy, she felt as if the entire weight of the world was pressing down against her shoulders and trying to smother her in grief. After she'd met Damien in the forest yesterday, she'd returned to Sector Four under the cover of darkness to search for Vale. She'd even dared to sneak through the back door of the orphanage to find him, but he wasn't there. He wasn't anywhere, and the few people Natalia trusted enough to ask hadn't seen or heard from him since the day Vayne's soldiers discovered them in the orphanage... Vale was gone. There was no trace of him, but she couldn't cry about it any more. There weren't any tears left in her.

Natalia started up the slope, brushing past the thick bushes and low-hanging branches and stepping into the clearing. Her eyes immediately found the sleeping figure lying in the shade of the largest tree bordering the tall grass and wildflowers swaying in the breeze. She studied him closely. He looked so peaceful—so different from the angry boy fighting for survival that she'd met yesterday. His dark hair was blowing across his forehead, and his eyelashes were so long, they nearly touched his cheeks. Natalia sucked in a breath. A large bruise was beginning to form under the skin of his left cheek.

"Damien?" She knelt next to him, lightly shaking his shoulder. His hazel eyes shot open as he jumped up, knocking her to the ground. "By the Aether!"

"Natalia?" Damien faced her, confusion clouding his gaze. He rubbed his eyes and blinked furiously, attempting to chase the sleep away. His eyes widened at the sight of her on the ground, and he extended his hand. "Oh, I'm sorry."

Natalia rolled her eyes and took his hand. He pulled her up easily. "I have a feeling that's rare."

"What is?" Damien asked, brows furrowing.

She smirked. "You saying sorry."

"Yeah." He shrugged with a smirk. "Don't get used to it."

"What happened to your cheek?"

Damien's smirk immediately fell into a deep frown as he shoved his hands into the pockets of his brown pants. "I work at the mill in Three... Vayne always has his dogs there watching us, and one of them decided to bite today."

"At least tell me you hit him back," she said, clenching her fists at her sides. Just the mention of the president's name sent a wave of rage simmering through her. Vayne had taken everything from her—freedom, happiness, family, Vale... And he was hurting people. It seemed that was all their president ever did. She understood why the people of Araedia were terrified of him. He could have someone executed with the snap of his fingers, but they couldn't just let him get away with it. They had to fight back somehow... But Natalia had already lost everyone she loved. She had nothing to lose, and everything to gain by fighting back. The civilians, however, still had loved ones... They had consequences for their actions.

"Of course, I did." Damien turned, gazing out over the rolling hills and trees beyond. With a jerk of his head, he motioned for her to follow as he walked toward the edge of the overhang, where he then sat, feet dangling. A nervous excitement at the height and far drop below filled Natalia when she sat down next to him. "Did you find your brother?" he asked.

"No..." She shook her head. "I didn't... There was no sign of him anywhere. It's like they took him and just disappeared."

The clearing fell silent as they sat, feet swaying. Natalia picked at the long grass and tore a blade from the dirt, sticking the end in her mouth and chewing on it.

"I lost my father to Vayne, too," Damien whispered. "And in a sense, it feels like I've lost my little brothers to my mother."

The blade of grass slipped from Natalia's mouth, falling to the ground as she looked at him. Damien merely kept his absentminded stare on the horizon. She could see the memories replaying through his head, haunting his mind.

"How old are they?" she asked.

The ghost of a small smile lifted the corners of his lips. "Nine and seven."

"How did you lose them?"

"It all started with my father's death. It was my fault... He took the fall for me, and..." Damien's voice cracked, and he dipped his head down, biting his bottom lip before clearing his throat. "...my brothers—and my mother especially—were never the same after that. She won't let me stay in a room with them for more than five minutes, and if she does, it's because she's yelling and berating me. She threatens to hurt them if they try to talk to me... My house isn't a home, and I've been miserable ever since my father's death. But I can't just abandon them. I'm the man of the house now. It's my responsibility to care for them, so I can't leave... But *you can*."

Shock flooded through her. "What?"

"Leave. Go find the rebels and make a better life for yourself. You have nothing holding you here any more."

"But Vale—"

"Vale is gone." He finally met her gaze, his hazel eyes burning with so many different emotions—grief, anger, grit, defiance, envy, regret. "You said it yourself. There's no sign of him. Vayne's men took him and disappeared, and I hate to say it, Natalia, but they've most likely already killed him. If they haven't already, they will soon, and I'm speaking from experience when I say there's nothing you can do to get him back. So, leave. Go find the rebels."

Natalia blinked back tears. She would not cry again. She'd already done enough crying... But Damien... A part of her knew he was right. She *should* leave to find the rebels, but what if she couldn't do it? What if she failed and was still alone in the end? She'd be better off sticking to what she knew because she couldn't handle the thought of being alone. Out of all the things to fear in their world, solitude and loneliness were what terrified her most. It was too great of a risk... Besides, what if Damien was the anchor she needed? She couldn't leave him here with Vayne and his dreadful mother. He had everyone to care for, but no one to care for him. She couldn't leave him like everyone else in his life. She wouldn't. Vale wouldn't leave him if he were here.

"No," she said with a scowl.

"What?" Damien's brows furrowed as he stood in anger. "What do you mean no?"

"I mean no," she said, standing as well. Damien took a step forward, and so did she, refusing to back down. Inches separated them now. "I have no idea what I'll find out there. At least here I'm not so alone if you're here... I don't want to just leave you here, either. I'm not going to do that."

Damien's face softened, and for a moment, he looked as if he were merely a little boy—young and dependent. The shock and confusion that were clear in his eyes were quickly blinked away, replaced by the angry mask he wore constantly.

"You're a fool, Talia," he said softly.

"Maybe." She shrugged, barely recognizing the nickname—the nickname Vale had always called her. It had sounded so natural rolling off Damien's tongue that it'd been nearly undetectable.

Damien rolled his eyes, running his hands through his hair as he stepped away and turned his back to her.

"Are you still going to train with me?" Natalia prayed to the Aether that he couldn't hear the pathetic desperation in her voice. She didn't want him to think she was weak, but she needed him—needed *someone*. "If you do, whenever your brothers come of age, you...you can come with me. We can find the rebels together."

The clearing fell utterly silent as Damien's back stiffened before her, and Natalia could hear a single word echoing over and over through her head: *please, please, please*. Please, turn around. Say yes.

"It'll take a few years," Damien said. He faced her once more, gaze hardened with the attempt to hide his emotions. "We'd both be done with the testings by the time we could leave."

"Then we wait...," she whispered. "And when it's time to leave, we'll leave."

A smirk lifted a corner of his lips. "Are you hungry?"

"Starving." Natalia smiled.

"Come on," he said, walking to the edge of the clearing. "I found an apple tree on the way here yesterday."

Natalia's smile widened, and together, she and Damien wandered off into the forest in search of the apple tree. She couldn't help the soft laugh that escaped her lips—a mixture of love, memories, and grief. *Vale loved apples...*

～

For weeks, Natalia and Damien met in the clearing, training, talking, and exploring the surrounding forest together. It had become their routine. Every day after Damien finished his work and Natalia finished gathering and selling apples in Sector Four's market picked from the apple tree, they'd find each other. Natalia hadn't gone back to the orphanage. She'd stayed far away, claiming one of the little, one-roomed wooden shacks as her own. The few neighbors she had didn't turn her in to the orphanage matron or to Vayne's soldiers. Some of them even helped by showing her who to trade with at the market and offering a warm bowl of soup or plate of leftovers whenever the rare occasion occurred. No matter what Vayne took from the people of Araedia, he couldn't take their humanity—their sense of community.

Though the sun was setting behind the tall trees in the clearing, it was still blazing out. Sweat dripped down Natalia's face. The summer was coming to an end, and the leaves were beginning to transition from a vibrant green to a molten yellow-brown, but the weather was hot today. Natalia and Damien trudged through the forest, several yards away from the clearing and overhang. She glanced at Damien. Shadows cast by the branches above flickered and danced across his face, shading his hazel eyes. He turned his head, smirking at her. Natalia rolled her eyes and elbowed him in the shoulder. He playfully shoved her back, and the next thing Natalia knew, their arms were locked and pushing against each other as they wrestled to the ground. A grin lit up her face as pure joy filled her being.

Suddenly, a twig snapped nearby. Natalia and Damien shot apart, falling as still as the trees around them. She held her breath, strained her ears, and listened, turning in a slow circle to survey the surrounding wood. The only thing she could hear was the pounding of her heart. Natalia looked at Damien, watching his eyes dart around before meeting her own. His jaw hardened, and he shook his head slightly. He clearly didn't see or hear anything either, but something—or *someone*—was out there. It wasn't an animal. No, it had been too loud. Could it be the rebels, or had Vayne's soldiers discovered them somehow? A shadow hidden within the trees to Natalia's right caught the corner of her eye, sending her whirling around.

"Show yourself!" she exclaimed. "We know you're there."

Damien took a step closer to her and whispered, "Are you sure that was a good idea?"

"No, but it's better than just standing here," she whispered back.

The shadow moved again, stepping out from behind the tree. Natalia's lips parted in surprise at the sight of a girl dressed in dirty white clothes—the clothes of Sector One. She couldn't have been older than them, with big, dark molten brown eyes and matching hair. A few small patches of freckles were splattered across her pale cheeks like paint.

"Who are you?" Damien exclaimed, taking a protective step forward. "Stay where you are!"

The girl scowled, and defiance was so clear in her eyes that Natalia nearly laughed. Damien was the most stubborn person she'd ever met, but this girl might have him beat. The girl took a step toward them. "And why should I listen to you?"

"Because you're the one stalking us!" Damien's brows knit together, and anger filled his voice. Natalia watched him clench his fists at his sides when another shadow—rather, two—walked out from behind another large tree.

"Please." The girl rolled her eyes. "I'm not stalking *you*. I can't help that you're the loudest creature to ever roam this forest. Sorry I have ears."

The two shadows took a few hesitant steps forward before joining the girl. A boy and another girl. They were both younger—Natalia guessed the age of eleven or twelve—and around the same height, with the same platinum-blonde hair, vibrant blue eyes, and warm complexion. They stood close to each other, clutching hands nervously. Natalia glanced between the boy and girl, studying them and their beige clothes from Sector Two. They were twins. But how did they get out here with a girl from One?

"I'm not going to ask again," Damien said, his voice turning deep and threatening. "Who are you, and how many of you are there?"

"There's only us. Please," the platinum-blonde girl begged softly. Her fear was plain in her trembling voice. "We don't want any trouble."

Damien's eyes narrowed, never breaking contact with the first girl. "You might not, but *she* does."

"My name is Lavelle Dalnum," the blonde girl said before nodding to her twin. "And this is my brother, Ren. We're from Sector Two."

The brunette beside them smirked. She clearly knew how badly she was getting under Damien's skin. "Aurum Everrett, Sector One." Her eyes flicked between Natalia and Damien, finally breaking away from their staring match. "And judging by your clothes, I think it's safe to say that you two are from Three and Four."

"Yes," Natalia said. "I'm Natalia Rhys, and this is Damien Mendax."

"Pleasure." Aurum dipped her head to Natalia before turning to Damien. "You, not so much."

Damien's frown deepened.

"How did you get out here?" Natalia asked, trying to change the subject before Damien exploded. She was utterly astonished and confused. How was it possible that they were all here?

"I met an old lady in One," Aurum said, crossing her arms. "She told me about a prophecy, Elementals, the rebels... Everything beyond the walls... I wanted to see what was really out here." She shrugged. "I got out, then ran into these two near Sector Two's wall. They were wandering around like lost puppies."

"And you two?" Natalia turned to the twins. "Did an old lady speak to you as well?"

Ren and Lavelle exchanged brief glances.

"Yes," the boy whispered, still clutching his sister's hand.

"How is this possible?" Natalia asked, looking at Damien. "How is she traveling between the sectors?"

"I don't know...," he mumbled.

"You met her, too?" Lavelle questioned. Her voice was stronger now, yet still quiet. She reminded Natalia of wind. She was soft and calm but also firm and guiding.

Damien nodded. "And let me guess, no one knows her name either."

"Nope," Aurum said, nonchalant arms still folded across her chest. Natalia bit the inside of her cheek as she studied Aurum. She didn't seem like any of this bothered her at all. There was no fear of being caught or killed in her eyes. She was acting as if she'd taken a mere walk outside—not beyond the walls. Natalia wondered if Aurum even knew what the consequences of her actions would be if she were caught. Surely the twins didn't know. If they had, they would've never stepped a foot beyond the walls. They were too scared—too sheltered by the comforts and more fortunate lifestyles of One and Two.

"How long have you been out here?" Ren asked, still clinging to his sister's hand mercilessly like he was afraid she was going to disappear if he ever let go.

"A few weeks now. There's this overhang..." Natalia lifted her hand and pointed toward the clearing. "...over that way. Damien and I meet there everyday. You can see for miles."

Lavelle's face lit up with a gorgeous smile full of warmth and kindness. "Can we see it?"

Damien turned to Natalia with a scowl, but she ignored him. She knew he'd say no—that it was too dangerous to show them, but what would they do? It's not like they could turn her and Damien in to Vayne's soldiers. They'd be in trouble for sneaking outside the walls themselves. Besides, Natalia was tired of living in a world full of division where the sectors had no interaction with each other. This was the freedom that the rebels were fighting for—that she was fighting for, too.

Natalia returned Lavelle's smile, observing her and the others. They were the beginning of a new era—a new family... She could feel it in her bones. They were all different, and maybe some day in the future, they could make a stand against Vayne.

"Follow me," she said.

CHAPTER FOUR

THE OVERHANG

Natalia walked toward the door of her small, one-roomed wooden shack that she called home in the outskirts of Sector Four, tucking a tiny package into her gray coat. Her room was small and empty, and her bed sat in the corner by a tiny window. A rickety table with a few dented pots and cups leaned against the wall by the door. A few pairs of gray pants, shirts, and coats hung over the two chairs beside the table. She had gotten some of the furniture from an old, abandoned shack farther down the dirt road. The rest, she'd learned to build by herself through trial and error. She opened the door and stepped outside, gently closing it behind her.

Tall grass and wildflowers tugged at her pant legs, the wind blowing her dark hair across her face as she gazed across the land. The grass was swaying in the breeze like billowing waves over the hills, and the trees and their branches danced along with it. She smiled to herself, appreciating the overlooked beauty of her home. It might be a cold place full of corruption and hunger, but it was still a lovely sight. Natalia took a deep breath before turning and jogging toward the looming wall.

It had been four years since Natalia and Damien had first met in the forest.

Four years since she'd lost Vale. Four years since she'd met Aurum and the twins—since she'd found and created a whole new family born of the most unlikely circumstances. Natalia was now eighteen like Damien and Aurum, and their first two mandatory tests had passed with little memory. It was as Vale had said all those years ago. Natalia's name had been announced over the mandatory projectors kept in every household, so she'd gone to the testing center in Sector Four, where Vayne's soldiers had asked a few questions and drawn a little blood. She'd then filled out simple paperwork about her life and left. It had been easy and hadn't lasted more than two hours. Aurum and Damien's two tests had been the same. So had Ren and Lavelle's first test at fourteen, though the twins' second tests would be soon since they were now sixteen. Natalia only had one test to go before she was declared a non-Elemental and forced to work in the fields with the rest of the adults in Sector Four.

She scoffed to herself. The Aether forbid, *all* of their tests were coming up. Her final test would commence in two days, in fact... For Damien, Natalia, and Aurum, however, the stakes were high. If the Elemental gene was ever found in someone, it was almost always found in the eighteen-year-olds. Their maturity, concept of danger and fear, and emotions were more developed—all possible triggers for the elements. They were at the highest risk for positive results... Panic squeezed Natalia's chest at the thought of Damien, Aurum, or the twins testing positive.

She passed a cluster of houses on the outskirts of Sector Four. Some of the houses were empty while others housed the few citizens who had survived over the years. Four had become quite empty compared to four years ago. Several of the elderly had been worked to death during the construction of one of Vayne's new buildings—of which Natalia had yet to find—and others had died of starvation. She'd resorted to stealing food from Vayne's soldiers to keep herself and her neighbors around her alive. Most of them were too sick and weak or too young or old to do anything... She'd even managed to get a part-time job selling knives and other small weapons crafted by the only blacksmith in the tiny marketplace in Four, which allowed her to buy more food. Natalia tried her best to smile at a starved, elderly man as she passed the houses, but all she could muster was a tight, thin-lipped grimace. His head dipped slightly, acknowledging her before she continued on.

The houses and shacks quickly began to dwindle out into nothing but grass, rolling hills, and trees. A few minutes later, an abandoned shack at the top of a hill came into view along with the towering wall. Natalia kept her eyes up on the top of the wall, searching for the pitch-black suits of armor of Vayne's guards, who occasionally patrolled. There were none today, which was no surprise. Four was no target to anyone—Vayne and rebels alike. It was too small, and its people were so broken, there was no fear of them attempting escape or aiding the rebels. The other sectors, however, were a different story.

Over the years, security had increased drastically in One, Two, and Three. The rebels had become very successful in sneaking over the walls with grappling hooks and spreading their influence throughout the sectors. They had allies within the walls now—allies who would sneak them food, information, weapons, or whatever they could. Rumors claimed their army in the woods was slowly growing stronger, but Natalia knew it would have to become especially strong to overthrow Vayne and his army of brainwashed dogs. A part of her still hoped that one day she could complete the plan she'd made with Damien—the plan to run away and join the rebels. Natalia would take Aurum and the twins, too, if she ever found the rebels, but no matter how long or how far she and Damien searched, they'd never found any trace of them or their camp. That didn't mean she was willing to give up, though. After the testings were over, she planned to find them one way or another.

Natalia passed the shack and began the descent down the slope that led to the tree she'd used to escape four years ago. It was the same tree Vale had told her to crawl through before he was... Taken. The same panic from before surged, filling her being with a paralyzing fear of losing everyone she loved. *Again.* She stopped halfway down the slope, taking deep breaths and twisting a small silver ring garnished with a lavender gemstone around her finger. Four smaller gems of baby blue and carmine red sat among the intertwining vines and leaves that wove around the metal. It had been a birthday present from Damien, and her nervous habit of twisting it had nearly rubbed her finger raw.

You're not thirteen any more. You can fight back. You won't let anyone take them, Natalia said in her head as she always did when her fear became all too consuming. She pushed her fear back far into the depths of her mind and knelt next to the twisted roots of the tree. Repeating her words over and over to herself, she crawled under the roots as she had so many times before and slipped between the cold concrete. The warm sun lit her face when she came out on the other side of the wall, and the next thing Natalia knew, she was sprinting through the trees toward the overhang... Toward her only sense of family and safety.

A few minutes passed before she slowed at the slope leading up the hill to the clearing. She paused for a moment near the top, listening to the rustle of the leaves in the branches and the sounds of life—the birds flapping their wings above, the squirrels and rabbits leaping along the ground. Natalia then stepped into the clearing to find Damien sitting on the edge of the overhang with his feet dangling back and forth. She smiled as she walked toward him, the constant security and trust she felt around him warming her heart and chasing away the fear and panic. He turned around to meet her gaze, rising from the grass.

"First one here?" she asked, hugging him tightly.

Damien nodded and slowly pulled away. He trailed his hand down her arm, pausing when his fingers met hers. "Always am," he muttered, staring at their joined fingers.

"Damien?" Natalia felt the color drain from her face. Something was *wrong.* He never displayed his emotions like this... She knew he loved her in more ways than one—a way that she couldn't love him in return even if she tried—but he was never so... *forward* about it like he was now. She hated to disappoint him, but she was too scared to try to love him like that. She wasn't ready... "What's wrong?"

"I don't know, I just..." His eyes widened, and he drew away his hand as if he'd only just realized that he'd grabbed hers. "The testings... I have a bad feeling about this one."

"Damien—"

"Vayne's increased security in Three." He cleared his throat. "It was nearly impossible to jump across the wall today."

"Then we'll find another way to get you across." She shook her head, silently cursing Vayne. All he did was ruin lives. He tore people—*families*—apart, and she hated him for it. She hated him so much she could hardly comprehend it. "I'm not losing you, too," she whispered.

"I'm afraid, Talia...," Damien murmured, turning away from her. He gazed out over the rolling hills and forest as if he were imagining himself far, far away from the sectors in some land that was safe and free. He turned to face her once more. "I'm afraid I'll never see you again... So, I have to tell you something. Something important—"

"Is Damien being dramatic again?" a raspy feminine voice suddenly blurted, echoing around the clearing. Twigs snapped, and bushes rustled as Aurum stumbled through the tree line with a smirk.

Damien rolled his eyes with a frown. "Says the dramatic one."

Natalia didn't smile or laugh at their banter as she normally would. Instead, she simply stood there. She knew Damien better than she knew herself... She knew *exactly* what he was going to say—what he was going to confess. But why was he so afraid that he felt like he had to tell her now?

"Oh, please," Aurum said, sauntering over to them and throwing an arm over Natalia's shoulders. "What did you do *this* time?"

"*I* didn't *do* anything," Damien said, crossing his arms and reverting to his normal, brooding self again. "Vayne increased security in Three again."

Aurum scoffed. "What else is new?"

"It's bad this time, Aurum," Natalia said.

"Bad as in you can't sneak out any more?" Aurum questioned, brows furrowed.

Natalia searched Damien's hazel eyes, finding nothing but a growing hopelessness. It was one of the many questions she'd been itching to ask him, but she knew his answer. He didn't believe he could, and Natalia's heart felt as if it had dropped into her stomach...

"Yes," he muttered with a scowl. "And if I'm able to get out, it won't be as often..."

"It's bad in Two as well," Lavelle said, stepping into the clearing with Ren at her side. Natalia, Aurum, and Damien turned to face the twins and watched Ren nod in agreement as they joined them near the edge of the overhang. "The rebels are really getting under Vayne's skin. He's getting more and more paranoid."

"The walls are crawling with soldiers now...," Ren added with a frown. "He sent them in yesterday."

Aurum cursed. "The rebels are getting stronger... That's good and bad."

"The more the rebels grow, the more Vayne will want to find the Aether," Natalia said, running a hand through the small knots left in her hair by the wind. "The Aether's the only way he could really wipe them out—wipe all of us out."

Damien scoffed. "The Aether doesn't exist, and if it does, then whoever it is, is a coward. They don't care about us. If they did, they'd help."

"Damien...," Lavelle whispered, face falling. "Don't say that..."

"I'm sorry, Lavelle, but it's true." He shrugged before facing her. His face immediately softened, and Natalia could see the guilt building in his eyes. He'd never meant to hurt or insult her in any way. He just wasn't going to get his hopes up for someone or something that they didn't know was real or not. Damien had never been the optimist in the group...

"What are we supposed to do?" Ren asked, glancing between everyone.

"There's nothing we can do," Aurum said. She put her hands on her hips. "Vayne's tried so hard to keep the sectors in the dark, but everyone knows that the rebels are growing stronger. He can't hide that. I think we'll go to full-out war soon, and Vayne will draft us all."

"What?" Lavelle exclaimed, fear plain in her vibrant eyes.

Ren grabbed both of her hands. "No, that's not happening."

Natalia looked at Ren. He'd grown over the past few weeks, shooting past Lavelle by a few inches. But heavy bags hung under his bright blue eyes, and instead of the usual calm and easygoing gaze, there was a hardened anger and fear. The sight wasn't welcoming. They were all scared, even Aurum. Natalia could tell by the way she was shifting her weight back and forth between her feet. They all knew the danger spread before them, and they knew that Aurum was right. There wasn't anything they could do about it.

"If the rebels' army was big enough," Lavelle said, meeting each of their gazes. "Do you think they'd be able to overthrow Vayne?"

Aurum frowned. "They'd need a lot of Elementals for that."

"Agreed." Natalia nodded. "Especially since they're fighting some of Vayne's mindless drones."

"I wouldn't count on the rebels saving us," Damien said, turning and walking toward the shade of a tree. He sat down against the bark, folding his hands behind his head. "The only people who can save us is ourselves."

Aurum turned away, wandering to the edge of the overhang, and a silence fell across the clearing. A breeze drifted through the trees, pinning Natalia's hair and coat tight to her body. The package she'd placed in the coat's inside pocket pressed against her ribs, and she cursed herself for forgetting it was there. She slipped the package from the pocket, stepping toward the twins.

"Here, Lavelle," she said, extending it. "I brought you another book."

Lavelle smiled brightly, causing a warmth to spread through Natalia. "What's this one about?" she asked, taking the leather-bound pages.

"Which natural herbs in the area make medicines, stop bleeding, heal rashes... You'll love this one. It even has sketches in it."

"Thank you!" Lavelle broke away from Ren and wrapped her arms around Natalia, squeezing tight.

Natalia squeezed her back with a smile. No amount of books—stolen or fairly bought—could repay Lavelle for the acts of kindness and love she'd shown them. And after all, Lavelle had been the one to teach Natalia how to read.

"You're welcome...," she whispered, eyes wandering to Ren, then Damien under the tree, and finally Aurum near the overhang. A pit formed in Natalia's stomach, and she knew that their sun-filled days in the forest were coming to an end. No matter what they did now, they'd begin to see less and less of each other. If Vayne continued to increase security, they wouldn't have more than a week—a week and a half if they were lucky—before they wouldn't be able to meet. They'd stay with their families in their sectors... Anger and fear wrapped around her heart like a snare. Vayne was taking away her family. Again. And then she would be alone... Again.

～

Natalia walked down the wide dirt road through the heart of Sector Four, scattered with Araedians dressed in multiple shades of gray. Hours had passed since she'd left Damien, Aurum, and the twins in the woods, and the last rays of the sun were sinking behind the walls and illuminating the small wooden buildings of the market in fire-like oranges and reds. Soldiers clad in the deepest black with guns and spears of electricity marched through the thinning throng as they always did. She kept her head low as she always did in the market and turned down one of the many branching alleyways, winding and cutting behind and between dozens and dozens of tiny wooden shacks and houses.

A few minutes passed before Natalia came upon a small, square cobblestone courtyard surrounded by crumbling stone walls and crawling with children of all ages and social status as they ran back and forth while others stood and talked. It was a mutual ground they met on frequently. The majority of the children Natalia recognized from the orphanage and the outskirts of Four, but a few belonged to those who lived in the Circle of Sector Four—the walled encirclement that housed Four's governor and Vayne's superior officers, who dressed in black armor with stark-white bands curling around their right biceps. Every sector had their Circles, but the citizens of Four referred to theirs as the Hive. Natalia gritted her teeth. To Vayne, they were no more than bees born to serve their queen. Unimportant and replaceable once their usefulness had been expended.

The courtyard was several blocks deep into the alleyways—far away from the prying eyes of Vayne's soldiers and the few loyalists he had, which were not many. Especially in Four. In the midst of the courtyard, a fire reached toward the night sky above, flames wild and hungry. Patches of dying grass stuck up between the cracked stones. A few feet from the fire, a rickety old projector had been propped up on a chipped and tilting wooden table, the light cast on the wall of the nearest shack. Natalia chuckled to herself as she wove between the crowd of kids and walked past a projector. There was no telling who had stolen it... Or how they'd done it.

All projectors were strictly built for homes and were used to try to fool the people into thinking that Vayne wasn't a tyrant and was good for their society. Every house had one, no matter how poor. This one was in rather good shape, and the children's cartoon—more propaganda drawn by Vayne's mindless slaves—projected upon the wall wasn't too blurry. But it was still forbidden to take it out of whatever home it had come from.

Natalia walked to one of the corners of the courtyard where a young boy sat with a pot of soup, handing out bowlfuls. She stopped in front of him with a soft smile, and the boy returned one before handing her a bowl of warm broth and milky potatoes. The boy was of a richer family as his clothes were nice and clean unlike the others around them, but he was sharing what he had, and she thanked him for it.

After quickly finishing her bowl and silencing her growling stomach, Natalia leaned against the crumbling stone wall and watched a few of the younger children toss a worn leather ball back and forth while another chased it. She allowed herself to become lost in their game, grateful for anything to distract herself from her thoughts and Damien's situation. If he truly could never escape again... What would she do without him? When would his problem become Aurum's and the twins' as well? Could they last until the twins completed their final testings, so they could run away into the forest? Would everyone be willing to leave the sectors behind? She knew Damien would. Aurum had her mother to look after, but she was growing fairly old... The twins, however, were a gamble. They still had both of their parents and a little sister... How could she ask Ren and Lavelle to leave them behind? Would it be possible to take their family, too, if they wished to go?

"Look!" a young voice called out from within the crowd. "The projector!"

Natalia turned, narrowing her eyes against the bright pictures on the wooden wall of the shack. Complete silence fell over the courtyard as everyone faced the screen. She scowled when Sector Four's squeaky-voiced governor appeared before them and began her daily ramble and countdown until the testings. She was halfway through her speech when the screen suddenly flickered. It returned to normal for a few moments, then flashed again. Natalia straightened, pushing off the wall. It was like the connection was being interrupted... Static hissed loudly through the air, causing some of the little ones to plug their ears.

"I can't see," a young boy whispered beside her, tugging at her gray pants. He appeared to be around three, and Natalia swore she'd seen him outside the orphanage before. "What's going on?"

"I don't know just yet." Natalia extended her arms and lifted the young boy up onto her shoulders. "Why don't we find out?"

The boy nodded, clutching her shoulders tight. "Okay."

"Are you here with anyone?" she asked softly while the screen continued to glitch, and the screen hissed more static.

"My older brother."

"Do you know where he is?"

The boy shook his head. "Somewhere in here."

Natalia nodded and turned back to the screen. The static finally faded away to reveal a frozen image of the governor. The image blurred, then refocused twice... Suddenly, a young man's voice rang out over the courtyard, echoing and bouncing off the walls.

"Araedians of Sector Four, do not be afraid," the voice began. The static returned even louder than before, cutting off some of the man's words.

"Vayne—doesn't—stand—chance with the rebels—don't—afraid—Growing stronger—day—"

Murmurs of fear, shock, excitement, confusion, intrigue, and panic swept through the crowd. Natalia simply stood there with the boy on her shoulders. Who was speaking to them? Were the rebels making contact with them, and if they were, why Sector Four? And if it wasn't the rebels, who was it?

"The testings—be strong—they—help—keep—fighting—I—" Sparks and smoke shot up from the projector, and the screen fell black. Not a soul in the courtyard moved. Natalia's breaths were short and shallow. What had just happened?

"Soldiers!" a voice exclaimed, throwing the crowd into action. Everyone immediately scattered and sprinted off in different directions. Natalia quickly grabbed the boy from her shoulders, cradling him in her arms and ducking into the nearest alley. Soldiers shouting commands and readying their guns and spears of crackling electricity sounded, sending spikes of adrenaline through her blood. Others ducked into the alley, and together, everyone ran, the wooden houses and soldiers passing and falling behind in rapid blurs. Natalia cut left then right, then right again before she burst into another stone courtyard. Unlike the one they'd just come from, this one was clean and well-kept. In fact, the more she stared at it, the more familiar it seemed... A few kids emerged from the alleyways and ran past her, running up the steps to the wooden building connected to the courtyard. Natalia gently set the little boy down. She hadn't stepped foot in this courtyard since she'd lost Vale... It was the orphanage.

"I can take him from here," a girl around the age of twelve said, stopping beside her. The boy extended his arms, and the girl picked him up. "I know his brother."

"Thanks," Natalia mumbled, eyes never leaving the building. She felt as if she were dreaming, staring at the place she'd once called home. It was bittersweet to see the pieces of her childhood—if that's what one could call it—she'd left behind. The nostalgia was almost enough to overcome the fear, confusion, and...*hope* she now felt. Someone—possibly a rebel—had interrupted Vayne's regularly scheduled propaganda and broadcasted an unauthorized message through the projector. Had the other sectors seen it, or had it been just for Four? Were the rebels planning to free them? Were they planning an attack?

"No." The girl shook her head and shifted the boy onto her hip. "Thank *you*."

Natalia watched as the girl turned and ran inside. The doors creaked behind her like they always did on their rusted hinges.

~

"Come on, Talia." Vale smiled. The dimples in his cheeks deepened as he watched eight-year-old Natalia stumble up the stone steps. Other orphans passed them, throwing the squeaky door open and disappearing inside. The day was growing darker and darker, and thunder rolled loudly in the distance.

"Sorry," she said.

Vale plopped down onto the steps, running a dirty hand through his dirty hair. They'd just returned from the market where they'd searched for food and medicine and other supplies that Vayne refused to provide to the orphanage. "What took you so long?"

"This," Natalia said, sitting beside him and digging inside the pocket of her gray jacket.

Vale laughed and took the small, red apple from her palm. "You got this for me?"

"Yes." She smiled proudly.

Vale returned her smile with his crooked grin and ruffled her hair. "I'll make a thief of you yet."

~

Natalia blinked away the memory, only to realize she now stood alone in the courtyard, and the crunch of boots against stone filled the air, growing closer. She wasn't eight any more, and no matter how badly she willed Vale to appear in one of the many windows, he didn't. So, Natalia took a deep breath, turned around, and left, knowing all that was waiting for her back home was her cold, empty house.

CHAPTER FIVE

SHAKEN

Natalia sprinted through the forest, sweat pouring down her reddening face. It had been nearly impossible for her to wait until noon so she could meet the others in the forest. Last night's events had shaken her to her core, and she needed to talk about it. Natalia still didn't know exactly who had interrupted Vayne's broadcast over the projector—no one in Sector Four really knew, and anyone who'd publicly tried to figure it out this morning had been taken into custody within the wall of the Hive. She burst through the brush, entering the clearing and scaring the birds out of the comfort of the high branches in the trees around her. They screeched in fear as they shot into the sky.

Damien, Aurum, and the twins whirled near the edge of the overhang, concern clear on all their faces once their eyes met Natalia's. Natalia twisted her ring nervously as she forced herself to slowly walk to them. She glanced at Damien and saw the utter fear and alarm in his gaze. She did her best to give him a smile, but all that she could muster was an awkward grimace.

Damien stepped forward and grabbed her arm eagerly, clearly too impatient to wait any longer. "What happened?"

"Relax, Damien," Aurum said, lightly elbowing him in his side. The twins followed after her.

"Don't tell me to relax." Damien turned, fixing a nasty glare at Aurum. She scowled in return. Natalia knew she should step in like she always did when they butted heads, but she just didn't have the energy. Not right now...

"Oh, enough, both of you!" Lavelle exclaimed. "She can't tell us what's wrong if you two can't stop going at each other's throats for five minutes!"

Aurum and Damien glanced at Lavelle, mouths slightly agape as if neither of them could believe she'd raised her voice. Even Ren's eyes had widened. Natalia would've laughed if she wasn't still freaking out.

"I think the rebels hacked the projector system last night," Natalia said, unable to keep it in any longer. Everyone faced her with wide eyes, and the clearing fell utterly silent as she told them what had happened.

"What?" Aurum whispered.

Lavelle's brows knit in confusion as she glanced between Natalia and Ren. "What does that mean?"

"Did it happen anywhere else?" Ren asked.

Aurum shook her head. "Not in One."

"Damien?" Ren looked at him.

"No," he said, eyes never leaving Natalia. "What else happened?"

"Soldiers came, but we all ran. No one has any idea what's going on, and those who've asked around haven't been seen since this morning... Apparently some soldiers overheard them." Natalia ran a hand through her hair, Lavelle's question echoing in her mind over and over. What did it all mean?

"What if the rebels are planning to storm Four?" Aurum blurted out suddenly. "It's the least-fortified sector. If they took it, they'd increase their army and gain complete access to a sector."

"No," Damien said. "There's no way they have the numbers for that."

Aurum frowned. "How do you know?"

"Because if they did, they would've done that by now, Aurum!" he exclaimed, throwing his hands up.

Lavelle tentatively stepped between Aurum and Damien. "There's no need to yell at each other—"

"Yelling is the only way you can get anything through her thick skull!" Damien neared Aurum, who lightly pushed Lavelle aside and took a step toward him.

"You're one to talk!" she snarled, face inches from his.

Natalia shoved them apart. "Both of you, shut up! Do *not* let Vayne tear us apart like this!"

Damien glared at Aurum for a few moments before finally meeting Natalia's gaze. She could see the churning anger inside him blazing like a fire. He rolled his eyes and turned around to face the rolling hills and forest in the far distance.

"We should just run." Aurum scoffed. "War is upon us. We should take our families and leave while we still can."

"Our parents would never...," Ren mumbled with a glance at Lavelle.

She nodded in agreement. "Ren's right, but even if we could convince them to leave somehow, where would we go?"

"To the rebels," Natalia said. Adrenaline shot through her veins. They were finally having the conversation she'd been waiting years for. She'd tried to talk the others into helping her find the rebels before. They'd agreed to look, but they'd never *truly searched*—not as they should have. But if she could convince them all to run and find the rebels now... They could escape Vayne and the sectors and wait until the time was right to take them back with the rebels themselves.

Lavelle gave Natalia a small, pitying smile. "Natalia, you've been searching for them for *years*. We've even tried to help you look a few times but..." She shook her head. "You all know I try my best to stay positive, but we're not going to find them. Besides, if we somehow did, they're trying to get into the sectors. We're trying to get out."

"And what about our friends and families?" Ren asked, looking from his twin to her, then Aurum and Damien, who now paced along the edge of the overhang. "They would all be too scared to—"

"We leave them behind," Damien said. He paused and turned toward them.

"Damien...," Aurum murmured.

Lavelle frowned. "Absolutely not."

"Leaving them behind isn't an option, and running away is pointless." Ren shrugged. "We have nowhere to go..."

"We have nowhere to go right now," Natalia said. "But we'd have somewhere to go once we find the rebels. You just have to be brave enough to take the chance."

Ren shook his head. "It's too risky."

"If I find them and come back for you, then would you leave?" Natalia asked, desperation clear in her voice.

"Maybe," he said. "It's still risky."

"What about the other societies?" Aurum asked, nervously twisting a lock of her dark brown hair.

"We don't even know if they truly exist, Aurum," Lavelle said. "They could all be rumors. We don't know what's out there."

Natalia turned away from Aurum and the twins, allowing their conversation to disappear with the breeze flowing through the clearing. Their words were nothing but whispers on the wind as she paused beside Damien, who stared out over the expanse of Araedia. Aurum had a point about the other societies, but so did Lavelle. Who knew if they still existed, and how in the Aether's name would they find them without a map? And there were no maps in the sectors. Ren was right, too. None of their friends or families would leave, and no matter how badly Aurum didn't want to admit it, Natalia knew Aurum's mother would stay, too.

She rubbed her temples in frustration. The testings looming in the back of her mind didn't do anything to soothe her either. They were out of options at this point. Natalia wouldn't leave Aurum or the twins, and she knew Damien wouldn't leave without her. They were stuck. Completely and utterly stuck. A hand grabbing hers jolted her from her thoughts. She looked at Damien at her side. He gave her a small smile—an extremely *rare* smile. Natalia cursed herself. She must really look pathetic to be receiving a smile from Damien. Damien pulled Natalia back over to Aurum, Ren, and Lavelle, who were all still debating their circumstances. The three paused and faced them, Aurum's eyes going directly to her and Damien's intertwined fingers. He hesitantly let go, and Natalia could've sworn she'd seen a flash of irritation and disappointment in his eyes. She chose to ignore it as she always did when he dropped hints of his feelings. She simply just didn't know how to respond.

"We're not going to decide anything today, so I say we get through these next testings," Damien said, his tone and stance way calmer than before. "And after that, we can make a final decision regarding what we're going to do—if we're going to stay or not. We all have a lot to think about... But either way, I doubt we'll be able to meet out here for much longer anyways, so we can discuss that as well. Arrangements will need to be made..."

A pit formed in Natalia's stomach. The thought of living in the sectors without being able to see them was... unbearable. She knew she wouldn't be able to do it— wouldn't be able to *survive* it. Besides losing those she loved, being alone was the thing she feared most. She wouldn't be able to live without them. Damien knew that. Could his arrangements involve trying to sneak her into one of their sectors? It was far past risky. It was nearly impossible, but... they could do it. Couldn't they?

"I agree," Natalia said. "We can't rush into any decisions."

The twins exchanged glances. Ren nodded, giving Lavelle a playful nudge before she nodded in return. "We agree," Lavelle smiled warmly.

"Well, Mendax," Aurum said. "For once in your life, it seems you're right."

Damien smirked. "I'm always right. You just can't admit it half the time."

"Sure." Aurum rolled her eyes. "I'll let you believe that."

"Now that this is all settled..." A devious glint lit up Ren's eyes. "Can we please go to the apple tree?"

Natalia laughed. "You just want to try to catch that squirrel again!"

"What?" Ren threw his hands up in mock innocence. "I'd never. I'm just... hungry."

"Come on," Aurum said, throwing an arm over Ren's shoulder and walking toward the tree line.

"Wait!" Lavelle cried. Everyone turned to her, confusion and concern on all of their faces. Lavelle's constant grin widened as she extended her arms. "Group hug."

Damien rolled his eyes, opening his mouth to complain, but Natalia grabbed his arm and yanked him forward. Aurum and Ren were there a moment later, and they were all squished together in each other's arms. Damien squirmed, causing everyone to laugh. Natalia watched as he dipped his head to hide his own smile. She flicked his ear, and he glanced at her, a dangerous playfulness gleaming in his eyes. He looked back to the others before finally pushing away.

"All right, enough of that." Damien ran a hand through his dark hair. "Let's go catch Ren's squirrel."

The twins grinned, grabbing Aurum's hands and immediately dragging her into the forest. Natalia chuckled lightly as she began to walk after them.

"Wait," Damien said and grabbed her arm, turning her around.

Natalia's heart rate increased, and nerves flowed through her like a poison. A few moments of silence passed. Damien simply stood there, hazel eyes flickering over and studying the features of her face. Somewhere within his gaze, a sadness seemed to lurk along with a thousand hidden secrets.

"Damien—"

Damien cupped Natalia's cheeks, placing his lips upon hers, and closed the small space between them. Her eyes widened in shock as he kissed her, and she merely stood there, too dumbfounded to do anything at all. He pulled away a second later, leaving her lips stinging with warmth.

"What?" Natalia asked breathlessly. It was the only word or thought she could muster. She couldn't even begin to untangle the web of emotions clouding her head and her heart. The only thing she was truly certain of was that she was flustered. Every other emotion was caught up in the web. Natalia knew she cared for him, but how deeply? Was it the way he wanted her to care for him, or was it the way a sister cared for a brother?

"I've been meaning to tell you this for so long... I was going to yesterday, but I was interrupted..." Damien brushed his thumb over her cheek, leaving a prickling trail of fire. "Talia, you know I have a bad feeling about these next tests. None of us know what's going to happen, and we especially don't know what's going to happen after them... So, I just have to say this because if I don't, and something happens to me—or worse, to you—I'd never forgive myself."

"Damien," Natalia whispered, shaking her head slightly. "Don't. You know how I feel about this sort of thing... You know how I feel about you..."

"Just let me say, Talia, please."

"No, don't." She shook her head more clearly, too confused to make any level-headed decisions. All she knew was that he was her friend—her family—and she loved him and couldn't bear to lose him.

"I love you," he said, staring directly into her eyes—her very soul. "No matter what happens, remember that. I love you, and I will always love you until the day I die."

Natalia swore her feet had been rooted in the ground as he leaned down and placed a kiss on her reddened cheeks. Damien finally stepped away before walking off into the depths of the forest after Aurum and the twins and their apple tree. She turned and watched him disappear within the trees and brush when a realization dawned upon her. This was her last day with everyone before the testings. She'd been too caught up in everything that had happened to notice. Natalia cursed herself, eyes flitting toward the wall in the distance. Toward the testings. Toward their fate...

CHAPTER SIX

ROMAN

He had two days. Only two before the rebels would strike again. Security had drastically increased in Sectors One, Two, and Three, and it had become nearly impossible to continue to sneak civilians out of the sectors like they had been over the past few years. He was failing... Vayne had grown much more attuned to his strategies. Now, Roman showed many signs of weariness. His black hair was a mess, along with the stubble that grew rapidly around his sharp jawline from lack of shaving. Bags hung under his brown eyes, full of gold, amber, and honey highlights.

He walked through the square tents, wooden shacks, and small buildings that made the rebels' camp, cursing himself for not doing more. He had so much to make up for because of Vayne—*his father*. All the guilt over his father's actions weighed heavily upon him like a ball and chain around his ankle. Every time news of another atrocity reached the camp, the chain grew heavier. Rebels greeted him as he passed, their eyes twinkling with admiration and respect for him. He could never begin to understand why they looked at him that way, but he was thankful for it and returned their greetings with a wave and a gentle smile that hid his exhaustion. He had to look strong for his people. If he lost hope, so would they.

He trudged through the river that flowed through the middle to the outskirts of the camp, starting into the surrounding forest. A few yards in, several small hills with wildflowers growing upon them began their steady ascents around the camp. Roman smiled at the flowers that reminded him of the ones he'd picked for his mother all those years ago. A slight pang of pain shot through his heart. He missed her every day...

Roman slowly made his way up the inclining hill, taking deep breaths to try to calm the swirling chaos of nerves and memories plaguing his mind. The forest grew denser the higher he trekked, and at the top, in the highest branches of the tallest tree, sat his right hand. Fraiser Hale. She was a year younger than the twenty-year-old Roman. They had escaped Sector One together nearly ten years ago and had grown so close that Roman thought of her as his sister. Fraiser's black hair was pulled back into a tight braid that ran an inch below her shoulders. She squinted her green eyes, scanning the area before landing on him. Dirt covered her light brown skin.

"Why do you always pick the highest tree?" Roman questioned as he began to climb, his muscular arms quickly pulling him up into the high branches.

"It's the best lookout point." She shrugged. "I'm an air Elemental, too, remember? We like heights."

"I know, I know," Roman said, sitting next to her and picking at the bark on the branch below him. He found it ironic that Fraiser's element was air when she was his rock. His nerves were already dimming at her presence... She steadied him in so many ways as he, too, steadied her, and he knew that the only reason he was here today was because of her.

Fraiser sighed, eyes never leaving her surroundings. "Roman, we're taking a huge risk tomorrow."

"High risk, high reward... Besides, it's our only option left," he countered, following Fraiser's gaze out over the hills and forest. Somewhere in the far distance stood the four walls encasing the sectors and the people they were trying to save. He *would* save them. After all the pain his family had caused, he had to, and after he saved them, he'd help them establish a fair government where they'd be able to find out if they were Elementals on their own. It would be fulfilling instead of terrifying and potentially fatal like the testings were. They would be free. "Is everyone ready to head out soon?"

"Yes, but we still haven't fully recovered from the loss of numbers from our last attempt," Fraiser said as she faced him, and her green eyes suddenly began to glow. Her irises shined gray while her pupils swam with silver. Roman studied her eyes, remembering the words his father had spoken to him so long ago.

"Elementals' eyes change colors if they're emotional or readying to use their powers. Black pupils symbolize a simple Elemental. Silver pupils, however, symbolize a powerful Elemental that is more adept and deadly. Silver symbolizes strength."

"If we can pull this off..." Roman paused. "...we'll have enough numbers to finally take him down. We're getting so close. Just two more testings, that's all we need. If we can succeed on the next two, then I truly believe we can defeat him."

"I hope you're right," she said. A silence filled the air before her eyes returned to their haunted normal green.

Leading the rebels was no easy task, and it had resulted in an immense amount of physical and mental pain for them both. Sometimes, Roman wondered which of the two scarred them the deepest...

Fraiser elbowed him, a playfulness flickering across her face. "Now, oh great and wise leader of the rebels, it's time for your uplifting and inspiring speech to the people!"

"Shut up, Fraiser." He rolled his eyes as she laughed.

~

It had taken the army of around two hundred rebels two days to reach the thirty-foot walls of the sectors that broke through the dense forest trees ahead. The sun had set and casted them all into dusk and dark shadows. Roman glanced to his right to find Fraiser beside him, eyes glowing gray and silver. She wasn't the only one who was ready. He could see a rainbow of glowing eyes around them—shades of green, gray, and a few reds and oranges. Fraiser met Roman's gaze, and he felt the familiar sting of his dark-blue irises and silver pupils beginning to glow. She gave him a nod. Everyone was in position. The rebels were ready to enter enemy territory.

Slowly, Roman crept through the forest with Fraiser close behind him. It was dark and quiet besides the rustling of leaves in the wind. Suddenly, a beam of light flashed across a bush a few feet ahead of him, and he immediately ducked behind a tree. Fraiser and the nearby rebels did the same, hiding behind trunks, bushes, and large rocks scattered around. Roman cursed Vayne as he watched the searchlights positioned atop the walls sweep through the forest like hounds on a scent. No one had been seen, but it didn't stop the fear from flowing through his veins.

Taking a deep breath, Roman continued on and watched as the rebels slipped from tree to bush from bush to rock. He prayed to the Aether that they'd get through this section of the forest quickly. If they were seen, Vayne's soldiers would deploy from the walls and chase them. There would be a battle, and though the rebels would have the advantage of the terrain, the soldiers would have the numbers—and deadly guns and spears of electricity. Roman pushed the negative thoughts deep down. He didn't feel like losing any of his people tonight.

Suddenly, Fraiser tackled Roman from behind. He froze, lying against the soft grass as a spotlight hovered over the spot where he'd crouched seconds before. The light wavered, then continued along to another patch of grass and bushes. He nodded at Fraiser thankfully, and she nodded back, a cocky smile upon her lips. He rolled his eyes. There went another point to her in their game of how many times one could save the other. Roman really needed to step up his game. Fraiser was leading by three points now. She quickly got up and helped him to his feet before they crept closer to the walls of Sector Four.

Roman's gaze landed on a large boulder between two thick trees a few yards ahead, and he couldn't help the small smile that pulled at the corners of his lips. He sprinted to it, ducking behind it before any beams of light could catch him. Fraiser joined him a moment later, and both of their eyes began to glow again as they slowly pushed against the boulder. It would only take the two of them to move the large rock because of their silver pupils. They were stronger than the other Elementals, and without them, it would've taken at least five black-eyed Elementals to move it.

Beneath the boulder was a small wooden trapdoor covered with grass, moss, ants, and a few writhing worms. Roman grabbed the cold metal handle in the center and lifted it open. This door would lead the rebels into the underground tunnel system that spread all throughout the sectors. They had access to every sector except for One and parts of Two, but this particular set of tunnels would take them under Sector Four and out to another door that'd put the rebels near the new train station where the children who'd tested positive during the testings would be sent. Vayne had built a new station as a precaution since the rebels had grown so successful at sneaking into the sectors.

Roman turned back toward the dark forest, lifted his hands to his mouth, and whistled a bird call—the signal for the rebels to climb down into the tunnels. Multiple groups of shadows darted closer, carefully making their way to the trapdoor as he'd instructed them. Patience was key now. They couldn't afford to have Vayne's soldiers spot them here. If they did, they'd never reach the train station in time to save the children from being brainwashed into Vayne's army—or if they were powerful Elementals, from becoming one of his personal guardian slaves. Slowly, the rebels began to climb down a small metal ladder into the cold depths of the earth. Several nerve-wracking minutes passed before Roman, Fraiser, and three other rebels remained.

Roman held a hand up to them as they stepped forward. "I need your help."

The three stopped, exchanging quick glances. Roman studied the young woman and two young men carefully. They were all strong and capable of accompanying him and Fraiser on the next leg of the plan.

"What is it?" the young woman asked worriedly.

"Fraiser and I need you three to come with us. We'll be staying above ground to push the boulder back over the door and travel to the other side of Sector Four. We have to open the exit on the other side for everyone underground. Our arrival to the exit is crucial. If for some reason we don't make it—or worse, we die—then everyone will be trapped in the tunnels. It's a dangerous path and a lot of responsibility, so if anyone doesn't want to help, I understand. I'll find someone else... But—"

"We'll do it." One of the young men known around the camp as Alec stepped forward. His skin was a dark brown, and his dark hair was cropped close to his head. His wide brown eyes were full of determination. He looked at the young man and woman to his sides and nodded at them. They dipped their heads in return before facing Roman. "We'll help."

"All right then," Roman said, pleased. He turned to Fraiser, who knelt next to the door. "Let's get that closed so we can move the boulder back. We need to head out within the next few minutes... The survival of the rebels rests in our hands..."

~

The day was dark, and thunderclouds rolled overhead while a constant tumult of rain pummeled the earth. Roman, Fraiser, and their companions snuck through the forest, keeping several yards between them and the tree line near the walls of Sector Four. They walked on in silence, and Roman allowed his thoughts to run rampant through his mind, never really settling on any clear path. All he knew was that he was wet and cold... But he was doing the right thing, and if this was all he had to suffer for it, he gladly would. Fraiser was a few feet ahead with Alec and the others when Roman suddenly paused to examine the dark sky, droplets of rain splashing against his face.

"Roman?" Fraiser called out as she stopped, raising a brow in confusion. The others halted a few feet behind her before turning to glance back.

"Hm?" he answered, not daring to break his gaze from the sky.

"We need to keep moving, or we won't make it in time," she said.

"What do you mean? We have an entire day until the testings," the woman questioned.

"We have to be there by the end of today," Roman answered, breaking his gaze away. "We have to let the others out of the tunnels, sneak past the guards, and get to the station. It's much more time-consuming than it sounds... Trust me."

The woman nodded, Roman motioned everyone forward, and they continued on.

As they trudged through the mud and rain, memories came flooding back to Roman. The rain had pounded hard against the earth that day as it did today... He'd been around fourteen when he and Fraiser had fled Sector One. He remembered walking into his father's office an hour before noon and accidentally interrupting an important meeting. He'd quickly ducked behind one of the enormous curtains that decorated the windows of Vayne's office, avoiding the eyes of the governors and his father. He'd listened as they'd discussed the growing situation with the Elementals—there had been a spike of positives in the most recent tests, and his father's impatience and fear of being overthrown had increased drastically.

~

Suddenly, someone pulled Roman out from behind the curtain to reveal the large wooden table and desk that occupied his father's office. He thought he'd been quick, but he hadn't been quick enough. The governor of Sector Four—a burly man with a bushy mustache—held him by the throat, dragging him to the center of the room. He stumbled over the ornate red-and-gold rug, wincing at the governor's grip. Fear shot throughout Roman's entire being, along with a strange burning sensation that ran up and down his limbs. His eyes began to sting and water as the man squeezed his throat tighter. He hit at the governor's arm, but his hold didn't loosen. The stinging in his eyes increased until he cried out in pain. He could hear voices shouting and chairs screeching backward, but they all sounded faint and far away. It was like someone had put hands over his ears.

Then Roman's eyes began to glow dark blue and silver. The governor of Sector Four was no longer holding him as he looked up and stared into his father's white pupils with black veins reaching toward his barely visible white irises. It felt as if he'd been electrocuted. Energy and power surged throughout his veins as the stinging in his eyes flared, and he was suddenly aware of the governor's hand reaching for his neck once more. Roman whirled and grabbed the man's hand, freezing his skin. The governor jumped back in pain, screeching viciously while he clutched at his arm. Frostbite raced over his jacket sleeve, spreading all the way to his shoulder. Roman turned back to face his father. The governor of Four had just triggered his element—the rarest element found in Elementals... Water.

The entire room froze as everyone looked between Roman and Vayne. Then his father spoke two words, his voice calm and even, "Seize him."

The office lurched into action, and Roman ducked under a punch thrown his way before countering with a punch of his own. His glowing eyes widened in amazement when the water from the vase on his father's desk shot forward, shattering the vase into pieces and knocking the governors of One and Four to the cool marble floor.

"Get him!" a man exclaimed, and the other governors charged him, along with the guards from the hallway who'd burst through the door.

Roman inhaled deeply, attempting to settle his rapid breathing. His father had always been so obsessed with trying to become a water Elemental. He'd let it drive him mad and had gone from a loving father and husband to an abuser. He'd neglected and hit Roman and his mother whenever they'd tried to convince him that conducting unusual experiments on himself wouldn't work. Those experiments had led to his white eyes and the black veins that stretched all over his body like poisonous snakes.

Years of anger toward his father came bubbling to the surface. Roman had never been able to stop his father. He'd fought back, especially when he'd hit his mother, but he'd never won. There was nothing he could do about any of it... Until now. The burning in Roman's eyes extended down to his arms before spreading to his torso and legs. He knew what the burning wanted. It wanted him to give in—to surrender his control and let it take over. So Roman did.

The next thing he knew, he was opening his normal brown eyes to an office soaked in water with large shards of ice sticking out of the walls and furniture. Sector Four's governor had been impaled with one of the large spikes of ice, and other bodies were strewn across the floor in pools of blood. Roman turned around to find his father leaning against the shattered front of his desk, unconscious. His hands shook as he merely stood there. What had he done? What was he supposed to do now?

Suddenly, an elderly woman—a servant he'd frequently seen around the mansion— entered the office and ran to him. She grabbed his arm and began to lead him down the golden halls lined with fancy furnishings and paintings. They quickly turned down hall after hall before reaching the open gates of the courtyard and fleeing into the nearby forest that began a few yards away from the mansion gates. Roman couldn't comprehend what was happening. All he felt was a cold shock seeping through him, and he didn't know what to do to stop it. The woman tugged at his arm, silently begging him to run faster, but where were they running? There was nowhere to go but—the walls. They were running toward the walls...

Soldiers shouting after them snapped Roman out of his stupor. He could hear the soldiers' footsteps pounding against the foliage of the forest, growing closer by the second. He leaped over an upturned root only to turn and watch as the woman tripped. He turned to help her, but she stuck out her hand in refusal.

"No! Keep running! Get to the wall!" she shouted. Roman's eyes widened in fear as the soldiers burst through the brush. He whirled and began to run once more, leaving the woman behind. Not staying to help her would become one of his biggest regrets in life...

~

Roman ran for what felt like hours until he finally stumbled out of the forest. Though the soldiers were still chasing him, he couldn't help but gaze at the concrete wall before him in awe. It was the first time he'd ever seen the wall this closely. Suddenly, the ground began to shake while his father's soldiers appeared in the tree line behind him. An explosion several yards to his left rattled the earth, knocking him and the soldiers to the grass. Dust and smoke billowed through the air for a few long moments before clearing. Roman's mouth fell open as rebels began to pour through an enormous hole in the wall dressed in their mismatched clothing—a symbol to Vayne and everyone else that they were against his reign.

"Mom!" Roman exclaimed, recognizing the soft face and black hair of his mother as she sprinted to him. The brightest grin spread across his face. He hadn't seen her since she'd disappeared several years ago. His father had always told Roman of his mother's apparent betrayal, but he'd never believed it. Joining the rebels wasn't a betrayal. It was a rescue— not only for herself but for Roman, too. He knew that if his mother could've escaped with him as well all those years ago, she would've. She'd warned Vayne not to intervene with nature and the elements—that it would result in terrible things. She'd been right. His father's inhumane experiments had convinced his mother of his father's insanity, and the experiments had given her a reason to stop it. So, his mother had escaped and helped form the rebels.

She pulled Roman up from the ground as the president's personal guard of brainwashed Elementals dressed in stark-white armor with a red band around their right biceps joined the soldiers that battled the rebels, and Roman's eyes glowed dark blue once more, his pupils silver. His mother touched his cheek and smiled. It was a smile full of joy, love, and pride—pride for him and what he was.

~

For what felt like an eternity, Roman fought alongside his mother and the rebels in their mismatched clothes and armor, pushing back against the soldiers trying to capture them. He found it surprisingly easy to wield his element. It came to him naturally. He'd throw a punch and the water would follow. It was a beautiful extension of his body and mind. The majority of the rebels wielded their elements, too, but others used guns and spears of electricity stolen from Vayne's army.

Roman dodged the tip of an electric spear when a column of air suddenly smacked into the soldier holding it, knocking the spear from his hands. A young girl stood over the man and used a grabbing motion to suck the air from the soldier's lungs as he scrambled after the spear. Roman's eyes darted between the lifeless body and the girl. Her eyes were glowing gray and silver—a stark contrast to her brown skin and black hair.

A scream pierced the air, causing Roman to whirl to face his mother across the battlefield. A spear of ice protruded through her abdomen. The world seemed to fall deathly silent, and the only thing he could hear was a ringing in his ears. He didn't know when he'd started running, or when the girl had started following him. Roman leaped over two bodies piled on top of each other, drawing his hands back past his right hip. He released a vicious scream, throwing all his power and emotions into the blow. He thrust forward, and daggers of ice flew from his hands, piercing the Elemental who'd speared his mother.

Roman stood over the young man, who fell to his knees and gasped for air through the blood filling his mouth. A knife of ice formed inside Roman's fist as he knelt next to him. With a single stroke of pure rage, he slit the man's throat, tears pooling in both of their eyes. Roman turned to his mother while the tears spilled over and down his face. Rebels suddenly began to surround them and lift his mother off the ground, and the girl tugged against his shoulder, pulling him back to the hole in the wall. They were retreating... Roman glanced back at his father's mansion—the only home he'd ever known—in the distance. He could taste the bile rising in his mouth. That wasn't his home. It never truly had been. Saying goodbye, he turned and followed the girl and the rebels into the forest...

~

Pain radiated through Roman's chest. His mother had died that night, and ever since that day, Roman and Fraiser had vowed to work together to lead the rebels and finish what she'd started. Though not a day passed when he didn't feel the echoes of her death, he couldn't help but smile to himself at the memory of the love she'd shown him—of the peace she'd given him when the entire world seemed to be against him. It was because of her love and memory that he vowed to accomplish her goal. If he couldn't do it, no one could. He would save the sectors and defeat his father. He didn't care how long it took, and he didn't care if it cost him his life. He'd do it.

~

Hours later, Roman and the others had successfully made their way around the entirety of Sector Four, and soon, the train station would be in sight. They ran throughout the dense woods, searching the hills for Sector Four's sewer drain.

"There!" Fraiser exclaimed, pointing toward a hill near the corner of the walls. There, in the side of the hill, sat the rusted metal drain. Water fell between the bars of the dark tunnel opening, and to the left of the opening was a metal door that locked from the outside. Fraiser quickly sprinted over, clearing away the branches and brush that covered the door before flinging the latch open. Roman slid to a stop beside her, sending pebbles and small chunks of concrete mixed in the dirt flying.

Waiting on the other side with a smile was seventeen-year-old Napoleon Wright with his light brown hair, blue eyes, and freckles that dotted his face. Roman smiled at Napoleon, and the memory of how he and Fraiser saved the young earth Elemental from the train station last year played through his head. He loved the boy he'd come to know as his little brother. He was always smiling—always a bright ray of sun in the darkest of hours.

Napoleon sighed, relief clear on his face. "What took you guys so long? We thought something had happened."

"We had a close call with a guard or two." Fraiser shrugged. "Security's tight, but we made it."

"We're here now, Napoleon. Is everyone ready to go?" Roman asked, clapping him on the shoulder as they began to lead the squinting rebels out of the tunnel.

"Yes, we're ready."

"Good," Roman said, watching the rain pound against the ground even harder than before. He couldn't shake the feeling that today would be like that fateful day so many years ago. It would be difficult and *deadly*. "I hope everyone is prepared..."

"We can do this," Napoleon assured him as they gazed out over the forest and hills.

"This is the right thing to do, isn't it?" he questioned, considering the lives that would be taken tonight—the deaths that would fall upon him. Deaths that *he* had caused.

Fraiser stood on the opposite side of Roman. She glanced at him, then at Napoleon. "You always make the decision you think is best for us. If this wasn't right, then we wouldn't be here."

Roman nodded, but he was far from convinced. He'd tried so hard over the years to be the best leader he could and make up for all the wrongs he felt responsible for. But how many had he led to their deaths? How was he any different than his father?

"I know that look, Roman." Fraiser nudged him. "You are *nothing* like him."

"She's right, boss man," Napoleon said. "You've done so well. You truly have saved us... Never forget that."

Fraiser nodded in agreement. "Your mother would be proud."

Roman looked at them, his heart swelling with love. He didn't deserve them, but he thanked the Aether every day that he had them. He gave them a small smile before beginning the march back into the forest. They needed to leave. The testings would be tonight... "Let's move out. We need to be in position soon."

Napoleon glanced at Fraiser solemnly. "He's never going to stop blaming himself for everything that's happened."

"He has to at some point," she said. "If he doesn't, he's going to end up getting himself killed..."

"We won't let that happen."

Fraiser smiled before ruffling Napoleon's hair. "No, we won't."

CHAPTER SEVEN

THE TESTINGS

The rain pounded viciously against Natalia's wooden shack, and thunder roared in the distance. She sat on her cot in the growing dark, glancing at the mandatory projector that sat on her small wooden table every few minutes. The testings would be announced tonight... She shivered, feeling trapped inside the cage she called a house. The storm was too bad to take a walk, and it wasn't like she could risk slipping through the crack in the wall today. Security would be on high alert because of the testings.

Natalia bounced her leg impatiently against the floorboards. She'd always hated the little shack, though she knew she'd been fortunate to find it after running away from the orphanage. A neighbor had helped her fix up some of the broken areas, but the shack had always made her feel claustrophobic. Like the orphanage, it was plain and sad and empty of those she loved—which was why she spent most of her time outside. Coming home after the day was over was just so...depressing...

Natalia rose from her bed and walked to one of the hooded, gray jackets upon the chair. She didn't care how bad the storm was. She needed to walk—to escape the overbearing heaviness that was threatening to smother her. Wishing Damien and the others were with her, she stepped outside, shrinking into the warm jacket. It was cold and the dark clouds blotted out the sun completely. She inhaled, appreciating the sweet scent the rain left as it pounded against the dirt road. Natalia then turned her back to the distant center of Sector Four and began to walk toward the walls. She wouldn't get too close, but she needed to see it. She needed to see the treetops of the world beyond the towering sentries just to know that it was still there. As she walked, worry crept into her mind, and she couldn't shake the feeling that someone was watching her. Then Natalia noticed the dozens of Vayne's soldiers patrolling her street—and the streets beyond. They were everywhere... But why?

Suddenly, a hand grabbed Natalia's arm from behind. She whirled to find a guard looming over her, clutching her arm tight.

"Return to your hovel," the man under the helmet sneered as he began to pull her back toward her shack.

"Let me go!" Natalia exclaimed, thrashing to free herself. "I didn't do anything!"

"Enough!" he yelled, causing the other soldiers around them to turn and face them.

Natalia could feel their eyes on her as she reared her free hand back and punched the soldier. Her knuckles connected against the dark helmet, scraping across it and ripping them open. Blood trickled down her hand, and the soldier stumbled backward. She turned to run only to slam into another soldier, who wrapped their arms around her. She struggled and thrashed about once more until the first soldier, having regained his footing, stood before her. He waved off the soldiers that had begun to surround them and returned Natalia's punch to the face.

The world swam, and the ground came rushing to meet her, but before she could collide with it, two sets of hands grabbed her. Together, the two soldiers dragged Natalia back to her shack, kicked open the door, and shoved her inside. She stumbled, collapsing to her knees. A warm trickle of blood leaked out of her right nostril, splattering onto the wooden floorboards. She looked up to find her once dark room now alight with a soft blue-gray light. Natalia stood and turned to the glowing projector on the table, reading the bold words on the screen.

MANDATORY CURFEW

Her jaw dropped, and she plopped down into the rickety chair. Her thoughts immediately ran to her friends. Were they okay? Were they under a curfew, too, or were the people of Sector Four the only ones? Had the rebels attacked? Or maybe President Vayne had something bigger planned tonight... She sat on the edge of the chair, hands clutching the wooden seat. She felt like a caged animal awaiting the slaughter.

Natalia closed her eyes with a sigh, attempting to calm herself. A few moments passed before her fingers returned to the ring Damien had given her, twisting it nervously. She grunted in frustration as her thoughts then wandered to Damien and the confusion he made her feel. She'd never really thought of him the way he wanted her to—she never allowed herself to think like that. She already loved him, but if she was *in* love with him... What would she do if someone took him from her? How would she be able to live without him? Would they work together if they tried? She shook her head, attempting to rid herself of the thoughts. Thinking of him now wouldn't do her any good...

~

Ren sat on the couch between Lavelle and their ten-year-old sister, eyes glued to the projector in front of them. Their parents stood in their tiny kitchen, holding each other in anticipation. Ren nervously bit his bottom lip until he tasted blood. Lavelle grabbed his hand and smiled. It was a forced, weary smile. She was nervous. They both were. The mandatory curfew had set everyone on edge. Those brave enough had attempted to escape their homes to run and hide, but they'd quickly been thwarted and hunted down by soldiers. Ren squeezed Lavelle's hand tighter, trying to keep his own from shaking. Suddenly, the blue-gray projector screen changed, and the bold letters signaling the curfew faded, replaced by the governor of Sector Two. Ren scowled as Lavelle shot him a surprised look. He only shook his head in response. What was going on? The testings never started like this... He glanced between Lavelle; their little sister, Claire; and their parents. Tears were welling in his mother's and Claire's eyes, his father was unusually still, and Lavelle had set her nervous smile in place. Everyone was so afraid—including himself.

"You should read something to us," Ren said to Lavelle, attempting to distract everyone.

Claire, who had the same blue eyes as the twins, nodded.

Lavelle's smile brightened a bit, and she stood. "Help me pick."

Ren nodded and followed her past their kitchen and down the beige hall to the room they shared. He watched from the doorway while she knelt between their two ivory beds that occupied the tiny room. A small ray of light peeked through the single window, casting Lavelle's shadow upon the floor. It danced as she slid under her bed. Lying on her back, Lavelle reached up, ripping one of the small wooden beams from the frame to reveal a large hole cut into her mattress.

Ren couldn't help the small chuckle that escaped his lips. Many of the books she had were stolen from Sector Four by Natalia. If they were ever found in her possession—for most books were banned to keep the people of Araedia as helpless and weak as possible—she'd be executed. She reached into her mattress, digging through the books he knew she had memorized by feel.

Lavelle's head poked out from underneath the bed. "History or poetry?"

"Poetry," Ren said with a genuine smile that only his twin could put on his face.

Her head disappeared back under the bed, and she rustled around for a few moments before reemerging with a small leather book of poetry that Natalia had given her for their birthday. Ren walked over, helping her to her feet before following his sister back into the living room and returning to their spots on the couch. Lavelle then flipped the book open and began to read. Ren leaned his head back against the cushions, closing his eyes. He focused on his sister's voice—the voice he loved the most and could listen to for hours. The voice he was terrified he would never hear again...

~

Damien stared out of the window in his small living room. His mother—as usual—was gone, leaving her three boys to care for themselves until she came stumbling home with a man even drunker than she would be. Damien's brothers hid in their room, too frightened to watch the projector—or to be caught near him when their mother did decide to come home. Damien knew his brothers loved him, but his mother had made sure that they'd never trust him. She'd told them so many lies about him and their father's death... Even though it *was* his fault, he'd never done it to purposefully get his father killed like his mother always said.

Damien rubbed his red, stinging left cheek as he walked over to their tiny kitchen table surrounded by four wooden chairs. His mother had left him with a parting gift a few hours ago. He hated to admit it, but she'd gotten him good that time. He grabbed one of the chairs and dragged it over to their projector that sat on a low wooden table. He took a seat, glancing back at the door to his parents' room. Their house had four rooms total, which was rare for a house on the outskirts of Sector Three. But he and his father had spent many hours building his brothers' room during the summer several years ago. It was one of his favorite projects that he'd helped his father with. They'd also fixed the back door and had even added a window to Damien's room. He slept with it open every night.

Ever since his father's death, Damien had been on his own while in Sector Three. He never considered his house a home. It felt more like a cage keeping him from his real home—the home which he thought of now. Had he messed everything up with Natalia? Was she angry with him? Would she disown him like his mother had? He should've never said how he felt. It made him vulnerable. It made him weak... But if he never saw her again, he knew he'd regret not saying anything. After all, he never expected her to love him back. But no matter what, he knew he'd always love her. Even unto his dying breath...

"It's all right," Damien whispered to himself. "Everything will work out. Be strong and courageous like Dad always said."

~

"Remember, Damien," the memory of his father spoke, placing his large hands on six-year-old Damien's shoulders. "You are strong and courageous, and I will always love you..."

~

Damien sighed. "I miss you, Dad..."

Suddenly, one of Damien's dark-headed younger brothers ran from their room into the kitchen. The other followed quickly behind; looks of terror were on both their faces. Damien stiffened as he faced the projector he'd neglected for the past few minutes. He froze, trying to comprehend the words upon the screen. He didn't know when he'd stood, or when his brothers had run to him with tears pouring down their cheeks... Or when they'd started hugging him... Damien numbly knelt on the wooden floor and held his brothers as they cried.

~

Aurum sat upon her white couch, mindlessly watching the projector images flash across the wall. She exhaled nervously as Sector One's governor read from a white sheet of paper. Her mother walked into the room from their white kitchen, questioning the date. She had her apron on, and Aurum could smell steak cooking.

"It's not time already, is it?" her mother asked before rambling on to her next question. None of her mother's words pierced her ears, and a knot began to form in Aurum's stomach. She picked at the fuzzy blanket on the couch next to her, unable to bear her mother's anxious chattering.

"Mom, I'm scared," she heard herself whisper. She didn't even remember forming the words. Her mother threw her arms around her, hugging her tightly. She smelled of the floral perfume Aurum had gifted her for her birthday last year. Tears welled in Aurum's brown eyes. The bad feeling Damien had talked about... She felt it, too. She felt like the entire world was pressing down on her shoulders, and there was nothing she could do to keep it from crushing her. She was suffocating. She couldn't breathe.

"Everything will be all right." Her mother grabbed her face gently, trying to stop her hyperventilating. "You'll be all right..."

"My friends—what about my friends?" Aurum mumbled more to herself than her mother. Her mind raced to Natalia, Damien, and the twins. "Please be okay..."

"Honey, I need you to calm down, please," her mother pleaded.

Aurum blinked, shaking her head. She hadn't noticed how rapid her breathing had gotten. She rose from the couch and walked down the blindingly white hallway to her bathroom. She slid inside, closing and leaning against the door. She glanced at the square mirror that hung over her sink. A frightened, pale-faced little girl with shaking hands stared back.

"Let the testings begin!" the governor's loud voice echoed throughout the house.

Aurum sprang away from the door, bending over in front of the toilet beside her sink. She wrapped her arms around her stomach as she hurled into the toilet. A few tears escaped her eyes as a cold sweat began to envelop her. Suddenly, a sob escaped her mother from the living room. Aurum's blood ran cold. Slowly, she rose from the toilet before darting back into the hallway. She froze as her eyes met the screen and the name that flashed upon it...

~

"It's past time for Sector Four... Get on with it," Natalia whispered to herself, staring at the blank screen. The testing announcement was running late. They should've already begun in Sector Four... *What was going on?* If something had happened in one of the other sectors, she wouldn't find out anytime soon. Vayne had made sure that communication between the sectors was impossible. They couldn't even watch each other's testing announcements. Without warning, the screen flickered, and the skinny face of Sector Four's governor appeared. Natalia plugged her ears, ignoring the woman's irritable voice. The screen flashed again, showing the pictures and names of the children of Four. One, two, three... The names went on and on. Seven, eight... Nine... Natalia stared at the ninth name and face upon her screen.

NATALIA RHYS

Breathe, Natalia told herself, shakily rising from her chair. She would be fine. Her friends would be fine, too. It was just another test. *In and out.*

Natalia began to walk toward her jacket when four soldiers burst through the door, knocking it off its hinges. She jumped back in shock and reached for the knife on the table. The closest soldier lunged for her, slamming the hand she'd closed around the knife's hilt onto the table. Adrenaline spread through her veins, and she swung her free hand at the soldiers only for it to collide with a gloved hand. She'd been too slow... But why were they here? Usually, the soldiers would simply wait outside for her. Was this because of her confrontation earlier, or was Damien's bad feeling about these testings right?

"No! Get off of me!" Natalia yelled as two soldiers flanked her and pinned her arms behind her back. "No!"

They dragged her through the door and out into the pouring rain and wind that tore at her hair. Waiting in the street were two additional guards and a large, black armored truck. The two additional soldiers threw open the back doors while the others slammed her down against one of the many cold metal seats that lined the inside. Fear and anger were all she felt as she struggled and pushed against them. How could she let them take her so easily? She had to keep fighting—not only for herself but for her family. The two soldiers pinned Natalia's arms against her seat, while the third and fourth locked her into the seat. Then they exited the truck, slamming and locking the doors behind them.

Natalia glanced around for the first time to find nine other children in the truck with her—all selected to be tested... If that was what they were even doing. She honestly didn't know at this point. Several of the children around her wept. Some sat and stared into worlds of their imaginations far away where they foolishly thought they'd be safe. Others pulled at their harnesses strapped across their thighs and chests as Natalia did, but unlike her, they quickly stopped and gave up.

Natalia never gave up. She spent twenty minutes pulling at the harness before the truck came to a jarring halt. She frantically swung her head to the doors, her black hair that had fallen from her braid crowding and sticking to her face. The doors flung open, and ten soldiers—one for each child—began to unlock the harnesses. As soon as the lock clicked open, Natalia popped up and swung, but the soldier quickly twisted her arm before throwing her against the side of the truck. She winced when her head smacked into the jarring metal. Thick, warm blood began to slowly trickle down her face. The soldier then grabbed Natalia, locking her hands behind her back before leading her from the truck.

The rain pounded against the earth viciously, and raindrops stung Natalia's face when she looked at the black sky above. Night had fallen... She could tell, despite the clouds blotting out everything. The wind violently ripped at her loose hair and clothes while her soldier pushed her forward. Bolts of lightning struck all around, glittering across the sky in scattering tendrils and casting a blue light upon her bloody face and the long metal building before her. Dense forest surrounded the entire building. They were deep into the woods—possibly a few miles out from the sectors...

But chaos had ensued. Children screaming and crying pierced her ears amongst the raging storm, and she could see soldiers beating those who tried to escape as they were all dragged toward the metal building. She didn't know what to do. She struggled and thrashed about, but it was no use. She was going into that building whether she wanted to or not.

"Natalia!" a familiar voice yelled from her left. Natalia turned her head to see Ren being forced to the ground, his face covered in mud, bruises, and blood.

"No..." Natalia whispered. It couldn't be... She was dreaming. That wasn't Ren. It was someone else. No, no, no, no... She couldn't have her family taken from her again. She couldn't. Natalia yanked harder against the soldier's grip on her hands. The man behind the helmet grunted as he shoved her to the ground, sending a kick into her side. She gasped and coughed for the air that escaped her lungs.

"Leave her alone!" Ren exclaimed, and his soldier struck him across the face. Natalia and Ren were then pulled up from the ground, once again heading toward the building. Enormous metal doors had been lifted to the ceiling by chains, opening their metal cage. Natalia's eyes followed the chains to the ceiling as she and Ren were dragged under. The soldiers led them in the direction of the dozens of lines of gathering soldiers and children wearing shades of gray, brown, white, and beige and cream. Beyond the lines, Natalia could see other children being loaded onto two trains. She searched the rows frantically, praying to the Aether that she wouldn't find another familiar face. But then her heart sank.

"Aurum!" Natalia shouted. Aurum glanced over her shoulder, a terrified look upon her face before her soldier yanked her brown hair and forced her to turn back around. Natalia released a shaky breath. "Ren, where's Lavelle?"

Ren shook his head. "She wasn't chosen."

"Thank the Aether," Natalia mumbled before searching the crowd for one last face. The relief that momentarily filled her mind immediately vanished, replaced by the fear and anger she had felt before. She was scared for herself and for her family. How could she protect them now? She was helpless. She cursed Vayne with every ounce of anger and hatred in her soul. She cursed and cursed and cursed him. This was all happening because of him. "Please, don't be here. Please, don't be here. *Please.* Don't. Be. Here."

It felt like her heart had been ripped from her chest, and tears filled her eyes as they met his. Blood trickled from his mouth and nose, and bruises were already forming on his face. Damien sighed in defeat when he saw her. She'd always been able to read him, and she could still read him through the crowd now. He'd done the exact same thing she had. He'd fought back, he'd gotten scared and angry, but he'd also hoped with every fiber of his being that she was the last person that he'd ever see in that building.

"Walk!" Natalia's soldier yelled before turning and slapping her across the face. Natalia yelped in surprise more than pain. Damien roared in anger before stomping on his soldier's foot and elbowing them in the abdomen.

"Talia!" he screamed as soldiers began to surround him. They collapsed inward, beating him to the ground.

"No! Stop! *Stop!* You'll kill him!" Natalia screamed, pushing and fighting against the mindless dog clad in black armor once more.

As soon as the words left her lips, an explosion near the trains rocked the entire building, knocking everyone to the cold concrete floor. Natalia rose to a knee before being knocked back to the ground by a second explosion. The fire of the soldiers' guns, screams, and war cries filled the air. The electric bolts lit up the clouds of smoke and dust billowing through the air. Natalia gasped when the rebels in their mismatched clothing and armor poured into the building from two gaping holes created by the explosions. Vayne's soldiers amongst the crowd of children pulled their guns from their shoulders and began to fire blue-purple bolts of deadly electricity toward the rebels, who quickly spread throughout the building. Some blocked and attacked with their elements and stolen spears and guns of electricity, while others ran into the crowd.

Natalia watched wide-eyed as the rebels began to help the children through the holes away from the fighting. *The rebels were saving them.* Adrenaline coursed through Natalia's veins, and she couldn't help the smile that spread across her face. She wouldn't have to find them because they'd come to her. She could join them now—fight alongside them and save her family. *She could finally be free.*

Natalia turned, elbowing her soldier's black helmet. The tinted glass hiding the eyes of the man beneath shattered, piercing his skin. She threw her weight into a kick that sent him to the floor before stomping on the glass in his eyes and face. The man screamed horridly, completely blinded. She whirled, searching the chaotic crowd, and watched as a woman with light brown skin, black hair, and glowing gray eyes sprinted at Aurum. The woman used a grabbing motion to suck the air from Aurum's soldier's throat. She then went to Aurum, who knelt on the floor, clutching her eyes in pain. The woman helped her to her feet to reveal Aurum's silver pupils and glowing red irises before leading her to one of the gaping holes.

Natalia laughed to herself in awe and shock. What in the Aether's name was happening? Aurum, catching the woman by surprise, yanked away and pointed back at Natalia and Ren. The woman nodded before turning and calling for someone amongst the crowd of fighting rebels. The action snapped Natalia out of her stupor, and she searched for Ren and Damien through the crowd. Aurum was safe now. She had to make sure they were, too.

It didn't take her long to spot Ren swinging at a soldier, who ducked easily before reaching for the gun strapped across the back of their armor. Natalia pushed her way toward him as fast as she could, and panic filled her like a disease. She had to get there. She had to get to him. Ren grabbed the gun, struggling and pulling against the soldier. He just had to hang on a little longer. She was almost there. The soldier knocked Ren to the ground, pointing the gun at his abdomen. She watched as Ren looked up in terror. Then his blue eyes began to glow dark green around pupils as black as the night sky.

Suddenly, a spear of ice shot through the soldier's chest, and the bodied toppled over. Natalia sprinted to Ren, pushing the body off him and yanking him up from the cold concrete floor. He immediately wrapped his shaking arms around her. His breathing was rapid, and his glowing eyes were wide with a fear that hurt her heart. She hated to see him like that. She faced the holes left by the rebels' explosions— the direction the spear of ice had come from—where a tall, muscular man with black hair and glowing dark blue irises and silver pupils ran. Two rebels followed behind him, weaving their way to her and Ren. Natalia gently unpeeled his arms and squeezed his hands reassuringly. The rebels weren't going to hurt him. They were his best chance of getting out of here.

"I'm going to go find Damien. Go with them. Be brave. I'll meet up with you after I find him," she said, disappearing into the chaos of the battling crowd. She tore her way through, pushing and shoving around rebels, children, and Vayne's soldiers. High-pitched screams dragged her attention back to the doors of the train station, and fear gripped her being. The soldiers had begun dragging as many Araedians as they could carry back to the armored trucks.

Without warning, something smashed into Natalia's side, sending her tumbling to the floor. She slid to a stop a few feet away and looked up to watch a soldier and a rebel fighting. The soldier ducked under the rebel's fist before flipping the young man onto the concrete and repeatedly beating him with a crackling spear of electricity. Her eyes widened in horror as the rebel's warm blood splattered across her face, and the soldier turned to her. Was she going to die? What would happen to Damien if she didn't find him? What about Ren and Aurum?

The soldier lifted the visor hiding their eyes to reveal the bearded face of a man hungry for violence—a man that *delighted* in it. He swung his spear at her, and Natalia rolled. Sparks exploded from the ground where the tip of the spear scraped against the concrete with an ear-piercing screech. She immediately bounded up from the ground and faced him. She blinked rapidly as her eyes began to sting slightly, and the room around her seemed to brighten. The stinging grew more and more painful, but Natalia couldn't close her eyes. She refused to die here—to die today.

A new adrenaline coursed through her veins, which she swore were on fire, and all the muscles in her body felt as if they'd grown five times stronger. She could feel her body changing—like a part of her that had been hidden away for years was finally releasing. She felt whole. She felt different. Then her pupils began to glow the purest silver, surrounded by ice-blue irises.

Natalia was an Elemental.

The sadistic man swung his spear again, and tendrils of electricity singed her gray clothes as she leaped back. She watched in amazement while something inside her called the rainwater toward her. It cut through the air like a blade, curling and wrapping around her arm. She met the man's gaze, full of anger and—fear. That was fear. Natalia lunged forward, throwing her fist at the soldier. A column of water shot from her hand and collided against his chest, sending him flying back into the crowd. Her lips parted in shock. She was an Elemental... And she had something that she'd never had before. *Power.*

Natalia turned, slamming into a firm chest. She lifted her head to find the tall man who'd saved Ren. He grabbed her arm and attempted to pull her back to the rebels' escape.

"Let go!" Natalia exclaimed as she tried to pry his hand from her wrist.

"We're saving you!" he yelled over the battle surrounding them.

"My friend is back there!" Natalia glanced back, pausing when her eyes found Damien. Two soldiers had already dragged him from the building and were nearing one of the many armored trucks. He fought them with every ounce of strength he had, but when the third and fourth soldiers came... He didn't stand a chance no matter how many punches he landed, and Natalia could only watch as they threw him inside the truck. Damien's eyes met hers a moment before the doors slammed shut.

She gasped when the tall man suddenly picked her up, tossing her over his right shoulder and sprinting toward the exit. She didn't know what to do. Tears of anger at herself and the man filled her eyes. If he hadn't intervened, she could've made it.

She could've stopped them from taking him. Damien. They'd taken him—*Vayne had taken him*. Just a he'd taken Damien just as he'd taken Vale. She didn't know what to do. She'd let it happen again. Why had she let it happen again? Vale was gone. Lavelle was still in Sector Two. Ren was gone. Aurum was gone. Damien. Was. *Gone.*

"Go back! We have to go back!" she screamed, battering the man's strong back. Her fists merely bounced off his black shirt. She was useless again. Even with the power she'd gained, she was still *useless.* "I can't leave him! Please, don't leave him!"

"We have to! Vayne already has him," the man said as he spared a glance back at her. His eyes had stopped glowing and were now brown with gold, amber, and honey highlights. With those mesmerizing eyes, he pleaded with her to comply—to let him help her.

Without warning, a column of raging fire shot past them, missing by an inch and sending them tumbling to the ground. Natalia winced, pushing herself up. Beside her, Brown Eyes—the name she'd settled on calling him for now—grunted in pain and clutched at his left calf. He hissed as blood and puss spilled from a nasty burn. She glanced over in the direction the fire had come from to find a young girl around the age of sixteen clad in stark-white armor with a blood-red band around her right bicep. Her heart sank into her stomach. She'd heard the awful stories behind that armor—the armor that Vayne's brainwashed personal guards wore.

The girl stalked toward them numbly, shooting spheres of vicious flames with glowing orange and silver eyes deprived of all emotions. Natalia squeezed her eyes shut and threw her arms up like a shield, awaiting the scorching flames... But they never came. All she felt was cool water. She opened her stinging eyes to watch steam rise from a circular shield of rotating water that floated before her. Had she done that? She moved her hands to the side, and the water followed. She rose from the ground, and the shield rose with her. Yes, she had...

From the ground, Brown Eyes flung large spikes of ice at the young girl. She dove to the side, countering with a wave of hungry flames. Natalia quickly knelt next to him and held her shield out. The flames collided against it, splitting and flying to the sides. The girl scowled. It was the only emotion she'd shown yet. A wall of ice appeared in front of Natalia, blocking the blows the girl viciously threw at them. Natalia turned to find Brown Eyes on one knee with his hand extended. He nodded, and as the wall shrank, Natalia sprinted at it. She jumped, using the top of the wall to leap and throw her shield at the girl. She watched the shield mold and freeze into a spike of ice that pierced the girl through the ribs. The girl sighed before collapsing to the ground, the ice shattering into a million pieces beneath her.

Natalia then turned and ran back to Brown Eyes, slipping his arm around her shoulders and pulling him up. She did her best to ignore the corpse that was lying on the ground because of her. It wouldn't be the last time she saw it. No, she'd see it in her nightmares. She was sure of it. Together, they hobbled toward the smoking craters. Slowly, the rebels began to fall back. With the majority of their army behind the wall, earth Elementals began to block one of the craters with mounds of hardened rock. Natalia grunted as she dragged him faster and stumbled into the last crater and out into the cold rain and wind.

"Where do I go?" she asked while the rebels closed in behind them, blocking in the rest of Vayne's soldiers and the children they couldn't rescue before fleeing into the forest.

"Follow." He grunted in pain. "Just follow."

Natalia nodded and followed after the rebels disappearing within the tree line. The night was pitch-black besides the occasional strikes of lightning, and the rain and blood falling into her eyes clouded her vision, making it nearly impossible to see. Suddenly, a boy around the age of seventeen with light brown hair, freckles, and glowing green and black eyes ran to them from the depths of the forest. His pupils remained black when his irises faded to a normal blue, and he ducked, throwing Brown Eyes' other arm around his shoulder.

The boy smiled. "Looks like Fraiser's not the only one you owe now, boss man."

"I saved her first." Brown Eyes shrugged. "We're even."

"Thank you." The boy nodded at Natalia. "I'm Napoleon Wright, and this is our leader, Roman. We're with the rebels."

"I think she's figured that out by now, Napoleon," Roman said, the corners of his mouth lifting slightly.

"Oh, right."

"You're the *leader* of the rebels?" Natalia blurted as she came to a jarring halt, causing Roman to wince when his leg hit the ground. The leader she'd been searching for—the person who'd kept her going and full of hope for so many years—was barely older than her.

"Yep." He frowned. "That's me."

Natalia truly studied him for the first time. He looked so tired—tired of being considered more valuable than others. He looked as if he wished he could be a normal rebel like Napoleon, who simply fought for what he believed in and didn't have to carry the burdens of leadership. But she couldn't help but be angry with him. She gritted her teeth. In fact, she wished she could punch him, but the fight wouldn't have been fair. He was currently crippled. Her burning gaze met his, and instantly, the fire and anger burning inside her were put out. Whether she liked to admit it or not, he'd saved her with his terrible timing. He'd kept her from Damien even though she knew she would've never made it to him in time... Though she still wished she could've done more to try to save him...

However, if she were being perfectly honest with herself, she really wasn't angry with *him* at all. Roman had saved her, Ren, and Aurum. Natalia sighed, softening her gaze. No, she wasn't angry with him... She was angry with *herself.*

"I'm sorry," she whispered.

Roman shook his head, studying her as she'd studied him. "You have nothing to apologize for... But we should keep walking..."

Natalia nodded in agreement, and they continued on deeper into the forest away from the train station. He was right. They needed to put as much distance between themselves and Vayne's soldiers as possible just in case they decided to give chase.

Napoleon nudged Roman's shoulder gently, raising a brow. "So, what happened to you?"

"He was burned," Natalia answered. She tightened her grip and pulled his arm farther around her shoulders. "Badly," she added with a shrug.

"Don't worry, boss man," Napoleon said as he patted Roman's chest. "We'll get you fixed up when we get back to camp."

Roman rolled his eyes, huffing in amusement. "You better be glad I can't run right now."

"He hates when I call him that," Napoleon said to Natalia with a cheeky smile.

She couldn't help but smile in return. She didn't know what was going on or what would happen, but she did know that in a world full of darkness, Napoleon seemed to be one of the only lights left. He was pure and fragile, and he reminded her of Lavelle—two rays of sunshine. Thinking of Lavelle brought Ren and Aurum to the forefront of her mind. She knew they made it out of the station... But where were they now? Were they going to the rebels' camp, too? Surely, they'd stuck with the rebels. They'd be stupid to seclude themselves out in the forest like this.

"Where is your camp? Will we be safe there?" Natalia asked, meeting Roman's gaze once more.

"Of course, you will," Roman said with determination.

"Don't worry. It's a day-and-a-half journey from here," Napoleon said. "No one will find us out that deep in the forest."

Natalia nodded as they trudged on through the now light rain, thoughts of Damien running rampant throughout her mind. Where was he, and what were they doing to him? Was he even still alive? No one had ever returned from Vayne's clutches, but maybe Damien could survive until she found a way to get to him. Besides, they never made it to the actual testing part, so maybe that would buy them time... But what kind of testing was that? It was nothing like her previous testings, but then again, she didn't really remember much about them. Was that the result of some kind of brainwashing? Knowing Vayne's methods, it was highly likely, but what was he *really* doing?

She wondered what Damien would think about the fact that she was an Elemental. She'd never really had the time to process it, however, she smiled at the thought of it. She knew exactly what he would've said—what Vale would've said, too. They both wouldn't have been surprised. Vale would've told her to embrace it because it only made her more special, and Damien would've told her to do whatever she wanted and to fear no one because *she was finally free.* He'd tell her how much he still loved her, and how he'd always have her back...

So, why didn't she have his when he'd needed it most?

You didn't try to save him. You were afraid. You're a coward. You always have been, and you always will be, the voice in her head screamed.

Natalia imagined explaining what had happened to Damien to Ren and Aurum. She imagined them telling her that it wasn't her fault, and there was nothing she could've done. No one could've saved him.

But you could have, the voice said again.

She glanced between Roman and Napoleon and the dark path ahead. The darkness of the forest seemed to crash toward her from all around, but it didn't near those two. It seemed as if nothing could darken the light that they shared—the warmth that surrounded them. Maybe it was the strong bond the two clearly shared. But whatever it was, Natalia wished she had it. Without Aurum, the twins, Damien, and Vale, she felt completely barren. She felt as if the darkness had swallowed her whole...

CHAPTER EIGHT

VULNERABLE

Natalia winced as one of the rebels' medics wiped the dried blood from her forehead. The cut was deep and had only stopped bleeding early yesterday morning. She'd had to take breaks while they'd traveled through the forest because she'd gotten so dizzy. Napoleon had nearly carried both her *and* Roman for the last hour of the trip. The day-and-a-half journey they'd promised had felt more like an entire week, and she still hadn't seen Aurum or Ren. Roman reassured her that they were somewhere within the throng of rebels marching through the woods, but she refused to relax until she laid eyes upon them. She'd tried to go find them as soon as they'd entered the camp, but Roman and Napoleon hadn't allowed it—not until she'd seen a medic first.

There were dozens and dozens of wounded who'd been immediately rushed through the tents and small shacks to the hospital. It was the largest wooden building in the entire camp. Rays from the setting sun leaked through the many windows set about, and small cotton beds lined the walls while two additional rows of beds split the middle of the tall room. It was nearly as tall as the sectors' walls. According to Napoleon, the building had been there since the first rebels. It had been abandoned when they'd discovered it, so they'd repaired it and started their rebellion from within.

The few doctors and medics amongst the rebels ran from bed to bed, tending to the wounded, which was a mixture of rebels and children alike. Across from Natalia sat Roman. Napoleon stood next to him, watching a doctor wrap a damp bandage around the burn on his calf. He winced when it touched his skin.

"Don't freeze all of it," the doctor warned. Roman nodded before extending his left hand for the bandage. His brown eyes began to glow their dark blue and silver as the damp cloth froze. "Perfect. Now I'm just going to wrap an extra layer, then you'll be good to go."

"Thank you," Roman said, glancing at Napoleon. He merely smiled in return.

Natalia looked away, feeling herself teetering back toward the edge of shock. The past day and a half had been exhausting, and she hadn't sat still long enough to process any of it at all. Her hands shook slightly when she tried to recall the events. Remembering only made it worse. The edge was far too near. She needed a distraction, so she stared at the ice on Roman's bandage. One day she could learn to do that. After all, like Roman, she was an Elemental. She could make water do anything she wanted. She could use it as a weapon, a shield, or she could not use it at all. It was her choice, but why throw away such power?

She exhaled unsteadily, attempting to calm the thousands of thoughts racing through her head. She could save Damien with this new power—and Lavelle. Once they got them back, they could do anything they wanted. They finally had something to rely on that they could always use, and they were finally free... Natalia wouldn't have to be afraid of losing those she loved any more. She could finally protect them once she learned to truly control it. Everything she'd done with the water yesterday had been luck and pure instinct. If she wanted to fight with the rebels to free the sectors, she'd have to practice. But she was more than willing to do so. These powers weren't a curse to lock away. They were a blessing.

"Natalia?" Napoleon questioned, pulling her from her stupor.

She met his blue eyes with a raised brow. "Sorry?"

"You need stitches," the medic standing before her repeated.

"No, I don't," Natalia said. Her heart rate picked up as she rose from the cot, ignoring the dizziness that hadn't quite faded. "I'll be fine without them."

Roman stood as well, cutting her off before she could slip out into the walkway. "That cut's bad. You need stitches," he said, authority ringing through his tone like an annoying bell.

She straightened defensively, attempting to look taller regardless of the fact that Roman stood a whole head over her. "What are you going to do, force me to get them?"

"I'm not going to force you to do anything. You have your own free will here unless you're trying to harm someone." He frowned and looked her up and down before turning and limping toward the door with Napoleon by his side. "But if you were smart, you'd get them."

Natalia glanced at the medic, who sighed. "How about we put a steri-strip over it? It will pull the laceration together and stop the bleeding."

"Here," she said, extending her palm. "I'll put them on later."

The medic frowned, reluctantly handing her the small strips of white cloth from a nearby wooden table. "Just at least come back tomorrow morning, please. I want to make sure it's healing correctly."

"I'll make sure she does!" Roman called out, exiting the hospital.

Natalia grunted in frustration and followed after them, barely slipping through the door before it closed. The storm clouds had finally cleared out and left behind a gorgeous orange, yellow, and pink sky, and the rays of the setting sun set the hundreds of square tents that made up the camp ablaze. Wooden shacks stood every few yards, and the rebels in their mismatched clothes bustled about between them all.

"How many did we lose last night, Napoleon?" Roman asked, turning and limping down one of the many paths carved between the large tents. She caught up to them easily but remained a few steps behind. It wasn't exactly a conversation she wanted to intrude on.

"Fifteen," Napoleon whispered solemnly. "Nine rebels and six children, and as you know, many are wounded... Overall, however, it was a successful operation..."

Roman frowned. He clearly wasn't as convinced as Napoleon regarding the successfulness. A smothering silence fell between them, the only noise being the racket of clanging pots and pans, fires, and people around them. Roman cut to the right and turned down another path woven in the grass. He seemed to be leading them further away from the heart of the camp. Napoleon stopped, laying a hand on Roman's shoulder.

"Don't beat yourself up about it." He smiled. "You're making the hard decisions, but they're the right ones."

Roman glanced at her with no particular emotion before turning back to Napoleon and ruffling his light-brown hair. "Aren't you supposed to be helping Alec?"

"Maybe." He swatted at Roman's hand, his smile widening into a grin.

"I'll see you in a bit," Roman said.

Natalia watched Napoleon dip his head and disappear into the throng of tents. When she turned around, Roman was already three tents away. She trotted after him, and the same silence from earlier was so loud now that it was deafening. She could feel the anger of being clearly ignored bubbling under her skin.

"I'm like you, right?" she asked, determined to shatter that silence and make him acknowledge her fully. "We're both water Elementals."

"Yes," he answered with a curt nod. "We're rare Elementals."

"Is that good or bad?"

"Both." Roman quickened his pace as they passed a group of rebels, who all greeted him with nods and small smiles. He nodded in return, and Natalia scowled when he began to walk even faster. Did he really think he could outrun her—especially with a limp?

"Hey!" she exclaimed, stopping. "Care to elaborate, or am I going to have to find someone man enough to turn and talk to me?"

Roman whirled and stared directly into her eyes with an intensity she'd never felt before. It was powerful and... Irritated. She had to bite the inside of her cheek to keep from smirking. She'd gotten under his skin. "You'll be a great target for Vayne, which is bad, but if you train hard, you *could* be a powerful Elemental. *That* is good because you can protect yourself and those around you."

"Wait!" Natalia called as he began to walk again, his limp already beginning to fade. She cursed at his stubbornness. "Will you just stop for one minute? Explain what's going on! I still don't know where my friends are, and I have people I need to help back in the sectors! I would've saved one of them if you hadn't dragged me away!"

"You're welcome," he said, facing her. "For saving you that is."

She scoffed. "You should've saved him instead."

"He wasn't savable. The soldiers had already thrown him in the truck."

"Everyone is savable." Natalia scowled. "I was supposed to protect him—and my friends—and I failed. I have to go and get them back."

"You can't just march into the sectors. It's not that simple. It's not that easy." Roman shook his head. "You wouldn't make it past security in Three."

Anger rushed through her like a poison, and she gritted her teeth. "I can handle myself."

Roman glanced to his right where a pitcher of water sat next to someone's tent. He punched forward, sending a column of water hurling at her. Natalia brought her hands up like a shield, repeating the motion she'd done against Vayne's personal guard—the girl she'd killed. By the Aether... She'd *killed* that girl—

Her eyes widened as the water ignored her command and slammed into her, knocking her straight to the ground. For a moment, she simply sat there, rooted to the spot by that girl's face as her last breath had left her body. She shook the thoughts away and pushed them deep down inside, locking them up where they could never escape again. She already felt enough guilt about Damien. There was no need to add more, and besides, the girl had attacked her. Was she not supposed to defend herself and Roman, even if she wished she could knock him on his ass? Natalia jumped up, gaze full of raw fury.

"You don't have enough control yet. Vayne's personal guard would cut through you in seconds." Roman held his hand up as Natalia opened her mouth to argue. "You had help with the one you faced at the station, and she was as green as they get. But if you stay here and let me help you, we can get your friends back. You can't just march into the sectors untrained, though. You wouldn't be saving anyone."

"I see the feisty one survived," a woman's voice called from behind.

Roman walked over to Natalia, extending his hand. She lightly batted it away and stood as the woman who had saved Aurum joined them.

"Fraiser." Roman nodded. "Glad to know you're alive."

"I always am." She returned what Natalia assumed was supposed to be a smile, but it was more like a barring of teeth than anything. Fraiser's piercing green eyes flicked to her, looking her up and down with a raised brow.

"Fraiser, this is Natalia. Natalia, this is Fraiser Hale. She's my right hand," Roman said.

Natalia and Fraiser watched each other for a long time, neither willing to break their staring contest. She could feel the hostility rolling off Fraiser in waves. She clearly thought highly of herself, and Natalia had never really gotten along with people like that. They were selfish and only cared about themselves... A few more moments passed before Roman cleared his throat.

"Your friends are in that tent over there," Fraiser said, pointing a few tents down back toward the hospital.

Natalia lifted her chin before glancing in the direction Fraiser had pointed. She was glad she was taller than her. It allowed her to feel somewhat intimidating when standing next to her, and though she hated the idea of backing down to Fraiser, she wanted—no, *needed*—to see Aurum and Ren. She couldn't last another minute without them.

"Thanks," Natalia said as she cut between her and Roman.

Fraiser's overly happy smile widened with mock kindness. "You're welcome."

"Natalia!" Roman called. Oh, so *now* he wanted to talk... Natalia paused, but refused to turn around, mimicking his previous actions. She could hear the hesitation in his voice when he spoke. He'd noticed. "I promise I'll explain everything later... Just try to settle in for now. Please."

She nodded and continued through the rows of gray square tents. Though she hated to admit it, Roman was right. Without more control over her element, she'd never make it to Lavelle and Damien. It didn't matter how badly she wanted to save them. She simply wouldn't be able to. They'd have to wait to be rescued a little longer than she'd planned.

Natalia studied the rebels as she passed them. Most were dirty and wore mismatched clothes that had been dyed different colors. Some even wore pieces of black armor most likely stolen from Vayne's soldiers, but unlike the people of the sectors, they looked happy. Several met her gaze with warm, welcoming smiles, and she smiled—truly smiled—in return. It was exciting to finally be in the rebels' camp, and the aura surrounding it was so... Open and happy. After searching and dreaming of it for so long, she'd finally found it. If only Vale and Damien were there to see it, too...

She could tell that Roman was good to his people and did everything in his power to keep them safe and happy. It was written all over him and the rebels. They loved and respected him greatly because he helped them be who they wanted. With him, they were all free. *Natalia* was finally free. She finally had a say in what she wanted to do with her life. Her opinion mattered, and she was no longer confined by walls and an oppressive leader.

It didn't take her long to get to the large tent Fraiser had pointed out. Natalia jogged to it, excitement and eagerness filling her, but then something inside her had her pausing at the flap. Would Aurum and Ren be angry with her for not saving Damien? Would they even want to see or talk to her? She took a deep breath. Whatever they decided, she still owed it to them to tell them what had happened. Releasing that breath, Natalia slipped inside the tent.

"Natalia!" Ren and Aurum exclaimed simultaneously, jumping up from the floor strewn with blankets and pillows and embracing her tightly.

A sob escaped her throat as she threw her arms around them. It felt like the weight of the world had been lifted from her shoulders. "Please, tell me you two are all right."

"We are now," Aurum said, voice cracking with emotion.

Natalia squeezed them tighter before finally taking a step back. She observed each of them carefully. Other than a few scrapes and bruises, they were both fine. Ren's brows furrowed as he glanced behind her at the flap of the tent.

"Where's Damien?" he asked. "Is he with you?"

"No," Natalia whispered. "No, he's not."

Aurum shook her head in shock. "What?"

"I couldn't get to him." Natalia clenched her fists, digging her fingernails into her palms. Don't break. Don't break. She couldn't break down—not in front of them.

They needed her to be strong, but she wasn't strong enough to keep the tears of anger from pooling in her eyes. However, the tears would not fall. She refused to let them. "Vayne's soldiers threw him back into a truck, and I..." She looked up, biting the inside of her cheek. She would *not* let the tears fall. "I was too late. It's my fault he's gone."

"No," Aurum said, tears spilling down her face as she embraced her again. "Natalia, there's nothing you could've done."

Ren wrapped his arms around them and leaned his head against Natalia's shoulder. "You did everything you could... We'll get him back..."

"Ren, what happened to Lavelle?" Natalia asked, and she felt him stiffen.

"We were listening to her read when the announcements started." He took a step back, turning away from them to face the gray wall of the tent. "My name was called. Hers wasn't. The soldiers came into our house and dragged me out. She tried to fight them, but... I think they left her there... I think she's safe..."

A haunting silence as cold as ice enveloped them, and Natalia shuddered. They needed a distraction—anything else to talk about. But what? She replayed the testings over and over through her head. Was finding the rebels the only positive? She sucked in a breath. No... No, it wasn't.

"I'm an Elemental," she said. "A water Elemental to be exact. I saw both of your eyes glowing, too..."

Aurum and Ren froze, exchanging glances full of fear and disgust. Natalia's heart dropped. They didn't see their newfound powers as a positive. She could see it written all over their faces. To them, the powers weren't a blessing. They were a curse full of danger, death, and destruction.

"I'm an earth Elemental," Ren said, intimidation and fear replacing his usual calm and stoicism.

"Fire." Aurum stared down at her hands with exasperation. "And I hate it. I can't control it, and it's terrifying... I reached for a blanket earlier and burnt it to a crisp. What if that had been one of you guys?"

"You just hugged both of us, and you were fine," Natalia said. It hurt her soul to see her friends so afraid of this new part of them.

"I wasn't thinking." She shook her head. "I was so surprised to see you standing there... I didn't realize what I'd done. I could've hurt you..."

Natalia took a step toward her. "But you didn't."

"That doesn't mean it's any less terrifying," Ren said. "The risk is still there. Like right now—I'm trying *so hard* to stay calm because I feel like if I get too angry or upset, I'm going to cause an earthquake or something awful. I could tear this entire camp apart by accident."

"That's why we're going to learn to control it." Natalia smiled, attempting to show them the good she could see—the endless opportunities. Roman had mentioned training, too. She knew she could convince him or find someone else to help Aurum and Ren. "Elements don't merely destroy everything. You can use them to protect people. I somehow used mine to protect Roman. I don't even know how I did it. It just kind of happened... It felt natural, like my body and instincts had taken over. Just think about it. If we can learn to control our elements, we could use them to save Lavelle and Damien. We could fight alongside the rebels and stop Vayne, or we could leave all of this and the sectors behind. We could use them to survive out in the wild.

But our elements are a gift. They come with power and free will. You can make it do whatever you want if you learn to control it. Aurum, Ren, we can finally be free. We can finally fight back against Vayne. For once in our lives, we have the power and the opportunity to make a difference. We can't just let that slip through our fingers..."

"Natalia...," Ren whispered, doubt clear in his voice.

"What if we hurt or kill someone trying to learn to control them? Have you thought about the lives that are possibly at stake if we try to do that?" Aurum questioned. The light from a lantern hanging from one of the tent's support beams reflected in her dark, chocolate-brown eyes.

"I know the lives that *are* at stake if we don't try... Damien and Lavelle need us, and I *know* Roman will train us if we ask. Or at least, he'll find someone else to help us. But we don't have to be scared." Natalia took Aurum's hands. "Neither of you will hurt anyone. Please, trust me. Damien and Lavelle need us. This is our way to get them back... And I don't know about you, but I'm tired of living in fear. It's all I've done all my life, and now that I have this opportunity to change that... I'm not going to pass it up."

"Okay." Aurum nodded. "I trust you."

"Ren?" Natalia said, turning to face him.

His vibrant blue eyes flicked between her and Aurum before he nodded as well. "I trust you, too. And I want my sister, my family, and Damien back."

"So, who's this Roman you keep mentioning?" Aurum asked with a mischievous smirk. Natalia was overjoyed to see the life and spirit reentering her friend's eyes. "It sounds like we need to meet him."

"He's the leader of the rebels," she said. "He's quite aggravating so far, but the people adore him."

Aurum winked at her. *"Aggravating,* huh?"

Natalia turned to snap at Aurum for being ridiculous when Napoleon suddenly slipped inside the tent with a sheepish grin.

"Roman is about to address the camp." He smiled. "Come on, I'll lead you to the square."

Natalia, Aurum, and Ren exited the tent and followed after Napoleon. He led them between dozens of tents and tiny wooden shacks until they came to the main dirt path carved into the constantly trampled grass. They passed the hospital, the river that flowed throughout the camp, and dozens upon dozens of more tents and shacks before arriving at wooden stands arranged to make a square.

The stands were full of fruits, vegetables, and other goods and supplies. Napoleon turned back, motioning toward the stands. Every rebel, which now included them, stood in the square. Some sat on small barrels, while others leaned against wooden crutches and sticks. The crowd began to quiet as Roman dragged a large wooden crate to the center of the square. Napoleon pushed his way around the crowd, bringing them closer as Roman stood upon the crate and cleared his throat.

"First off..."

"There's hardly a thousand people here," Aurum whispered to Natalia and Ren. Vayne's army in the sectors was made up of nearly five thousand brainwashed soldiers. "This can't be it. There has to be more of them."

"I think this is it...," Ren returned softly.

Natalia watched as the little hope Ren and Aurum had drained from their faces. She felt her own hope drop along with theirs. The rebels weren't as strong as they had been made out to be... But could that change? After all, they'd gained more Araedians last night when they'd interrupted the testings. Could that be enough to make a difference for them?

~

Roman continued. "I'd like to welcome all our newcomers. I know you all must be confused and have several questions, but just know that you will all be safe here. You will not be forced to stay, and if you wish to leave, you may do so with a pack of food and supplies provided. But, if you would like to stay and help our cause, then you are most welcome to do so. If you simply wish to live amongst us in peace and not fight, then you are welcome to do that as well. Our camp is different from the sectors you came from. Here, we treat everyone the same, and you are actually allowed to have your own opinion." A mixture of laughs and cheers erupted from the crowd as Roman spoke those words. Among the new faces in the crowd was children Natalia recognized from the train station. The rebels had saved more than she had thought. "Everyone has a voice and an opinion, and you are free to share it whenever. The only reason I stand before you is because of the loving people you see around you. They rescued me, brought me into their home after my mother's death, and took care of me when I needed it the most. Then, they honored me by choosing me as their new leader. I will do everything in my power to lead you the way you should all be led. I will give my life for you if need be. Please, feel free to reach out to me or anyone else if needed...

"I would also like to congratulate my fellow rebels. We did it. We accomplished another one of our many goals, but it was not achieved without sacrifice. And we will always remember those of us who have fallen... However, their deaths are not in vain. Now we have more numbers than ever, and we will continue to grow stronger. We will be able to do so much more than before. We will take care of each other, fight for each other, and, one day, we will overthrow Vayne and free the sectors! That day will come soon, I promise. Now, everyone rest up and be safe!"

The crowd erupted into a frenzy of shouting, clapping, and whooping, and Roman descended from the crate. He made his way through the dispersing crowd toward Natalia, Napoleon, Ren, and Aurum, with Fraiser following closely behind him.

"Nice speech," Aurum said, studying Roman. She looked at Natalia with a smirk and wiggled her eyebrows.

Natalia rolled her eyes. What was Aurum getting at? Whatever it was, it was sure to lead to trouble. After all, it was her middle name.

Roman nodded. "Thank you."

"I'll only give it to you because you didn't stutter." Fraiser elbowed Roman. "You still forgot nearly all of the points you were supposed to go over."

"The stutter happened once," he said, clearly fighting back a smile.

"Oh, cut him some slack, Fraiser," Napoleon said with a shrug. "He only forgot about five points this time."

Everyone burst into laughter, except Roman and Natalia, who studied each other carefully. She felt a small pang of jealousy shoot through her. He and Fraiser seemed close—almost in the way that she and Damien had been close—but how close were they exactly? What did they mean to each other? Why did she want to know so badly? Her eyes met his golden-brown ones, both filled with curiosity. Something about him seemed to catch her off-guard. She couldn't tell what he was going to do or say, and she couldn't tell if that terrified or intrigued her. Natalia finally tore her eyes away, feeling vulnerable under his intense stare. A sudden anger accompanied that vulnerability. She *despised* feeling vulnerable.

"Everyone, this is Fraiser. You've all met Napoleon, I assume," Roman said, not taking his eyes from Natalia.

"I'm Aurum Everrett, this is Ren Dalnum, and that's Natalia Rhys," Aurum said to Fraiser. Natalia watched as Fraiser smiled at Aurum and Ren. It looked like it felt unnatural for her to smile—like she wasn't used to it. Fraiser then turned and glared at Natalia while Napoleon talked to Ren and Aurum. A few moments passed before Roman stepped between them.

"We'd like to help you all set up your tents if that's all right," he said, completely blocking Fraiser. Ah. So, he was observant, too. He knew she and Fraiser already didn't like each other.

Aurum suddenly leaned against Natalia's shoulder, causing her to jump slightly. "That'd be great."

Roman nodded. "Follow me."

"What are you doing?" Natalia whispered to Aurum as everyone followed Roman out of the square and back toward the hospital.

"Testing something," she smirked. Natalia frowned, nearly frightened of Aurum's newfound antic that involved Roman. There was no telling what she would do either, but why the sudden interest? What could she see that Natalia couldn't?

Maybe she finds him attractive, Natalia thought, confused by Aurum's actions. *What else would she be doing?* For some reason, the thought annoyed her, and she looked away, concentrating on the trees in the distance.

Roman turned off the main path, once again weaving down the small paths between the tents. He stopped in front of an old wooden shack and opened the door to reveal stacks of gray fabric, stakes, mallets, and other supplies.

"You can pitch your tents wherever you'd like," Roman said, pulling out armfuls of supplies. "For the most part, everyone prefers to stay together around the hospital and the square. A few are camped out beyond the square, and some are by the river, but feel free to go anywhere."

"The river?" Natalia questioned, turning to Aurum and Ren. She knew they wouldn't want to be too close to anyone just in case they had an accident regarding their elements. They'd *all* be more comfortable farther away.

"You read my mind," Aurum said with a smile, and Ren nodded.

Natalia frowned at Aurum's smile. She could tell it was forced. Ren and Aurum were both struggling a lot more than they were letting on. She felt it because she was, too. She'd pushed all the fear and worry *deep* down, hoping to never deal with it again. If she could focus on getting Lavelle out of the sectors and saving Damien, then she would be okay. It wouldn't matter how she felt or what she feared any more. She had people she needed to take care of and save, and they would take priority over everything... Especially herself.

Roman led them back in the direction of the hospital before cutting left behind another group of small shacks. They kept straight until they came upon the river. They followed it downstream for about a minute before crossing over. Roman's eyes began to glow dark blue, and he extended his arm, parting the waist-high water for them to cross. Natalia watched him carefully. The simple action took no effort from him. It had been as simple as blinking. The stinging in Natalia's eyes returned as she attempted to levitate the water up to her hand. Her fingers began to tingle while the water collected in one spot. It hovered above the river for a moment before splashing back down into the current. She grunted in frustration. She hardly had any control... A few yards from the water was an open area of tall grass, upon which sat three gray tents, each a few feet apart.

Napoleon plopped down into the soft grass with a sigh. Natalia smiled at him, and he returned a toothy grin. He was always happy, and she liked that about him.

"What sector were you from, Natalia?" Napoleon asked.

"Four," she said with pride and walked behind the tents, setting her supplies down.

Napoleon sat up in a flash. "I'm from Sector Four!"

"Really?" Natalia's smile widened. "Where did you live?"

"My parents died when I was young, but a family friend that taught at the school in the Hive took me in. I spent most of my time there. Where did you live?"

Natalia remembered the numerous times she'd gazed upon the Hive's walls with a mixture of envy and hatred—envy for the warm comfortable beds and living conditions, and hatred for Vayne's soldiers housed within. Though, it was clear that not everyone inside the Hive was loyal to Vayne. Not everyone was so harsh and cold and... Evil. "I lived in the orphanage."

"Oh." His face dropped. "I'm sorry..."

"Don't be," Natalia said softly. "I was happy there and wouldn't have had it any other way."

Memories of Vale flashed through her head like a phantom. She still felt the echoes of his hauntings, and there wasn't a single day that she didn't think about him—his crooked grin and the way he saw the world. She missed that gaze full of light, adventure, and love. She missed it every minute of every hour... But she knew he'd be happy to see her here. He would've loved Napoleon and Roman. The Aether knew he would've probably even liked Fraiser, too. She fought the urge to roll her eyes and chuckle.

Ren cleared his throat, clearly attempting to change the subject. Natalia was grateful for it. She'd never told Aurum or the twins about Vale—only Damien. All the others knew was that talking about her childhood was always hard on her, and that was enough for Ren to enact what she liked to call the Dalnum twin way. It didn't matter what conversation or circumstance she was in. Ren and Lavelle would help her get out of it. They were always kind and considerate like that. "So, where do you guys use the bathroom?"

Fraiser snickered and pointed back toward the square. "There are some small shacks off behind the square. Earth Elementals shift the hole when it gets full."

"That's why it's so green back there," Roman said, and Napoleon burst into laughter, causing the others to laugh as well. "The showers are that way, too."

"It's not exactly a shower, though," Napoleon said breathlessly, fighting against another laughing fit. "It's really just a pool that the river flows through, so just don't drink from the river too far downstream."

Ren chuckled. "Good to know."

Suddenly, Aurum cursed, and Natalia and the others turned to watch a tent—Aurum's tent—collapse inward. Aurum huffed, facing them. "Is anyone going to help me?"

"Nice tent." Fraiser huffed in amusement as she, Napoleon, and Ren walked over to her.

Natalia shook her head in mock disappointment before grabbing her own supplies from the ground and getting to work. She grabbed a stake, meaning to drive it into the ground when a warm hand gently grabbed hers.

"I got it," Roman said. "The ground's hard here."

Natalia's brow furrowed slightly, and she frowned. "I can do it."

"I know," he returned with a smirk.

Natalia released the stake, her frown deepening as Roman shoved the stake deep into the ground. Aurum stood in front of her fully pitched tent while the others moved on to Ren's. She wriggled her eyebrows at Natalia again. Natalia raised an eyebrow in confusion, handing Roman the next stake before Aurum burst into laughter.

"What sectors are you two from?" Roman questioned, gesturing at Aurum and Ren and accepting the stake.

"One," Aurum said. She was still grinning like a fiend.

Roman smiled. "Fraiser and I are from One as well. You don't happen to be familiar with the guards' atop the walls schedules, do you?"

"I know them like the back of my hand." Aurum shrugged. "I had to know them. It was the only way I could escape to see the others."

"Escape?" Roman stood, a ravenous curiosity filling his gaze.

"Ren; his twin sister, Lavelle; Aurum; and Damien and I would sneak out of our sectors and meet each other in the woods," Natalia said. "We've been doing it for years."

"What?" Napoleon and Fraiser exclaimed simultaneously.

"How?" Roman asked.

"I kept up with the guard schedules in One," Aurum said, glancing at Natalia and Ren. "Whenever they changed, I'd jump from the roof of this tall building to the tree branches on the other side."

Ren smiled sadly. "Lavelle and I used the old sewer systems, but Vayne's been slowly repairing them for months. I don't know how many are left."

"I see..." Roman mumbled. "Do you know the guard schedules for Two?"

"Yes." Ren nodded.

Roman grabbed another stake. "That's perfect. What about Three and Four? The more guard rotations we know, the better. It makes sneaking into the sectors a lot easier for us."

"Damien kept up with Three," Aurum said softly before turning to face Natalia.

Natalia sucked in a breath. It felt like she'd been punched in the gut. It took everything she had not to topple over.

Be strong for them. Be strong for Damien, she repeated. His name tore a hole right through her chest. She knew Roman was right earlier. No matter how badly she wanted to, she couldn't just march into the sectors and tear through Vayne's entire army. She needed more control over her element, but how much longer could Lavelle and especially Damien last?

"Damien was the one captured, wasn't he?" Roman said, searching Natalia's face carefully. She glanced up, meeting his gaze with fire in her eyes. She was so angry with herself for not saving him.

"Yes," she whispered.

A few moments of heavy silence passed before Ren spoke. "Natalia knows the schedule for Four. She also has the best way to sneak in and out of the sectors."

Natalia bit her lip to keep from smiling at the second distraction he'd offered her. The Dalnum twin way was pulling through once again. All eyes turned to Natalia, and she nodded. She hated that she'd have to leave Vale out of the story, but what point was there in talking about him? It only made the pain worse... It only made her seem more... Broken. Unguarded. However, she couldn't help but feel that his memory died a little more each time she left him out.   "When I was thirteen," she said, "an old woman taught me the history of Araedia. She knew I wanted to escape the walls, so she pointed me in the direction of a tree half-grown into the wall. Under its roots is a crack large enough for someone to slip through."

"You're joking." Roman's mouth dropped in disbelief, and he stood.

"Did you just say there's been a crack in that damn wall this *entire time*?" Fraiser exclaimed, throwing her arms up.

"Yes," Natalia answered.

Fraiser whirled to face Roman, her furious eyes burning through him. "Roman, you're an idiot."

He smiled, holding his hands up in mock innocence as he tried to stifle a laugh. "How was I supposed to know it was there? If you're going to blame someone, blame Napoleon. He's the earth Elemental."

"Hey!" Napoleon exclaimed, playfully chucking a small stake at Roman.

Roman caught it, and the three smiled at each other before Roman turned back to Natalia. "Can you take me to it?"

"Yes, on two conditions."

Fraiser rolled her eyes and snorted, earning a quick glare from Roman. "Of course, *you* have conditions."

"Ignore her," Napoleon whispered as he walked past Natalia and leaned an arm on Fraiser's shoulder. Fraiser shoved him away, and he winked. "That's what I do."

"Name them," Roman said, his gaze so intense that Natalia had to take a deep breath.

"Help us learn how to control our elements as quickly as possible."

He nodded. "Done."

"And..." She took another deep breath, fighting back the overwhelming emotions swirling to the surface. "...when I take you to the sectors, help me get in and find the friends we left behind."

"Also done," he said.

"When you go, I'm going, too," Ren announced suddenly. "I want my sister back."

Natalia gave him a soft smile. She could see how hard he was trying to hide the fear in his blue eyes. He wanted so badly to be strong for them and Lavelle, but he was struggling. He was intimidated by the power he had, as was Aurum, but her fear was less visible. The only sign of it was the constant tapping of her thumb against her four fingers.

"You two sure as hell aren't leaving me behind," Aurum said, determination chasing away the fear.

Natalia nodded at them, hope filling her. She prayed they could read the message hidden within her eyes—that everything would be okay. They would learn to control their elements. They would get Damien and Lavelle back, and everything would be okay... She would make sure of it.

"All right, then." Roman smiled, and Fraiser, Napoleon, Aurum, and Ren walked back over to finish setting up Aurum and Ren's tents.

Natalia grabbed the gray fabric of her own tent, unrolling it out onto the soft grass. Roman didn't walk away. In fact, he knelt down and grabbed another stake and the wooden mallet.

"You know," he said. "You didn't need to make conditions. I would've helped you with both even if you'd never told us about the crack in the wall."

She shrugged. "I'm just trying to take care of my friends."

"So am I."

"I'll stay for five days of training, and not a day more," she said. "After that, I'm heading for the sectors with or without you. I can't afford to waste time."

Roman frowned. "I know I'm not going to change your mind, and you know that five days isn't enough time to really teach anything. I understand that we can't afford to waste time, but just know this: I'm going to help you as much as I can. But I'm not going to let you get yourself and the others killed by trying to save someone who can't—"

"He can be saved, and he will be." Natalia wouldn't accept anything else. She met Roman's gaze. The vulnerability returned with his stare making her skin crawl. She immediately tore her eyes away and prayed to the Aether that he couldn't see the fear she was trying so hard to hide. Lavelle was alive. Damien was alive. They were still alive, and she'd save them. She'd sacrifice herself if she had to. She wouldn't let what happened to Vale happen again.

CHAPTER NINE

DAMIEN

The dark stone floor was damp and cold as ice, and the metallic odor of blood filled the musty air. Damien opened his hazel eyes to find his own blood smeared across the floor of the cell, a small, dim light above keeping him from complete blindness. The only noise was the heavy rising and falling of his chest. Damien licked his lips, dry as sand, just like his throat. His brown hair was coated in a layer of thick sweat, and his entire body ached as he sat up, recalling the previous day's events.

"Talia...," he whispered desperately as his last glimpse of her face appeared in his mind. He saw her blue-gray eyes, full of distress, and her black hair that had stuck to her sweaty face and neck. He remembered how even in that moment he had thought she was beautiful. Then a series of horrific images replaced the calm. He remembered being dragged into a truck by soldiers and his eyes reflecting off the metal inside. He could feel the same stinging in his eyes now that he'd felt as fire had uncontrollably left his fists when he'd punched the truck doors in anger.

Sweat from the surges of heat had dripped from his hair and face by the time the trucks had rolled to a stop. The last thing he remembered was the truck filling with gas. After that, there was nothing but darkness. He knew what he'd become, but he wasn't about to admit it out loud. He couldn't untangle the web of emotions he felt. Fear suddenly filled him at the thought of Natalia. Was she okay? Where was he, and what was going to happen to him? Would he ever see her again? Panic rapidly spread throughout him.

Please, be okay. Talia, please... He would rather distract himself by worrying about her than fearing what would happen to him. He'd push his emotions and needs deep down until he was ready to deal with them later—if there would even be a later for him.

Echoes of footsteps marching down the hall beyond filled the air. Damien slowly began to drag himself up from the cell floor as the footsteps neared. Suddenly, his cell door flung open, and a tall man with hair darker than the night itself stood in the doorway. A shiver ran down Damien's spine as he studied the horrifying man before him. His skin was unnaturally pale—nearly translucent—and scaly. The veins running throughout his body were as black as his hair. His eyes, however, frightened Damien the most. The man's eyes were white like snow, with thick black veins stretching out across them as if they were snakes. Damien could barely make out a faint gray line, outlining his irises. Even his pupils were white. This could only be one man... Damien now knew where he was. He was in Sector One, and standing before him was President Vayne Averie...

"Don't look at my eyes with such disgust." Vayne smiled a nasty grin. "You should see your own."

The unnerving man reached into the pocket of his black suit, withdrawing a small square mirror. Damien's mouth parted in shock as he stared into the unrecognizable reflection. Amongst the blood and dirt, he saw glowing orange irises and silver pupils. His breathing quickened while he continued to stare into the mirror.

"What did you do to me?" Damien hissed, anger flooding through him. The angrier he became, the brighter his eyes glowed. What was happening to him? What had this disgusting excuse for a human being done to him?

"I didn't do this to you, Damien—"

"How do you know my name?" he exclaimed, blinking furiously at the stinging in his eyes. It felt as if they would burst into flames.

Vayne smiled sadistically. He was wallowing in Damien's pain—basking in the joy of Damien's suffering. "Do you even know what you've become?"

"*I'm an Elemental*," Damien whispered, finally allowing himself to say it out loud. He didn't know what to think. He didn't care about his newfound powers or what they could possibly mean. He wished he knew whether Natalia and the others were safe. He wished he wasn't in such agonizing pain. All he wanted was to go *home*.

"Do you know where you are, Damien?"

He shook his head. "Stop saying my name."

"You're in the dungeons of my mansion in Sector One... Do you know why you're here?"

"Why don't you stop asking and just tell me?" Damien scowled, mustering all his hatred into a glare.

"Like you said, you're an Elemental, but not just any Elemental. You're a silver-eyed, fire Elemental. You're powerful, and you're going to join me and my army."

"*No*," Damien snarled. The burning spread, erupting through the tips of his fingers. It grew warmer with each passing second.

"You can have power and glory. You can have *everything* you've ever wanted. You can defend your home against the scum that try to steal it from us everyday. You can have status, Damien. You can go from being a little boy no one knows from the sawmills of Sector Three to one of the most powerful men alive."

"*I'll never join you.*"

Vayne sighed. "We could have done this the easy way. Don't bother trying anything," he warned, waving the guards behind him forward. They quickly seized Damien, dragging him out into the hallway. He blinked furiously, trying to adjust to the light of the pure-white hall as they followed after President Vayne. The hall was disorienting after being inside the dark cell: a smart design. Fear ran throughout Damien while Vayne led them down the hall toward a large, armored black door. The president's nasty grin returned, and he paused, watching the guards drag Damien inside.

The floor, ceiling, and walls of the room were as pitch-black as the cell, which was even more disorienting than the hall. Damien couldn't tell where the walls began or ended. His glowing eyes searched the room for means of escape. There were none. The guards quickly strapped him down against a barely visible black chair. Restraints clung to his wrists, abdomen, and ankles, and he watched as President Vayne stalked into the room and tightened a band around his head, strapping it down to the headrest of the chair. Damien's fingertips erupted into flames as he pulled and grunted against the restraints. The flames seemed to flare with his fear and anger, pulsing with his heartbeat.

He could feel all his emotions building up and channeling energy into the fire. It grew in size and heat as more anger and fear flowed through him. He hadn't meant to use his powers against the restraints. It had just happened, and even though he liked that his new power wanted to help him, it was no use. The restraints were fireproof...

"So much raw power... You will be perfect," Vayne whispered with a hideous smile that revealed black gums. He turned, nodding to someone behind him. "You may begin."

"Thank you, sir." A skinny man dressed in a white robe nodded as he entered Damien's sight. He held several large syringes in his hands. Another man, dressed identically, rolled a large cart into the room. Upon the cart sat dozens of syringes, small sticks of electricity, and an assortment of other painful-looking objects. The two men stalked toward Damien, syringes in hand.

"No... No, no, no, no! I'll kill you! No!" Damien screamed and thrashed about, his breathing rapidly accelerating. Vayne walked out the door, and a guard slammed it shut behind him. The men stood over Damien and stabbed the syringes through his skin. He screamed in pain. The liquid was as cold as ice, yet it still burned throughout his entire body, which began to spasm. Each movement felt like ice on a burn wound. All he felt was pain. There was no more room for fear or anger, only pain. "What are you doing?" Damien exclaimed through gritted teeth.

The skinny man glanced at Damien. "You're going to tell us everything about you."

"No, I won't."

"Believe me, boy, you won't have any choice." The man smiled. He walked around the chair with another syringe in hand. He stopped near Damien's face, bringing the syringe toward his eyes. His screams echoed down the hall. He was full of so much pain, he could feel the brink of unconsciousness creeping closer and closer. He'd let himself fall into the darkness if it meant he could escape this torture. He'd fall into it with open arms. His last thought was of Natalia and the day he'd found her in the forest. It had been the happiest day of his entire life. He clung onto the picture while his vision blurred and eventually blackened...

~

Damien opened his eyes, feeling empty, afraid, and alone. He stared into the dark abyss of the ceiling, sweat dripping from his shaking body. He could see the burning orange reflection of his eyes, which stared back at him. In the corners of his eyes, black veins began to reach out across the white toward his irises. His eyes were heavy, and he was mentally and physically *exhausted*.

"Welcome back," the skinny man purred. A small baton of electricity buzzed in his hands. "Don't worry, you weren't out long. Are you ready to continue?"

No... Damien's fear grew. He thought he'd escaped the pain, but this was only the beginning. And he didn't know how long he could go without breaking. They wanted to know everything about him, and they weren't going to stop until they got it. The question wasn't what they were going to do to him. It was what *weren't* they going to do to him. He'd never felt such pain before in his entire life. His body was scorching-hot, and it felt as if he'd been stabbed with thousands of fiery swords while electricity ate away at his bones and tight muscles. How long could he last like this?

Damien was never the one who needed saving. He was always helping or saving someone else. But for once in his life, Damien wished someone would come save him as the electric currents crackled through him and he screamed. Tears filled his eyes, and he felt the black veins creep further toward his irises. He'd seen what the veins would look like when he gave up—but he wouldn't give up. Not yet. He had to give Natalia and the others time. They would come for him. He *knew* they would. Natalia would fight back, so he would, too. He would rather die than let them get into his head. He would fight until he could fight no more. Damien gritted his teeth as the electricity continued to crackle through him. He stared into the sadistic eyes of the skinny man and smirked. One way or another, he would make sure he escaped, and when he did, he would kill the man. He would kill him for torturing him, and he would kill him for taking him from Natalia.

"So, you've got some spirit now?" the man scowled.

"What's your name?" Damien asked.

The man studied him for a moment before chuckling wickedly. "Remus."

"When I get out of here, Remus... I'll kill you."

"When you get out of here, you'll be so broken you won't be anything more than an obedient dog," Remus spat. He turned to his partner in the coat with an upturned hand. Remus' partner handed him another small baton of electricity and two more syringes. "Now, tell me about Natalia and the forest. I think that's where we left off."

Damien's eyes widened. He'd never said anything. He'd let himself pass out before he did. Remus laughed as Damien cursed him and himself. He had been stupid. He had let himself fall into the comfort of unconsciousness to escape the pain when that was what Remus had wanted him to do all along. Damien had been sleep-talking, giving them the information they wanted the entire time.

Stay awake. Stay awake. Damien told himself when Remus stabbed the two syringes into his skin. The two batons of electricity followed, and the comfort of the darkness began to creep in again. Damien fought against it desperately, but no matter how hard he tried, his eyelids still grew heavier. He could feel himself losing. *No, fight it! Fight it, Damien, come on!*

Damien? Natalia's voice called from within the darkness. It wasn't her. He knew it wasn't, but he couldn't stop himself from going to her. He'd always go to her... She was the only one he'd ever truly known, and she was the only one who'd ever truly known him. Closing his eyes, Damien lost and allowed the darkness to take over once more...

~

The door to the black room swung open, the light from the hallway illuminating Damien's reflection against the dark ceiling. His skin was pale, and the black veins had spread across his eyes, meeting at the outline of his glowing irises. He looked like Vayne, though he wasn't as pale, nor were the veins as dark. Someone walked over to him and loosened the restraints around his wrists. He felt the tension break as they were ripped off his body. He sat up, watching soldiers drag a man into the room. The man's dark blue eyes met Damien's. He was screaming, but no sound pierced Damien's ears. All he heard was ringing. He felt numb and empty, and all he remembered was lying down in the chair. He tried to remember more. How had he gotten in the chair? How had he gotten into President Vayne's mansion? No, he was being silly now. He'd always been inside the mansion... Right?

Damien's head began to ache as he tried to push past the muddled haze that seemed to surround his mind like a cage. He turned toward a tall, young woman standing in the doorway. Like Damien, she clearly couldn't have cared less what the soldiers were doing with the screaming man. He stared into the woman's green eyes. Her dirty-blonde hair had been tied into a long braid, the yellow-gold highlights nearly identical to the highlights that shot throughout her eyes. She flashed a wicked smile, the green of her eyes fading and turning to a glowing ice-blue around silver pupils. Black veins reached toward her irises like his. Damien swung his legs off the side of the chair and slowly set them on the floor. She tossed him a clean, black shirt.

"President Vayne is ready to see you." She studied him as he stood. "I'm Zyra Vaathe."

Damien pushed past her, throwing his old shirt to the floor and replacing it with the new.

Zyra scoffed. "You didn't even let me enjoy the show," she purred.

"I want to leave."

"Fine." Zyra sighed disappointedly. "Follow me. Maybe you'll gain some personality on the walk."

Damien frowned as they marched down the hall past the dozens of black-doored cells. His thoughts felt empty and emotionless besides the dangerous combination of anger and hate swelling inside. But anger and hate for what or who, he hadn't figured out yet. However, he was able to sort out some frustration. He was frustrated that he couldn't remember *anything* besides lying in the stupid chair. But the more he pushed against the haze, the more it began to recede. With time, he knew he would remember.

Zyra pushed a white door at the end of the hall open, continuing into a white, dome-like room. Dozens of doors branched in all directions, and Damien glanced up to the ceiling of the dome. It was carved with pictures of the four elements. Suddenly, he bumped into Zyra, who faced him. He frowned at their closeness. She'd let him run into her on purpose so they could touch, and her touch caused him to feel something... Annoyance. She was keeping him from President Vayne.

"Come on," she said with a flirtatious smile. She led Damien straight ahead, swinging the door open to reveal red, velvet curtains. She glanced at him before drawing them back to reveal President Vayne's office. Light from several windows bathed the room, and President Vayne sat behind a large wooden desk, the sun giving his skin a sickening glow that made him appear reptile-like. He smiled wickedly as he studied Damien, who nodded toward him as if he were greeting an old friend. And that was what the president felt like to him. It was like they'd known each other for years. They had, though. Hadn't they? Damien knew he could trust Vayne. He could *always* trust Vayne. Zyra nudged him forward, closing the golden door and letting the curtains fall behind them. She then walked to the desk, sitting on the corner.

"Welcome, Damien," Vayne began. "I assume you've reconsidered your options regarding our conversation earlier."

"I have, sir." Damien silently cursed himself for not accepting the president's offer the first time. How could he have been so stupid? President Vayne was only trying to help him make up for his mistakes. Suddenly, memories came flooding back through the haze, shattering it like glass. Damien remembered everything: his childhood, Natalia and the others, their overhang, and fighting back during the testings—all of his mistakes. He had to prove his loyalty to Vayne.

"Say it," Vayne commanded as he leaned forward in his chair, hands viciously clutching the arms.

"It would be the greatest honor to serve you, sir, if you would have me."

Vayne nodded, pleased. "I will, Damien. Now, I need you to tell me everything you know about the girl with the ice-blue eyes."

"Natalia," Zyra said with a smirk, letting the name roll off her tongue. "That's her name, I believe. You were screaming it in the beginning."

"Yes, tell me of her," Vayne commanded. "I rewatched the security footage from the attack on the train station. She was the water Elemental who fought alongside Roman."

Damien hesitated. Deep down inside him, somewhere hidden far away, he thought he felt surprise, shock, and a warning. Surprise and shock over the fact that Natalia had become an Elemental, and a warning to not tell them anything... But the emotions were too distant, and he had to be loyal to Vayne. Vayne was the only one who'd ever supported him. "I knew her before my time with you here, sir."

"Come now, Damien," Zyra said, hopping off the desk and walking toward him. She slowly drew a line across his chest with her finger before slipping behind him. She spoke softly into his ear, "We need more details than that."

The words seemed to spill out from Damien now. He couldn't stop. "She has no biological family in Sector Four. She had an adoptive brother at one point, but he's been dead for years. She cares for her friends deeply and thinks of them as her family. Her feelings for them are her downfall. She has moments of a bold anger, which causes her to be irrational at times—another one of her weaknesses. It's easy to get under her skin if you know her well. She can be impatient and impulsive, but she's strong and determined. She's breakable, but she shouldn't be underestimated."

"She *is* powerful. She killed one of my personal guards in battle within minutes of discovering her element, though that's no real bother since you've filled that spot, Damien. But she'd add greatly to my army...," Vayne mumbled, lifting a hand to his chin. "I want you and Zyra to capture her and my son *alive*."

"Of course, sir." Zyra nodded with a wicked smile. Damien nodded beside her in agreement. "Roman won't get the better of us this time."

"Good. Now...," Vayne began, rising from his desk with a fist down upon the table. "I want you two to oversee the construction of the new station. You are also to double-check security in each sector. I don't know how they found out about the change in location, but I assume it was somehow through the sectors. We cannot allow this to happen again."

"Yes, sir." Zyra and Damien nodded.

"Oh, and one last thing, Zyra," Vayne said, lifting his fist from the desk. "You are to train Damien so that he's even more deadly than you..."

~

Zyra led Damien down a plain, light-gray hallway in the undergrounds of Vayne's mansion. At the end sat large, black double doors. She pushed them open and entered the enormous room waiting beyond. The room—nearly twenty yards long with a high ceiling—was full of training equipment. Wrestling mats dotted the floor, along with training dummies and tall, silver tables, upon which sat stacks of black armor and plastic spears.

He followed Zyra as she marched past the dozens of people sparring on the mats and finally stopped near the back of the room where they could train undisturbed. All the while, Damien's mind was entirely blank. He felt cold and empty. He felt as if far away, tucked deep down in the darkest part of his mind, there was a cage around his old self. The cage blocked all contact with the boy he used to be and the people he loved. He remembered his life before, but the glossy haze surrounded every memory. He could no longer tell what feelings were behind those memories, and every time he tried to untangle the web of emotions, he only found hate, anger, loyalty to Vayne, and a desire to kill.

"Tell me about your family, Damien. You didn't talk much about them earlier." Zyra turned with a smirk, studying Damien. His empty eyes observed the room, scanning all around. He finally met her gaze and frowned.

"Why do you care?"

"Tell me about them," she repeated, stepping closer.

"I don't want to get to know you."

"Oh, come now, Damien. Don't be so serious. Have fun with the game," Zyra said, pursing her lips. "If you don't, it will consume you."

"What if it already has?" he asked as a sharp stinging filled his head. He winced.

"It won't. This is only the beginning." Zyra tilted her head. "Don't worry, though. The aches and pains will fade over the next day or two... Now, tell me about your brothers."

"We were all very close until my father's death, which my brothers—and my mother especially—blame me for." Damien huffed, feeling no remorse. He didn't really know why he'd let it bother him so much before. He didn't need them. They were useless distractions and had kept him from reaching Vayne sooner. He clenched his fists. All of those years *wasted*...

"Was it your fault?"

"Yes, but it was an accident. We were starving in Three—" He paused. No, that couldn't be right. Vayne would've never let him starve. It must have been his mother's doing... He cursed her viciously before continuing. "I think... So, I stole a loaf of bread. Long story short, the soldiers came for me, but my father turned himself in in my place. They killed him, then my mother convinced my brothers I did it on purpose."

The soldiers had been right in their actions. It was what his family had deserved, though he couldn't stop himself from wishing that it had been his mother instead. His father would've made a great servant to Vayne—a loyal servant.

"I see...," Zyra murmured. She ran her eyes over him again as if she were seeing something he couldn't. It felt like something had been placed over him, but what?

Damien shrugged, indifference taking over. "Now it's my turn to ask a question."

"I thought you didn't want to get to know me." She smiled.

"Just shut up and tell me what sector you're from."

"One."

"That makes sense. Ones *are* the most annoying little pests," Damien jeered. He nearly jumped in surprise as a shock of electricity seemed to run throughout him. The shock was familiar. He'd felt it before in the room with Vayne when he'd hesitated for that slight moment while talking about Natalia. Just thinking about her name sent unyielding waves of anger through him. He wanted her dead. But why did he feel the shock now? It wasn't because of her this time... The cage imprisoning his old life seemed to tighten. He knew a girl from One... She'd been annoying, too, but in a good way. Aurum. Her name was Aurum, and all he wanted to do was kill her. He wanted to kill Natalia and the twins, too. He wanted them all dead... So, he would kill them, and once they were all dead, the anchor trapping his mind, drowning it underwater, would be lifted.

"So, what's with the Natalia girl?"

"Do you have any family?" he countered, distracting himself from the electric current and the anchor drowning him. He needed to think about something other than his desire to kill, and if this was the game he had to play to do so, he would.

"Tell me about the girl."

"Tell me about your family."

"I have two older brothers," she said. Her green eyes pierced his as her blonde braid fell off her shoulder. "They're both high-ranking officials."

"Do you miss them?"

"I feel the same way as you do regarding family. I don't care."

"Fair enough," he said. "Can we train now?"

"You're no fun." Zyra rolled her eyes. "But fine. Today, I'm going to teach you how to form a solid weapon from your element. It's extremely difficult, but Vayne thinks you possess a large sum of power. He felt it inside you, so maybe you *can* do it. But you have to focus. You have to feel the fire flowing throughout your veins." She closed her eyes, and Damien did the same. "Feel the fire throughout your very heart and soul... Call upon it. Bend it to your will. It is yours, and no one can take it from you. It's always been a part of you and always will be. It only listens to you. Now, Damien, form a flame inside your palm."

Damien inhaled deeply. She was right. He could feel the fire coursing throughout his body from head to toe. He was surprised he'd never felt its presence before. It was so vibrant and full of life. In fact, it was currently the only thing reminding him that he was still alive. He turned his palm upward and exhaled, flames licking high into the air.

"Good. Now, tell it what you want it to be," Zyra said as she reached her arm out, pulling water from a nearby bucket. It shot at her, curling around her arms before forming a spear and hardening into packed ice. Her irises glowed ice-blue, surrounding her silver pupils. Her eyes looked so cold and... Deadly.

The flames in Damien's hand whirled into a tornado of fire before straightening into a long sword. He opened his glowing, orange eyes to find Zyra smirking. She nodded in approval and then charged. Damien brought his sword up, barely blocking the spear of ice. A *crunch* filled the air as their weapons collided, pushing against each other, though neither of them gained any ground. He had done it. And the raw power flowing through his veins... It was like a drug. One taste, and he was already addicted. He could bask in this power forever. He *wanted* to. Damien smiled wickedly, enjoying the rush of adrenaline and letting out a low chuckle.

"It looks like Vayne was right."

～

Several days of intense training passed before Damien and Zyra began their trip around the sectors as Vayne had commanded. They made their way from Sector One to Four, increasing security drastically. Damien exploited each flaw and escape route in the walls that he and his friends had used before. Zyra had found it extremely interesting that he'd seen the forest beyond the walls before, and he'd told her how the land stretched for miles atop the overhang. All four of the sectors could be seen. Additional soldiers were ordered into main squares and atop the walls, and the sectors were becoming impenetrable one by one. Only one stop remained on their trip, and Damien dreaded it most. He knew Sector Four would bring back the electric shock. Four would try to bring out everything that was buried. Everything that was bad. Everything that Vayne did not like.

Terrified stares followed Damien and Zyra as they marched through the square of Four. The people dressed in all different shades of gray jumped, clearing a large path for them. Whispers filled the air, and Damien could hear them all. The people were afraid, and he liked that they feared him. He liked being powerful, but he mostly liked being *deadly*.

Soldiers in black armor and helmets followed after Damien and Zyra as they exited the square and began the trek down the dirt road toward the edge of Sector Four. Damien knew exactly which flaw to expose here, but he still sent the soldiers out to search all four corners of the walls. He would be especially thorough with Four. Damien and Zyra walked on throughout the sea of grass and small hills.

The electric shock hit him like a wave. The anchor seemed to sink deeper, dragging him under the heavy waves and smothering him. Natalia had told him of her home and how she loved the landscape. He scowled before thrusting his hands forward, scorching the grass around him in anger. He had to stop the anchor from pulling him too deep. He had to stop the pain Natalia had caused and would cause him. Because of her, he hadn't been loyal to Vayne, and he refused to make that mistake again. Zyra simply glanced at him with a smirk before continuing on, letting the grass burn behind her. They walked on until they reached a lone, abandoned house at the top of a hill. He peeked inside the broken windows before turning to find a worn path in the tall grass leading down the sloping hill. They were in the right spot. He slowly made his way over, following the path.

"Where are you going?" Zyra crossed her arms. "We've done enough sightseeing. We need to find your stupid little flaw, fix it, and head to the construction site." He ignored her continuing down the hill. Zyra rolled her eyes with an annoyed groan. "Damien, nothing's down there! Let's go."

"Call it a hunch," Damien returned, nearly at the bottom. He turned, beckoning her after him. Zyra huffed before following. He knew it was here. Natalia had described it to him many times. They followed the path down to a large tree that had grown into the wall. Damien raised a brow as he circled the tree, studying it. It was *exactly* as she'd said.

"There's nothing here. It's just a tree." She turned, starting back up the hill. "This was a waste of time. We need to check on the site, then get back to One before Vayne gets pissed at us for taking too long."

Damien's hazel eyes suddenly landed on a cluster of roots sticking out from the ground. He walked closer, bending down next to the branches. He set his hand down upon the disturbed soil, and with a smirk, he poked his head underneath the roots. He'd found the flaw... He'd found the *crack*. A strange sense of joy filled him. The cage that had ensnared his life before Vayne would open for information he could use against Natalia. It brought him joy to betray her. His eyes narrowed against the crack in the cold concrete.

"But there *is* something, Zyra."

CHAPTER TEN

CONTROL

The sun was beginning to set behind the tall trees upon the hills, and soon the rebel camp would be engulfed in darkness. Small lights within the grass flashed every few seconds. Natalia peered closely as one flashed near her black boots and smiled when a small firefly flew toward her from its place in the tall blades of grass. She had never seen a firefly before, but Lavelle had read to her about them many years ago. It amazed her as it blinked about, and all Natalia wished for in that moment was that Lavelle was here, seeing it with her. Her chest throbbed at the thought.

"What do you guys do with the tents when it rains?" Aurum questioned as Fraiser stalked into their encirclement, throwing a pile of blankets and pillows into Natalia's, Aurum's, and Ren's tents.

"They're made of waterproof material, so they don't collapse."

"Interesting." Aurum turned back to Roman, who sat across from her in the grass. Between them were piles of kindling and tinder. She bit her lip in frustration. "I don't think I can do this."

"You can," Roman said. "Just don't be scared. Fear won't help you control it. I assume you've noticed a change in your body temperature ever since your eyes changed, right?"

Aurum nodded. "Yes, but will I have to go through that pain again?"

Natalia looked away from the firefly at Ren, who sat a few feet from her. His eyes darkened, and she could practically see the memories from a few nights ago playing through his head. How badly had it hurt them to discover their elements? Natalia's own eyes had stung, but it hadn't been unbearable. It wasn't so awful that she didn't want to use her element ever again... Why hadn't they said anything to her about it? She leaned over and took Ren's hand, wishing she could take their pain away. His vibrant blue eyes met hers, and the darkness disappeared. She'd pulled him out. He was all right, and he was safe.

"It won't hurt, Aurum, I promise," Roman said. "Now, I need you to focus on the heat. You should feel it somewhere inside you."

Aurum closed her eyes, clearly trying her best to keep her breathing steady. Her dark eyebrows narrowed. "I found it."

"Good, now I need you to focus on moving the heat to one of your fingertips."

Fraiser returned from their tents and plopped down next to Napoleon a few feet from Aurum and Roman. She reached across him, grabbing a leather water-skin and one of the many wooden cups on the ground. She bit off the cap of the water-skin and poured a shining fluorescent liquid into her cup. Natalia watched Napoleon bite into a small loaf of brown bread before reaching for Fraiser's cup.

She rolled her eyes. "Only one sip, or I'll have your head."

"I feel like I should be saying that to you," Napoleon said with a laugh.

"Good," Roman mumbled, drawing Natalia's attention back to them. Sweat dripped down Aurum's paling face. "You can do it."

Suddenly, a small flame burst forth from Aurum's pointer finger, and her eyes, now glowing a burning red around silver pupils, flashed open. Her breathing increased rapidly as pure fear spread across her face. Each breath made the flame grow bigger until it hungrily blazed inside her palm. Natalia shot up from her spot in the grass and ran over, kneeling next to her.

"Stay calm," she whispered. "You're all right."

"The flames won't burn you," Roman said. "Do you feel it burning you?"

Aurum shook her head. "No, I know it won't, but it's not me I'm worried about."

He chuckled. "You've got two water and earth Elementals and one air Elemental with you. We can put out the flame if you lose control."

"But you won't." Natalia smiled reassuringly.

Aurum took a deep breath, slowing her breathing, and the flames began to grow smaller. They crawled back up the sides of her fingers, gently weaving between them.

"Now, stick your hand into the kindling, and then let go of the flame. Tell it to retreat back to its source inside you," Roman instructed.

Aurum stuck her hand into the tinder, igniting them into a whirlwind of flames. She gently pulled her unscathed hand back, and the flames upon her fingertips, along with her glowing eyes disappeared. And a small, warm fire kindled to life.

"Perfect." Roman smiled. "That was perfect."

Aurum sighed in relief. "Thank you."

"Anytime."

Natalia threw an arm around her as Napoleon scooted closer to them and the fire with a bright, infectious smile. "Great job, Aurum!"

Fraiser stumbled over after him, still drinking the fluorescent liquid from her cup. Ren followed a moment later and sat behind Natalia and Aurum with an expressionless face. Natalia knew who he was thinking about—who he wished were here with them. She was thinking about it, too. Both Damien and Lavelle would be marveling at the sight before them as she was now. Aurum had taken a step forward. Though it was a small step, it was still a step. Natalia's eyes slid to Roman across the fire. His head was turned, and he was studying the dark forest a few yards away. He'd stuck true to his word. He'd helped Aurum... He turned to face her, meeting her gaze. Natalia bristled and glanced away.

"How's it even possible that we're Elementals?" Ren asked no one in particular.

"That's a question I wish we had the answer to," Fraiser said, lifting her cup into the air as if she were toasting. "Maybe one day we'll find out."

Napoleon shrugged. "There's been a sudden spike in Elementals over the past few years, though, which is very interesting."

"How many Elementals are there?" Ren ripped at the grass.

"It's impossible to tell," Roman answered.

"He's right," Napoleon said, taking another bite of bread. "It's impossible to tell, but I saw these old documents in the Hive before I joined the rebels. The statistics showed that around one in twenty Araedians test positive for the Elemental gene."

"How'd you get your hands on those documents?" Natalia asked. It was impossible to get into the Hive's government buildings unless you served Vayne.

"Let's just say I was curious." He shrugged.

"That's one way to put it." Fraiser said, shaking her head and huffing in amusement before extending her wooden cup toward Aurum. "Here, try some of this."

"What is it?" Aurum asked, accepting the cup and sniffing the fluorescent liquid.

"I wouldn't if I were you," Roman warned.

Aurum turned to him with a smirk. Natalia cursed to herself. She knew that smirk. It was nothing but trouble. She watched as Aurum threw her head back, taking three large gulps. She immediately began to cough and shoved the cup back toward Fraiser. Aurum shot up from the grass and sprinted for the river a few yards away, cupping the water with her hands and drinking. Roman, Fraiser, and Napoleon were cackling, and even Ren had released a small chuckle—nothing like his true laugh, though. Natalia simply smiled as Aurum walked back to the fire.

"He did warn you," she said.

"Shut up, Natalia." Aurum laughed, only to be interrupted by another coughing fit. "What in the Aether's name is that?"

"Brennivan," Napoleon answered. "It's alcohol."

Aurum lifted a brow before sitting down between Fraiser and Napoleon and asking them more questions. Natalia watched Roman add smaller sticks to the fire. The flames grew higher, and she found herself trying to fit together the puzzle pieces that made up the rebels' leader. He'd been so reluctant to talk to her before... Why? Why was he now so eager to help them learn to control their elements? She frowned. He was so confusing. Suddenly, Ren slid closer to Natalia and leaned over, dragging her from her thoughts.

"Did it hurt when your eyes changed?" he mumbled.

"No, but yours did?"

"Yeah," he said with a nod.

"I'm so sorry, Ren," Natalia whispered. "About everything."

He studied her face. "Can you show me what yours look like?"

"I can try," she said, mustering a smile for him. This was her chance to show Ren that he didn't have to be afraid. It was a chance to take away some of his fear. Natalia took a deep breath, focusing on the flowing river water. She extended her left hand, twirling her fingers with the currents she could feel weaving between each other. She took another deep breath, and three small spheres the size of marbles rose from the river, slowly and wobbly flying toward them. They paused and hovered in front of Ren's face, who stared at Natalia, wide-eyed. She wrinkled her nose, attempting to keep the spheres steady. To keep her control. They began to rotate, spinning faster and faster. Ren smiled as he reached out and poked one, sending it splashing to the ground. The two remaining spheres shrank back before launching into the tip of his nose. This time, they both laughed—full and utterly happy laughs. It was nice to hear him truly laugh.

"What color are mine?" Natalia asked.

"Ice-blue," Roman replied, sitting down in front of them. "And your pupils are silver... You have a lot of control for a new Elemental."

"It wasn't as easy to control as it looked," she said.

"It will get easier with training."

"I'm not afraid of it. I love it. It makes me feel so much stronger than I was before." Natalia paused, glancing between Ren and Roman. They studied her, listening intently, but she could see the internal battle in Ren's eyes. He was trying so hard to convince himself not to be scared—to be brave enough to try out his own element. "Show us your eyes, Ren," she said softly.

"I don't know, Natalia. What if—"

"I know you can do it." She gently nudged his shoulder. "Just try."

Ren sighed, nodding before tentatively closing his eyes. He took a deep breath, placing his hand on top of a small pile of rocks he'd been stacking. He scowled, then slowly lifted his hand, a single rock levitating underneath it. He opened his eyes and glanced at Natalia's normal, blue-gray eyes.

She smiled. "They're pretty."

"What color?" he asked.

"Dark-green... Like the forest."

He smiled, letting the rock fall back to the ground as his eyes returned to their normal blue. "What color are yours, Roman?"

"Dark-blue," Natalia answered. She looked to Roman, who closed his brown eyes. "They're what I imagine the deepest parts of an ocean to look like. Your pupils are silver, too."

He opened his eyes, staring into hers. She stared back. Natalia felt the vulnerability return. It felt as if he'd torn through her piece by piece to the point that he knew her better than she knew herself—like he could see through all the walls she'd been building her entire life. Fear shot through her. It was utterly terrifying. How could he read her so easily? Or was she just overthinking? Maybe he didn't see through her at all. She hoped her face didn't give away the fear she felt. The fear of being vulnerable...

With the same motion Natalia had used, Roman sent a small sphere of water from the river flying toward her. She ducked, and the sphere flew past her, splattering in the soft grass. Ren and Roman laughed as she sat up. Her initial reaction had been annoyance. Slight anger even, but hearing them laugh... It took away the anger, the aggravation, the fear, and turned it all into joy. But then the guilt hit, drowning and smothering her like a tsunami. She knew for a fact that Damien wasn't laughing right now. He was most likely facing unbearable horrors that she couldn't save him from.

"Hey! You guys," Fraiser yelled from across the fire, her words beginning to slur together. "Come try some Brennivan!"

"Oh, great." Roman sighed, pushing himself up from the ground. Fraiser began to snicker as he walked over, falling backward off the rock she sat upon. Natalia and Ren rose and followed after him.

For the remainder of the night, they all sat around Aurum's fire, exchanging stories and getting to know each other. And for a slight moment, Natalia felt normal. She felt like an eighteen-year-old girl hanging out with new friends. Because that's what the rebels were now. They were her friends—her allies—and she knew if Vale were here, he'd tell her to bask in the moment and enjoy it. Tomorrow was when everything would change, when the real work would begin.

An hour later, Natalia was under the blankets in her tent, twisting her ring and staring at the fabric above. Her hand felt ten times heavier, and everywhere she looked, she saw Damien. He was surrounded by the enemy with no friends in sight and completely and utterly alone. She had been stupid to laugh earlier when he was in such danger. She shouldn't be enjoying herself. Her focus had to be him, and from now on, it would be. If he was even still alive...

~

It was nearing late morning when Natalia sat upon the thin mattress of the hospital cot, clenching her fists until they turned white. Aurum stood behind Napoleon, who held a sharp needle near Natalia's forehead. Natalia dug her fingernails into her palms, drawing blood as she tightened her fists. She swore Damien's ring around her finger was about to burst into pieces from the pressure.

Four difficult days of training had passed since she and her friends had arrived at the rebels' camp. Natalia had somehow allowed Roman and Napoleon to convince her to get stitches for her cut, which had been reopened that morning in a training accident with Fraiser. She still suspected Fraiser had aimed for her head on purpose.

"Are you okay, Natalia?" Napoleon questioned, eyeing her clenched fists.

"I'm fine," she said through gritted teeth, ignoring the slight dizziness clouding her head.

"You're not squeamish...," Aurum mumbled, crossing her arms over her chest and tilting her head. "What's wrong with you? Does it hurt that badly?"

Aurum's fear of her element had disappeared almost as quickly as it had formed. Once Roman had helped her with that small fire, she'd been more than eager to learn more. She was still cautious whenever she practiced around others, but when she and Natalia trained together alone... She was an embodiment of wildfire—strong, fierce, and a little reckless at times... But she respected her element, nonetheless.

"It doesn't hurt," Natalia said. "The needle is just making me lightheaded."

Aurum snickered. "I've known you for years, and not once have you mentioned a fear of needles." Her snicker turned to a full-out laugh. "The great and mighty Natalia, scared of needles!"

"Shut up, Aurum," Natalia hissed.

"It's all right." Napoleon smiled, clearly fighting back his own laughter. He wasn't strong enough to hide the humorous gleam in his eyes, though. "You're almost done."

"Hey, guys," Ren said as he and Roman, drenched in sweat from training, walked through the hospital doors and joined them beside the cot. It had still taken some convincing to get Ren to agree to training, and Natalia knew the only reason he'd agreed was because of Lavelle. It was more than strange to see Ren without his twin. His other half had been ripped from him, and he was visibly miserable. His skin had grown sickly pale, and large bags hung under his dull eyes. His usual calm demeanor had become twitchy and nervous like that of a caged wild animal.

Natalia frowned. He'd stopped eating as much as he used to as well, and she was tired of it—tired of stupid stitches, training, and taking orders. She was tired of wasting time. Today was the fifth day she'd promised Roman, and if he didn't allow them to leave tonight, she'd leave by herself. She stood on wobbly legs, and Napoleon and the dreadful needle disappeared into the far corner of the hospital. Roman stepped toward her, but she stuck a hand up in protest. "I'm fine."

"You look pale," he said, clearly unconvinced.

Natalia lifted her chin, allowing cold steel to enter her tone. "I'll be better once we leave for the sectors tonight."

"We're not leaving tonight." Roman straightened, face as unreadable as it always was. Behind him, Aurum whispered to Ren, and the two disappeared in the direction Napoleon had gone.

"What do you mean?" she questioned, anger flooding through her. "Today's day five, and you said—"

"You're right. Today *is* day five." He took a step closer to her. "And tomorrow—after day five is over—we can leave for the sectors whenever you want."

～

Natalia scowled. His training, regardless of how helpful it was, was taking too long. The more time they wasted, the higher Damien's chances of dying rose—if he wasn't dead already. Those thoughts never failed to haunt her every night in her dreams. She had Lavelle to worry about, too. She was most likely still with the rest of her family, but even living in the sectors with them was an enormous risk. A risk that Natalia couldn't stomach for one more day. The helplessness she felt was threatening to swallow her whole if she didn't do *something.*

Natalia met Roman's gaze. His mesmerizing brown eyes, full of hypnotizing honey and amber highlights, studied her carefully as if they were trying to guess what she would do. She shivered before diverting her gaze and pushing past Roman out into the sunlight of the rebel camp. She'd been training with him for the majority of the past few days, and if she didn't get away from him soon, she was going to throttle him. She jogged through the tall grass, following the river that flowed through the rebel camp upstream. She knew where to find Fraiser. She would be training the new recruits. Roman clearly didn't think Natalia was ready to return to the sectors, so she'd prove she was. Her anger flared as her thoughts wandered back to Damien. She needed to push herself even harder than she had been. He was her family, and she *had* to get him back.

Natalia clenched her fists, rounding a bend in the river that opened up into an area of flat grass. A cheering crowd was gathered around Fraiser and a young man in the middle. The crowd gasped as Fraiser knocked the young man—who stood nearly a foot taller than her—to the ground with a column of wind. She clasped her hands together with a smirk and watched a few of the young man's friends help him up before staggering back into the crowd.

"Who's next?" Fraiser questioned, turning in a slow circle and searching the crowd. A long pause filled the air. "No one?"

Natalia stalked into the crowd, making her way through it as quickly as she could. She came to the edge of the ring in the center and stepped out to meet her. "Me."

All eyes turned to Natalia, the rebels' stares pinning her to the spot. Fraiser was notorious for her brutal training sessions, but she was the best of the best. Her only rival was Roman himself, and they never sparred in public. In fact, Natalia had never seen them spar in private. She had heard and felt it, though, and that alone was enough to tell her it was a sight to behold. What better way was there to prove she was ready than by beating Roman's right hand? Besides, she had to admit to herself, the thought of getting to fight Fraiser made her smile.

"Are you sure?" Fraiser smirked. "I don't want to give you more stitches." Natalia frowned and took another step forward, but Fraiser just shrugged, completely unbothered by the challenge. "All right, sweetheart, don't say I didn't warn you."

"Oh, I'll be fine," she said with a grin promising violence.

Natalia and Fraiser began to circle each other slowly, and Natalia thought back to her training with Roman over the past few days. They'd spent hours going over the basics, which she'd mastered easily thanks to her previous training with Vale and Damien. Fighting with her element wasn't too different from regular fighting. The only real challenge behind it was balancing her energy and focus because controlling her element ate up so much of the two. Roman had actually started going over some more advanced techniques with her, but the message he preached every session was clear: The only thing that *truly mattered* was *control*.

The one time she'd lost control during training was when Roman had purposely pissed her off. She had let her emotions run wild and had ended up making an impulsive decision for which she paid the price with a hard jet of water to the stomach. All Natalia had to do to beat Fraiser was keep her emotions in check. The water would follow as she commanded. She took a deep breath and focused on the currents flowing through the nearby river. Adrenaline and power coursed through her veins, and her eyes began to sting as they glowed ice-blue and silver.

Fraiser smirked, jabbing forward playfully. Natalia refused to budge, and Fraiser snickered. "Oh, lighten up, Natalia."

Natalia rolled her eyes. Suddenly, Fraiser, irises glowing gray around silver pupils, shot a column of air toward her. She easily sidestepped and reached out to the water with her mind, commanding it to obey her. A snake of water from the river shot through the air, parting the crowd and circling Natalia like a shield. Fraiser smiled, forming two rotating discs of air in front of her hands. Natalia jumped into the air, flipped, and kicked at her own shield. A spear of water tipped with ice shot at Fraiser, who raised her shields and shattered it. Natalia continued her attack, jumping and jabbing and flipping and kicking a series of spears from the water as Fraiser rolled, ducked, and blocked.

The snake of water before her quickly diminished down to a single sphere, and Natalia met Fraiser's eyes. Fraiser drew her arms back and pushed them forward, sending the rotating discs of wind flying toward Natalia with deadly accuracy. Fraiser's first disc collided with Natalia's sphere, destroying them both while the second shield struck Natalia's abdomen. She flew backward, landing on the ground and gasping for the air that had been knocked from her lungs. Her glowing eyes began to water as she lifted her head from the ground, loose strands of black hair falling in front of her face.

"I really expected more of a fight." Fraiser laughed, turning to face the cheering crowd. Natalia, anger filling her like a poison, sat up and slowly began to rotate her hands in a circle. Roman was right in the sense that she couldn't let her emotions control her, but that didn't mean she couldn't use them at all. What if it was better if she used them? What if she used her anger to hone her control into a dangerous advantage?

Natalia felt the water resist her will at first, but she wouldn't accept defeat. It *would* listen to her. She took a deep breath, drawing on as much power as she could and focusing it on the currents forming in front of her. An enormous sphere of water silently formed behind Fraiser while she continued laughing and working up the crowd. Those among the crowd began to gasp and fall silent, causing Fraiser to turn to watch the mass of water engulf her. A thin shell of ice formed and cradled the water, making it impossible for Fraiser to swim out and escape. Natalia stood for a moment, hands outstretched, before dropping the sphere to the ground. Ice scattered amongst the grass and dirt, and Frasier gasped and coughed, her wet hair clinging to her neck and shoulders.

"I really expected more of a fight," Natalia said, her voice deathly quiet.

Fraiser stood with a scowl and formed another disc in her hand while Natalia formed her own matching disc of ice. They sprinted at each other, and—

Suddenly, a step before they collided, a wall of ice from the water on the ground shot up. Fraiser and Natalia both gasped, and they slammed into the wall, bouncing off and tumbling to the ground. Natalia sat up, the taste of metallic blood on her stinging lips. Fraiser rose to one knee as a small stream of blood from a cut on her forehead raced for her right eyebrow. Anger burned through Natalia, and she whirled to the crowd, searching for the only one who could have stopped them.

Where is he?

Roman stepped out from within the crowd, arm outstretched. The wall of ice melted as he pulled his hand back to his side. "Enough," he spat. "Training is over. Everyone, go back to what you were doing."

The crowd quickly dispersed, leaving Natalia, Roman, Fraiser, Ren, Aurum, and Napoleon in the patch of grass. Aurum helped Fraiser to her feet while Roman started toward Natalia, who stuck out a resistant hand. She stood, locking eyes with a furious and scowling Fraiser. Natalia returned her own glare. Everyone was utterly silent, and the tension was so thick, she could've cut it with a knife.

"How about we all go get lunch in the square?" Napoleon asked with an awkward smile, clearly doing his best to smooth things over.

Fraiser held Natalia's stare for a few more moments before glancing at the others and rolling her eyes. "I'm not hungry," she said, turning and storming off into the tree line of the forest a few yards away.

Aurum marched over to Natalia and grabbed her arm, whispering, "What's going on with you? You've been so angry lately."

"I'm fine." Natalia pulled her arm from Aurum's grip.

"You know you can't get away with lying to me," she said. "I know you like the back of my hand... I also know that when you act like an immature child, there's a reason behind it, so why don't you just tell me now?"

"No." Natalia shook her head, staring at the currents as they weaved throughout the river. She knew she couldn't get away with lying to Aurum, but it was easier to lie than to tell her what was wrong—that she was angry that they hadn't left to rescue Damien yet. She was angry she'd let Vayne take him in the first place, but she was also afraid. She was overwhelmingly terrified that Damien was dead, and that they wouldn't be able to find him or Lavelle... She was terrified of the vulnerability that never left her whenever Roman was around. Her fear and anger were beginning to eat her alive, and nothing Aurum could say or do would stop it.

Aurum sighed, pinching the bridge of her nose. "Just do something for me, okay? Try *not* to cause any more trouble with Fraiser. You know how much fighting and conflict freaks Ren out, especially when he's not with Lavelle. We both know how badly he's struggling right now. Let's not make it any worse for him."

Natalia looked at Ren, who stood between Roman and Napoleon a few feet away. The three were glancing between her and Aurum, not bothering to pretend that they weren't arguing. The last thing Natalia wanted was to make things worse... Guilt and shame washed over her. Aurum was right. She was being childish. In fact, she was proving Roman's point. She wasn't ready, but that didn't mean she was staying any longer. She'd still leave tonight even if she had to leave alone.

"I never wanted to hurt or scare him," Natalia said.

"I know." Aurum offered her a small smile. "You didn't because he's stronger than that, but you did freak him out a little bit. It's all right. Just try to relax, and you and I can talk more about this later..."

Natalia nodded, biting her lip in slight embarrassment. "I'm sorry."

"You're forgiven," Aurum said with a small chuckle. She turned to face the others. "I'm going to go track down Fraiser."

Roman huffed. "Be careful. She's not in the best mood today if that wasn't obvious."

"If I can handle this one *and* Damien," Aurum said, nodding at Natalia, "I can handle her, too."

"Good luck!" Napoleon smiled.

Natalia watched Aurum disappear into the forest before facing Roman, Ren, and Napoleon, who was still smiling. Roman opened his mouth to say something, but Natalia shook her head. "I know, I know. This proves I'm not ready, but I don't want to hear it. I don't need scolding."

"After that little stunt, you do." He smirked. "But it seems Aurum beat me to it."

"You're unbearable sometimes, do you know that?"

Roman chuckled. "I could say the same for you."

"Hey, guys?" Napoleon asked, glancing at them all. "I wasn't just trying to break the tension when I mentioned getting lunch... I'm *starving*."

"Then let's go eat." Roman turned and ruffled Napoleon's hair before playfully locking his arms around his head and leading him in the direction of the square.

Ren appeared next to Natalia a moment later, and together, they began to follow after them. "What happened?"

"I'm sorry, Ren, I was just blowing off some steam."

"It's Damien and Lavelle...," he whispered. "Isn't it?"

She sighed as they trudged through the river, nearing the beginnings of the hundreds of gray tents. She glanced down at the colorful gemstones on her ring glistening in the sunlight. "Yes... Yes, it is..."

"Trust me, I get it. Sitting here while they're stuck in the sectors... It's killing me," Ren said as he looked up at the clear sky above.

"How are you, Ren?" she whispered. "Truly, how are you?"

"I'm surviving... Even if I don't really feel like I am." He shrugged. "It's hard without her. She's always been there, and now she's just...gone... I feel powerless. But somehow, I keep telling myself to keep going because we're going to save them. Both of them."

They wound through the tents and small shacks, nearing the square. Natalia offered him a sad smile. "I understand the feeling..."

Roman and Napoleon entered the square, and Natalia and Ren followed a moment later. She glanced around, watching as the rebels bustled about between the wooden stands, tables, and crates. Together, the four headed toward the stands and tables with boxes of fruits, breads, meats, and vegetables stacked upon them, and were soon back across the river, sitting around the fire pit within their encirclement of tents. The soft grass grabbed at Natalia's legs in the growing breeze as she reached for one of the apples that sat in the wooden bowl between them. There were also strawberries, dried venison, loaves of brown bread, and a small assortment of cooked vegetables.

She winced when she bit into the apple, blood flowing from the split in her lip. The fruit was still delicious regardless of the taste of iron accompanying it. All of the food was delicious and freshly picked from the small gardens spread throughout the camp. Even the bread was still warm from its cooking stone. For a long time, they ate in silence—until Aurum and Fraiser crossed the river, food in their hands and smiles on their faces. They walked over and sat between Ren and Napoleon. Natalia looked at Aurum, who merely smiled.

She fought the urge to roll her eyes and laugh. Of course, Aurum had befriended the most stubborn and arrogant rebel of them all. Maybe Aurum could help Natalia and Frasier get along better. After all, if Aurum liked Fraiser, there had to be at least one redeeming quality that she could like about her, too.

"Now that we're all back," Roman began, shooting a pointed look at Fraiser. She returned his glare with a wicked grin. "I'd like to discuss our next move."

Napoleon smiled. "Let's hear it, boss man."

Roman set down the wooden cup of water he'd been holding and straightened, meeting each of their gazes. "As you're all aware, the rebels destroyed most of the last train station during the testings. Vayne has undoubtedly already begun construction on a new one, which means we have another station to locate before the next testings. To locate it, we need to get inside one of the sectors."

"Why?" Aurum questioned before taking a bite of her strip of dried venison.

"The sectors always send workers and supplies to the stations," Fraiser said. "They'll lead us right to the construction site."

Natalia raised a brow. "I've never seen any Araedians work outside the walls, nor have I ever seen the supplies it would take to build a train station. We don't have those kinds of materials."

"The reason you don't see or hear about it is because they brainwash the workers, so they don't remember anything." Fraiser took a sip from her cup, which was likely filled with more Brennivan.

Ren froze, his face paling. "Really?"

Fraiser nodded.

"The point of all of this," Roman said, drawing all eyes back to him, "is that we can look for your friends while we're in the sectors.

"We can use the crack in the wall to easily get into Four." Natalia immediately set her bloody apple on the ground, and adrenaline rushed through her veins. She'd finally get her chance to look for Damien and Lavelle. She'd finally get her chance to save them. "It will be the easiest to sneak into."

Roman nodded. "Yes, exactly."

"So, when do we leave?" Ren questioned.

"We'll leave tonight," he answered, glancing at Natalia.

She sucked in a breath. He'd changed his mind... But why? Had her outburst with Fraiser been enough to convince him? Was it because of Ren's obvious agony, or some other reason—some other agenda? She searched his golden-brown eyes for the truth but found nothing. Absolutely nothing. Natalia bit the inside of her cheek in frustration. She couldn't read him at all, and it bothered her to no end.

Roman looked away, turning back to Ren. "I'm sorry, but you're not coming, Ren."

"What?" Ren exclaimed, shooting up from the grass. "No, I have to go! My sister, my *twin sister*, is in there!"

"What are you going to do if you run into soldiers, or Aether forbid, Vayne's personal guard? They'll cut you down within seconds," Roman said, rising as well.

The next thing Natalia knew, they were all on their feet. Fraiser stood beside Roman while Napoleon shrunk back behind them with a nervous, unsure expression. Aurum walked over to Ren and grabbed his balled fists, which shook with anger. He winced as his irises began to glow dark-green around pupils as black as tar and his breathing accelerated. She knew he wasn't ready. None of them were, but Roman was talking about Ren's sister. There was no way in hell Ren would stay here while they went after Lavelle—*if* Roman allowed her and Aurum to go.

Ren scowled, ripping his hands from Aurum's. "I don't care who I have to go through to get her back. It's Lavelle. I'll *die* before I let anyone hurt her, and I'll be damned if I just sit here while others rescue her for me."

"Calm down." Roman lifted his hands in peace. "I'm trying to save you both."

"I'm not the one who needs saving," Ren said, squeezing his knuckles until they turned white.

Natalia watched Fraiser shift into a lower stance, readying to attack. Beside Ren, Aurum did the same, and her eyes began to glow orange and silver as her gaze locked onto Fraiser. By the way they looked at each other, she knew there would be no hard feelings between them if it came down to a fight. They were both simply protecting those they loved. And then she realized that *that* was Fraiser's one redeeming quality.

"I'm going, Roman." Ren looked at Aurum and then Natalia, who hadn't moved from her spot between everyone. "Even if I have to go through you."

~

Roman followed Ren's gaze to Natalia who simply stood between everyone, her hands at her sides. He'd planned on bringing her and Aurum along, but not Ren. Unlike Aurum and Natalia, he was too weak physically and mentally, and his control over his element hadn't improved much at all. The other two had mastered the basics extremely quickly. They connected with their elements on a much deeper level than the twin. They weren't afraid of it like he was.

Roman didn't want to start any more conflict. Today had already been full of it, but bringing Ren would be like personally signing his death sentence. He understood Ren's anger and desperation, but he couldn't allow him to go. He just couldn't, and he wasn't going to fight him about it either.

"Ren—"

"Walk with me," Natalia cut in, looking directly into Roman's eyes.

He froze for a split second, caught up in her mesmerizing blue-gray gaze. He'd never get over how unpredictable she was to him. He could always somewhat read everyone he encountered, but she was a closed book. Everything she did surprised him, especially now. She hadn't physically picked a side like Aurum and Fraiser had. She hadn't drawn a line in the sand even though he already knew whose side she was on. She walked past him, and he turned, following her toward the river that flowed through the camp. Once they were a few yards away, she turned to face him.

"You have to let him go," she said. "If you don't, he'll find a way in by himself, and that *will* get him killed."

Roman bit the inside of his cheek. He couldn't help the guilt that formed a pit in his stomach every time he looked at her—a reminder that he'd failed her already by keeping her from her friend, Damien. But he knew that neither of them could've saved him. They'd both been too late that night. He shook his head. "What if he runs into Vayne's personal guard?"

"If it's a risk he's willing to take, then let him take it." She ran a hand through her black hair and sighed. "I think we both know Ren's not a fighter, but he'll fight tooth and nail for Lavelle. He'll give everything he has and more for her."

"I'd be signing his death sentence if I let him go."

"We can protect him, Roman. We *will* protect him."

It was aggravating how convincing her words were. It was like everything she'd said was coated in honey and sugar, and he was a starving man. He'd be going against his instincts by letting Ren go. Everything—his heart, his mind—told him no. Everything except for her, of course. But she was right about the fact that Ren wouldn't just stay at the camp, and Roman refused to lock him up. That's what his father would do, and he was not his father.

"Please, Roman." She finally tore her eyes away from his, glancing back at Ren and the others. They'd only relaxed a little bit, and Roman knew when they returned that Fraiser would be even more riled up. She hated when he spoke to Natalia, but he couldn't figure out why.

"I just don't want any of you to get hurt," he said softly but not weakly. He cursed the Aether. She was changing his mind, and he was letting her. What was he doing? Fraiser would've slapped him twice by now if she'd been in on this conversation.

She turned back to Roman. "I know, but it's our lives. You said it yourself. This isn't the sectors, and we have free will here."

"Fine." He sighed. It would complicate things a little bit more, but he'd allow it. She was right again. This wasn't the sectors. They had free will here, and he didn't want them to think that they didn't.

"Thank you," she said, nodding quickly and heading back toward the others as if she couldn't stand being next to him for a moment longer. The thought made his chest feel tight, and he waited until she was a few steps ahead before following. She was so confusing.

"Well?" Fraiser asked with a frown when he finally rejoined them all.

Roman didn't meet her gaze and instead turned to Ren, Aurum, and Natalia. "You three are coming with me to pack supplies. We'll be gone for a few days."

Ren smiled, turning to Aurum and Natalia, who grinned back. Roman finally met Fraiser's gaze. The fire burning within it was scorching, and he wondered why her element had been air and not flames. It took all his self-control not to smirk. If her element had been fire, Vayne and the sectors wouldn't exist. He couldn't decide whether that would have been a good or bad thing.

Fraiser scowled and shook her head as if to say, *You're the biggest idiot I've ever met in my entire life.*

He shrugged. She was probably right. "Fraiser, Napoleon, I'll speak with you two after we're done."

Neither of them would be accompanying him. Someone had to stay with the rebels and lead while he was gone. They both knew that, but he also knew Fraiser would be angry that he'd allowed Natalia to convince him to let Ren go. As if on cue, Fraiser turned on her heels and disappeared into her tent. Napoleon merely smiled innocently before following her. Aurum grabbed Ren's and Natalia's hands, leading them toward the river. The life filling all of them—the sense of hope and determination to fight for those they loved—reminded him how much he valued Napoleon and Fraiser. How he would die before he let anything happen to them as well.

"Come on, slowpoke!" Aurum called from across the river.

A small smile graced Roman's lips as he jogged after them, and together, they wove between the wooden shacks and tents, a cool breeze nipping at their backs. They arrived at the square, Natalia glancing back over her shoulder before disappearing into the small crowd of rebels strolling about. All these former citizens of Araedia were here under his protection. His leadership. He couldn't begin to fathom why they'd chosen to follow him after his mother's death, but they had. They'd entrusted their lives to the son of the very president they were trying so hard to defeat. Roman fought back a shudder. He hadn't told Natalia and the others about his heritage—not yet. How could he? He'd seen the look in her eyes every time his father's name was mentioned. The hatred behind them... What was to stop her from hating him, too? How could she trust him when his father had caused her and her family so much pain?

Roman hadn't realized he'd stopped at the entrance to the square until Aurum and Ren passed him. Ren hesitated, allowing Aurum to slip into the crowd and leaving them alone.

"Are you all right?" he questioned tentatively.

"Who was Damien?" Roman returned. He wanted to know exactly who his father had taken away from Natalia. From all of them. He'd always been curious, but now it was personal. However, he couldn't lie to himself either. He also wanted to know how deeply connected she and Damien were.

"Six years ago," Ren began, falling into step beside Roman as he walked to a stand of leather, backpacks, satchels, and other smaller bags, "an old woman convinced each of us to leave our sectors and venture out into the woods. Damien and

Natalia met first. Then Aurum, then me and Lavelle..." Roman grabbed a backpack from the highest hanging notch on the stand and handed it to him before grabbing another. "It was an interesting dynamic at first, but we all learned to survive with each other—*because* of each other. We ended up forming unbreakable bonds, but Natalia and Damien always had something special. They could finish each other's sentences without even trying. They were always on the same wavelength. Kind of like me and Lavelle. Like twins."

Roman didn't know why, but his jaw locked, and he found it hard to nod along as Ren continued.

"Aurum likes to tease them for it. She thinks they're in love with each other, but I could never really tell. Lavelle always said that Natalia did love him, but not the way that Damien wanted her to." He let out a small chuckle. "She always said that she thought Natalia was too independent for him, and Damien loved her too much—to the point where he scared her, and she pushed him away."

"What do *you* think?" Roman asked, the answer suddenly very important.

"I think they were both so desperately in need of someone when they found each other. I think that for them, it was like finding a gallon of ice water in the hottest desert before you're about to pass out—"

"What about passing out?" Aurum cut in with a raised brow.

Roman and Ren turned to find the girls behind them, carrying six metal canteens. Ren opened the backpack he held, and Aurum dumped the canteens inside.

"Oh, we were just talking about how if Natalia gets any angrier, she might burst a blood vessel and pass out." Ren winked.

Roman bit the inside of his bottom lip. It was a stupid lie, but it was better than what he would've come up with because he was completely dumbfounded. No matter how unpredictable and unreadable she was, he couldn't help but like Natalia— even if she got under his skin worse than Fraiser. But he had the feeling he did the same to her, and it made him smile.

He chuckled to himself. *Maybe we shouldn't save Damien.*

"You're so weird," Natalia said, dumping the remaining canteens into the backpack with a small laugh. She then turned and reached up for the last two backpacks hanging on the notches... But she was too short. Roman smirked, easily grabbing the backpacks and handing them to her. She made a face, scrunching her nose in frustration. Aurum snickered behind her, causing Natalia to pinch her.

"Hey!" Aurum exclaimed, a playful gleam in her eyes. Natalia grinned and dodged Aurum's hand before running into the crowd back in the direction of their encirclement of tents. Ren laughed, and Roman began to lead them out of the square. Ren's laughter died almost immediately as he stopped at the edge of the maze of gray tents.

Roman turned around, studying him carefully. The bags under the boy's eyes hadn't gone unnoticed. "What is it?"

"Do you think he's still alive?" he whispered.

"I don't know..." A few moments of silence passed before Roman continued, chewing on the words he didn't want to say aloud. "If he is, he's most likely been brainwashed... She knows that, right?"

Ren glanced in the direction Natalia and Aurum had run. "It was always rumored in the sectors that brainwashing occurred under Vayne's rule. We always thought it was true... All of us did. She knows it's a possibility that it's happened to Damien, but I don't think she wants to admit it... Is there any way to fix it if he has been?"

"As far as I know," Roman whispered, "there's no cure..."

He remembered encountering those under his father's brainwashing before. Out of those he'd encountered when he was little and those he'd seen recently, they were all the same. There was only one cure. And it was death.

But I haven't been home in a long time..., Roman thought.

CHAPTER ELEVEN

THE RETURN

Roman watched Natalia and Napoleon describe the best bakery in Sector Four to Ren as they all sat around another small fire Aurum had constructed and lit. A small dinner of dried beef and an assortment of fruits and vegetables left over from lunch sat on wooden plates, the setting sun casting everything around them in a blood-orange hue. The dark shadows of the trees danced and waved their branches against the grass as a breeze wove between them.

Roman glanced at Fraiser and Aurum, who sat shoulder-to-shoulder across from him. Aurum's eyes glowed, and her brows knit together in concentration while she focused on trying to weave a small line of flames through her fingers. Fraiser smirked mischievously, her own eyes beginning to glow gray and silver as she formed a small tornado of winds in her palm and sent it flying into the flames. The flame and wind collided before swirling up into the air and dissipating. The two girls chuckled, and he couldn't help but smile at them.

He was glad that Fraiser had found another friend, especially a girl. She'd never really bothered to try to make friends with anyone besides Roman and Napoleon after her little sister had died. Though Roman would always be there to love and support her like a brother, he knew that sometimes she just needed another girl. And some part of him couldn't help but think that Aurum reminded Fraiser of her little sister because of Aurum's heart of wildfire.

Out of the corner of Roman's eye, movement caught his attention. He turned to find Natalia walking back toward the river, the canteens from the square in her arms. He shook his head and rose. She was so eager to save her friends. He hoped he wouldn't fail her in that sense. Again. As leader of the rebels, he couldn't afford to fail. If he did, people got hurt—or worse. They died, and he didn't particularly feel like adding Damien and Lavelle's names to the list. But he sure as hell wouldn't be adding Natalia's. Or Aurum's and Ren's.

He followed her to the bank of the river, not quite sure what exactly he was doing. But he did know that he wanted to talk to her and figure out what she was thinking. If he understood her better, maybe she'd finally open up enough to the point that he could read her a little bit. A little bit was better than nothing because nothing was absolutely agonizing.

"Do you need help?" Roman asked, sticking his hands in the pockets of his dark pants.

Natalia turned and ran her eyes over him before shaking her head. "It's all right, I've got it."

She kept walking, only a few feet away from the river when one of the six canteens slipped out from under her elbow and clanged on the ground. Roman picked it up with a chuckle and met her frowning face. He didn't miss the twinkle of amusement hiding in her eyes, though she was clearly reluctant to laugh as if she thought it would expose her in some way. He gave her a soft smile. The gray-blue shade of her eyes was calm, yet intriguing. It reminded him of a stormy day and the rain—he *loved* when it rained. He'd always wondered whether the reason he loved the rain so much was because he was a water Elemental, but his father had proved him wrong. Vayne was an Elemental and originally born to air. He hated anything and everything that had to do with it, always expressing how useless it was. It was one of the many things that had fueled his father's obsession with the other elements, but no element was useless. They were all important and powerful and created a fragile balance that held everything together.

Natalia returned Roman's gaze. What was she about to do? Would she tear her eyes away like before, or would she wait for him to do so? Some part of him hoped she wouldn't. But then she did before setting the canteens down by the riverside and kneeling beside them. He joined her on the grass, hands casually resting on his knees.

He watched as she extended her arms out in front of her toward the flowing currents. Her eyes began to glow, and she twisted her hands to form a rising sphere of water. Its balance was wobbly, causing her to scrunch her nose in concentration. She then swung her arms outward and split the sphere into six streams of water that floated to each unscrewed canteen, including the one he now held in his hand. Roman smirked and his own eyes began to glow as he commandeered two of the streams. He wiggled his fingers around, sending the water flying and spinning about frantically. The two streams circled around Natalia's head while she finished screwing the lids on the other four canteens. She swatted at the water with a smirk, but

Roman shot them out of her reach. She then looked to the water, moving her arms once more to fire two of her own small jets of water at his. They missed, but she'd gotten closer than he'd thought.

"You use it as often as you can," he observed, twirling the now combined stream through his fingers.

"I'm trying to learn to control it as soon as possible." She formed another set of jets and rotated her wrist. They circled each other slowly.

"It won't take you long," Roman said, finally sending the water into his two canteens. "A lot of people have a hard time accepting their elements, but you don't, which is good. You can't control things you're afraid of. It's something I hope I can help Ren understand, so he can start improving his training."

"He'll get it, especially when he gets Lavelle back. He's not complete without her." She stood and faced him. Roman rose as well, taking another canteen from her arms so they were even. "Will we leave soon?"

He nodded. "After everyone finishes eating. Filling these..." He lifted the canteens. "...was the last thing I had to do."

Together, they walked over to the flap of his tent where the four backpacks sat in the tall grass, splitting the cans of water between them. Aurum joined them a moment later followed by Ren, Napoleon, and Fraiser, who was frowning. Roman fought the urge to roll his eyes. When was she not frowning? He knew she was just concerned for him...and still a little angry that he'd let Natalia convince him to bring Ren, which Fraiser had thought was a horrible idea. It wasn't that she didn't trust Ren—or Aurum. Natalia was the one she didn't trust, but Roman did.

"We're ready when you are, Roman," Aurum said.

Roman nodded and distributed their backpacks. "It will be a little over a day's journey from here to Sector Four."

"Not that bad of a haul." Ren shrugged on his backpack.

Napoleon smiled at them. "Be careful."

"Hold the fort down," Roman said, leaning against Napoleon's shoulder as an older brother would and ruffling his hair. He gave Fraiser a smirk. "Oh, and make sure Fraiser doesn't destroy the place while I'm gone."

She shot him a glare that could burn down the entire forest around them before rolling her green eyes. "Don't die."

"I won't." Roman turned to help Aurum with her bag, leaving the others to say their goodbyes if they wanted to. Natalia and Napoleon spoke for a moment before Fraiser walked over. Napoleon immediately found somewhere else to be as Fraiser grabbed Natalia's elbow and whispered into her ear. Fraiser leaned away a second later, and the two girls stared each other down. Roman frowned, irritation nipping at him. What had she said to Natalia? Why couldn't they just get along? It was really starting to piss him off.

Natalia looked at Napoleon, ignoring Fraiser completely and strapping on the last backpack. "We'll see you in a few days."

Aurum and Fraiser exchanged two playful punches, and the next thing Roman knew, he was leading Aurum, Ren, and Natalia toward the tree line—toward the sectors, his father, their friends, and possibly death. He said a quick prayer to the Aether that everything would work out. That they would all be okay. He paused at the edge of the forest and glanced back at Fraiser, who was already marching back into the heart of the camp while Napoleon waved. He chuckled to himself. The camp was in good hands. And then, they entered the forest, his camp disappearing behind them.

~

The sun had finished setting thirty minutes after Natalia and the others had left the camp. They were an hour into their journey, and the forest around them was encased in a calming darkness, the moonlight illuminating patches of the ground through the canopy. Natalia studied Roman while she and Aurum followed a few feet behind him and Ren. Even through the dark, she could see the shape of his strong back and muscular arms. Ren had grown much taller over the past few months, but beside Roman, he looked small and scrawny. The two passed under a patch of moonlight, igniting their black and blond hair in silver highlights.

Aurum looked at Natalia and whispered, "What did Fraiser tell you before we left?"

"That if I hurt him in any way, she'll gut me." Natalia snorted. "That's the nice version."

"You know, she's not *that* bad once you get to know her a little bit," Aurum said with a sheepish grin.

"I'm excited for Damien and Lavelle to meet everyone but her." She frowned.

"Oh, come on, Natalia—"

"Aurum." Natalia gave her a pointed look. "She hates me."

"Hate is a strong word..." Aurum glanced ahead at Roman and smirked. "I think I know why she hates you, though."

"What?" Natalia questioned, following her gaze and knitting her brows.

"Don't look at me like that." Aurum snickered. "You know exactly what I'm talking about."

"No, I really don't," she said and looked away, suddenly finding their surroundings a lot more interesting... What Aurum was implying was...crazy. It was absolutely crazy. Fraiser was not jealous, especially not of her and Roman because there was nothing to be jealous of. Roman was the leader of the rebels and annoying, and that was it. She wouldn't let herself believe anything else. She couldn't—not while Damien and Lavelle were still out there at least.

"Please." Aurum raised a brow. "You mean to tell me that he's not even slightly attractive? You mean to tell me that you two aren't staring into each other's souls every second of every minute you're around each other?"

"I don't know him at all," Natalia said with a shrug, fighting the slight heating in her cheeks. "I'm just trying to figure him out because—"

"Because he's unpredictable, and you can't read him to save your life?"

Natalia frowned. "And because he's confusing and nearly as aggravating as you are."

"It's all right." Aurum chuckled. "He's doing the same thing to you. And I'm not aggravating. I'm *amazing*."

"And humble," she said.

"You have to admit, though, there's a little something there—"

"Aurum, I don't want to talk about this." Even if Aurum was right, which Natalia wouldn't allow herself to believe or consider for a moment, Roman would never go for her. Besides, she and Roman were strictly training. It wasn't like there was another water Elemental to teach her, and she had one sole focus: save Damien and Lavelle. There couldn't be distractions or anything of the sort until they were safe. However, a part of Natalia—the side of her that always felt exposed in Roman's presence—couldn't deny that a hint of *something* was there. But what was that something? Was it simply the fact that she never had a clue what he was going to say or do? Like Aurum said, he was unpredictable to her, and it was frightening not knowing what either of them felt. Maybe that was the something Aurum was talking about... They walked on in silence for a few minutes when Aurum faced her again.

"What are we going to do about Damien?" she asked, her usual happy dark brown eyes cold and cast in shadow.

Natalia bit the inside of her cheek and hesitated. "What do you mean?"

"We don't know for sure, but if I had to guess, he's most likely imprisoned in One. We're sneaking into Four."

"Well, once we find the location of the next station, we'll have to go to Two for Lavelle. Why not pay Vayne a visit while we're close by?" Natalia suggested, mustering as much confidence as she could. Even if it was fake. She ran her fingers over her ring. Damien was the first family she'd had since Vale. She couldn't just let him go—couldn't give up on him. She'd never stop trying to save him until one of them was dead.

"What happens if something goes wrong?" Ren asked, causing Natalia to jump. She hadn't known he'd been listening.

"We have friends within the sectors who are willing to hide us," Roman said.

Aurum's eyes widened in surprise. "People have hidden you before?"

"There's always Araedians in each sector who are willing to help us. Though it might not seem like it, a lot of the population supports the rebels... They're just silent. Most are too terrified to speak their minds and stand up for what they believe in." Roman scoffed in disgust. "But I don't blame them. They have to protect themselves and their families. As you all know, Vayne is particularly fond of *and* good at putting down rebel sympathizers."

"That's why he can't always find you when you sneak in, though," Natalia said, meeting Roman's golden-brown eyes. They gleamed with a mischievous light that reminded her of Vale the one time he'd successfully pulled a prank on the matron of the orphanage.

He nodded with a crooked grin. "That's one reason. The other is that we're just that good at sneaking around."

It was somewhat comforting to know that they wouldn't be entirely alone and without support when they entered the sectors, but there was only so much the Araedians could do. Vayne was indeed fond of and very good at putting down sympathizers. Natalia prayed to the Aether that nothing would go wrong and that they wouldn't have to put anyone else in danger. She didn't want to risk other lives trying to rescue someone she should've already saved. She'd risk her own, but that was it. And any lives taken because of them would be on her hands and her hands alone. Natalia took a long, deep breath as they continued on through the forest.

~

Hours of traversing the forest and climbing rolling hills passed before the sky began to lighten, dawn approaching. Natalia rubbed at her heavy eyelids, trying to chase away the sleep pulling at them. All conversation had died about an hour ago, and everyone's exhaustion was clear on their faces. Roman had asked if they would like to break, but Natalia, Aurum, and Ren had shaken their heads, not wanting to make the journey any longer. She was beginning to regret that decision as they trudged up a particularly tall and steep hill littered with trees, bushes, and rocks. The opposite side of the hill was so steep, it was a near drop-off. They reached the top and paused, surveying the landscape cast in dark navy and blue-gray shadows.

Natalia blinked at the sight before her—at the walls of the sectors peeking through the treetops in the distance. A reserve of energy burst through her veins. They only had a few more hours to go, then they could rest for a bit before continuing on to Four. She took a step forward when Roman suddenly tackled her to the ground.

"Everyone down!" he snapped in a forceful whisper.

Aurum immediately dropped, pulling Ren down with her. Natalia's heart thrummed in her ears as the forest fell deathly quiet. Through the bushes and rocks atop the hill, the four watched three soldiers clad in black armor with guns that shot crackling, blue electricity wander through the forest. The soldiers turned, beginning to navigate their way up the hill. She gritted her teeth. What in the Aether's name were Vayne's soldiers doing this far away from the walls? She silently cursed. They shouldn't even be *outside* the walls. Everyone froze, the soldiers slowly making their way higher and higher. She cursed again and looked at Roman. They needed to move. Now. He met her gaze and gave her the slightest of nods before grabbing her arm and pulling her up into a low crouch.

Aurum and Ren rose, too, and together, Roman slowly began to lead them down the other side of the hill—down the drop-off. Every step was critical. One mistake would have them tumbling down amongst the trees and rocks. The echo of the soldiers speaking to each other bounced around as they grew closer to the crest of the hill. Without warning, Aurum stumbled behind them and landed on a large stick with a loud *snap*. They collectively sucked in a breath, rooted to the spot.

"What was that?" a masculine voice questioned.

Then three dark helmets appeared atop the hill and stared directly at them. The next thing Natalia knew, they were all sprinting down the hill, using the trees and larger rocks to keep from tumbling down. She grabbed a low-hanging branch and steadied herself. It snapped. Roman lunged for her as she fell, grabbing her waist and pulling her in as close as he could. Behind them, Aurum and Ren shrieked when they, too, slipped and rolled down the steep drop-off. Natalia squeezed her eyes shut and winced while she and Roman knocked against bushes and small rocks. They were only a few seconds from the bottom of the hill when Roman's back slammed into a large tree trunk, hitting so hard that they dislodged from each other. A loud *crash* echoed through the forest, and Natalia rolled to a violent stop, finally on even ground. She looked up dizzily to watch Ren and Aurum fly through a patch of bushes and collide at the bottom. She winced for them.

Ren groaned as Aurum rolled off him. "Ren, are you all right?"

"Yep." He gasped for breath. "Perfectly fine."

Natalia shuffled to her knees and turned to Roman, who hissed painfully a few feet away. She slid over in the foliage and glanced to the top of the hill. Vayne's soldiers were cursing and yelling at each other as they tried to navigate down the drop-off and not repeat their own actions. Panic flooded through her. She slipped an arm underneath Roman, helping him rise to his feet.

"Can you run?" she asked. Aurum and Ren—leaves, dirt, and grass in their hair—rose, too.

He winced. "Yes."

Natalia looked at Ren, and he nodded, answering her nonverbal question. They were okay. She returned his nod. A scream pierced the air, and they all whirled to watch the three soldiers plummet down the hill, their guns flying off their backs and scattering.

"Run!" Aurum exclaimed, and they were off, but a mangled cry of pain stopped Natalia dead in her tracks. Roman writhed in pain on the forest floor, clutching at a spot under his backpack on his lower back. The spot that had hit that tree. She ran back to him, fear and panic pounding through her like a drum.

"What's wrong?" She unstrapped his backpack and flung it to the side. Aurum and Ren were at her side a moment later.

"I don't know," he said with a gasp. He cried out in pain again as his back suddenly began to spasm.

"Natalia...," Aurum mumbled.

"What?" She lifted her head and followed Aurum's gaze to the bottom of the hill where the soldiers had stopped rolling. They quickly stood, scrambling after their guns. Natalia gritted her teeth. They needed to get Roman out of there, but even if they could, where would they go? And leaving him was *not* an option.

Roman groaned in agony. "Just—"

"Shut up," Natalia and Aurum said simultaneously as Natalia rolled him over onto his side and lifted his black shirt. Her eyes widened at the bruising that had already formed down his spine. She ran a hand over a large knot near the lower half of his back and winced at the broken bone underneath his warm skin. She shivered, feeling a sudden rush of power. There was no moving him. They'd have to fight their way out.

Aurum had concluded the same thing as she stepped forward to meet the three soldiers now rushing at them. Her irises glowed red around silver pupils, and she shrugged off her backpack, sprinting to meet the soldiers. Flames erupted inside her palms before they flew toward them. A second before the flames scorched the ground, the soldiers dove to the sides. One soldier set his hand against the earth to stand when the forest floor around it rose and encased his arm, trapping him. He screamed when a large rock suddenly rose from the ground and struck him across the face. The visor of his black helmet cracked. The rock struck and struck the soldier until he fell back to the ground, blood leaking through the cracks in the helmet.

Natalia whirled to look at Ren, whose glowing green and black eyes returned to their normal blue, full of fear. Sweat trickled down his paling face, and she hoped that Aurum could take the other two soldiers by herself. Ren's energy was already depleted. Natalia set her hand back down on the knot of Roman's broken bone. It was as if a magnet was drawing her to it. She could feel that something was missing between her hand and his body. The rest of his body felt alive, but that one spot felt like all life had been drained of it. It was cold, dark, and in desperate need of *something* to survive. And Natalia knew what that something was.

In that moment, there was a connection between her and Roman telling her what to do—like instincts but even deeper than that. She reached into her backpack, grabbing her canteen and then opening it. Water climbed out, piling into her palms while her eyes began to glow ice-blue and silver. She set her hands gently against the knot and waited. She could feel it in the air between them—sparks and pricks of electricity along her skin—something was happening. Another rush of energy coursed through her as the water in her palms began to glow dark blue—the color of Roman's now glowing eyes. It gently pulled away from her hands, along with the rush of energy, and began to swirl around his back over his injuries. Roman winced, and a pop suddenly sounded from his lower back, causing him to yelp in pain.

"Roman?" Natalia exclaimed in terror. What was happening? She laid her arm on his shoulder as he finally stopped spasming, and the water collapsed to the forest floor. His breathing was slow and labored.

Behind them, Aurum had singed one of the soldiers into a pile of burning bones, the stench of burning flesh filling the air. Natalia watched her duck under the last soldier's fist and send her own fist flying into their side. The soldier stumbled back with a muted grunt and straightened. Then Aurum sent a column of flames shooting at the soldier's exposed throat. The flames wrapped around it, constricting like a snake choking its prey. The soldier collapsed to the ground with a strangled cry, and smoke rose from his sizzling neck. Everyone froze, and the forest fell entirely silent.

Natalia bit the inside of her cheek. Her heart felt heavy and cold. She'd just watched her friends kill three of Vayne's soldiers to survive. She clenched her fists, and a familiar, all-consuming anger filled her—hatred filled her. This was all because of Vayne. Every bit of pain and suffering—past, present, and future—was because of him. She knew Aurum's and Ren's actions today would haunt them just as that girl she'd killed haunted her. Aurum would try to hide it, but Ren... She feared Ren would snap if he didn't get to Lavelle soon. By the way his hands were shaking, she knew she was right. He needed her badly, and the horror on his face... It was gut-wrenching to see it there. He glanced at her with shadowed eyes.

"Is everyone okay?" Aurum whispered.

Natalia nodded, but she wasn't just answering the question. She was convincing Ren, Roman, Aurum, and herself that they were, in fact, okay. They were all alive, and that was what mattered. She looked at Roman, who was staring at her with wide brown eyes. "Can you sit up?"

"Yes," he said, doing so with a small wince.

"Wait, what happened?" Aurum glanced between them in shock. She shook her head in disbelief. "Did you—Roman, did you *heal* yourself?"

Natalia's brows furrowed. He had... But how? And at what cost? His usually tan face was paler than death, and bags had formed under his dull eyes. He didn't look like he was even fully awake yet.

"I don't know," he mumbled.

"You look pale." Natalia held the back of her hand against his forehead. It wasn't hot. If anything, it was cold...

He looked so weak, but when he turned to peer at her, she felt as if he saw right through her—as if he wasn't weak at all. As if he held all the power, and *she* was the fragile one. "You look tired."

"I'm fine." She shrugged. It wasn't a lie. Not entirely. She felt a little drained—like some of her energy had been taken from her. Other than that, she truly was fine. "Do you want to stand?"

He nodded, and she rose, extending her hands to him. Roman stood on wobbly legs but remained upright.

"Thank you," he said.

"I didn't really do anything." She grabbed her canteen from where she'd discarded it on the ground and slipped it back into her backpack.

He gave her a knowing look. "I think you did more than you realize."

"What do you mean?" Ren asked tentatively.

Natalia watched as Ren handed Roman his backpack. Roman grabbed his own canteen, taking a few gulps before closing it and zipping it back inside. "I read about it once before I fled Sector One. The power is very rare in Elementals, but some of us have the ability to transfer energy to heal." He took a steadying breath. "And, obviously, it's very tiring. I also read that it's possible that if an Elemental is injured, another Elemental of the same element can help them heal themselves by simply being in their presence. You made me stronger because of how strong you are yourself. We all feed off each other because we're all connected."

"Incredible," Natalia whispered.

Aurum walked over to the smoking corpses littered along the forest floor. Hesitantly, she knelt beside them and began to unstrap their armor. "I wonder what they were doing out here... We've never seen soldiers beyond the walls before."

"I don't know, but I'd rather not stay and find out," Roman said as he limped over and helped her with the buckles, dividing the armor into their four backpacks. They were only able to carry two of the three sets.

"Agreed...," Ren said softly, staring into the distance.

Natalia grabbed his hand and mustered a small smile. "Then let's get going."

～

Two and a half uneventful hours of walking through the forest passed before Natalia spotted a familiar incline. She, Aurum, and Ren suddenly sprinted up the side of the sloping hill, leaving Roman confused as he hurried after them. They reached the clearing within seconds and gazed out over their overhang. Natalia smiled brightly, closing her eyes when the breeze lifted her hair around her face. It was nice to be back and feel the rush of nostalgia and memories connected to the land here—even if parts of it were missing.

"This is where we'd meet whenever we escaped the walls," she explained to Roman, who slightly limped up beside her with a smile. They hadn't seen or heard any additional soldiers, and he'd gained most of his strength back quickly. It was a great relief to see the life and color enter his eyes and skin again. She turned to Ren and Aurum, who rested a hand on Ren's shoulder. Tears filled his eyes, and Natalia could've sworn her heart cracked a little. She knew how badly he was struggling without Lavelle. He'd hardly eaten over the past few days, and she'd even heard him rustle out of his tent several times in the late hours of the night when she couldn't sleep either. Natalia twisted her ring. He only had to make it another day or two—maybe even just a few more hours... It was time to save Damien and Lavelle. No matter what, she vowed she wouldn't leave the sectors without them.

"Come on," Aurum said, leading him back to the tree line. "We're almost there."

Natalia and Roman followed, and as they approached, the walls seemed more looming and foreboding than ever. They knelt behind a cluster of thick bushes near the tree line, and she studied the dozens of soldiers who patrolled the top of the wall with guns and spears. She frowned. She'd never seen that many soldiers atop the walls in her entire life. If Vale were here, he'd agree. What had happened during the eight days they'd been gone? Were the other sectors like this, too, or was it just Four?

Natalia crept west, leading them toward the crack in the wall. A few minutes of dodging twigs and crunchy leaves passed before she suddenly stopped and blinked. What she was seeing was impossible. Utterly impossible. She ran her eyes over the light-gray cement that filled the crack, a scar against the pavement. More soldiers paced above as she glanced back at Aurum, Roman, and Ren. Roman and Aurum had fallen eerily still, clearly going through any and every idea for another plan. Ren simply stared at the scar, his eyes an empty and hopeless void. Natalia gritted her teeth and ran her hands through her hair, attempting to calm the thousands of thoughts racing through her mind.

"I have an idea," Aurum whispered. Everyone turned to face her. "But I don't think you're going to like it."

"What is it?" Natalia asked eagerly.

"Ren and I will create a distraction farther down the wall. The guards will chase after us, and while they're occupied, you two find a way in."

"What do you plan on doing when they chase you?" Natalia asked, fear creeping into her voice. Splitting up wasn't a good idea. It was too big of a risk, and if something happened to them, she'd—

"Natalia, I know what you're going to say, but we'll have to split up to look for Damien and Lavelle and the train station anyway." Aurum slung her backpack off her shoulder and unzipped it, revealing the soldiers' armor. "Besides, we have these.

Once we lose the guards, Ren and I will use these to sneak in to go find Damien and Lavelle."

Roman nodded. "And Natalia and I will look for the location of the next station."

"Exactly," Aurum returned, meeting Natalia's gaze. "Then we'll all meet back at the overhang tomorrow. If one group isn't back by the following day, the group at the overhang will return to camp."

"What?" Natalia exclaimed. This was crazy. What if something happened, and more of them were captured? She couldn't chance it, and she had to be the one to save Damien. She owed him that. "Aurum—"

"Natalia, there's no other way in," Ren interrupted, light and energy filling his eyes. "If you want to save Damien and Lavelle, this is what we have to do to do it. You know Aurum's right."

"We'll be fine," Aurum said with a smile of love and confidence. "You don't have to worry so much about us. Not any more. We'll get them back. You know we will."

Natalia sighed. She hated to admit it, but she knew Aurum was right. It was impossible to accomplish what they wanted without splitting up. She just hated the thought of not saving Lavelle and Damien herself, but she had to let go of her fear. It was holding her back and keeping her from making the hard decisions—something Aurum had always been good at. She admired and trusted her for it. Damien had always said that it was because of Aurum's golden heart that she couldn't be cutthroat, but she was cutthroat now. It wasn't the time for kindness and peace. Natalia wasn't entirely sure there would ever be a time for that again—not while Vayne was still breathing. Not while they were at *war*. It was time to step up. They weren't little children any more. They were grown, and it was time to start making the difficult decisions. Natalia finally nodded in agreement. Aurum was right. It was the only way.

"Will you be able to find your way back to the camp if something goes wrong?" Roman asked.

"I can find it," Ren said. "Ever since my element kicked in, I've been more attuned to the earth and the trails woven into the dirt. I can get us back."

"All right." Aurum nodded with a feral grin, pulling out the armor. "Let's do this."

They all stood, and Natalia embraced Aurum and Ren. They squeezed her tightly in return. "I'll see you two soon. Be careful."

"We're always careful." Aurum winked. Ren smiled, seeming to finally come alive. He was ready to save his sister, and so was everyone else. But in that moment, Natalia saw something click. He was different... He was no longer the innocent, young boy who'd followed Lavelle into the woods. He had killed, and it seemed it had finally set in with him, but he hadn't run from it. He'd accepted it. He didn't seem to care at all because he had done it for those he loved, and he would do it again if he had to. Ren—like all of them in some way—had grown, but for better or worse, Natalia could not yet tell. Aurum and Ren gave small waves and then disappeared into the forest.

Roman faced Natalia, his eyes meeting hers. They both studied each other carefully. He didn't seem afraid, so why was she? They could do this. She clenched her fists and dipped her head toward him. He smiled encouragingly in return, and together, they waited for five long minutes until shouts could be heard in the distance. The soldiers atop the wall froze, glancing back and forth before sprinting off in the direction of the commotion. Roman gently grabbed Natalia's hand and bounded between two trees, breaking into a sprint toward the scar of cement.

Natalia, eyes glowing as she reached for the power inside her, paused just before the wall, reared back, and sent her foot flying into the cement. A crack sounded, and tiny pieces caved inward. She flexed her toes, trying to stretch out the tense sting in her foot, and scowled. This needed to be quick. She would have to deal with the pain later. She kicked the cement once more, stumbling backward as more pieces fell to the ground. Behind her, Roman opened his canteen and formed an enormous icicle in his palm. He grunted, slamming the icicle down. Large shards exploded to the ground, and the remaining concrete collapsed. Natalia grabbed his shoulder, gently turning him to face sideways.

She led the way between the cold concrete and then under the roots of the familiar tree. It was oddly comforting to slide under as she had so many times before, but it was like a rock had been lifted off her shoulders when she and Roman emerged on the other side. They were by no means safe, but she was home. She turned to him, nodding at the sloping path that led up the hill to the heart of Sector Four, and they began the sprint up the path. At the top of the sloping hill sat the abandoned shack she'd passed nearly every day.

"There!" She pointed at it. They could hide in there until they knew for certain the coast was clear. Roman, overtaking Natalia, reached the house first and swung the door open, surveying the area while she ducked inside. Clearly satisfied no one was around, he followed in after her.

"Hello?" Natalia whispered.

Her only answer was the wind stirring the dust up from the floor. A small makeshift kitchen sat in the left corner, accompanied by a broken cot at the right where a small closet had been built. The mandatory projector sat on the floor along with shards of glass from the shattered windows. It appeared tampered with... Parts were missing. Natalia's eyes widened and fear shot through her when the sound of boots pounding against the earth filled the air and neared. Quickly, she whirled to Roman, who reached over and grabbed her arm while he swung the closet door open and dragged her inside. He slowly shut the door, darkness enveloping them like a heavy quilt. Natalia sighed in relief as she listened for the heavy footfalls. They had slowed but were growing closer. She didn't think any of the guards had seen them, but she could've been wrong. It hadn't taken them long at all to cross the distance between the wall and the shack, though.

Roman, giving into his clear exhaustion, sat his chin on the top of her head and closed his eyes. Natalia's heart raced and her cheeks heated. They fit perfectly in place. She couldn't stop the meek smile that danced across her lips. But why was she smiling when they were in danger? They could be caught at any moment. Yet for the first time in forever, Natalia simply stood there without a thought. It had been so long since her mind was quiet... It was...very nice. However, it didn't last long, and a sense of betrayal washed over her. Damien... Yes, she loved him, but it wasn't the same way he loved her. So why did she feel like she'd betrayed him? She bit the inside of her lip.

"Really?" Natalia rolled her eyes.

"My apologies," Roman drawled. He chuckled as he lifted his chin. "I'm a little drained."

Natalia huffed in amusement, allowing a smile to break through. "Me, too."

A few moments of silence passed before she hesitantly opened her mouth to speak and glanced up. Their noses were almost touching. She hadn't realized exactly how close they were in the tiny closet. In spite of herself, her cheeks heated once more.

"What is it?" he asked.

She slightly tilted her head back down. "How did you sneak into the sectors before?"

"During the late hours of the night, we would throw grappling hooks over the walls and climb them. The guards were always asleep or being lazy and not patrolling at all. They never bothered to keep diligent watch until we got too good at it." Suddenly, the heavy footsteps were upon them. Whoever was outside—which Natalia presumed was reinforcements for the walls—was running past the shack. They stood in heavy silence until the last of the footfalls were gone.

Natalia sighed and whispered, "How are we supposed to do this?"

"I don't know," Roman admitted, his voice solemn and soft. "We'll figure it out, though... We always do."

CHAPTER TWELVE

HOMECOMING

Ren and Aurum sprinted through the forest, ducking under low-hanging branches and leaping over fallen logs and rocks. Soldiers clad in black armor with guns and spears of electricity chased after them like vicious hounds. The two paused atop the overhang, turning to face the forest. The soldiers had been on their tails ever since Ren and Aurum had chucked rocks at them from below the walls. It had been a good distraction—maybe too good.

Ren glanced at Aurum nervously. Sweat dripped from both of their brows while they waited. He stretched his arms outward, squeezing his glowing green and black eyes shut, and then inhaled deeply, concentrating as his mind connected with the earth around them. It was a distant connection at first, but it grew stronger as each moment trickled by. Soldiers suddenly burst into the clearing, firing bolts of crackling blue-purple electricity. Eyes glowing, Aurum lunged forward and sent two columns of fire toward the bolts. They collided with a thunderous *crack*. Smoke billowed through the air, covering everything. A few seconds later, it dissipated, and Aurum's jaw dropped as she looked at Ren.

But he didn't dare meet her stare. He couldn't. Ren strained, doing everything in his power to keep the rock wall that had formed between them and the soldiers from slipping back into the earth. The wall dropped a few inches, and he cursed. "I don't know how long I can hold it."

"You don't have to hold it," Aurum said, running to his side and grabbing his arm. Never taking his eyes from the earthen wall, he let her lead him a few steps backward toward the edge of the overhang. He risked a glance at her, then at the drop several feet behind them. She gave him a wild grin, and he nodded. He knew what that look meant.

Ren took Aurum's hand and turned, sprinting for the overhang. The earthen wall dropped as he flicked his hand outward, focusing all his energy on creating a flat board of rock. Together, they leaped onto the board, and it tipped over the edge, sending them surfing down the steep dirt. Bolts of electricity flew over their heads, and they screamed while the wind raced past them. Ren's knees wobbled as his energy drained. He clutched Aurum tightly, his only anchor to the spinning world around him. The ground flattened out into the forest, and she wrapped her arms around him before jumping. They landed in the soft grass and could only watch as the board collided against a tree.

Ren's eyes returned to their normal blue, and he bent over with his hands on his knees, gasping for air. Suddenly, two figures flashed behind a cluster of trees to their left. Ren froze, and Aurum's eyes began to glow as flames erupted in her palms and slowly curled into whips. Two soldiers stepped out from the trees and sent bolts of electricity flying at Aurum and Ren, who each dove to one side. Aurum rolled before throwing and coiling her whips of fire around the soldiers' necks. He marveled at the additional power and control she had because of her silver pupils. She didn't look like she was even trying, but...he had to admit it was terrifying to see her like this—to see her kill.

She snapped the whips, slinging their bodies off into the forest without a second glance. Ren studied her with a dumbfounded look. It was as if he couldn't recognize her until her normal dark-brown eyes reappeared. He knew she was doing what she had to for them to survive. It's what he was doing, too. But the fear was still there, and it hurt his heart that they were having to change to protect themselves. If he could, he'd give what little power he had away; however, that power was vital if he wanted to save Lavelle and Damien. And if he had to destroy himself to save them—to save her—he would.

"Ren?" Aurum was at his side immediately, helping him up. "Are you all right?"

He nodded. "Are you?"

"Yeah," she mumbled, glancing in the direction she'd chucked the soldiers' bodies. He didn't miss the shadows that flickered in her eyes.

"Aurum—"

"I'm fine, I promise." She gave him a forced smile, and he frowned. "Hey, don't give me that look..." She met his gaze with a sigh. "I just—I just wish we didn't have to become monsters to survive."

"You're not a monster," he said. "We're doing what we have to do... The sacrifice is worth it."

He wasn't only trying to convince Aurum of his words. He was trying to convince himself, too.

She cleared her throat. "We should go take those soldiers' armor...and change into the armor we already have."

Ren nodded as Aurum led them back into the forest. Ren's frown deepened, and her words echoed through his head. *I just wish we didn't have to become monsters to survive...*

"*Monsters...,*" he repeated to himself.

~

After the soldiers passed, Roman and Natalia slowly stepped out of the tiny closet inside the abandoned shack. She walked over to the busted windows, carefully peeking out while Roman dug around inside the closet.

"Would these look suspicious?" he asked, holding up two long, gray, hooded coats.

"Not at all," she answered, taking one from him and slipping it on. Natalia stepped outside the house and threw the hood over her head. Roman followed behind her. The world suddenly fell darker, and they both lifted their heads to the sky. Dark clouds began to block the sun, piling in from the horizon. A storm was brewing.

"We need to find construction workers, or anything that could lead us to the new station. Any idea where to look?" Roman questioned, the cluster of buildings that made up Four growing closer as they sauntered up one of the many dirt roads woven within the waving tall grass, hills, and trees.

"The Hive's our best bet," she replied.

A few minutes later, they passed the wooden shacks and huts that made the outskirts of Four and entered one of the nearly empty main streets that led to the square. Natalia peered down an alleyway with furrowed brows. It was empty. Where was everyone? It wasn't even midday, yet the usual vendors weren't out. The bakery was closed for the day, too, and the only people wandering the streets were those without any home or shack to go to.

"Why does Four call their circle the Hive?" Roman whispered as they turned at an intersection.

"We've never been heavily controlled here compared to the other sectors." Natalia glanced at two burly men who passed with scowls embedded on their worn faces. "Our disgust for Vayne is more public here. We don't usually have to watch our backs about what we say because the soldiers know they've been sent to the slums of the four sectors, so if they hear anything, they don't really care. It's a quick reprimand, then they go waste their time somewhere else until they can be promoted.

But we call it the Hive because we think of Vayne's soldiers and guards as his bees. They're his workers, and the only place they feel safe here is their nest, the Hive."

"I see," Roman murmured.

"We can take the backroads. I know there's not a lot of people out right now, but I'd rather not be seen by *anyone*. They'll get us there faster, too." Natalia ducked into a small alley between two houses, and they began to weave their way between wooden shacks and buildings, keeping their distance from the few soldiers that patrolled the main street.

They rounded three corners until they came upon a circular, light-gray wall around fifteen feet high. The roofs of nice, wooden and brick houses shot into the sky, along with tall chimneys. Natalia peeked over a stack of crates and watched as soldiers at the front gates swiftly escorted men and women carrying tools and supplies around the left side of the Hive in the direction of the far corner of Sector Four. She grabbed Roman's elbow, leading him from the comforts of the alleyways to the clusters of trees to the right of the Hive that began one of the several forests inside the walls of Four.

They ducked inside the foliage, following a barely visible, worn path around the circular wall. Natalia frowned at the line of workers and soldiers stretched out from behind the Hive into the denser parts of the forest. How had she never seen this before? They stalked the line of Araedians for a quarter of an hour before they paused behind a large cluster of bushes and trees. Natalia frowned when soldiers began to force the workers and supplies into five black, armored trucks. Nothing like this had ever happened in Four. Ever. Vale hadn't mentioned anything like this before, either. In the other sectors, forced labor was more common, but Vayne never bothered with Four, so why would he now? Unless...

Natalia sucked in a breath. The new station had to be close. Why else would he come all the way out here? Everyone would expect him to stay close to One, especially because of the rebels, but he was doing the opposite.

She smirked. *He's getting desperate for more Elementals. He needs more for his army to make up for what we—I mean, the rebels—stole...*

"We'll never get on one of those trucks," Roman said softly.

Natalia raised her brows and looked at him. Since when did he give up so easily? "What now, then?"

"I don't know." He shook his head.

Suddenly, his eyes widened, and he froze, jaw locked in place. Natalia followed his gaze to the path at the edge of the tree line that led back to the Hive.

Two soldiers were heading into the forest. Straight toward them. Chills ran down her spine when Roman slipped his hand behind her and unzipped her backpack. He drew out a canteen—a source of water so they could fight—and slowly unscrewed the lid. Natalia sucked in a breath, her hands beginning to twitch with adrenaline.

"Do you think we'll be able to find them?" a familiar masculine voice asked.

Natalia paused. The voice had come from the soldier, but... It couldn't be...

"I know we can find Lavelle," the second soldier, another familiar feminine voice, answered.

"Aurum? Ren?" Natalia stood from her hiding spot in the bushes.

Roman stood up with her, grabbing her elbow cautiously. "What?"

The two soldiers froze, scanning the tree line before the feminine voice called, "Natalia?"

Natalia walked out from behind the cover of the bushes and trees, and Roman followed immediately. The two soldiers took off their helmets and revealed two of her favorite smiling faces. She sighed in relief as she grabbed Ren and Aurum and led them a few yards deeper into the forest before embracing them.

She blinked away her shock. "How did you...?"

"We stole some more armor." Aurum winked.

"After our distraction, we came back to the walls and were escorted here by the soldiers who were supposed to capture us. We said we had run into us, but we had escaped," Ren explained, gesturing to the singed plates of armor near his neck and shoulders. "We were planning on heading to Two on one of the transport trucks we heard about on the way over."

Roman ruffled Ren's hair with a broad smile. "We'll make fine rebels of you yet."

Natalia laughed, and joy filled her heart. She couldn't find the words to express how glad she was that they were here and safe.

"Actually," Roman began, realization shining in his eyes, "do you have any more armor?"

Aurum nodded. "Bits and pieces."

"Can I have it?"

"Here, take mine," Ren began peeling off pieces of his own armor. "We only managed to salvage two full sets between the soldiers that found us this morning and now. Natalia can pose as a worker, and you can be the guard escorting her. Aurum and I can do the same at the transport in the Hive."

"Brilliant," Roman said, already strapping the black armor on.

Natalia glanced between the three of them. Ren and Aurum were unharmed, which was more than she could've ever asked for, but...would this plan work? Could Ren really get onto the transport without armor? What if people started asking questions, and they got caught in a lie? They'd be stranded. Alone.

She twisted the ring around her finger nervously, and Aurum met her gaze, chasing the panic away. Natalia took a steadying breath. She knew she wasn't going to change their minds, so there was no point in arguing. All she could do was pray to the Aether that they'd be all right. She walked over to Roman, helping him secure a shoulder pad.

Don't think about what could go wrong, she told herself. *Focus on your part, and everything will work out.*

She nearly laughed at herself. That was exactly what Damien would have said to her if he were here. Maybe in a few hours, he would be... She winced when a throb of pain shot through her chest. Or maybe he wouldn't, and neither would Ren and Aurum. Natalia frowned at herself. She had to stop thinking like that. If she didn't, her fear would eat her alive. So, she promised herself she would stop... But then again, promises are the sweetest lies... Aren't they?

"Once you find Lavelle and Damien, get over the walls however you can," Roman instructed, taking Ren's helmet. "And remember, meet at the hill tomorrow. If one group isn't back by the following day, then return to camp."

Aurum nodded. "We will."

"We'll see you soon." Ren looked at Natalia.

"I know." She smiled. She knew he could see right through the mask she was trying to hide behind. Hell, all of them probably could. She felt like an open book, especially with Roman. Together, she and Roman watched Aurum and Ren disappear into the forest once more. She faced him. The armor Ren had given him fit like a glove, and she was surprised to find a small pit forming in her stomach. It was frightening that there was something oddly familiar about the look of him in Vayne's armor. He was posing as the very thing he wanted to destroy.

"Are you ready?" he asked.

"I'm ready if you're ready."

He smiled. "I'm going to need you to put your hands behind your back."

"What?"

Roman grabbed her arms, gently pinning them behind her as they stepped out beyond the cover of the trees toward the armored trucks and soldiers. He leaned down and whispered into her ear, "I'll be next to you the whole time. They won't separate us."

Natalia felt her cheeks heat, and her heart seemed like it would beat out of her chest. The vulnerability returned to her, only this time, it felt as if it had increased tenfold. She cursed herself. She needed to pull it together. Roman gave her hand an assuring squeeze when they neared the trucks.

What was she getting herself into?

CHAPTER THIRTEEN

THE TRAIN STATION

Aurum and Ren stood in the tree line, watching soldiers enter and exit through the Hive's thick metal gates. Ren popped his knuckles nervously before sparing a glance at Aurum. She appeared calm and composed. He wondered if anything ever made her nervous. With Lavelle, he'd never had a problem with being brave because he had to be brave for her, but now that she wasn't here, it was so hard to *not* be afraid. There were so many things that could go wrong, yet they still left the safety of the tree line and made for the Hive's gates. Aurum locked her hands around Ren's wrist, restraining them behind his back.

"Don't be nervous," she whispered to him.

He stifled a nod as they passed two soldiers heading down the main road toward the market of Four. One of the soldiers huffed in annoyance. "I don't know why Vayne's calling for more engineers from here. There aren't any left."

"I know," the second soldier agreed. "Why would he need them in One and Two? The few that were here were sent off to the new station."

"Shut up!" the first soldier exclaimed, smacking the back of the soldier's helmet. "You could be tortured for mumbling that."

"Sorry! I'm sorry!"

Ren glanced back at Aurum, and she mentioned him forward. "Keep moving."

Together, they passed through the metal gates into the Hive. The buildings were tall and made of wood and brick—a luxury in Sector Four. The streets were surprisingly busy, and soldiers, officials, and their families hurried about. The majority of the soldiers marched down the main road back in the direction of the Hive. Aurum and Ren followed after them. Side roads branched out in all directions, and the alleys were decorated with tall lampposts from which flowers hung—a privilege that only the families of the officers, soldiers, and governor that inhabited the Hive were permitted to see. The Hive was a colorful maze of streets, an intricately woven city within the walls of Four.

Aurum steered Ren through the crowd to a cluster of tables filled with papers; soldiers had gathered and formed lines in front of these tables, along with a few chained prisoners who sat in the center of the Hive's square. At the tables sat women dressed in different shades of gray, stamping and signing papers. The lines moved quickly, and soon, they were facing a stout woman somewhere around her late forties.

"Where's your destination?" she asked.

Ren pulled against Aurum's hands, and she tightened them around his wrists. He dropped his head, smiling to himself. Lavelle would be having a blast, laughing at his dramatics. He squeezed his knuckles until they turned white. He'd give anything to hear her laugh right now.

"Sector One," Aurum answered. "He's an engineer for Vayne."

Ren's eyes widened. They couldn't go to One. Lavelle would be in Two, and going to One would only get them caught, though there was a possibility that Damien would be there. But did Aurum really plan to search for him when they didn't even know if he was still alive? Lavelle *was* alive, and they knew where to find her.

"Engineers get first priority. Make sure he gets there in one piece." The woman nodded, scribbling on her paper before stamping it with Sector Four's dark-gray seal—a large number four surrounded by a sun to its right, a crescent moon to its left, a tree stemming from the top, and a rose on the bottom. "Your truck leaves in the next ten minutes, so hurry to the waiting area." She pointed at a large concrete building near the back gate of the Hive similar in shape to the station the rebels had saved them from.

Aurum nodded. "Thank you."

This time, Ren's struggling wasn't for dramatics. He pulled against Aurum as she dragged him toward the waiting area.

"What are you doing?" she hissed under her breath.

"What am *I* doing? What are *you* doing, Aurum? We can't go to One. Lavelle's in Two, and we'll get caught if we—"

"We're not actually going to One, brick-head."

"Thank the Aether." Ren sighed in relief. He couldn't help the smile that played on his lips. They were going to save his sister. "But why didn't you just say we were going to Two, and what are we going to do about Damien?"

"I don't want them to be expecting us. If we say we're going to One and get off at Two, by the time they try to look for their missing engineer, we'll be long gone. Regarding Damien..." Her voice dropped to a barely audible whisper when they passed a group of soldiers. "...we have absolutely nothing to go off of with him. My plan is to get Lavelle and then look for information on Damien. We need to find out if he's still alive. If he is, we can try to find him, or we can meet Natalia and Roman back at the overhang and decide what to do from there."

He nodded, and Aurum nudged him forward. The crowd of soldiers surrounding the waiting area parted for them as they entered the building and walked up to another set of lines and tables. Each table was labeled with a sector's number, and they headed toward the one for Sector One. A man in a black uniform sitting there didn't even spare them a glance as he asked, "What are your purposes for transfer?"

"I'm escorting this engineer to—"

"Last truck on the left."

Aurum frowned. "Thanks."

Ren glanced back at the man at the table. He seemed so bored. If only he knew how big of a mistake he'd just made. He'd probably be killed for letting them through security, if that's what one could call it. It had been so easy to sneak in. Aurum led them down the rows of humming trucks with large white numbers painted on the sides. She paused, standing between the last two trucks at the end of the building. A large metal door sat a few yards away from them, leading outside into Four. A white *One* was painted on the truck closest to it, followed by a truck with a *Two*.

Ren's eyes traveled between Aurum and the trucks. Their engines suddenly roared to life, preparing to begin their journey. A whistle blew out over a speaker, signaling their nearing departure. Ren turned to Aurum, and she nodded. They ran toward the truck with the white *Two*, throwing themselves in and slamming the doors shut. The powerful machine took off, jostling them while they scrambled into the empty seats. The next thing Ren knew, they were all alone in the truck, riding to Sector Two.

He sighed. After everything he'd been through, he was finally going to see Lavelle. The relief and adrenaline that flowed through his veins made his body feel heavy as he leaned his head back against the cool metal. He refused to think about the last time he'd been in one of these trucks—memories of that day had scarred and haunted him. And his friends. But with Lavelle back by his side, he'd finally be able to sleep at night, use his element without fear of hurting others because she would be there to get him through it. He could learn control over the powers he had never wanted, and maybe she could even teach him to love them at some point. With Lavelle, he'd finally be able to find some peace in the world he was drowning in...

~

Over an hour later, the truck finally rolled to a stop, and Ren's heart began to speed. What would they tell the driver or other soldiers if they asked questions? Aurum hopped to her feet, helping him up. She nodded to him reassuringly. He had to trust her. She'd always been good at thinking on her feet. With one hand, she grabbed Ren's arms, which he had put behind his back again, and opened the truck doors with the other. They were met with the beginnings of a brilliant sunset of oranges, yellows, and pinks shining in through the open doors of the transport station. It was identical to the transport station in the Hive, except now they were in the Circle of Sector Two, and soldiers bustled about *everywhere*.

"I've never seen this many soldiers in my life," Aurum whispered to Ren.

He bit the inside of his cheek. "How are we supposed to get out of here?"

"I don't know..." Aurum glanced around with a frown.

Suddenly, two soldiers walked over to them, and fear filled Ren like a disease. Why had Vayne increased security so drastically? Was he afraid of the rebels? Or his people? There had never been many civilian riots or uprisings in the sectors. Rebellious Araedians were usually dealt with by soldiers, but could something have changed? Could the people have heard about what happened at the last testings?

"You there! What are you doing?" a voice exclaimed.

Ren glanced up. The two soldiers stood inches from Aurum, hostility rolling off them in waves. One of the soldiers pointed at him. "We haven't received orders for another engineer."

Aurum rolled her eyes. "He had to take a piss. What was I supposed to do? Let him go in the truck?"

The soldiers scowled and exchanged glances beneath their visors before one of them pointed toward the door the trucks exited and entered through. "Bathroom's over there to the left. Be quick about it."

"Thanks," Aurum said, no hint of gratitude in her voice. She shoved Ren in the direction the soldier had pointed. Ren could feel the soldiers' eyes fixed on their backs as they walked down a few yards and turned. Two small metal doors sat side-by-side in the corner of the building. Ren glanced at Aurum over his shoulder.

"Check and see if there's a window in that one," she said, nodding at the door to the right. "I'll check this one."

"Okay." Ren slowly opened the door to find a single stall and sink in the small gray room before him. A bright light above cast a blue hue, making it appear unnaturally clean. He frowned. There were no windows. It was a simple, bland bathroom, and Aurum was likely to find the same result behind her door.

Think like Lavelle..., he told himself. She was always so creative and inventive, always coming up with new ideas and schemes. He had to see the bathroom as she would. Ren turned in a slow circle, observing everything carefully. His eyes fell on the large, square drain in the middle of the tile floor. Without warning, the door to the bathroom flung open, and Aurum silently slipped inside before locking it behind her.

"Hopefully you had better luck than I did," she said, observing the room. She sighed at the answer that greeted her. "Great, no windows... I'm starting to run out of ideas."

Ren smirked. "I'm not."

"What did you find?"

He tapped his foot against the drain. "I don't think we would've had much luck walking down the streets once we climbed out of a window anyway... No one goes down in the sewers, though."

She blinked several times, scrunching her nose. "*Absolutely not.*"

"Come on, Aurum, do you have any better ideas?"

"Fine," Aurum grumbled, kneeling to the cold tile floor. "Let's get this drain up."

The unnaturally clean feel of the room quickly dissipated when Ren knelt and stuck his fingers between the bars. Aurum gagged beside him as she did the same. Mud stuck to them like glue.

"Wait a second...," Ren mumbled. He sat back on his heels for a few silent moments. Aurum raised her brows at him in confusion.

Mud! The word echoed through his mind like a tolling bell. *If I can use my element, we can get this up easily.*

"What is it, Ren?"

"Get back," he said, closing his eyes. He felt Aurum step away as he reached out for the earth with his entire being, mustering the power that remain deep inside him. His fingers and eyes began to sting, and an eerie sense of unfamiliarity filled Ren. His powers felt weird and distant, but the thought of seeing Lavelle again immediately buried the feelings, replacing them with strength and his love for his sister. The cold, damp earth underneath the tile hit him like a tsunami, burying him in raw strength, power, and energy. He opened his glowing, forest-green irises, now surrounded by the deepest black pupils. He balled his fists and watched the tiles around the drain crumble inward with his movements. Tiles, rocks, and the drain crashed into the water below. Aurum and Ren—eyes now their normal vibrant blue—leaned over, peering into the gaping hole.

Aurum smiled. "You did it."

"I did it…"

"But we're not in the clear just yet." Aurum extended her hand. Ren took it, and they stood. Then, they jumped, landing with a *splash* in the cold water ten feet below. He snickered when Aurum gaged again at the horrid smell. She turned to him, pinching her nose with one hand and pointing up with the other. "Do you think you can plug that hole up?"

He nodded when a shout suddenly rang through the air, and the door to the bathroom rattled. Fear filled him. Those soldiers were trying to get in. They had taken too long. His eyes began to glow again as he lifted the rocks, tile, and drain back to their original places. The fix wasn't perfect, but he doubted the soldiers would notice. Finished and drained of nearly all his energy, he turned to face Aurum, and together, they began their trek through the musty sewers of Sector Two in search of Lavelle.

~

Natalia and Roman stood amongst the other soldiers and construction workers gathered around the five armored trucks. Roman had stuck to what he'd promised. He hadn't left Natalia's side. She almost wished he would. Whenever he was around, she felt he could see right through her, and she needed to have her guard up now more than ever. They couldn't afford to be caught. There couldn't be any mistakes.

"Everyone in!" a tall, muscular man clad in black armor with a white band around his right bicep—a superior officer—boomed through his helmet. The workers flinched at the sound of his voice, quickly piling into the trucks with supplies and tools in their hands. "I want one soldier in the back of each truck!"

Roman walked Natalia to the nearest truck, helping her and then the others up into it. Natalia extended her hand to an elderly woman and helped pull her inside. Natalia scowled, watching the other workers shoved into trucks, and hatred filled her. Vayne was hurting and corrupting so many people and families. She gritted her teeth. She had wanted to go look for Damien so badly, she had forgotten how many others needed the rebels' help, too. She grabbed a young boy's hand, pulling him into the truck as well.

"Sit down!" the tall man yelled and walked over to their truck. "They don't need your help! Get in a seat, now!"

Her scowl deepened, and she hopped down from the truck, allowing the anger flooding through her to take over. She could feel a distant stinging in her eyes. Her element was *begging* to be used, but she couldn't... At least not yet. She recalled every training session with Roman where he'd lectured her about control. She had to stay calm. Natalia looked at the man's visor covering his eyes. *"No."*

"What did you just say to me?" His helmet was a mere inch from hers now, and she could see the scratches and small dents embedded in the black metal.

Roman suddenly stepped between them, pulling Natalia back into the truck. "Don't waste your time with this one, sir."

"Ride on the outside of the truck, soldier. Don't degrade yourself by riding inside with them," the man said to Roman before scoffing and spitting at Natalia's feet. She pushed against Roman, but he held her firmly to him. The stinging had grown, and she could feel her being searching for a source of water. She quickly looked down at the ground, squeezing her eyes shut. She could feel them glowing beneath her lids.

Control, Natalia thought. *Control yourself.*

"Yes, sir." Roman turned Natalia around before whispering, "Get in the truck, Natalia."

She quickly scrambled back in with her head down and strapped herself in to the first available seat. Roman leaned against the frame of the door. "I know you want to help these people. Believe me, I do, too, but we have to lay low. I can't have you getting arrested for fighting a soldier, though I'll admit, it would be rather entertaining to watch."

"Oh, ha-ha. You're so funny," she deadpanned. She was unable to stop a smirk from lifting her lips, though when Roman took his helmet off and smiled, his brown eyes glinting with amusement. Her smirk turned to a cheesy grin, and she shook her head at him. *So unpredictable...*

He then hopped down from the truck and closed the doors, shutting out the rays of setting sunlight. The truck's engine revved before starting deeper into the forest of Four. Natalia squinted and watched through the doors' blacked-out windows as Roman clung to a bar on the side. The trucks were on a wide path that she didn't even know existed. It was taking them toward the northeast corner of the walls, which meant the new station must be northeast of the sectors.

The truck hit a large bump, jostling everyone inside viciously. She whipped her head back to Roman outside, but he was fine. He was still there, simply observing the forest as they flew by. Earlier, she had wished he would leave her alone for a moment, but now that they were separated—though it was by a mere metal door—all she wanted was him next to her.

She'd slowly begun to enjoy how unpredictable he was, and the more she thought about it, the more she realized she could always expect him to do what she least expected. He was predictable in his unpredictability, but she knew she could count on him to make the right and loyal decisions—compassionate decisions that were such a contrast to the society of the sectors. He wasn't as unreadable as she thought he was, and maybe the vulnerability she felt wasn't so bad now that she could *somewhat* read him. But if she could read him, he could definitely read her. Which meant they both had one thing over each other: *power...*

~

A half-hour passed before they reached the northeast corner of the wall. The trucks idled in front of the cold concrete for a few moments before an arched pathway suddenly sunk into the grass below, opening a tunnel through the walls for the trucks that now hummed through. Natalia turned to Roman, who stared wide-eyed as the arch of concrete shot back into place, perfectly concealing their path. She knew that Vayne had incredible technological power, but the hidden door within the wall was astonishing. What else did he have that they didn't know about? They rumbled on for a few more minutes, and she watched Roman turn and lightly knock on the window.

"North," he mouthed. The truck bounced over rocks, roots, and fallen branches, slamming Natalia against the back of her seat. For a couple of miles, they rode on through the dense forest and hills, which grew less steep as they continued on. The trucks soon broke out into a clearing where a metal building, identical to the first train station, sat nearly finished. They screeched to a stop, and she could see the muscular man hop out of a truck and into the mud through the small windows on the doors. The mud flew from his boots while he marched around to the back of the trucks.

"Open the doors!" he boomed.

Roman quickly hopped down, throwing the doors open. Natalia turned toward her fellow passengers and helped them gather their tools and supplies before helping them out. Roman extended his hand to her after the last passenger had walked away. She accepted it and jumped down into the slick mud. Her foot hit the ground, and she slipped, throwing her arms out and clutching Roman's arm. Her feet danced as if she were running on ice. He laughed and steadied her with a hand on the small of her back.

Natalia rolled her eyes while Roman continued to snicker, then, together, they followed the line of construction workers toward the building. An additional company of soldiers trailed behind them, guns at the ready in their arms. They entered the building to watch the tall commander spit at the feet of a worker.

"You *will* do as I say, or I'll see to it that you suffer a slow and agonizing death. Now, get to work!" he snarled. "I'm not afraid to whip you right here and now."

Roman reached out, gently grabbing Natalia's arm and leading her to the closest group of workers and soldiers. She studied the different groups piled together throughout the building. Some were off working on the pipe system while others carried and laid bricks and fiddled with colorful electrical wiring. She knelt next to the young boy—by the Aether, he couldn't have been a day over thirteen—who handed her a brick with a small smile. His shining hazel eyes reminded her of Damien, and she paused. It was like looking at a ghost...

She blinked away the memories threatening to swallow her whole and returned a smile of her own, waiting for him to apply the mortar before setting the brick down on top of it. Natalia glanced back at Roman as the boy spread more mortar. He stood a few feet away, his eyes never leaving her. He subtly dipped his head in acknowledgment to let her know that he was there and that he wasn't leaving. Warmth spread through her chest. It was nice to have someone who truly had her back—who would refuse to leave her no matter what circumstances they might face. But they had done it, she realized. They'd found the location of the new station, and now all they had to do was play their parts, survive the day, and get the information back to the rebels. Then they could hopefully stop the next testings. Natalia turned back to the boy.

"What's your name?"

~

Ren led the way through the sewers, following the recognizable names of streets above carved into every intersection of the tunnels. Dark, foul-smelling water sloshed at their feet as they trudged under a web of dripping pipes. Aurum, eyes glowing, kept a constant flame in her hands, lighting their way. Ren glanced up, pausing at another intersection. Four dark tunnels branched outward, all leading into a smothering darkness. She lifted her hand above her head, illuminating the names carved into the hardened earth.

Ren grinned and took off. "We're a block away from my house. Come on!"

"Wait!" Aurum called, sprinting after him. The flame in her hands snuffed out, plunging them into pure darkness. She quickly created another and cupped her hands around it. Ren was yards ahead of her, nearing another intersection of three roads. He hesitated for a moment before cutting down the dimly lit left tunnel. He paused next to a metal ladder halfway down, waiting for Aurum to round the corner. His heart felt as if it would beat out of his chest, and adrenaline flushed through his veins. The last rays of sunlight peeking in from the drain above warmed his skin, and he closed his eyes, allowing the warmth to wash and spread over him. He turned and watched Aurum finally round the turn and extinguish her flame.

"Should I take the armor off?" she asked.

"No, keep it on." Ren grabbed the cold metal bars, pulling himself up to the metal drain. He peeked between the bars to find wooden crates stacked on top of each other, and he heard the busy main street off to the right. They were under an alleyway near his house. Ren closed his eyes again, focusing on the earth around the drain. His eyes began to glow as he pushed a hand up, while clinging to the ladder with the other. The drain and the earth surrounding it slowly lifted, sending small rocks and chunks of dirt splashing into the water below. Ren strained, using what little reserves he had to push the earth and metal onto the dirt path. A smile lit his face, and he climbed up to the street. He reached a hand down, helping Aurum out of the hole in the ground he'd created. Quickly, they slid the chunk of rock and metal back into place before ducking deeper into the alleyway behind several beige houses.

Ren led the way through the maze of beige, taking them toward the outskirts of the bulk of the city. Here, the houses began to space out, allowing the tall grass to wave in the breeze that wove between the houses like a phantom. The closer they got, the faster he increased his pace. Finally, he rounded a corner and suddenly stopped behind a medium-sized house. He couldn't stop the tears from filling his eyes as he gazed upon his home. A small stream of smoke rose from the chimney. His chest began to rise and fall heavily, and Aurum laid a hand on his shoulder. He turned to her to find a bright smile and shining brown eyes. Ren returned the smile before facing the house and walking to one of the windows in the back wall.

He hopped up onto a wooden garbage crate, holding his breath and peeking inside. His heart hammered in his chest, and he released a shaky breath, overcome with joy as he quietly tapped on the window. He watched Lavelle turn, wide-eyed and mouth agape. She dropped the book she was holding before running to the window, throwing it open and pulling him inside. Ren squeezed her tightly, digging his head into her shoulder as sobs racked her small form. All the pain and loneliness he'd felt after their separation diminished to rubble. It was nothing but dust on the wind now, and he could feel himself being put back together. His heart was full again. His other half was here with him, and, in that moment, they were perfectly safe.

"I thought you were dead," Lavelle whispered, shaking.

Ren chuckled and warmth and happiness spread across his chest. "You can't get rid of me that easily, Lavelle."

She somehow managed to laugh through the sobs escaping her. Then without warning, she stiffened in his grasp and gasped, spinning Ren around to face the window. Her terror was plain in her vibrant blue eyes—their eyes. "Ren!"

Ren's eyes began to glow as he turned to watch Aurum tumble through the window. Lavelle grabbed his hand, throwing the door to their room open and dragging him down the bland, beige hall.

"Wait, Lavelle!" Ren slammed his heels into the wooden floor.

"What are you doing? We have to get out of here!"

"But, Lavelle—"

Aurum removed her helmet and stepped into the doorway. "So after all this time, *that's* how you greet your best friend?"

"Aurum?" Lavelle exclaimed, and tears began to pour down her cheeks once more. She glanced between Aurum and Ren several times. "No, I'm dreaming again. This isn't real."

"Nope." Aurum walked over and pinched her arm. "You're not dreaming." Lavelle threw her arms around her neck, squeezing her tightly. Aurum grinned, squeezing back. "I missed you, too."

"How is this even possible? I—I thought you two and Natalia were dead," Lavelle said as she stepped back.

Ren's eyebrows rose in curiosity. "Wait, aren't you forgetting someone?"

"Yeah..." Aurum nodded.

"No?" Lavelle glanced between them. "What are you talking about?"

"Damien?" Aurum frowned. "Does the name ring a bell?"

Lavelle's face hardened, and pain flickered over her eyes. "I saw Damien. He was with *them*."

Ren and Aurum shared a look at each other, dread and fear passing over their faces. What did his twin mean by that? "Who was he with?" he asked.

"The soldiers."

Aurum shook her head. "That's impossible. How could you have seen him? Vayne took him. He should be dead or imprisoned."

"They were on the walls..." Lavelle's eyes dropped to the floor. "Ren, tell me what happened that night... What happened after they took you?"

~

The day passed by quickly for Natalia. She and the young boy, Idris, laid dozens and dozens of bricks until they ran out, and when they did, they ventured outside into the boiling sun with Roman close behind them to carry in more. Natalia smiled down at Idris while he talked about his family in Sector Four. His bright hazel eyes twinkled with love and amusement when he told a funny story about his younger sister. Damien's eyes used to do that whenever he was scheming...

A dull ache spread throughout her chest. She missed Damien more than she could've ever imagined. It was weird not being the one to search for him and find him, because that was how she'd dreamed it. They'd embrace each other with open arms, and their family would finally be reunited again. But not everything always worked out the way she wanted it to, and sometimes it was better that way. However, Idris reminded her of everything she had wanted but could never have—siblings and a mother and father—but at least she'd gotten to grow up with Vale and Damien and her friends. They were her family, and she wouldn't trade them for the entire world. It didn't matter that they weren't exactly what she had imagined. In fact, they were *better*.

The three walked back into the station to watch a soldier throw a man who was working on electrical wires to the floor. Natalia, Roman, and Idris froze, and the building fell silent as all eyes turned to the soldier kicking the man repeatedly. What had happened? Natalia glanced at Roman worriedly. After one look at her face, he ran over to the soldier who now had the man by his throat with his fist reared back. Roman grabbed the soldier's fist from behind, turning him away.

"All right, I think he's had enough," Roman said.

The soldier shoved Roman back. "He's had enough when I say he's had enough."

"Don't make me stop you," Roman threatened, straightening. He towered nearly a whole head above the soldier. "He has to be able to work, so cut it out and just leave him alone."

The soldier turned toward where the tall commander was standing. His glare met the soldier's eyes. "This isn't over," he said, spitting at Roman's feet before walking away.

"Everyone back to work!" the commander's voice boomed.

~

An hour passed before the sun set. Sweat dripped down Natalia's nose as she bent over next to Idris. Their day was nearly done. A few feet behind them, Roman stood with another soldier, discussing several different things. She knew he was digging for any information he could get on Vayne and security in the sectors. Nothing of importance had come up so far.

"What happens to the workers when they're taken back to the sectors?" Roman asked.

"You don't know?" The soldier raised a brow. "You must be new."

Roman rubbed the back of his neck. "Uh, yeah."

"You should've had a superior officer explain it to you. Did yours not?"

"Nope." Roman shook his head.

"Well, once their day is done," the soldier said, motioning at Natalia and her fellow workers. "We take them back to headquarters to have their memories of what happened here wiped. Then we return them to their homes as if nothing ever happened, and their families simply believe that they were off on business for the testings."

"What kind of business?"

The soldier shrugged. "We usually say they're filling out paperwork, or that some file was misplaced, and we need to re-enter their information."

"I see..." Roman met Natalia's gaze.

Fraiser had told the truth. She'd been right... The horror struck Natalia like one of the armored trucks outside. Vayne really was brainwashing the workers, and if he was brainwashing the workers... Who else had fallen under his spell? Who was safe to talk to, and who was compromised? Fear shot through her at the thought of

Damien's imprisonment. What awful things had been done to him? She chewed the inside of her cheek. They had other problems, too. Everything had just gotten a lot more complicated. What were she and Roman supposed to do when they returned to Four? They couldn't go back to the Hive. It would be crawling with more soldiers, Natalia would have to have her memory wiped, and the soldiers would have to pull her information to know which house to return her to, which would alert them to the fact that she'd "gone missing" during her testings. They would be captured and brought to Vayne before midnight.

Suddenly, a loud whistle rang through the air, drawing everyone's eyes to the commander. He marched over into the middle of the room, and the white band around his right bicep shone in the lights above.

"Attention!" he yelled.

The soldiers straightened and replied in unison, "Yes, sir?"

"Round up your workers and take them to the trucks. We return to Four immediately."

Another collective answer. "Yessir!"

"Yes, sir…" Roman mumbled.

Natalia turned to Idris, a sadness filling her. He wouldn't remember her. He wouldn't remember laughing with her and telling her about his family… This was what Vayne did. He tampered with the minds of his people and made them his puppets, and she couldn't let it stand—*wouldn't* let it stand. They had to do something. If they didn't, they weren't any better than Vayne himself. Natalia gave Idris a small smile while Roman led them back toward the trucks. Twilight was upon them, casting a blue glow on everything. She sat her hand on Idris's back and steadied him as he climbed up into the truck. Roman took a step forward, offering her his hand. She took it, and he helped her inside, then a soldier suddenly appeared beside him.

"We need you in another truck."

Roman straightened defensively. "No, I'm supposed to be in this one."

"We need you—"

"I heard you, but the commander assigned me to this truck himself. If you want to question him, be my guest, but I'm staying here."

The soldier glanced between Roman and the truck twice before finally turning and walking away. Roman then climbed up in the truck next to Natalia, leaving the door slightly cracked open. She had to clench her fists to keep from grabbing his hand in thanks. Throughout all of this, he'd still kept his promise and showed no signs of breaking it. He was constant, and he was there.

She leaned over and whispered, "Roman, what are we going to do about the Hive? We can't go in there."

"I know..." He took off his helmet, revealing sweaty, damp hair and worried eyes. He turned to meet her gaze. "We could jump?"

Natalia's brow raised. "Out of the trucks?"

He nodded. "We can ride them back into Four, jump out before they stop at the Hive to unload, and book it to the crack in the wall."

"Or we could jump out *before* we get inside the walls."

"It would take too long to get back to the overhang, and I'm not as familiar with this part of the forest. We'd have to stay closer to the walls and risk being seen just to know where we were going. I'd rather take our chances in Four where you know where everything is," he said, hopping out of the truck. "I'll knock twice before I open the doors, then we'll jump."

Natalia nodded before turning to Idris and the other workers. They were laughing and whispering amongst themselves. She let out a shaky breath she hadn't realized she'd been holding. They had no clue what was going to happen to them. They didn't know their memories of today were about to be erased, and even though it made her feel like the worst human being in the world, she knew they couldn't take them. They'd never all survive the trek through the woods to the rebels' camp, and many probably wouldn't want to leave. They'd be too scared; however, she still made herself promise to save them one day.

We'll come back and free you. Vayne won't hurt you any more, and you'll finally be okay. You'll be alive, she promised and promised. *You're only losing one day...*

But a lot could happen in one day.

~

Ren watched Lavelle bite the inside of her cheek. "So everyone got out except for Damien...," she mumbled.

"Natalia and Roman did all they could. No one could have saved him..." Aurum frowned.

Ren ran a hand through his blond hair. "After that, the rebels took us back to their camp out in the woods. You should see it, Lavelle. It's amazing. There's all kinds of Araedians and Elementals from each sector. Everyone there is free from this hell..." He gestured around their beige bedroom. "We're free to do whatever we want out there."

"And we're free to fight back." Aurum smirked. She snapped her fingers, producing a dancing flame on her fingertips. Her eyes began to glow their red and silver as Lavelle gasped in awe.

"Aurum... It's stunning..." Lavelle grinned.

"All right, now tell us more about Damien," Ren requested. He couldn't fathom how it was possible that she'd seen him. Had it really been Damien, or had it been someone else?

Lavelle shook her head. "Wait, hold on. Does this mean we're *all* Elementals?"

"I mean it's possible." Ren shrugged. "No one really knows, though. It kind of just happens. Some people have elements, and some don't."

Aurum nodded. "But Vayne doesn't know what's coming for him, Lavelle. With the rebels and the elements, we can beat him... Which is why you have to come with us."

"What about Mom, Dad, and Claire?" Lavelle blinked several times. "They've already lost you, Ren. They can't lose me, too..."

Ren tried not to think about his little sister. She would be at school right now, and their father would be at work while their mother was out doing her daily chores. "Lavelle—"

"No," she held up a hand. "You've explained what happened to you. Now it's my turn. Besides, you want to know about Damien, don't you?"

"Sorry, go ahead." Ren sighed.

Lavelle gave him a small, melancholy smile. "A few days after you disappeared, soldiers came to Two. They started increasing security everywhere, especially at the walls. Claire and I were picking berries at the farms by the wall we used to sneak over when we saw a group of soldiers. It didn't look like much at first, but..."

"But what?" Aurum questioned eagerly.

"Damien was with them."

"Are you sure it was him? The Damien I know would *never* help Vayne. He'd rather die. Besides, Vayne would never let him out if he's still alive," Aurum said, pacing.

Ren glanced between Aurum and Lavelle, watching in silence. He tried to picture the last time he'd seen Damien. It had been the night the rebels had rescued them, but Damien had fought against Vayne's guard with every fiber of his being. Aurum was right, too. Vayne wouldn't let him out, so why would he help them?

"I heard him, and he knew exactly where to position the soldiers," Lavelle said. "He knew the weak spots because we told him about them! All those weaknesses we found in the wall so we could sneak over are gone. Who else would know about that? It was him, but he wasn't the same. His mannerisms were too straight, too perfect. He looked like a puppet on strings…"

Ren's thoughts turned dark. There was only one answer to their question, but it wasn't a pleasant one… Had Damien betrayed them, or had he been brainwashed?

Lavelle pinched the bridge of her nose, squeezing her eyes shut. "And he was with this girl… I can't remember her name, but she's one of Vayne's lapdogs. I think Hero said it was Zyra."

"Who's Hero?" Ren asked, raising a brow.

"Oh!" Lavelle's blue eyes widened. "I forgot to tell you. Another reason security is being increased is because of the rumors of growing rebel sympathizers… And it's true. Do you two remember Natalia telling us about that broadcast that was interrupted before the testings?"

Ren nodded, recalling the look on Natalia's face the next day. The usual testing announcements had been running in Sector Four when the broadcast was interrupted by someone. Natalia had thought that the voice was with the rebels, but Roman had never mentioned anything about it. Besides, Ren didn't think the rebels had enough technology to do anything like that. "Yeah, what about it?"

"There's been more, and Hero and his friends are behind them. Come on. I can show you." Lavelle rushed through their bedroom door and down the hallway, Ren and Aurum on her heels. "I don't know what sector he's from, but he's the one interrupting the broadcasts. He's the voice, and he supports the rebels, but he hasn't been able to make direct contact with them yet. He's trying, though, so—"

"He hasn't been able to contact the rebels because they don't have that kind of tech," Ren interrupted. "But, Lavelle, how did you…?"

"You'll just have to see." She led them into the beige living room, kneeling next to the projector that sat in front of their small beige couch. Ren and Aurum joined her, watching her movements carefully. She flicked on the projector and began to cycle through the channels. There were only five channels for each sector as Vayne wanted to control and influence his people as much as possible. Propaganda cartoons and different Sector Two news channels flickered by until Lavelle finally settled on the channel where the testing announcements were broadcasted. She then began fiddling with the knobs and buttons on the projector until a loud static began crackling through the tiny speakers. Without warning, the screen fell black, and a white line stretched across it.

Lavelle leaned closer to the projector speakers and whispered, "Hero?"

The white line jumped and curved in multiple spots at the sound of her voice, then ran flat again as silence enveloped the room.

"Hero? Are you there?" she repeated. There was no answer.

"What is this?" Aurum questioned.

"It's a hidden channel. Vayne doesn't even know it exists. Well, a lot of people don't, but it's how Hero and his friends communicate between the sectors. He's trying to convince people to fight back."

Static suddenly spat through the speakers, and she turned back to the projector, twisting one of the knobs a little more to the right.

"La—elle—Are—there?" a masculine voice broke through, the white line jumping and curving once more. "Lavelle? Are you there?"

She smiled. "Yes, I'm here."

"Is everything all right?"

"Hero, there's some people I think you need to meet." Lavelle waved Aurum and Ren closer. "This is my brother, Ren Dalnum, and my friend, Aurum Everrett. Aurum, Ren, this is Hero Ellisaire."

Aurum raised a brow. "Uh, hi."

"Hello," Ren added.

"Wait, Lavelle," Hero said, his voice crackling. "I thought you said they were part of the last testings?"

"They were, but you were right, Hero! The rebels *did* save them!" Her smile widened. "And Aurum and Ren both know their leader."

"By the Aether...," Hero whispered. The curved lines grew smaller with the volume of his voice. "Ren, Aurum, I wish we could be meeting in person, but this will have to do for now. Is there any way that I could meet your leader? I need to speak with him. It's important."

Ren turned to Aurum, who shook her head. Ren bit down on his lower lip. "Hero, this is Ren. I don't think it will be possible to sneak Roman into the sectors, and with security increasing each day, we won't be able to get you out either."

"But," Aurum added, "if you have a message for him, we can deliver it. We'll be heading back to the camp soon, and if Roman has a projector, we can try to fix it up so we can communicate with you."

"Okay, that could work," Hero murmured.

"What do you want us to tell him?" Ren asked.

"Tell him that rebel support is growing. We're beginning to unite, and we're ready to start fighting back. If he plans on interrupting the next testings, we'll be with him, and we'll be prepared to fight. Now, I have to go. Something's going on outside, and soldiers are everywhere. Be safe."

"You too, Hero," Lavelle replied, flicking off the projector.

"We need to get this information to Roman as soon as possible." Aurum turned to face the twins.

"I know, but what about Damien?" Ren knew what Aurum would say, but he had to be able to tell Natalia that they had tried to find him.

"He's been compromised. We can't go around storming the sectors looking for someone who's most likely been brainwashed."

Ren frowned. "We don't know that for certain, Aurum."

"You're starting to sound like Natalia..." She sighed. "Ren, we all know something's happened to him. He's not the same Damien any more."

"What if he's being forced?" Ren exclaimed. "What if Vayne's told him he's captured us too, and he thinks by complying he's saving us? We just don't know!"

Lavelle grabbed Ren's hand. "You're right, Ren, we don't know. But we can't go looking for him. It would be a suicide mission..."

"Fine." Ren gritted his teeth. "But I'm not leaving without you, Lavelle."

"Our parents—"

"Will be fine," Aurum interrupted. "I'm with your brother. We're not leaving without you."

Lavelle faced Ren, and he felt as if he'd been punched in the gut as she uttered, "What about Claire?"

"She has to stay here." He fought back the tears threatening to gather in his eyes. "It's too dangerous for her to come with us."

"Okay..." His twin dropped her eyes to the floor. "I need to get a few things first."

Lavelle ran back in the direction of their room and knelt next to her bed before sliding under it. Aurum shot Ren a confused look. He smiled as they waited. A few moments later, she slid back out from under the mattress, piles of small books and tiny bottles of herbs in her hands. Ren walked over to the tiny nightstand between their two beds, opening the tiny drawer and then grabbing Lavelle's brown, leather satchel. He held it open, and she dumped the books and bottles inside.

"Is this everything?" he asked.

She nodded. Suddenly, the sound of their front door opening pierced their ears. They all froze, holding their breaths as they listened.

"Lavelle?" the twins' mother called.

Ren turned to his sister. She frowned and tears filled her eyes. Aurum quietly crept toward the window, slowly and silently easing herself outside. Ren gave Lavelle what he hoped was an encouraging smile. He knew how hard it would be for her to abandon their family, but it was impossible to safely get everyone back to camp. They couldn't tell them where they were going or why because it, too, would put them in danger. They had to leave them behind. It was for their own good. He grabbed Lavelle's hand and helped her out the window. His mother's footsteps echoed down the hall as a heaviness suddenly fell over his chest. He paused near the sill.

"Ren, come on!" Aurum whispered roughly.

With one last glance at his home, he turned and hopped out the window, landing unnaturally more silently than Aurum and Lavelle. He reached up, quickly closing the window before his mother opened the twins' bedroom door. Aurum, Ren, and Lavelle shrank against the wall of the house. Aurum slipped her black helmet on before peeking up at the window. She nodded, pointing back at the alley they had followed earlier. The three bolted toward it, only pausing after they were a few houses away.

"How are we supposed to get out of here?" Lavelle asked. Aurum turned to Ren, flipping up the visor of her helmet to reveal two confused brown eyes.

Ren glanced at the darkening sky behind the walls. "I have an idea."

CHAPTER FOURTEEN

DECEPTION

Ren, Aurum, and Lavelle knelt behind a large pile of crates on the outskirts of the berry farm near the walls. Large cherries painted on the crates glowed red in the fading rays of sunlight. A few trees dotted the tall sea of grass, making the large barn between them and the wall appear like a looming cathedral. Workers clothed in beige were finishing their rounds between the rows and rows of berry bushes that surrounded the farm. Only a little longer; then the coast would be clear. Ren closed his eyes, inhaling deeply as he reached out to the earth with his mind. He felt nothing. He was still so excited and happy from finding Lavelle that he couldn't concentrate, and he hadn't fully recovered from using his powers earlier. Adrenaline flowed through his veins, and his mind was a jumbled mess of emotions.

Breathe, Ren, he told himself, taking another deep breath and forcing his head to clear. His irises then began to glow their dark, forest-green while he searched for the easiest path to take to the wall.

"All of the workers are heading back to the barn. We should be good to go in a few more minutes," he said, feeling the vibrations of the workers' footsteps flowing through the soil. He opened his eyes and glanced between Aurum and Lavelle. Lavelle stared at him, her widened eyes reflecting the glowing green, her face a mix of shock and awe. He watched the reflection fade as his shifted back to their normal blue—identical to hers. He hoped she was taking this well. She seemed to be doing fine, but Lavelle never wanted anyone worrying about her, so she wouldn't say anything even if she wasn't okay. But at least she wasn't scared of his and Aurum's powers. In fact, she seemed to love them.

Aurum turned toward the twins. "It's nearly dark enough. Let's get closer to the wall."

Ren nodded, slipping around the boxes. Lavelle followed after him, and Aurum took up the rear as he led them through the rows of bushes. He held up his hand, crouching low to the ground as a worker passed a few feet ahead of them. Aurum crawled up to Lavelle, picked a berry from the bush next to her, and lifted her helmet, popping the berry in her mouth. Lavelle rolled her eyes, stifling a giggle. Ren waved them forward, and the three ran a few more yards before crouching down next to another pile of crates that were even with the barn.

The workers were starting on the road back to the center of Two when Ren urged them forward again. They stood up, now fully running through the rows of berries. The rows quickly turned to the tall grass waving in the wind. Ren watched Lavelle glance up at the walls as they neared their base. She tugged at his and Aurum's arms and pointed. He immediately inched closer to her while his eyes followed her finger. He would not lose her again. Soldiers patrolling the tops of the walls were starting to move in their direction, and they had nowhere to hide amongst the sea of grass. If they didn't find cover quickly, they'd be seen.

Aurum cursed under her breath. "Ren, do it now."

Ren paused, focusing hard on his surroundings, and his eyes began to glow again. They were only a few yards from the base of the wall, and Aurum and Lavelle stood as close to him as possible, sharing a nervous glance. Suddenly, the earth below them opened up, swallowing them in darkness. Aurum's eyes glowed red and silver, and a flame burst to life in her palms. Ren stood from the damp earth and helped Lavelle, who stared at Aurum curiously, to her feet. He ruffled her hair, knocking dirt from it. He laughed when she swatted at his hand.

"What you two can do... It's so...incredible," she whispered, astonished.

Ren smiled. "I'm glad you're not scared of us."

"I could never be scared of you."

"Okay, let's keep moving, twins. This is making me feel claustrophobic." Aurum shivered.

"Don't worry." Ren put his hand on her shoulder. "We'll be out soon."

If he was strong enough to control his powers...

"I wish you had found out about these powers earlier, Ren. They would've made sneaking out so much easier," Lavelle said as Ren extended his hands at the wall of earth in front of them. It shrunk back a few feet, allowing them to walk a little farther. He repeated the motion several times before he paused, resting. A thick sheet of sweat already covered his face, and he was panting hard.

"I can feel the concrete above us," he said between gasping breaths, but he had to keep pushing. He couldn't let Vayne's soldiers find and take them, especially Lavelle. He'd die before he let that happen. However, his determination couldn't stop the sweat from dripping from the tip of his nose. The frequent use of his element over the past few hours was taking its toll on him. Dirt clung to his face amongst the sweat like glue. "We're almost there. Just a few more pushes," he said to not only Aurum but himself too. He could do it. He had to hang on just a little bit longer, then he would be able to rest. Ren took a deep breath, mustering up his strength and digging deep down within his power. He lunged forward, extending his hands, and the earth tunneled back farther than before.

One more... Come on, he grunted as he pushed one final time. "Okay, I'm about to open it back up. Be ready to run."

"Hurry, please," Aurum squeaked. She had squeezed her eyes shut the entire time.

Ren looked up and focused on the earth above him. He lifted his hands above his head and quickly swung them out to his shoulders. The ground opened as quickly as it had swallowed them, and the three shot out into the grass beyond the wall, sprinting toward the woods. Ren turned as they ran, slinging his arm out in a flat line. The hole he'd opened closed, leaving no trace of them, but it didn't stop a booming voice atop the wall from exclaiming, "Rebels!"

Fear shot throughout him, and without warning, a bolt of electricity landed near his feet, sending him flying. He grunted in pain when his body hit the ground with a hard *smack*. He groaned and clutched at the air that had been knocked from his lungs.

"Ren!" Lavelle's voice rang out from a distance.

"No, stay here, Lavelle. I'll get him." Aurum returned, her voice growing closer. A second later and she was at his side, lifting him up and pushing him in the direction of the tree line. The world spun as they ran. "Come on, Ren!"

Ren glanced back at the wall, eyes widening. He pointed behind her. "Aurum—"

Aurum screamed in pain when a bolt of electricity clipped her right shoulder, sending them both tumbling to the ground. The scent of burning flesh immediately filled the air. Ren stood on wobbly legs, grabbed her arm, and began pulling her toward the trees. Aurum stumbled to her feet only to fall back down after a few steps and clutch at her shoulder, silent tears streaming down her wincing face. Electricity sparked from the wound, causing her entire body to spasm. She struggled to bite back a scream. Lavelle sprinted toward them.

"No, Lavelle, go back!" Ren waved her away.

"I'm not going anywhere," she said, lifting Aurum to her feet and slinging her arm over her shoulder. Together, the twins ran into the forest, aiming for the overhang with an unconscious Aurum between them...

~

The world was cast in complete darkness by the time the armored trucks rumbled back into Four and Natalia sighed in relief. They had done it. They had figured out the location of the new station and survived the day, and she would soon be reunited with Lavelle and Damien. The thought of seeing them sent butterflies of excitement through her stomach, and she smiled. Everything had been worth it.

I can't wait to see you, she thought, picturing Lavelle's and Damien's smiling faces. She then turned to watch Roman gaze out the window. Moonlight painted everything with a beautiful pale glow, and the grass and trees swayed in the breeze. Even his skin seemed to be glowing. A slight panic seeped through Natalia when the back of the Hive's curved wall appeared in the break of the trees, and she jumped when Roman knocked twice on the window of the doors. She shakily unhooked her harnesses and stood.

"What are you doing?" the little boy, Idris, questioned, hazel eyes piercing her own.

Her heart ached as Roman opened one of the doors, and cool wind blew loose strands of hair around her face; suddenly, Idris's eyes looked all too familiar. For a moment, she didn't see him. Instead, she saw an older boy with dark hair and cautious hazel eyes. She saw Damien and the day she lost him in the testings. She imagined him screaming, "What are you doing, Talia? Please, don't leave me."

"Talia, come on!" Roman shouted over the wind, gently taking her hand.

She met his gaze, and in that moment, she swore he'd seen every part of her—the good and the bad—and not balked at a single thing she'd ever said or done. And the way he'd said her name... Not her full name, but *Talia*... She fought the urge to take one last look at Idris and the face that reminded her of Damien. She took a deep breath, refusing to break his stare. The trucks weren't going as fast as she had thought, probably because they were nearing the Hive. They had to jump. Now. She squeezed his hand tighter and slipped out onto the metal tailgate that the soldiers usually stood on.

"Ready?" Roman shouted, and she nodded. "On three! One!"

The wind ripped at her hair. "Two!"

"Three!"

And they jumped, colliding against the ground with a loud *thump* and rolling to an ungraceful stop. Natalia coughed, desperately trying to recover the air that had been knocked from her lungs. Roman did the same for a few moments before stumbling to his feet and helping her stand. Together, they sprinted at the cluster of buildings that made up Sector Four as fast as their feet would carry them. They'd only have a few minutes, maybe even less before soldiers came looking for them.

"Come on," Natalia urged when they reached the main dirt road that ran throughout most of Four. "We can take the back alleys."

Roman glanced back at the Hive, buzzing with searchlights and activity. "We need to hurry."

She clenched her fists. She could feel the darkness seeping out of the walls of the Hive. Everything involved with those damned concrete walls felt evil, and standing so close to your enemies' home was like standing next to a landmine that could explode at any second—like being rats in a pit of vipers. The thing was, the landmine had exploded and the vipers had sensed them.

"Follow me," she said, turning down the nearest alley. Two minutes of twists and turns passed until Natalia found the main set of alleys she was looking for. They had entered the maze a lot farther east than she'd hoped. Searchlights began filling the streets of Four and would soon find their way to the alleys, but Natalia had been running through them for a long time. No one could navigate them like her. For half an hour, they sprinted, turned, stopped, and waited, avoiding soldiers and flashlights at all costs.

They went to round a corner when Natalia suddenly grabbed Roman and yanked him back into the safety of the shadows. The beam of a flashlight passed over where he'd been seconds before. Together, they retreated behind dozens of boxes of flour sitting outside the bakery. They waited a few minutes before sprinting out from behind the boxes into the sea of grass toward the wall. Adrenaline and excitement pumped through Natalia's veins. Working with Roman was fun despite the possibility of their capture or death. They ran down the path past the abandoned shack and started down the sloping hill when Roman grabbed her arm.

"Wait!" he whispered.

"What is it?" Natalia questioned, both of them crouching down amongst the grass.

Roman pointed to the top of the wall. "Look."

She gasped. *Dozens* of soldiers manned the wall, pacing back and forth. "What happened? There are never this many guards." Her eyes widened, panic seeping through her veins as her heart began to beat faster and faster. What if something had happened to Ren and Aurum? Had they been caught? "Roman, what if Ren and Aurum...?"

He shook his head. "No, don't think like that. They're all right. They can take care of themselves. And think about it this way—if they'd been caught, soldiers wouldn't be out guarding the walls, so they must've gotten away."

"You're right." She inhaled deeply, slowing her breathing. "So, what do we do now? Do we try to sneak back through?"

"I don't know," Roman mumbled, running his hand through his hair. "Do you think the soldiers from the Hive will search for us in that abandoned house? We could stay in there."

Natalia faced the shack. It was far from the center of Four, and there was nothing of importance out this way, so why would the soldiers look for them this far away from the Hive? And as far as they knew, the crack was still plugged up. She nodded. "I think it'll work."

"Okay, let's go."

Natalia rose from the ground, and they walked into the abandoned shack. The dusty floorboards squeaked underneath their weight, and their footprints from hours before still sat in the coat of dirt and dust. Roman walked across the small room and knelt next to the shattered window. He wiped away the glass and took off his hooded coat, setting it down on the floor before sitting on it. Natalia followed after him, taking off her own hood and setting it down next to him. They leaned against the wall and watched the trees and grass wave in the wind through the shattered windows by the door.

Natalia twisted the ring on her finger. She hoped Ren and Aurum were okay, and she hoped they'd saved Lavelle and Damien. She couldn't wait to see them, but how would they react to Roman and the rebels and their Elemental powers? She was especially curious to see Damien's reaction. She knew he wouldn't like Roman. She knew Damien like the back of her hand. She could see him feeling threatened by Roman even though she told herself he had no reason to be.

Damien was like her brother, and she would never let anyone replace him... Or maybe that was it. Damien didn't want to be her friend or her brother. He wanted to be more, and the kiss before the testings confirmed that. Damien wouldn't like Roman because of the way Roman looked at her sometimes. Friends didn't look at each other like that. But Natalia didn't know what exactly that look meant, and they had too many other things to focus on right now. Besides, she wasn't even sure how she felt about anything—all she knew was that she wanted Damien back and to keep fighting alongside Roman. Never mind the look he'd given her before they'd jumped from the truck, or the name he called her. It was nothing. All those piercing glances were definitely nothing, and he was still annoying... She was not lying to herself, and she was not in denial...

"Where'd you get that ring?" Roman asked with a small smile, his brown eyes locked onto hers. "You twist it a lot."

"It was a birthday present." She smiled back. "I usually twist it when I'm nervous or excited."

"What are you nervous or excited about?"

"I can't wait to see Lavelle and Damien, but I don't know how they'll react to everything...to *us*. They don't know we're Elementals, and there's just so much they don't know. I don't want them to be scared, especially of us."

"They won't be scared of you. It'll take some time for them to wrap their heads around everything, but they'll be okay. We'll make sure they are."

"We will." Natalia smiled once again before leaning her head back against the wall. "It's crazy to think about how powerful love is and the lengths that people are willing to go for those they love."

"It *is* crazy." Roman chuckled. "I wish I had grown up with friends like you did."

"What was your childhood like?" she asked.

"I was an only child. My parents and I were a very fortunate and happy and loving family in Sector One, or at least I thought we were. After my father..." He hesitated, seemingly sorting out the right words to say. "...left us... It was just me and my mother."

"I'm so sorry...," Natalia said, feeling suddenly guilty for bringing about the subject.

He shrugged. "It's all right. He and I didn't get along very well anyway... But my mother and I..." Roman grinned, and it was the most genuine and joyous thing she'd ever seen. "We were so close. I could talk about her all day. I loved her more than anything in this world. Even though she's gone, I still see her everywhere I go. I see her in the world and elements around us. I see her in the rebels... She was so passionate and brave. She always made me feel like I could do anything."

"She sounds amazing."

He nodded. "She was. You actually remind me of her sometimes. You both make this face when you get angry. Your noses scrunch up and your eyebrows knit together," he said, scrunching his nose and knitting his brows.

Natalia laughed and elbowed his shoulder. "I don't do that!"

"Yes, you do!" Roman laughed too.

"Yeah, okay, whatever." She rolled her eyes, glaring playfully.

"See?" He pointed. "You're doing it right now!"

"No, I'm not!" She laughed again. For the next few minutes, she and Roman debated over different faces that they made and smiled and laughed at each other. They even thumb-wrestled a few rounds.

"No, that doesn't count!" Natalia exclaimed. "You're cheating!"

Roman burst into laughter. "How am I cheating? I think you're just bad at thumb-wrestling."

"No, you're tickling my palm! And how dare you say I'm bad at thumb-wrestling. I'll have you know that I was the champion of the thumb-wrestling tournament we had a few years ago."

"Ah, so you're just rusty?" He grinned.

"Sure." She shrugged. "Now come on, one more round."

"But you said best of two out of three, and I've won twice."

"Nope, you've cheated twice."

Roman smirked. "Fine, I'll just beat you a third time."

And he did. And a fourth and a fifth... After eventually giving up, Natalia told him about how she and Vale and the orphanage kids used to—and still do—run around the alleyways of Sector Four, and she told him about her small house in a cluster of small houses not too far from where they sat. It was weird to say Vale's name out loud. No one knew about him except for Damien, and they never brought him up. But it was nice at the same time. In a sense, it made her feel like Vale was still alive—still there with her... The last thing Natalia remembered before closing her eyes was the sound of Roman's soft humming.

~

Sunlight warmed Natalia's cheeks, causing her to stir. She snuggled closer to the soft fabric her head leaned against. Confusion filled her. What was she leaning on? She slowly opened her eyes to find her head resting on Roman's shoulder. His own head was bent down on top of hers. Her skin grew even warmer. How was she supposed to get up without waking him? For a few minutes, she simply sat there, sorting through the web of emotions running through her. She liked being next to him, but it felt dangerous. What was she doing? She knew she could trust him—she *did* trust him, but... Natalia winced embarrassingly as she stuck her hand up to his forehead, pushing him up. Roman jolted awake, blinking several times.

"Oh, sorry," he mumbled, rubbing the sleep from his eyes with a yawn.

Natalia smirked. "Not a morning person?"

"No." He laughed sleepily. "Definitely not."

"Neither am I." She rose from the floor and grabbed her coat. Today would be the day she was finally reunited with Lavelle and Damien. Her heart was set on seeing them today, and if she didn't—no, she couldn't think like that. She was *going* to see them. She refused to believe otherwise. A small laugh left her lips while she watched Roman groggily rise from the ground and sling his coat over his shoulder. The corner of his mouth rose as he glanced at Natalia, and they walked out of the small shack. The two squinted against the rays of the early morning sun, lifting their hands to their eyes. Natalia turned toward the wall. The soldiers who had paced atop it were now gone, replaced by only a single guard every few yards.

"If we stay quiet, we'll have no problem getting through," Roman said, the wind blowing his black hair in his face. He ran a hand through it and pushed it back.

"What about when we come out on the other side?" Natalia asked. Her eyes flickered between the soldiers.

"The wall's close enough to the forest that we can get behind the tree line before they even know we're there."

"Are you sure?" She raised a brow.

Roman nodded. "I mean, they already know the crack's there, so even if they do see us, it's not like they're discovering something new. We probably won't be able to use the crack again anyway, because they've been increasing security."

"Good point." Natalia shrugged before starting down the slope of the hill to the tree that guarded the crack. Together, they silently made their way down the hill and crouched behind the tree. Roman gestured Natalia toward the upturned root, and the déjà vu hit her like a punch to the gut. She shook her head. She didn't want to go first. She didn't know if she could... Not after Vale... Not after he hadn't come out.

She opened her mouth to protest, but the look he shot at her told her enough. He wasn't budging. Natalia bit the inside of her bottom lip in frustration and leaned in close, whispering, "As soon as I'm out of sight, start crawling. You have to be right behind me."

"Okay," Roman replied. "I'm right behind you. I promise."

Ignoring the familiar words, Natalia rolled onto her back and grabbed the roots, pushing herself under the tree and through the crack. She crawled out on the other side and sprinted toward the tree line. Once hidden within the safety of the brush, she turned back to face the wall. Panic surged. Where was he? By the Aether. *Where. Was. He?* Natalia cursed. She'd need to distract the guards to go back for him. She wasn't just going to wait. Not again.

She glanced up, and one of the soldiers above began walking in her direction. She unscrewed the lid of her canteen, and her eyes began to glow ice-blue around silver as a small sphere of water formed in her palms. Her brows furrowed and her hands curled into fists, hardening the sphere into ice. She then sent the sphere of ice sailing yards ahead of her. It collided against a rock with a *clash*, causing the soldiers on the walls to run toward it—in the opposite direction of the crack. She turned and sprinted back for the crack as soon as Roman slipped through.

"What the hell took you so long?" she exclaimed in a hushed voice. She swore her heart was about to pound out of her chest.

His brows furrowed. "What do you mean? I was right behind you."

"Nothing, I just..." Natalia's chest rose and fell rapidly, and she closed her eyes, forcing herself to take deep breaths. He was here. He was alive. That was all that mattered. They just needed to get into the forest before the guards came back. Everything was all right, and Roman wasn't Vale. He was fine. "You're just slow."

She could see the conflict in his eyes as they headed into the tree line, and he studied her. He clearly didn't believe her. Of course, he didn't... But instead of demanding more, he simply shrugged and asked, "Where'd all the guards go?"

Natalia allowed a cool swagger to fall over her panic and pulled a string of water out of her canteen, allowing her eyes to glow again. The snake-like string wove throughout her fingers twice before coiling around her index finger. Roman smirked and his eyes began to glow their mesmerizing dark-blue and silver. The snake around her finger suddenly broke apart into two marbles of water. They swirled around her hand before flying up at her nose. Natalia barely ducked in time to watch them splash against the tree behind her. She glared at Roman, who snickered, and by the Aether—it was the most relieving sound she'd ever heard. Then the two turned deeper into the forest and began making their way to the hill.

Natalia quickened her pace at the sight of familiar trees and landscape. She broke out into a run when the brush began to thin and open up into the clearing around the overhang. She burst through the trees to find Ren, Aurum, and *Lavelle*.

"Lavelle!" she exclaimed, running up and embracing her tightly.

"Natalia!" Lavelle squeezed her close. Tears spilled over her cheeks. "I didn't think I'd ever see you again."

"I missed you so much." Natalia pulled away, studying Lavelle's face as if she were seeing her for the first time. She smiled brightly, and tears filled her eyes. She glanced behind Lavelle at Ren and Aurum. *Just* Ren and Aurum. Natalia frantically searched the clearing, and her heart seemed to stop. "Where's Damien?"

Ren's and Aurum's eyes dropped to the grass, and they hung their heads. Natalia walked to them, more tears filling her eyes. Aurum bit the inside of her cheek, meeting Natalia's gaze. "Natalia..."

Natalia shook her head. "No..."

"Vayne has him," Aurum whispered hoarsely.

She laughed. "What? No, you're joking with me. I bet he's hiding and just trying to scare me. This is all a joke... You guys are playing pranks like we used to. Ha, ha, it's funny. You guys are *so* funny. You can come out now, Damien!" Natalia called, turning toward the edge of the clearing.

Ren glanced between Aurum and Lavelle nervously before walking over to Natalia and placing a hand on her shoulder. "It's not a joke..."

"No!" Natalia gritted her teeth, pulling away from him. She squeezed her eyes shut, fighting back the tears threatening to spill over. It wasn't true. It couldn't be. They were supposed to save him. How could they have not saved him?

"Natalia...," Aurum said again, her voice barely above a whisper. "He's gone. There's nothing we can—"

"There's *always* something we can do!" Natalia screamed, turning to face them. She could see it in their eyes now. It was no joke. They were here, and Damien was not. Vayne really did have him, and who knew what he was doing to him? She faced the walls and began marching toward them. Roman ran up, grabbing her arm. She yanked it free, and a few tears spilled over onto her cheeks. "Get off!"

"Talia, please." Roman reached for her again.

"No!" she swatted at his hand, continuing on. "I have to save him."

"I can't let you go," he said, slipping his arm around her waist and lifting her off the ground back into the clearing as she fought against him. "It's a suicide mission!"

"No, I don't care! I can't leave him again!" Natalia beat against his back until he finally set her down. She tried pushing past him, but his arms locked onto her shoulders, holding her in place. Tears ran down her face. "Roman, I can't..."

"Please, calm down," he pleaded. Fear and pain filled his eyes, surely mirroring her own. "We can't march back in there. My father will—"

Natalia jolted back, eyes widening. Everyone froze. The clearing was unnaturally still and silent. Anger and confusion suddenly flooded through her to the point where her vision blurred red. She gritted her teeth. "Did you just say *father*?"

Roman straightened and bit his lip. "Wait, please, just let me explain—"

"What do you mean, *father*?" she exclaimed.

He'd told her his father had left him and his mother, so what did he mean? Who was Roman's father? Did he work for Vayne? It would explain his hesitation in the shack last night. She slowly studied Roman's face, comparing it to the projections of all the important officers and governors from Sector One she'd seen... His brown eyes, his nose, the shape of his sharp jaw... His *black* hair, darker than the night itself... And then it clicked. Only one other man in all the sectors had hair darker than the night. She thought hard about the shape of the man's face and his nose. She had only seen him in pictures, but the similarities were uncanny. *Vayne is Roman's father...*

Aurum released a shaky breath. "It's not what it looks like..."

Natalia whirled around to face her. She hoped her eyes hid the pain and betrayal she felt. Roman's *father*—Vayne Averie—had Damien as his prisoner. Roman Averie was the leader of the rebels, and he was *Vayne's son*. Why hadn't he told them? Who all knew? She turned back to Roman. "Do the rebels know?"

Roman's eyes flickered between Natalia and the others behind her.

"Do they?" Natalia exclaimed.

"Yes, they do!" Aurum exclaimed.

Natalia's mouth dropped open as she turned to face Aurum once more. "What?"

"Everyone knows except for you and Ren. Fraiser told me who he is, and why he hasn't told you yet. He wanted to give you two—all of us—time to calm down and settle in. It was never a secret—it was just until he thought you were ready to know. He wanted you to trust him."

"Last night, you told me your father left you and your mother!" Natalia scowled.

"He did!" Roman retorted, pain evident in his eyes. "He did leave us..."

"When were you going to tell me?" she asked, her voice cracking on the last word. She knew he was hurting, too, but he had still withheld information from her. She didn't care how good his intentions were. He still hadn't told her. Could she even trust him any more?

"I was going to tell you and Ren when we got back, Natalia, I swear. I just didn't want you to hate me." His eyes were full of sadness and regret. "Look, I know I shouldn't have waited, but—"

"Roman, it's fine," Ren said, stepping forward. "It's your past, and it's your decision if and when you want to tell us. Do I wish you had told us sooner? Yes, but if
I've learned one thing over the past few days, it's that you are not one bit like your
father... Besides..." He turned to Aurum and Lavelle, then Natalia. "...we don't judge
based on pasts."

Natalia took a few steps back toward the edge of the overhang, blinking profusely. Her mind was racing. Everything she thought she knew about Roman was
wrong. He was Vayne's son, but he led the rebels... She rubbed her temples, fighting away a headache. She jumped when Lavelle's arms wrapped around her without
warning. She hesitated before turning into her hug. She couldn't deny that her heart
was aching. She was so happy to have Lavelle back, but the hole in her heart seemed
to rip deeper and deeper. She was in pain because of not only Roman but Damien,
too. They were all together—except for Damien, and it was tearing Natalia apart.
The pain resonated within the depths of her chest. Everyone in their family had
been reunited except for him. Her best friend was gone, and there was absolutely
nothing she could do to save him. Lavelle was currently the only thing holding her
together, keeping her from breaking down. She was a warm light in the cold, dark
world surrounding her. She was a safe house.

Lavelle rubbed Natalia's back before pulling away. "Hey, why don't you take me
back to this camp I've heard so much about? I heard there's a hospital, and I'd really
like to make sure Aurum's arm doesn't get infected."

"What happened to your arm?" Natalia jerked up, turning to Aurum. For the
first time, she noticed the bloody bandage around Aurum's shoulder. The sleeves of
her shirt were ragged and singed as she walked over to her. "Are you all right?"

She shrugged with a wince. "Yeah, just got clipped by a bolt. I'm okay, though."

Natalia frowned. "How did you guys get over the wall?"

"We didn't exactly go *over* it." Ren smiled. "It's a long story. I'll tell you on the
walk back to the camp."

"Oh," Lavelle said, walking up to Roman and extending her hand. "I'm Lavelle
Dalnum, by the way."

He took it with a sad smile before whispering, "Roman."

Just Roman. Not Roman Averie... He then turned and started into the forest
back toward the rebels' camp. Aurum followed after him, then Ren and Lavelle.
Natalia took a few steps before glancing back at the walls, the wind blowing loose
black hairs around her face. She was leaving Damien... *Again.* She cursed herself.
She should've gone looking for him herself, but she hadn't, and she knew she would

regret that for the rest of her life. She squeezed her eyes shut, forcing her feet to walk away. She winced as her heart shattered into a million pieces.

~

Night had fallen the next day by the time Roman led them into the rebel camp. They were quickly greeted by a watch party and Fraiser. Roman sighed and watched Natalia march off in the direction of their circle of tents, and his chest tightened with guilt. He was so angry with himself. He should have explained everything before they'd left. It was all his fault. He had failed her *again*, and he only hoped that she could somehow find it in herself to forgive him. But could she ever trust him again? By the look on her face when she'd turned toward him, and the way she'd ignored him the entire day's journey back, he didn't think she could.

He was an idiot. A complete and utter idiot. He'd really thought that something had changed between them during their trip—that they'd both finally begun to open themselves up to the idea of being vulnerable around each other—but he'd ruined it. Just like he ruined everyone around him because that was what his family did. Fraiser faced him and raised a brow. He simply shook his head before turning to Aurum, Ren, and Lavelle.

"Napoleon will be in the hospital. He can help with Aurum's shoulder. I'd take you myself, but I have some things I need to take care of," he said.

"That's perfectly fine." Lavelle smiled warmly. "Thank you, Roman. It was nice to meet you."

"Likewise." He dipped his head and watched the three walk past the circle of tents and toward the river.

"Did you find the station?" Fraiser asked.

He nodded. "Yes."

"What the hell is wrong with you? You look like someone just killed a puppy."

"She knows."

Fraiser rolled her eyes. "Let me guess... Oh! She's being dramatic about it." Roman glared at her, and she frowned. "Come on, Roman. You know I was joking."

"This is all my fault. If I had just saved both of them the first time, we wouldn't be in this mess. I shouldn't have told anyone who I am. I should have been better." He clenched his fists until his knuckles turned white.

"Roman..." Fraiser put a hand on his shoulder. "Who cares who your father is? It always takes everyone a little time to process it, but once they do, everything always works out. She knows you're nothing like Vayne." She scoffed. "I can't believe I'm actually defending her..."

"I can't either." He smiled. "The world might actually be ending."

Fraiser chuckled. "Jokes aside, you're trying to save everyone when sometimes not everyone can be saved. We have to take what we can get and work with it. No one blames you for any of the pain and suffering Vayne has caused. In fact, everyone loves and respects you, because you fight against him despite your heritage."

"But how do I defeat my father? How do I destroy a monster without becoming one myself?" Roman turned to face her, and she sighed, her green eyes filling with sadness. He wasn't truly asking her for an answer because no one had an answer to that question. It was the same question he'd been asking himself for years, and every time, the answer was the same. He didn't know. No one knew. "Natalia and I found the train station. It's a couple miles northeast of Four's wall."

"Do you think we can pull this off?"

He stood there for a few moments, contemplating the odds stacked against them. "Yes," he whispered. "Yes, Fraiser, I do."

"Hey, Roman! Fraiser!" Ren suddenly called, jogging across the river to meet them at the edge of the forest.

"Is everything all right?" Roman asked, concern filling him. "How's Aurum?"

"Lavelle and Napoleon are taking care of her, but I need to talk to you and Fraiser about something."

"What is it?" Fraiser questioned.

"Aurum and I were talking with Lavelle when we first found her, and she showed us something crazy." Roman studied the twin as he spoke. The nervous boy he'd come to know was gone. In his place stood a confident Elemental full of strength. Even the earth around Ren seemed to listen to him when he talked. "There's this hidden channel in the projectors that Vayne doesn't know about. A group of rebel sympathizers has been trying to use it to unite those within the sectors and convince them to fight back. Not many know about it, though, so they've been trying to contact the rebels."

Fraiser frowned. "We don't have that kind of tech."

"I know, but imagine what we could do if we did." Ren glanced between Roman and Fraiser. "Anyway, Lavelle showed us the channel, and we spoke with their leader, Hero Ellisaire. He wanted me to tell you that rebel support is growing. The people are beginning to unite, and they're ready to start fighting back. But most importantly, he wants you to know that if you plan on interrupting the next testings, they'll be with you. They'll be ready, and they'll fight, too."

Roman ran a hand through his hair. This was it, their chance. If they could rally the people in the sectors, they might have a chance at winning. "I wish I could speak with Hero directly, but I can't risk sending rebels back to the sectors for parts or a new projector. Not after the security increases, and the ones that have yet to come. After our stunts over the past few days, we won't be getting back in for a while."

"So, what's our next move?" Ren asked.

Fraiser glanced at Roman with a mischievous grin. "Give the order."

Roman smirked. "Begin preparations."

"For?" Ren's brows rose, the faintest glimpse of excitement shining in his eyes.

"A raid," he said. "We're going to raid the next testings."

CHAPTER FIFTEEN

ALONE

Damien stared into the square mirror that hung above his sink in his quarters. The room was dark, as it always was. Dark maroons and blacks and grays covered every inch of the room his eyes could see. Once again, her smile flitted through his mind. He knew he shouldn't think like that any more. He clutched his head, forcing the thoughts away. He had been taught to truly fight...to kill... His right arm twitched as the blurry vision of her grew slightly blurrier. It seemed as if every day, his eyes became more and more distant, empty, and emotionless. All he felt was anger. She had left him. She had abandoned him like everyone else, and he hated her for it. Or did he? He couldn't tell any more, because he couldn't help the overwhelming sense of what he assumed was love—as it was the only spark he could feel besides the unnaturally strong rage—he felt when her name was spoken. The way she had smiled and laughed in the forest...

A part of him had fought so hard—and was still fighting—to hold onto her, but the part was losing. Day by day, it lost more and more ground. Damien was loyal to Vayne, and Vayne alone. No one else. He studied his messy, uncut hair; the dark circles under his hazel eyes; and the new, unwanted paleness to his skin that made him appear sickly. He squeezed his fists into tight balls. His knuckles grew white, and his fingernails dug into his skin. He felt his right arm twitch once more before he flung it into the mirror in a fit of rage. Shards of glass clattered to the floor. As they did, a memory flashed through his head.

~

"Damien!" his mother exclaimed from inside their small, wooden kitchen in their home in Sector Three. His brothers hid, listening behind the small wooden door that led to their bedrooms. "You have to be more careful! We only have one plate now!"

"I'm sorry, Mom... I tripped," Damien mumbled as he stared at the shattered pieces that lay on the floor. It had taken four months of labor from him to buy the plate.

"You have to do better," his mother scolded, slamming a wooden cabinet shut.

Damien dipped his head down and studied the wooden floor. It had been two months since his father's death, and his once-loving mother had turned into his worst nightmare. She had quit showing up to her job in the heart of Sector Three, causing Damien to find work cutting down trees near the walls. Suddenly, a low chuckle filled the room. Damien glanced at his mother to see a dark figure emerge from the shadows. It was Vayne. The world began to grow darker before his mother whirled around, baring rows of razor-sharp teeth and glowing red eyes.

"I'll save you, Damien," Vayne smiled. "All you have to do is ask..."

Damien's mother inched closer, foam dripping from her mouth as if she were a rabid predator, and Damien was her prey... He knew how this particular beating ended, but now that his mother was even more of a monster... He wasn't sure he'd survive it this time.

"Save me, please!" Damien exclaimed. His voice sounded young and horrified.

Vayne smiled as his mother lurched toward him.

"Help!" Damien screamed before the image erupted into a smothering darkness. Vayne chuckled somewhere in the distance...

～

Damien jerked backward, his eyes flashing open. He scowled, sending both fists repeatedly into the remaining glass upon the wall. Tears formed in his eyes, but not tears of physical pain. The cuts on his hands were as numb as his heart, which felt as if it did not even beat. He was so tired of not being able to tell what was real and what was fake. Visions and nightmares constantly plagued him whether he was awake or asleep. His only break from them was when he was talking with Vayne, training, or carrying out one of Vayne's missions. And now he craved being with him, helping him, just to make the nightmares stop.

He had completed his first mission with excellence. Vayne had no idea how many weaknesses the walls really had, and once they'd been exploited, hardly any rebels had been able to get in. In fact, they hadn't even tried after their stunt in Two, though Damien and Zyra still hadn't figured out why they were in Two in the first place. The incident with the soldier and worker in Four had been dealt with, even though Damien still didn't believe the commander when he promised the two had been captured and killed. He'd thought the man had lied to cover up his own mistake. But how could Damien trust himself if he couldn't tell what was real and what wasn't?

"*You* should have done better, Mom. You didn't love me, and neither did my brothers. You all used me. But, no, *she* didn't... At first... But then she left me!" he hissed, his arms and neck twitching. His mind was a constant dark and vicious battlefield. It was as if thousands of swords pierced his mind as he tried to convince himself she was evil. Then, Vayne would appear, and each time, he would show Damien who was behind the swords. Natalia. She caused his pain. The happy memories he had weren't real. They were an illusion, a trap set by her to destroy him. "I did all I could. It's not my fault. Vayne saved me. I did all I could. It's not my fault... Vayne saved me..."

"He did save you, and you should be grateful for that," Zyra said, leaning against the doorframe of his bathroom.

"Get. Out," he snapped, whirling away from the shattered mirror to face her.

"It's time for training."

"We've already trained for five hours today."

"We don't have to train in combat." She winked.

Damien rolled his eyes. "Again with the flirting? I don't think you understand, Zyra. I don't *want* you."

"You *will*." She smiled sadistically as she sauntered out of his quarters. Her voice echoed back from the hallway. "I'll see you in ten."

Damien growled angrily, staring back into the remains of the mirror. His face appeared shattered like the shards of glass, and his bloody hands gripped the sink until he thought it would break. His eyes suddenly began to burn, glowing orange around silver pupils. He yanked a shard of glass from the wall, slicing it through his dark brown hair. He paused, watching the locks fall to meet the glass scattered upon the floor. He clenched his fists as his eyes narrowed in on the small, braided black cords with black rocks woven into them that now lay on the floor. The bracelet had been a birthday present from Natalia. He didn't even remember ripping it off...

～

Outside in the courtyard, Damien and Zyra trained for hours, beating each other until they bled. Damien slung his sword of fire toward her viciously, and she ducked out of the way, countering with a deadly spear of ice. Damien easily blocked her blows with his sword, eventually parrying behind her and kicking the back of her knee. She collapsed to the ground before quickly flipping over onto her back and glaring at him with her glowing ice-blue and silver eyes. He held his sword to her throat. Slow clapping filled the air as Vayne sauntered toward them with a look of satisfaction upon his unnatural face.

"Well done, Damien." He smiled. "Your skills have improved greatly. At this rate, you could become one of the strongest Elementals in all the sectors."

"Thank you, sir," Damien returned, studying the grass grabbing at the soles of his boots. Vayne took a step closer, causing him to flinch.

"Look at me when you speak," Vayne hissed.

Damien stared into Vayne's unnaturally white eyes. "Yes, sir."

"You two are dismissed." Vayne nonchalantly waved his hand and turned and walked back inside the great mansion doors. Damien fought the urge to follow after him. He was so afraid of him, yet all he wanted was to please him. The swords then returned, raging a vicious battle in his mind. Suddenly, Damien turned, unable to take the pain any more, and marched out of the mansion gates into the cold night. No one would care where he was going. They knew he'd come back. No matter how long he spent away trying to fight his own head, he always came back.

The stars above Sector One shone brightly, and a slight breeze blew through the remains of his hair. Damien exited through the gates, walking in the direction of the forest surrounding the inner walls that guarded the mansion. He broke into a sprint soon after entering the tree line. He ran deeper into the forest, only pausing when he finally felt pain from the lack of air in his lungs. He slumped down into the soft, tall grass, running his fingers through the sharp blades. For a few silent minutes, he sat there, his face emotionless and numb. He ripped a dead blade of grass from the ground, frowning. It reminded him of his father...

∼

"Good, Damien! Again!"

Damien smiled and repeated the jab against a brown sack full of dead grass. His father stood behind him, beaming with pride. Their house stood in the distance, jammed between other small, wooden houses on the outskirts of Sector Three. The forest was dense here compared to the thinning trees of the inner city. Without warning, the rumbling of an armored truck filled Damien's ears. He glanced at the dirt road leading into the heart of the sector. His heart dropped as the summer sun reflected off the deadly, black metal. The truck screeched to a stop in front of Damien's house.

"Stay here," his father whispered, walking back toward their home.

"But...," Damien began, but his father was already halfway up the small hill between the forest and their house. Damien watched from afar while his father greeted the four guards that hopped out of the truck. For a few minutes, they simply talked; then suddenly, one of the four punched Damien's father, sending him tumbling to the ground.

"No!" Damien screeched, sprinting toward them. Tears poured from his eyes while they announced his father's arrest and dragged him into the confines of the metal truck. Damien's mother, who had run outside due to the commotion, wept as Damien appeared next to her, and together, they helplessly watched the truck drive away, kicking up dust as it went.

~

A few tears slid down Damien's pale cheeks, and he leaned back against the ground. *That* was real. He knew it was, but he still felt cold and numb. The only warmth he could find was through his furious hatred for Natalia. But why did he hate her? They were family. Right?

~

"What are you doing?" Natalia exclaimed, an apple flying over her head. She clung onto one of the many branches of the apple tree they had a habit of climbing with a grin.

"You're not listening to me." Damien crossed his arms. He sat several branches higher than her. He'd always been the better climber, and he never let her forget it.

"I'm not listening because you're being absurd," she laughed, climbing higher. "Why do you doubt yourself so much?"

"You know why, Talia." Damien stared off into the dense forest. He wished the two of them could just run away and never look back, but he couldn't leave his family. And now that Aurum had come along, he knew Natalia wouldn't leave without her. He rolled his eyes. Aurum was so annoying, but at least she kept things interesting...

"Damien, you—" The branch Natalia had been standing on snapped. Damien lunged forward, grabbing her hand. He grunted and strained as he held up their weight and slung Natalia to the nearest branch. She dropped down onto it, and he climbed down to meet her.

"Talia, are you all right?" he questioned worriedly.

She plopped down on the branch, patting the bark beside her. Damien sat down next to her. "Damien, you have to stop letting your mother get in your head. It's your greatest weakness."

He scoffed. "Apparently, your weakness is climbing trees."

"Thank you for saving me." She nudged him with a laugh.

"Again," he added with a smirk.

She sighed. "Oh, what would I do without my dear brother?"

Damien shook his head, shoving her playfully. No matter what she felt, he loved her... And he always would.

~

No, she is the *enemy*. She is not family...," Damien told himself, bringing his hands up to his temples. The swords stabbed at his brain as he attempted to make sense of the black, entangled emotions clouding his mind. The darkness surrounded him, smothering him from the inside. He was falling apart... Damien winced as the pain intensified. He wrapped his fingers around the remains of his hair, pulling some strands loose. He gasped when Natalia suddenly appeared in front of him. He shot to his feet, studying her carefully. Her skin appeared cold and pale. The familiar and usual blush upon her cheeks was completely gone, and her eyes seemed dark and full of hatred.

"What are *you* doing here?" he exclaimed.

"What do you mean, Damien? We always meet here," Natalia replied, stretching her arms out toward her surroundings. They were back at the overhang. "See? You even have your bracelet on."

Damien glanced down at his wrist, finding the rocks braided into the simple, black cords—the same bracelet he had left on the floor of his chamber hours before, along with locks of his hair and shattered glass.

"No, no, no, no, no... You're not real. This can't be real."

"Of course, it's real, Damien." Natalia smiled, slowly approaching him. She cupped his face with her hands, slowly stroking her thumbs across his cheeks. She leaned forward, lightly placing her lips upon his. For a few fleeting moments, it was as if all the pain in his life had never happened. He was safe, happy, and he was good. But then he jerked back.

"As much as I want to... You're not real. The real Natalia would have never done that. She never felt the same—"

The vision of Natalia smiled sadistically as she plunged a knife deep into Damien's stomach. He winced, and her smile grew with his pain.

"You're right. The real Natalia would have done *this*," she whispered into his ear. Damien collapsed forward, colliding with the soft grass... His blood soaked into the ground, turning the nearby wildflowers crimson. Natalia's eyes began to glow a sickening white before she flashed rows of sharp teeth.

His eyes shot open, and cold sweat dripped from his forehead. Damien pushed himself up from the ground, his arms wrapping around his stomach. He briefly lifted his shirt, finding only muscle and clean skin. There was no wound and no blood. He glanced at the sky to find dawn approaching. He shivered and turned back toward the mansion. As he began to walk, he paused, straining to hear the faint whisper calling to him.

"Damien, come home..."

Damien's now orange, glowing eyes narrowed against the small patch of grass where he had lay only moments ago. He screamed in anger and pain as he turned and extended his palms at the grass, scorching it until it crumbled away in the breeze. He then faced the mansion again and began to walk, never once glancing back.

~

Damien passed through the gates of the Circle of Sector One. Once inside, he walked through the trimmed grass and up the gravel walkway that led to the double-paned doors of the mansion. Zyra greeted him there, a smirk upon her face. The morning sun had finally revealed itself on the horizon, casting an eerie, red-orange glow upon her face. The yellow highlights in her eyes were more prominent in the light. She was gorgeous but toxic and deadly. He must trust no one. Not even Vayne. No—he could trust Vayne... As the constant battle inside Damien's head raged on, he pushed past Zyra into the white marble and golden hallway.

"Did you not hear me?" she scoffed, following him toward his chambers.

"No," Damien answered, refusing to turn his head in acknowledgment.

"Vayne wants to see you in his office."

Damien took a left down one of the many branching hallways, passing the hall that led to his chamber, and continued on into the office. Zyra slipped in behind him before he could close the door. He cursed under his breath. Her eyes followed him as he walked over to the president's desk.

"You wanted to see me, sir?"

"Yes, Damien," Vayne answered, rising from his desk chair. "I did want to see you. Where have you been?"

"I needed some air, so I went to the forest outside of the Circle's walls."

"Why did you need air?"

"I—I...," Damien stuttered, fumbling for an answer. He winced when the swords in his mind began to stab even harder than before. He grunted and fell to a knee, his hands clutching his temples.

"I told you he was losing it." Zyra smirked.

Vayne rolled his white eyes. "I thought he was stronger than this."

"Well, in a way he is, sir," Zyra said. "Most patients don't require more than one session of brainwashing. It seems his feelings for the girl, Natalia, are keeping the effects from fully taking over. His will is so strong that the old him is still in there somewhere, and he's fighting. I think if we subject him to another session, there will be nothing left of him to remember her, thus rendering his feelings and will useless. Then he'd—"

"Then he'd be a mindless slave of no use to me," Vayne interrupted. "No, we can't subject him to another full session—it would destroy the weapon we've created. The scientists in the lab said they used his feelings for her and turned them into a hatred. Clearly, it didn't fully work. He loves and hates her. That's why there's a constant battle inside his head. Deep down he knows the truth... His *heart* knows the truth... But his brain is telling him what we want him to think. He needs a half-dose. Let the girl be the anchor he holds onto, but we have to fully twist that anchor of love into hate."

"That should be easy." Zyra peered down at him. "After all, there is such a thin line between love and hate..." Damien looked up at Zyra, feeling his stomach twist. A sadistic smirk appeared on her face as she spoke. "It's a shame, really. Doing so much damage... But, it must be done."

"Don't talk of me as if I am not here," Damien spat out before writhing in pain once more. His screams filled the office, and the battle in his head intensified.

She frowned. "It's getting worse."

"Zyra, take him down to the lab," Vayne commanded.

"*No!*" Damien bolted up from the floor, sprinting for the door. Suddenly, a dark cascade of wind began to surround him before tossing him against the marble floor. A small crack flittered across the marble where he landed. "Don't take me back. Don't take me back."

Zyra smiled while two Elementals from Vayne's personal guard clad in that sickening stark-white with the red band around their right arms entered the room, dragging him to his feet. Damien's hazel eyes began to glow orange and silver, and fire ignited in his palms. He thrust his hands outward, scorching the guards. Then he turned to face Vayne, watching his dark element retreat back toward him. As he did, a whip of water coiled around Damien's neck, pulling him down to Zyra's feet. He glanced up to watch her strike him with a fist of ice, clouding his vision in darkness. His last thoughts as the darkness closed in were of the old Damien—the Damien who'd met Natalia out in the forest—and of how much he wished he was back there with her, smelling the fresh grass and eating apples.

CHAPTER SIXTEEN

NIGHTMARES

The only thing Natalia could feel was soft grass beneath her. Everything was black. She crawled through the darkness, carefully feeling forward with her hands. She froze when she felt a puddle of thick, warm liquid seeping into the crooks of her fingers. She sucked in a breath, and a light suddenly flashed. Everything was bright and colorful once more. She found herself kneeling in a meadow full of tall, soft grass and wildflowers that blew in the wind. Trees surrounded the edge of the meadow, reminding her of the clearing around the overhang.

Natalia stood and glanced up at the bright sun, throwing a hand up to block it. Her eyes widened, and it felt as if her veins turned to ice as she watched blood trickle from her hand. She held both of her shaking hands out in front of her, examining the blood. A gasp escaped her lips, and she stumbled backward, her body coming to an abrupt stop as she slammed against something. She whirled around, peering at the boy who stood before her. It was Damien. His gaze was cold, and his eyes were entirely white with tangles of wicked black veins that looked like dark snakes poisoning him.

"Look what happened to me, Talia. All of this because you left me. You abandoned me," he whispered.

"No...I didn't. There was nothing I could do..."

"Liar!" Damien exclaimed, spit flying from his mouth. Natalia turned to run, but black snakes flew out from the tall grass, wrapping around her and pulling her to the ground. Her breath escaped her lungs as she collided with the earth. Slowly, she sat up to find herself in the forest of the Hive. It was unnaturally dark, and a single ray of sunlight peeked through the canopy of trees. Damien suddenly appeared in the sunlight, and five shadows stalked up behind him. Natalia cowered in fear as she watched a white-eyed Aurum, Ren, Napoleon, and Fraiser join him.

"Look what you did to us!" Aurum hissed.

Ren scowled. "You should've never let this happen…"

Natalia winced. "I tried to—"

"No, you're weak!" Napoleon spat. "How could I have ever trusted you? I thought you could help save us! I thought we would be family, but we're not!"

"You're an enemy!" Lavelle added, deep hatred filling her voice.

Natalia flinched at their words. "I'm sorry," she whispered, voice breaking. Her hands began to shake.

"You're not even putting up a fight." Fraiser scoffed and faced Damien. "Why should we bother killing her, Damien? She's useless dead or alive."

"We're killing her because she deserves it," he whispered. "But first we must make her suffer!"

He marched toward her with the others mere steps behind, and Natalia shut her eyes tight, awaiting the continued torture… Nothing happened. She continued to wait, but nothing ever came. She hesitantly opened her eyes to find herself at the edge of the overhang. She turned to face the forest when the sound of crashing footsteps neared, and without warning, Roman burst into the clearing.

"Natalia?" he whispered, fear clear in his eyes.

Damien and the others appeared behind him, smiling wickedly with rows of razor-sharp teeth. Natalia froze, sucking in a breath.

"Talia!" Roman exclaimed, reaching out to her. Then Damien lunged for him.

~

Natalia gasped, jerking up from the pillows and blankets scattered amongst her tent. She panted, and sweat dripped down the sides of her face while tears dampened the corners of her widened eyes. Her head fell into her hands. A week had passed since they'd returned from the sectors. Their next move would be raiding the upcoming testings, which would take place in a little over a month. All they could do now was train, wait, and prepare, but Natalia was already tired of waiting. She hated the anticipation, and each night since their return the same nightmare would haunt her. Every time Damien lunged for Roman, she would wake up. Her hands would shake, and uncontrollable tears and sweat would pour down her face. She would sit alone in her tent and overthink every single thing she'd ever done or said, but tonight was different…

Why? Why was the nightmare happening, and why did she wake up every single time Damien lunged for Roman? They hadn't spoken to each other since they'd returned from the sectors. She gritted her teeth, angrily clenching her fists. She didn't want to fall asleep ever again. And suddenly, it clicked. It was *anger*. Natalia was full of it, and she refused to sit and mope about it any more. She was tired of the sleepless nights and in need of a distraction, so she rose from the floor of her tent and quietly slipped through the flap.

The night was still very dark. It would be a few more hours until the sun finally began to rise above the trees, but a small fire crackled in the patch of grass between the seven tents that had become their common area. She walked toward it only to immediately stop at the sight of Fraiser with a bottle of Brennivan in her hand. Fraiser smirked at her, raising the bottle and gesturing at the log across from her. Natalia hesitantly walked over to the log and sat down to watch Fraiser toss the bottle over the flames. She jumped forward, barely catching it before it shattered on the ground.

"For your troubles." Fraiser smirked. A glaze seemed to cover her eyes.

Natalia frowned, unscrewing the cap and taking a long swig. She coughed several times before taking another quick sip and flinging the bottle back over to Fraiser. "Why are you out here?"

"We *all* get them, too, you know." She shrugged, taking a sip. "Don't think you're something special."

"Go to hell, Fraiser." Natalia scoffed.

Fraiser smiled. "Where do you think I came from?"

She rolled her eyes. "Just pass the bottle back."

"Your wish is my command, Your Highness," she mocked, passing the bottle over. A few moments of silence passed as Natalia drank. The effects of it slammed into her immediately, and she could feel a haze spreading through her. Fraiser picked at her nails.

"How do you do it?" Natalia asked.

Fraiser cocked her head to the side. "Do what?"

"Act like all the deaths and lives you take don't bother you..." The Brennivan washed down her throat like liquid fire, and she narrowed her brows. "Do they bother you?"

"Of course, they do," Fraiser said, extending her hand for the bottle. Natalia threw it to her again. "But it's their deaths or my family's. Or yours, I suppose." She smirked. "But I choose theirs. Every. Time. I will *always* choose theirs."

A few moments of deafening silence passed, and the girls simply stared at each other as if they were both entirely foreign and couldn't understand a word the other was saying. So, she decided to speak the one language they could always understand. She nodded at the Brennivan. "Pass that back."

Fraiser did, leaning back with a frown. "So, when are you and Roman going to stop acting like idiotic children and speak again?"

Natalia threw her head back, letting the remaining Brennivan pour out of the bottle and burn down her throat. "Since when do you care?"

"Well, I don't care about you, but I do care about Roman," she said with a shrug. "If he's not happy, then I'm not."

"Sounds an awful lot like a lapdog to me." Natalia smiled vindictively.

Fraiser chuckled. "I think you're just upset you got your own lapdog killed."

Natalia's face dropped. Anger began spreading through her like a wildfire, and the alcohol running through her veins wasn't helping. Fraiser *did not* just say that. She scowled. She knew Fraiser was a terrible person, but she didn't think she would have ever stooped that low... But she just had. Natalia's grip around the empty glass bottle tightened.

"What's the matter?" Fraiser pursed her lips. "Vayne got your tongue? Oh, no, wait, sorry. I forgot, it would be Damien's tongue—"

Natalia chucked the bottle at Fraiser, who barely scrambled out of the way in time. It shattered against the rock with a loud, ear-piercing *crash*. Fraiser rose from the grass, a small trickle of blood running down her cheek where a large shard of glass had clipped her. Roman, Aurum, Napoleon, and the twins rushed out of their tents, worry and confusion filling all of their tired eyes. Natalia turned and stalked off into the forest, while Fraiser turned and marched toward the river. The others simply stared at each other in a state of shock. What had just happened?

"Should we go after them?" Napoleon asked, concern filling his eyes.

Several worried glances were exchanged between the five of them before Aurum shook her head. "No, just let them both cool off..."

~

The sun was shining directly overhead when Roman walked through the hospital doors. He ran a hand through his hair with a sigh. He'd hardly gotten any sleep all week, especially after the events earlier this morning. He was stressed and very confused, especially since he hadn't really talked to Natalia since their screaming match about Damien and his father... He paused in one of the many aisles of cots, scanning for Napoleon. His eyes finally found the back of his light-brown hair in the front corner of the hospital. Roman walked up to the cot Napoleon stood over where a young boy sat, clutching his right wrist.

"What happened?" Roman asked, clapping Napoleon on the shoulder.

He turned with a smile. "Hey, boss man!"

"Sprained wrist. He was training with Fraiser." Lavelle frowned, walking up to the cot with bandages piled in her hands. He studied her as she set them down on the bedside table before raising a brow at him. Despite everything, she was fitting in nicely, and he'd noticed the huge difference she was making in the hospital. Her knowledge of natural herbs was astounding, and every patient who saw her said only good things. A rare frown pulled at Lavelle's lips. "He's the third one we've gotten today."

"Ah." Roman glanced at Napoleon, who shrugged.

"Roman, I need you to talk to her. Please, this is getting out of hand." Lavelle placed her hands on her hips.

Napoleon laughed. "Literally."

Roman and Napoleon snickered when a roll of bandages suddenly flew at them. Roman ducked in time to watch it hit Napoleon's forehead. He doubled over, laughing as Napoleon picked up the bandages and sent them back toward Lavelle with a mischievous grin. Roman watched her attempt to fight away a smile, but it was no use. Even the boy on the cot was laughing. Ever since Napoleon and Lavelle had been introduced, the two had immediately clicked. They never failed to bring a smile to Roman's face, so he'd spent nearly the entire week with them. He was certain they were the only thing keeping him sane at the moment.

"Get over here and help me wrap his wrist," she said.

Napoleon nodded, leaving Roman and crossing over to the other side of the cot. He nudged Lavelle before gently holding up the boy's hand. Lavelle quickly wrapped the boy's arm, cutting the bandage with a knife and tying the two loose ends together.

"All right, you're good to go. Just no more sparring or hand-to-hand combat for at least a week," Lavelle warned.

"How am I supposed to train then?" the boy asked with a frown.

"Focus on your element." She smiled warmly. The boy huffed before jumping off the cot and heading in the direction of the door. Lavelle turned to face Roman. "Seriously, though, Roman, can you please talk to Fraiser?"

He nodded. "I will."

"Thank you."

It was amazing how quickly Lavelle had adapted to the huge change in her life. She had gone from believing her brother and friends were dead to discovering the rebels within and outside the walls. She had taken the fact that they were Elementals well. She still loved each and every one of them, and their powers didn't scare her. She was fascinated with them really, but Roman suspected the change had been easier to accept because she'd been reunited with her family.

"Do you two want to come with me?" Roman said, eyes flicking between the pair. He knew if he left them, his smile would fade, and he wanted so badly to keep smiling.

Napoleon turned to Lavelle with a shrug. "Our shift's over."

She smirked, glancing at Roman. "You're so scared to run into Natalia alone."

Roman felt his cheeks heat. She was right. That was another reason why he'd been glued to them. He couldn't bare to run into Natalia alone. They hadn't talked outside of the group since they had returned from the sectors. He knew she needed space and time to think and process everything, so that's what he'd given her, but neither of them was ever alone now. There was always someone accompanying them just in case they ran into each other.

"You need to talk to her, Roman."

"She's right," Napoleon agreed. "You two can't avoid each other forever."

"I know..." He sighed. "I just...I—"

"She doesn't hate you," Lavelle said. The warmth in her vibrant blue eyes—the eyes she shared with Ren—seemed to fill the whole room. "She could never hate you even if she wanted to."

"Come on." Roman ran a hand through his dark hair, ignoring every word she'd just said. He had no idea what that meant and was a little scared to try to figure it out. "Let's go talk to Fraiser."

"Actually, can we stop by the tents first? I'm hungry," Napoleon said.

"That's a great idea," Lavelle agreed as they walked out of the hospital into the warm sunlight. "Oh, didn't you and Natalia make soup earlier, too? We can kill two birds with one stone."

"Yeah, we did." Napoleon elbowed Roman.

He chuckled, cringing internally. "You two are impossible."

Napoleon and Lavelle shared a smile while Roman created two walls of water within the river, blocking the flowing currents so they could cross. He released the water as soon as they stepped out of the damp riverbed and hit the tall, soft grass. They continued on toward their tents that surrounded the fire pit. Natalia and Aurum stood over the small crackling fire, talking and watching as a small pot of soup cooked on a large rock in the center.

Roman glanced between the two when they looked up, and Natalia's eyes immediately darted away while Aurum greeted them with a genuine smile. Roman chewed the inside of his lip nervously, repeating Lavelle's words to himself. *She doesn't hate you. She could never hate you even if she wanted to.* He hoped she was right about that, but he knew she was right about the other thing—he did need to talk to her and end this silence. He'd rather her just tell him how much she hated him. He studied her carefully as they drew closer. Her eyes met his for a split second before flicking back down to the grass.

"Lavelle, what's wrong?" Aurum asked, clearly noticing Lavelle's slight frown that everyone was so unaccustomed to. It was easy to notice when she was upset because she *always* had a smile on her face.

"Nothing, I just need to talk to Fraiser," she replied.

"Nope!" Natalia threw her hands up, turning and walking toward the forest. "I'm out. Good luck with that, Lavelle."

Napoleon chuckled, dipping a wooden bowl into the warm broth inside the pot. "She's forgetting our soup."

Roman's lips formed a flat line. He knew Fraiser wasn't the only reason she was walking away... He lifted his foot to start after her, but quickly set it down again. He'd deal with Fraiser first, even if it was the more cowardly thing to do. Well, now that he thought about it, it was probably just as terrifying to talk to Fraiser, too.

"It's all right." Aurum shrugged and picked up one of the many bowls next to the fire. "I'll eat her portion."

"I wouldn't recommend it," Napoleon warned. "I did that once... It didn't end well."

"Is that why you asked me to thaw that frozen pillow last week?" Aurum snickered.

Napoleon grinned. "Yes!"

Aurum rolled her eyes. "Anyway, what did Fraiser do this time?"

"We just had another young boy come to us with a sprained wrist." Lavelle crossed her arms. "It's the seventh one this week, and the girls are just as bad as the boys. She's training them too hard!"

"Speaking of training, you and I need to work on your hand-to-hand combat," Napoleon said, nudging her shoulder.

"Focus, please," she said.

"Right. Sorry." He smiled sheepishly as Lavelle shook her head with an amused smirk.

"I understand that we need to train, but we can't fight if we're all injured or recovering from injuries. Whether it be a small sprain or a broken bone, we all have to be 100 percent ready."

"You have a point." Aurum shrugged, rising with her soup. "All right, let's go talk to her. Roman, you go talk to Natalia. Napoleon, Lavelle, and I will handle this."

Roman's eyes widened. "But—"

"Nope!" Aurum grinned. "We're all tired of watching you two avoid each other. It's awkward for everyone, so just bite the bullet and talk it out."

"Agreed." Napoleon slapped Roman's back. "You got this, boss man!"

"I don't know, guys…" Roman rubbed the back of his neck, glancing off toward the forest. When he turned back around, Napoleon, Lavelle, and Aurum were halfway to the river. He watched Lavelle glance up at Napoleon.

"You need a haircut," she said.

"Ren needs one, too," Aurum added before they disappeared around the bend of the river. Roman took a deep breath. He could do this. He had survived so many difficult and life-threatening situations. He had faced death several times and survived, but it didn't stop his hands from sweating.

~

Napoleon wasn't very tall, but he towered over Lavelle by nearly a foot. He studied her as she laughed at Aurum's joke. He smiled at the sight of her dimples that only showed when she found something truly funny. She was a ray of sunshine wherever she went. He followed her and Aurum upstream in the direction of the training area, the running water a humming melody beside them. The camp had been bustling with activity over the past few days. Everyone was beginning to prepare after Roman's announcement the day they'd returned from the sectors. Napoleon hadn't even remembered the contents of the speech. His eyes had been fixed on Lavelle the entire time. Fraiser had elbowed him and repeated what Roman had said. Roman and Natalia had discovered the new train station, and the rebels would raid it during the next testings. Their orders were simple: train and prepare.

After a few short minutes, they rounded the bend in the river and came upon the training area. Crowds of young recruits stood in the clearing, watching Fraiser and a dark-haired boy. The boy charged at Fraiser and flung his fist up to her face. She easily sidestepped, grabbing the boy's wrist before flipping him over onto his back. Napoleon watched Lavelle's eyes widen before she took off toward the crowd.

"Oh, no…" Aurum glanced at Napoleon.

He met her worried brown eyes, and they both immediately started after her. "Lavelle, wait!"

"Stop!" Lavelle's voice angrily rang out from amongst the crowd. Everyone turned and froze, allowing her to push through with Napoleon and Aurum not far behind her.

"Wait, Napoleon." Aurum stuck her hand across his chest as Lavelle's blonde hair disappeared into the inside of the circle of rebels where Fraiser stood. They watched as Lavelle ran over to the boy and yanked him up off the ground. Fraiser smirked, shifting her weight to her right leg and placing a hand on her hip.

Napoleon shook his head. "We don't need to wait."

He'd known Fraiser for years, and he could tell by her stance that she was feeling threatened. The only person who was allowed to stop her training was Roman, and they had sent him after Natalia. Maybe that really had been a mistake… What if Fraiser tried to fight her like she'd done with Natalia? He balled his fists. He loved Fraiser like a sister, but he wouldn't let her touch Lavelle.

"What do you think you're doing?" Lavelle exclaimed, a heavy silence falling across the field. "And don't you *dare* say training! Do you know how many people you've sent to the hospital this week? This is not training!"

Napoleon began to push through the crowd as Fraiser rolled her green eyes. "Listen, darling—"

"Do *not* call me darling."

"They need it," Fraiser continued.

Suddenly, someone placed a hand on Napoleon's shoulder, causing him to jump. He whirled around to find Ren, worry filling his eyes.

"What's going on?" the twin asked.

Lavelle scoffed. "No, they don't, Fraiser. You're hurting them!"

"Vayne's army won't take it easy on them, so why should I? I have to prepare them to fight!"

"They can't fight with sprains and broken bones!"

"You listen carefully…" Fraiser pushed Lavelle to the ground and stood over her. "This is *my* training—"

Both Ren and Napoleon surged forward in an instant. Ren knelt behind Lavelle, lifting her up as Napoleon pushed Fraiser away and positioned himself between them. His eyes began to glow light-green around pupils as black as tar, and he could feel the earth around them building with energy—answering his call.

Fraiser frowned. "What are you doing, Napoleon?"

"Lavelle's right, Fraiser."

"The Aether, help me. Not you too," she scoffed. "These girls have you and Roman whipped. You're not really going to fight me over her, are you, Napoleon? You and I both know who will win that. Step aside." She took a menacing step toward him and glanced at Lavelle. "I'm sure Lavelle is big enough to handle her own problems, or does she always need someone to come save her?"

"Stop," Napoleon whispered. "Please, don't do this. Please, don't actually be as bad as you're made out to be. Prove me wrong. You're better than this." He shook his head, allowing the desperation to seep into his voice. "Prove to us you're better than this and just walk away."

Fraiser chuckled. "Oh, Napoleon... You always have been such the little peace-maker. You know better than to think I'll back down and just walk away. It's not happening. If I have to go through you, I will."

"Can you not let go of your pride for one *damn* second?" Napoleon exclaimed, feeling anger building up inside him. "Fraiser, we're family! How could you—"

"No, Napoleon. She is *not* my family, and if you choose her, then *you* are not my family."

"Fraiser, you're being ridiculous..." Napoleon bit the inside of his lip. He knew she was prideful and never backed down from a fight, but she'd never been this prone to starting one. This wasn't just about Lavelle interrupting her. This was about something else... But he was angry now. This was stupid, and Fraiser was beginning to cross the line. Someone needed to put her in her place...

"Choose, Napoleon! I don't have all day—"

Napoleon grunted as he sent a large chunk of earth flying at her. She barely had enough time to roll out of the way and watch it fly into the scattering crowd. It collided and shattered against the ground with a loud *crack*. He lifted his hands up and rotated them toward her, creating chains of hardened earth around her wrists. She glared at Napoleon with glowing gray irises and silver pupils. If looks could kill, he'd be dead.

"This isn't about choosing sides, and I refuse to do so," he said. A sudden sadness wrapped around his heart. He shouldn't have to fight her. "You're better than this... I know you are. I just hope you can fix whatever's bothering you so you can learn to let people in. Because if you don't, Fraiser, and you continue down this path... I'm scared you'll end up alone, and I think you're afraid of that, too."

Napoleon's eyes returned to their normal blue, intensified by the dark freckles that dotted his face. He turned his back to her and walked over to Ren and Lavelle, who both hadn't moved a muscle. The sound of the earth around Fraiser's wrists breaking apart caused him to whirl around and watch Fraiser shoot an enormous column of air at them. Without warning, Aurum leaped in front of them with glowing red and silver eyes and flung a whirlwind of fire at the column. They collided and violently spiraled up into a cascade of winds and flames that dissipated high into the air after climbing above the trees.

"Enough!" Aurum yelled. She frowned at Fraiser, pain filling her eyes as she turned to Napoleon and the twins. "Let's go..."

"Thank you," Napoleon whispered, and they all turned to start back toward the tents. The crowd disappeared as well, leaving Fraiser in the grass quiet and alone...

Aurum shook her head, her voice cracking with emotion. "Don't thank me for that."

He glanced back at Ren and Lavelle, who gave him a small smile as a token of her gratitude. She was all right. Most of them were, and that was all that mattered. He paused, taking in Lavelle's slightly reddened cheeks and the vibrant blue of her eyes. He feared he'd get lost in them forever if he stared for too long. They were a sea of blue, and she was a siren, pulling him in and trapping him under the waves. But he didn't care. In the few moments that he saw her face, it didn't matter that one of his closest friends was drowning.

~

Natalia quickened her pace at the sound of Roman's footsteps behind her. She still didn't want to talk to him, which she knew was childish, but she was just so angry. He had betrayed her, yet she felt like he was the one who couldn't trust her. He hadn't trusted her enough to tell her about his heritage until he'd had no other choice. She rolled her eyes as she broke through the edge of the forest into a small clearing she'd stumbled upon during the week. It seemed to be the only thing capable of calming her frantic mind these days. She scoffed at herself. She was being stupid. Everything about this was stupid. Stupid, stupid, *stupid*.

"Natalia!" Roman called, jogging through the brush to catch up to her.

She whirled around with her back facing the trunk of a large tree at the edge of the clearing. A small pool of freshwater sat not too far away. Natalia's eyes began to glow, and she slowly rotated her hand, weaving a snake of water between her fingers. Roman stopped dead in his tracks to watch it coil around her wrist as she locked eyes with him. She could feel her face heating with rage.

"Natalia, I'm so—" Roman barely ducked out of the way in time to watch the snake shoot over his head and crash into the forest behind him.

"If I hear you say you're sorry one more time..." She gritted her teeth and watched Roman shoot his own snake of water at her. She extended her arm, splitting the snake in half when it collided against her hand. Water sprayed to the sides. "I think I'm going to lose it..."

Roman's glowing eyes met hers once again. "I am, though. I should've told you before."

"And I should've gone looking for Damien myself, but I didn't! It's in the past, and there's nothing you can do about it now. It doesn't matter. I'm over it." She turned to walk toward the tree, but his warm hand caught her arm.

"No, you're not, Talia," he said.

That nickname. That damned nickname.

"Do *not* tell me how I do or don't feel!" She whirled around, yanking her arm free. "You have no idea what I feel!"

"Then tell me!" Roman replied, throwing his arms out helplessly. "I don't know how to fix it if you don't tell me what's wrong!"

Natalia scowled, taking a step toward him. "You betrayed me, Roman! You told Aurum who you were before you told me!"

"No, I didn't!" Roman exclaimed, also taking a step forward. "Fraiser told her, not me."

"You still knew that she knew, and you still withheld it from me *and* Ren—" Natalia suddenly froze, and her cheeks began to heat as she noticed just how close they were to each other. Their eyes locked, full of so many different emotions. Roman's head tilted slightly to the side, and Natalia found herself leaning closer. His eyes flickered down to her lips, and she felt her cheeks heat even more. Without warning, a raindrop hit the tip of her nose. They both jumped back with a start before lifting their heads toward the clouds above. Raindrops continued to fall slowly around them.

"We can't go on like this," Roman whispered. "*I* can't go on like this, Natalia."

"I just don't understand... Why didn't you tell me before?" Her voice broke with emotion. "Did you not trust me?"

"I was afraid you'd hate me." He let out a shaky breath.

She shook her head. "That's stupid, Roman. I couldn't hate you even if I wanted to."

He blinked, lips parting as if he'd heard her say it before—as if he were having déjà vu. A few moments of silence passed before he spoke softly but not weakly.

"Are you sure? Others hate me. Hell, I hate *myself* because of my *father*. Every part of me that I don't like comes from him. Vayne haunts me every day of my life, and sometimes even seeing my own reflection makes me sick."

"Roman...," Natalia mumbled.

"So many people have judged me because of my father and still do. I didn't want you to think any different of me... I'm still...me. I'm still the same Roman who dragged you out of the train station." He gave her a small smile. "The same Roman who absolutely destroyed you in a thumb war."

Natalia raised a brow. "I wouldn't say *destroyed*."

He chuckled, but his smile quickly faded. "The point is, I *never* want you to see or even think of me like him."

Sadness filled his gaze, and his eyes seemed a darker brown than usual. It was as if all his demons were at the surface now, clawing and scratching to break free. She now understood why he hadn't told her. He had wanted her to see him as his own, separate person. He wasn't a monster like his father, and she knew that. He was just Roman—not Roman *Averie*. It was that plain and simple. She was still upset with him, but she knew he never meant to hurt her. He never wanted to hurt anyone. He was kind, funny, loved his people, and tried to protect everyone. He put too much pressure on himself and worked himself too hard sometimes. As much as she hated to admit it, he was the thumb-war champion, too. But unlike his father, he was good... Truly good.

Natalia sighed. "I think I'm the one who owes you an apology."

"No." He shook his head. "You don't. I promise, you don't."

"So, we're all good now?"

Roman chuckled. "As long as you don't go and chuck another bottle at Fraiser, yes, we are."

She rolled her eyes. "She deserved it."

"I'm sure she did." Roman laughed again, and Natalia joined him, studying the faint dimples that popped up on his cheeks when he truly smiled. She was glad they had settled everything. She had been miserable the entire week, and it felt good to hear him laugh again.

The rain began to trickle down harder from the light-gray clouds above, growing heavier and heavier. Natalia blinked profusely and held her wet palms out with a large grin. She looked over at Roman, who returned her smile. His eyes began to glow dark-blue and silver before he playfully shot a sphere of raindrops at her. She sidestepped and fired her own sphere at him. Roman wiped his hand out across his body, recycling the throw and sending it back at Natalia. Together, they laughed as they ran around, launching spheres of water toward each other in the pouring rain...

~

When Natalia and Roman finally returned to the camp, the sun was beginning to set. The rain had lasted only a few minutes, but they were drenched.

"There you two are!" Napoleon waved with a grin as the two walked into the encirclement of tents. "Are we all good now?"

Natalia laughed with a nod at the sight of him. His hair was wet, and his eyes were sparkling with amusement. He looked like a drenched puppy. "Looks like the rain caught you guys, too."

"Well, I was trying to cut *someone's* hair, but..." Lavelle said, flicking Napoleon. "Of course, he picked the worst time to do it."

"Where are the others?" Roman asked, eyes twinkling with amusement.

"Aurum and Ren went to go get food for everyone," she answered.

"Hey, wait." Natalia raised a brow at the empty bowls on the ground. "Napoleon, where's my soup?"

Napoleon's eyes widened, and he threw his hands up defensively. "Uh, it wasn't me! I swear!"

"Aurum...," Natalia mumbled. "That little—"

"Who's hungry?" Ren announced as he and Aurum crossed over the river. Trays of hardened earth sat in their hands with food piled high.

"I brought you strawberries *and* blueberries to make up for the soup," Aurum offered with a cheeky smile when she passed Natalia.

Natalia smirked. "I'll accept them, but I'm still going to get you back."

"I'll help," Napoleon whispered with a wink.

"I don't know if you want to get involved in *that* war, Napoleon," Lavelle warned.

He shrugged. "I'll take my chances, but only after we've eaten."

Natalia, Napoleon, Lavelle, and Roman sat down while Aurum and Ren set the trays of food down around the fire pit. Aurum casually twisted her wrist, conjuring a flame on her fingertips. Her eyes began to glow red and silver, and she tossed the flame into the fire, setting it ablaze. Then the two joined the others on the ground, passing around plates and bowls. Natalia watched as all her friends laughed around her at whatever stupid joke Aurum had just told. But the laughter didn't pierce her ears, and neither did the fake laugh she added to the mix. Her thoughts wandered to Damien. She knew he'd be right up in the middle of the mischief if he were here.

"Are you all right?" Roman whispered, gently nudging her arm.

She looked over at him with a small smile. His hair was still damp, but his eyes seemed to be on fire, like the life and energy they usually held had crept back into them. Was that because of her? Was it because he, too, was happy that they had worked everything out? For a moment, she wished they were out in the forest again, dancing and playing in the rain. She wished that they were as close as they had been when screaming at each other... The thought of what could have happened between them sent shivers down her spine.

"Yeah, I'm good. Are you?" she returned, hoping he couldn't see her cheeks reddening.

He grinned. "I'm exactly where I want to be."

"We should start training again tomorrow," Natalia said. "We need to start preparing for the testings."

"Yeah, and you could definitely use some training." Roman smirked. "You looked rusty earlier today."

"Oh, shut up," Natalia said, elbowing him. He chuckled.

"Wait, did I hear you correctly?" Napoleon exclaimed at Aurum, eyes wide. "Did you just say that Natalia threw a knife at you?"

Natalia's face lit up. "No, no, no! That is *not* how it went!"

"Yeah, it is." Aurum said, but the gleam in her eyes said otherwise. "Come on, twins, back me up here."

"Oh, no." Ren shook his head.

Lavelle bit into her apple. "We're staying out of this one."

"Okay, but you need the context of the story first, Napoleon," Natalia said.

"I'd love to hear this." Roman laughed, leaning back against one of the logs that sat near the crackling fire. Aurum sat across from them with Ren, who kept nonchalantly trying to inch closer to Napoleon and Lavelle with an overly protective look on his face.

"Yes, do tell, Natalia," Fraiser's voice rang out. Everyone froze as she plopped down next to Natalia, who didn't even try to hide her scowl. Fraiser smirked. "Oh, please, don't let me stop you."

"Damien and I were throwing knives. Aurum scared us, and I threw a knife near her head. The end," Natalia spat, her good mood shattering within seconds. The camp fell silent, and she watched Napoleon glance around nervously. Aurum simply sat there while Roman and Ren picked at the grass. Lavelle joined Natalia in casting a glare at Fraiser.

"Look...," Fraiser sighed, standing. "I know I'm not the easiest to get along with..."

Natalia scoffed and rolled her eyes. "Yeah, we know."

Roman threw a handful of grass at her. She swatted the grass away and shook her head with a small smile as he flashed a quick wink.

"Just shut up and listen, please," Fraiser continued, her voice sincere. She turned to face Lavelle. "I'm sorry about today. I shouldn't have done what I did... Napoleon, Aurum, and Ren, my apologies to you all as well. I was angry, and if I'm being completely honest..." She took a deep breath. "I was scared, too. I still am, but that's no excuse. Just know, I'm sorry... Natalia, I shouldn't have said what I did to you, but I'm not sorry about it..."

Natalia locked eyes with her. They weren't friends. She didn't know if they ever could be, and she didn't really *want* to be. But there seemed to be some sort of mutual respect for each other now. They were both powerful, and they cared about a lot of the same people. Natalia dipped her head in acknowledgment, then returned her attention to her food. She didn't want to hear anything else Fraiser had to say...

~

Napoleon stood outside of his tent, watching everyone file into their own. He glanced across at Roman, who laughed at whatever Natalia had said. He smiled. He was so happy that they'd worked everything out. He'd never seen Roman look at anyone the way he looked at her. Aurum clapped Fraiser on the shoulder before getting up from her spot in the grass and heading into her tent. The hair on Napoleon's neck and arms rose, feeling a set of eyes boring into his back. He turned to find Ren staring at him scrutinizingly.

"Hey." Lavelle suddenly appeared next to him with a smile on her face. "Are you all right?"

He nodded, glad to have a reason to turn away from Ren. He'd been watching Napoleon all night, and he couldn't figure out why. "Yeah, I just wanted to talk to Fraiser before she went to bed. I'm scared that something's wrong, because she never apologizes... What about you? Are you okay?"

"Like you said, she apologized." Lavelle shrugged. "She's forgiven, but I won't forget what she did. I don't understand why she did it in the first place. It doesn't make sense to me."

"Fraiser's life has always been hard. She's never had it easy," Napoleon said, glancing at Fraiser, who sipped from a wooden cup presumably filled with Brennivan.

"What do you mean?" she asked.

Napoleon sighed. "Well, it's not really my story to tell..."

"Which is exactly why *you* shouldn't tell it," Fraiser said, stumbling over from the fire she'd just extinguished with a gust of wind. Her glowing gray and silver eyes returned to their normal green. She turned to Lavelle. "My whole life, I was an orphan in Sector One with my little sister. She was always sick, and I was always struggling to keep us both alive. When I was around ten, she passed away...

"A few weeks later, I fought against Vayne alongside Roman's mother. That's how I met him. His mother and the rebels had been sneaking over the walls to try and help those in the orphanage who were sick. It was no use, though, but that's how I knew they were good—how I knew I could trust them. They kept trying to save her even though they knew she was dying. I had no one left in One and nowhere to go, so I joined them. I knew they would keep me safe, and I wouldn't be alone. It was the perfect opportunity, and I took it..."

"Fraiser...," Lavelle mumbled. "I'm so sorry..."

Fraiser shrugged. "It was years ago. Besides, I don't need your pity."

"I didn't mean it like that...," she said. She took a hesitant step forward and wrapped her arms around Fraiser, embracing her in a hug. "I am sorry, though."

Fraiser pulled away gently. "Uh, thanks..."

"Fra—" Napoleon began, but Fraiser quickly cut him off.

"No, Napoleon." She frowned. "You need to know how truly sorry I am about today. I should've never put you in that position... I know I don't say it much, but I love you...so much. You remind me of my little sister, and I consider you my little brother. The last thing I wanted to do was hurt you."

Napoleon smiled. "I know, Fraiser, and I know how hard it can be for you to trust new people. Just take your time, okay?"

"See, that's one thing I don't have... None of us do." She chuckled morbidly. "Time..."

Napoleon and Lavelle glanced at each other as Fraiser drained the remains of her cup and walked over to Roman, who had been standing next to his tent and watching them. They watched Fraiser's head drop as she spoke before she grabbed and hugged him. Napoleon hoped that things would get easier for her. He knew she had major trust issues and rarely opened up to anyone at all, but what she told Lavelle tonight was a start. A *good* start. And he was so glad that she had chosen Lavelle.

Maybe she could even become friends with Natalia at some point. He would love it if she could, but he couldn't stop himself from worrying about what Fraiser has said.

See, that's one thing I don't have... None of us do.

Time...

CHAPTER SEVENTEEN

THE CALM BEFORE THE STORM

Natalia and Napoleon darted through the crowd of frantic rebels. Araedians and Elementals alike, all dressed in mismatched clothing, ran around everywhere. The camp was bustling, everyone packing supplies to travel for the upcoming battle. Fraiser was right. They didn't have any time left. The month of preparation had passed in a blur, and the testings would occur at the end of the week. Natalia was afraid they still weren't ready—weren't prepared for every possible obstacle or outcome.

"This is the second time this week!" Napoleon shouted, ducking under a pile of crates a group of rebels was moving.

"Hey, it's not my fault we're late for training today. You were the one who wanted to stop for cocoa cakes!" Natalia returned as the two continued to weave their way through the crowd and tents in the direction of the training area. She paused before the river, turning to watch Napoleon jog up beside her while he wiped cocoa powder from the tip of his nose.

He rolled his eyes. "You didn't exactly try to stop me."

"Oh, shut up," Natalia said, flicking her hand at him. Water shot up from the river, splashing his face, and her eyes shone ice-blue and silver for a brief moment before returning to their normal blue-gray. She watched a bright smile spread across his face as he shook his head in disbelief. Yet again, the gleam in his blue eyes—the gleam of adventure and life—reminded her of Damien, except he was a lot more calm and peaceful. Damien never seemed to be in reach of those two emotions, not with everything he had going on in his life.

"I'd get you back for that, but we're already late as it is," he said, playfully pushing her.

He would've loved you..., Natalia thought, shaking her head with a laugh. "Come on."

Napoleon's eyes began to glow light-green around his black pupils, and he extended his arms out toward the river. A section of the riverbed rose up from under the water, creating a small bridge for them to cross. Small railings a few inches high barred the sides.

Natalia clicked her tongue, throwing a glance at him over her shoulder. "Fancy."

"I told you." He shrugged. "I've been practicing."

She watched his eyes return to their normal blue, and they walked across to the others standing in the clearing. She stopped and rolled her eyes at the sight of Fraiser, who whirled to face them with a scowl on her face. *Big* shocker. Natalia's eyes immediately wandered behind Fraiser, where Roman stood next to Aurum and the twins, and she barely noticed when Fraiser marched up to her and Napoleon.

"You're late," she snapped, her voice laced with venom.

"Well, we're here now." Napoleon smiled, sheepishly rubbing the back of his neck.

Natalia's eyes flickered to Roman, who stifled a laugh behind Fraiser. Fraiser turned back to him with a vicious glare. "Roman, I swear—"

He coughed, attempting to hide his laughter. "Sorry."

"My sincerest apologies, Your Highness," Natalia mocked with a curtsey. "Could you ever find it in your miserable little heart to forgive us?"

Fraiser clenched her fists angrily.

"I think she can," Roman said, walking between Fraiser and Natalia with a cheeky grin. He winked at Natalia before turning to Fraiser. "Can we just start training already?"

"Fine," she returned with a forced smile—well, Natalia supposed it was more of a grimace than a smile. "Natalia, you can partner with *me*."

"Actually," Roman said, leaning against Fraiser's shoulder. "I think Elementals of the same element should train together today. We get more out of it."

Fraiser frowned and batted his arm away. "I train *everyone*. I always pick who trains with who."

"But I *lead* everyone." Roman nudged her, his grin widening. "And I say she trains with me."

Fraiser's tone grew low and serious. "You won't be leader for long if you keep acting like this." She threw a side-eyed glare at Natalia before turning, grabbing Napoleon's arm, and dragging him over to Aurum and the twins. "Aurum, you're with me. Napoleon, you're with the twins. Everyone will start with hand-to-hand combat. We need to be able to defend ourselves if we're somewhere we can't use our elements, or if you can't draw from a source."

Natalia noted the small canteen strapped to Roman's belt. He always kept one with him ever since they'd returned from the sectors. Earth and water Elementals had to have a constant source of their element to draw from. It was their only disadvantage. Without their sources, they were nearly powerless.

"After hand-to-hand, we'll move on to elements. When we do, we'll spar one pair at a time. It's just as valuable to observe a fight as it is to fight in one," Fraiser added before turning away from the pairs to talk with Aurum.

"Don't worry," Roman began, a mischievous glint in his golden-brown eyes. "I'll go easy on you."

Natalia scoffed. "Oh, please, we both know who's better at hand-to-hand."

"I never thought you'd admit to my superiority, but—"

"Now you're just being ridiculous," she interrupted as they started to circle each other slowly. She watched Roman's eyes search her body while she searched his, both looking for flaws or an opening to attack. Natalia pursed her lips. She found nothing but strong muscles and stubble on his chin. Fed up with the anticipation, she lunged out with her left fist. Roman swiftly ducked and countered with a jab of his own. The two circled and danced around each other, neither landing a blow. Natalia sidestepped one of his punches to counter with a kick toward his side. He caught the edge of her boot, yanking her to the ground.

She landed with a *thud*, only to swiftly sweep Roman's feet out from under him, taking him down with her. They swiftly rose and paused. Mischief gleamed in Roman's eyes, but Natalia was ready. Without warning, he unscrewed the cap to his canteen and shot a rocket of water toward her, eyes glowing dark blue and silver. Her own eyes glowing their silver and ice-blue, she extended her arms and flicked the water to the side before it circled around her. She then threw her hands forward, redirecting the blast of water back at him. Roman shot his hand out, splintering the blast into a cascade of mist and crystal-like raindrops. The two's laughter filled the air.

"Hey!" Fraiser exclaimed, standing over Aurum, who sat on the ground with a huff. "I told you two, no elements!"

"Relax, we're just having some fun," Natalia said.

Fraiser's eyes narrowed. "Oh, and I guess that's what Vayne and his soldiers are doing, too. It's all fun and games for you, isn't it? Do you think Damien is having fun right now?"

"Fraiser...," Aurum warned, getting up and stepping toward her with a cold look. "*Don't* go there."

"No." Fraiser held a hand up. "I'm sick and tired of everyone not taking training seriously. We won't be ready if you keep this up."

"We've been training for nearly an entire month—" Ren began before Natalia cut him off.

"Which is exactly why I think we could use some fun. Yes, the testings are soon, but there's no use in exhausting ourselves now. So, I don't know about you guys, but I'm done with training for today," Natalia said and turned to face the river.

"Fine," Fraiser sneered. "Come on, everyone. We can move on to elements now."

"Actually," Roman said with a shrug. "I think I'm done, too."

"What?" Fraiser spat between gritted teeth.

"Well, if you two are done..." Napoleon walked over to Roman and Natalia. "...I guess that means I'm done."

Natalia swore she could see steam seeping from Fraiser's ears. "We have *three* days left until we have to leave for the train station. *Three*, and you'd all rather run around like *children*?"

"Natalia has a point, Fraiser," Aurum said. "We've been nonstop training for weeks. I really don't think there's anything else you can teach us. We're either ready, or we're not."

"What are you smiling at?" Fraiser exclaimed angrily as a smirk appeared on Natalia's face. "This isn't a joke!"

Natalia's smirk grew into a full-out grin, and she turned, sprinting toward the river with the twins, Napoleon, Aurum, and Roman behind her. She glanced back to watch Fraiser exclaim in frustration and chase after them. She didn't disagree with Fraiser. Training was important, but like Aurum had said, it was all they'd done nonstop for weeks. They were ready whether Fraiser thought so or not, but she had to admit that the testings *had* snuck up on them. The camp had gone from peaceful to constant chaos within days. Everyone was nervous, and Fraiser's constant hounding wasn't helping at all. They needed a distraction. They needed some fun.

Natalia's eyes began to glow again when she extended her left hand, freezing a layer of ice on top of the river. She skipped onto it, sliding across to the other side with the others following swiftly after. Ren paused next to Natalia as Fraiser approached the river. He took a depth breath before opening his glowing dark-green and black eyes and stomping on the ground. The earth beneath him rippled at Fraiser like waves, knocking her off her feet. Natalia and Ren snickered and took off after the others, the bridge of ice disappearing behind them.

~

The sun had fallen behind the trees, and the night was growing cold as Roman walked through the rebel camp, firewood piled high in his arms. Natalia, Aurum, Napoleon, and the twins were all back at their encirclement of tents, eating and enjoying each other's company. Fraiser had made herself scarce since training earlier that day, which worried him, but Fraiser always worried him. It had been that way since they first met. She was brutally honest and unpredictable, yet reliable. She didn't like to open up and closed herself off as much as she could.

He needed to check on her and make sure she was all right. She was his closest friend, and he felt like he'd been abandoning her for weeks. He hadn't meant to. He'd just gotten too caught up in planning and training. But the clock was ticking. They had about a week left until the testings, and he needed to make sure she was ready. The others seemed to be. In fact, after today, the whole camp appeared prepared. The rebels had been training and gathering supplies for the past few weeks, and for once in his life, Roman wasn't scared to face his father and his army. He was confident in his people.

Lost in thought, he trudged straight through the river separating the main camp from their encirclement of tents. He cursed himself with a small laugh and walked through the tents to the fire and those gathered around it. The twins were laughing at some shared memory, while Napoleon, Aurum, and Natalia argued over which elemental weapon was the best. Roman's eyes locked with Natalia's as he passed them and set the wood down near the fire. She flashed him a quick smile.

"Hey, boss man," Napoleon said with a grin. "I need you to help me out here."

Roman chuckled. "What is it?"

"Please tell Napoleon and Natalia that they're wrong, and whips and swords are the best elemental weapons." Aurum shrugged.

"Okay, whips aren't *terrible*, but—" Natalia began only for Aurum to chuck a grape at her head.

"Nope! I'm right, and you two are wrong," she said.

Napoleon rolled his eyes. "Whatever, Aurum."

"Come sit with us," Natalia offered with another smile.

He returned the smile but remained standing. "I would, but I need to go find Fraiser. I'll see you guys in a little bit."

"Later, boss man!" Napoleon called as Roman turned toward the darkening forest.

He knew where Fraiser would be. She always went to the tallest tree at the top of the highest hill surrounding their camp. He trudged through the forest heavily. His feet were tired, and so was his mind. All the training and preparing were beginning to take a toll on him. Now what they needed was rest in order to be ready for the testings. Roman's calves began to burn halfway up the hill. He used the trees around him to pull himself further. He reached the top and sat down, leaning his back against the trunk of a tree.

"I could hear you coming from a mile away," Fraiser called down from among the branches. Roman glanced up, but he couldn't find her. She was too far up. "I seriously don't think you could've been any louder."

"Quit it." Roman chuckled.

"What do you mean?"

He smirked. "Quit rolling your eyes at me."

She swung down from her branch, landing a few feet to Roman's left with crossed arms. "You couldn't even see me. How do you know if I rolled my eyes?"

"Oh, come on, Fraiser. You know how well we know each other. Sometimes I know how you're feeling before you know it yourself."

She rolled her eyes. Again. "Why'd you come up here?"

"Do I have to have a reason to come talk to my best friend?"

"Oh, come on, Roman," she mocked, shifting her weight to her right leg. "We both know how well we know each other."

What am I going to do with you? Roman thought. She hadn't changed a bit since they'd met, and she never would. He could always count on her to be his constant, even if things had been changing lately. "Okay, so I may or may not have a reason, but it's a good one."

"I can't *wait* to hear this," Fraiser said, joining him on the ground. She tore at a blade of grass. "What do you want?"

"I just wanted to see how you were doing." He smiled. She raised a suspicious brow, and he held his hands up defensively. "What? I'm serious, Fraiser... I feel like we haven't had a chance to talk in forever, and the testings are coming up... How are you?"

Fraiser inhaled deeply before turning to face him. Her green eyes were sad and distant, and like him, she looked tired. "I'm afraid...," she whispered.

Roman's brows knitted. "Why?"

"I believe in our cause with all my heart, and I truly think we can pull this off. I know we can beat your father, especially if this next testing goes according to plan. If it's successful, and Lavelle is right about that Hero kid rallying the people, I think we'll win..."

"So why are you afraid?"

"Because even though I think *we* are winning, I feel like *I* am losing. No one has taken training seriously for the past few days. It's like the newbies don't realize we're about to risk our lives for this cause. To me, they're not true rebels because of that. They haven't risked what we've risked, and you and Napoleon have changed." She pulled at more grass. "I know I haven't been the easiest person to get along with, especially when it comes to the newbies—"

"You get along with Aurum just fine." Roman shrugged. "I think Natalia's the only one you have a real problem with."

Fraiser glared at him. "Let's not get into that tonight... I think we'd both like to walk away from this conversation as friends and not enemies."

"Agreed." He nodded. "I'm sorry, continue."

"You have to admit, though. You and Napoleon *have* changed, and that's okay. There's nothing wrong with that, but...I can't stop thinking about what Napoleon said to me when I tried to make him choose between me and Lavelle."

"What did he say?"

"He said that if I continue down the path I'm on, he's afraid I'll end up alone. He said that he thought I was afraid of that, too. Well, I think Napoleon may be right. I don't want to be alone, but sometimes I feel like I already am."

"Fraiser, I am *always* with you. You know I am," Roman said, leaning forward and grabbing her shoulders. "Look at me. I won't leave you, and you don't have to be afraid. You may not get along with *everyone*, but we *all* fight for each other."

She shook her head. "But someone has to be able to sacrifice and make the hard choices that no one wants to make, Roman. You have so many people that you care about, and there are so many people that care about you. You won't sacrifice them to win."

Roman pulled away. "And you will?" He shook his head. "You're not like that, Fraiser."

"But I am. If it came down to it, and I had to choose between you and Natalia, I'd choose you. You would hate me for the rest of our lives, but you'd be alive. If I have to choose between you and Napoleon and them, I will always choose to sacrifice them. I'm selfish, and I can't live without you two. I know that we're not all going to make it out of this... You and the others run around like children and act like we're all going to be here when this is over, but we're not. Some of us could die before this week is over."

Roman sighed. "Look, I know we haven't taken the past few days as seriously as we should have, but I think everyone's just frightened and looking for fun to lift the tension. A little fun before the big mission is good for us."

"I guess I can see where you're coming from, but I don't work like that. Raiding this station isn't going to be easy... To win, we'll have to do whatever it takes. I know you, Roman. You'll sacrifice yourself before you let anyone else do so, but I won't let you... I can't."

"Fraiser—"

"*That's* why I feel alone. *That's* why I feel like I'm losing, but it's worth it to me. If in order for us to win, I have to lose, then I'll lose." Fraiser rose from the ground, taking a few steps back toward the camp. "This is my way of showing that I care."

Roman sat up and watched Fraiser flash him a small smile before turning into the forest. He watched her disappear among the brush, wondering how his best friend had become so distant and cutthroat. Like she said, it was her way of showing that she cared... But it sucked. He ran a hand through his hair with a sigh. She was right. He'd sacrifice himself for any one of the rebels in a heartbeat. They were his people as were Fraiser, Napoleon, the twins, Aurum, and Natalia, so how could he save everyone? Whether he liked to admit it or not, Fraiser made a good point. Could they all make it out of this alive?

He leaned his head back against the tree, staring up into the night sky through the branches. In the distance, stars twinkled magnificently. He wished Natalia were here with him now to see them. He bit the inside of his cheek. He would make sure she got out of this. He would make sure they *all* got out of this, even if it was the last thing he ever did...

~

Two days remained. The rebels had two days to cover the distance between their camp and the new train station before the testings began. Natalia watched Roman as he stood atop a stack of barrels, shouting directions and assigning companies to the rebels gathered in the square. They were to meet at the training grounds near the edge of the forest within the half hour. All supplies, weapons, and armor had been gathered, and those who were going to stay were saying their goodbyes. She inhaled deeply, nerves settling over her. So many people depended on the rebels' success. If they failed to gather more rebels and inspire those inside the sectors to fight back, they'd lose momentum, and their revolution would crumble to pieces... Then there was Damien. She still had no idea where he was, or what had happened to him after his capture. Maybe she could find him during the testings...

Natalia shook the thought away. It was becoming too difficult to juggle the weight of what her heart and her mind were telling her. She knew she had to focus on the mission and the fate of the sectors, but she wanted to find Damien, too... She hadn't forgotten him during the past month, not for a single moment. She sighed. She had other things to worry about—like Lavelle accompanying them. With no element, how could she defend herself? Even though they had taught her hand-to-hand combat, she was just so tiny and...sweet. Would she *really* defend herself when it came down to it? What about the others? Were they ready for this? Was *she* ready for this?

"Are you all right?" Roman asked.

Natalia jumped, completely unaware that he'd walked up next to her. She held her hand to her chest, her heartbeat skyrocketing.

He grinned. "Sorry, I didn't mean to scare you."

"It's okay." She smiled. "And yes, I'm all right. I'm just a little worried about Lavelle... And everyone else, and you and Damien..."

"Hey." Roman grabbed her hand, holding it between his own. "We're going to be fi—"

"Let's move it." Fraiser sneered as she walked between them, tearing their hands apart. She turned back to them with a glare colder than ice. "Everyone is ready except for you two."

Natalia's brows narrowed, and she took a step toward her. Her nerves immediately disappeared, and anger flooded through her. Roman grabbed her arm, holding her in place. Fraiser waited a moment before sighing frustratingly and starting to the training grounds.

"We're going to be fine. I'm not going to let anything happen to us," he said with a small smile.

Natalia glanced after Fraiser. "I'm not going to either..."

Together, she and Roman walked through the eerily empty camp. Around thirty pairs of eyes of the ones who would be staying behind stared at them. Some in worry, some in confidence and pride, and some in awe, particularly the few children within the camp. A small blonde-headed girl smiled and waved at Natalia as she passed. She returned her own smile and gave a small wave. Not only was the camp empty, but it was also silent. She felt like the slightest noise would set off a time bomb. Even the gathering of rebels in the clearing was quiet when they parted for Natalia and Roman. Several rebels held guns and spears, and the majority wore different pieces of armor, all stolen from Vayne's army and his soldiers. Others wore their familiar mismatched clothing and held deadly looking makeshift weapons. They appeared prepared. Fraiser, the twins, Napoleon, and Aurum waited for them at the edge of the forest.

"About time," Fraiser huffed with a roll of her eyes.

"Are you incapable of doing anything other than complaining or rolling your eyes?" Natalia asked.

"All right," Roman began, ignoring Fraiser and Natalia. "Napoleon, you and the twins will lead our underground companies through the tunnels under the sectors. Fraiser, Aurum, and Natalia, you three will join me as my above-ground team. Our job is to get everyone into the tunnels, then find our way around the walls to the tunnel's exit. Any questions so far?"

Napoleon shook his head. "Nope, we've been over the plan a thousand times. We got it, boss man."

"The other rebels know what they're doing, too," Aurum added with a smile. "They've also been over the plan a thousand times. We're ready, Roman."

Fraiser nodded. "Just give the order."

Natalia looked at Roman as he faced her, their eyes locking. He studied her with such an intensity, she wondered if he thought this would be the last time they'd see each other. She nodded at him encouragingly. She didn't know what exactly had changed between them. Ever since that rainy day in the forest... Things had been noticeably different. She didn't mind the change, though. For once, being open around him didn't scare her so badly that she shook... She had absolutely no clue what would come of it, but she didn't really care. They could be dead by the week's end, and—no. She wouldn't think like that. She knew they would survive this. They were all ready.

Roman just had to say the words...

"Rebels!" he shouted, his golden-brown eyes never leaving hers. "Move out!"

The mass of rebels erupted into thunderous cheers, raising their weapons high into the air. Roman's hand found Natalia's, and together, they began to walk into the depths of the forest toward the sectors. His touch sent electrical currents throughout her body, and adrenaline pumped through her veins.

"I wouldn't be surprised if Vayne heard that all the way from One," Lavelle said.

"If he didn't, he'll hear it soon." Natalia smirked, the rebel camp disappearing amongst the trees behind them...

~

Hours passed before the sun finally set, concealing the rebels in complete darkness. They continued on through the forest toward the distant walls of Sector Four. Napoleon explained the underground teams' route through the tunnels to Natalia as they walked on. She shivered at the thought of being trapped underground.

She shook her head. "I'm never going down there."

"It's not as bad as it sounds." Napoleon chuckled. Natalia raised a brow at him, continuing on.

It was nearing dawn when Sector Four's walls and beaming searchlights became visible through the walls of trees. Natalia and Roman knelt behind a cluster of bushes, while the rest of the rebels waited several yards behind in the thick brush.

"Do you see that boulder over there?" Roman asked, tilting Natalia's head a little to the right.

"Yes." She nodded, squinting at the outline of the boulder that could be seen amongst the brush and trees.

"The entrance to the tunnels is underneath it. That's where we need to go."

"What about the searchlights?" she questioned, wondering how they'd get the entire army to the boulder without being spotted.

"I've sent some fire Elementals down that way," he began, pointing to the left. "They're going to light some small fires. We don't need a big distraction, we just need them to think they see scouts back that way. Come on, let's get closer."

Slowly, the two crept toward the boulder, jumping behind other rocks, trees, and bushes to avoid the dangerous beams of light sweeping across the forest like starving snakes.

"Has security always been this bad?" Natalia asked when they ducked behind two trees that had grown intertwined. A rustling in the bushes beside them made her jump, and she looked over to find Fraiser beside them.

"No," she answered. "It's gotten worse, but the guards on the walls should be gone any second."

Roman pointed at the searchlights. "Look!" The five beams dwindled to two, then to one. "They did it. Fraiser, signal the army forward and get Aurum to meet us at the boulder."

"On it." Fraiser nodded, disappearing into the dark forest.

The mass of rebels slowly began to follow after Roman and Natalia, who continued on to the boulder. Soon, Fraiser and Aurum met them beside it with glowing red-and-gray irises and silver pupils. Natalia's and Roman's eyes began to glow their blues and silvers as well, and the four began to push against the boulder, slowly moving it off the wooden trapdoor underneath. Fraiser knelt and yanked it open, and a cool breeze flew up, whipping Natalia's hair across her face. Fraiser made a short, sharp whistle, and rebels in small groups of five came running out of the forest, slowly descending into the tunnels. Different shades of oranges and reds filled the tunnels as the fire Elementals inside carried flames for light.

Several long minutes passed before the bulk of the rebels, which totaled a little over seven hundred, were below. Napoleon and the twins stood next to Roman, Natalia, Fraiser, and Aurum, waiting while the last few climbed down.

"Well, this is it...," Napoleon said.

"Please, be careful," Natalia said, squeezing the twins. She then turned to Napoleon, taking a step forward and hugging him tightly before whispering into his ear, "Promise me you won't let them die, and promise me *you* won't die, either."

"I will always promise you that," he whispered in return and hugged her tighter. He pulled away with a small smile before quickly hugging Aurum and Fraiser and clapping Roman on the shoulders. "Good luck."

"Good luck," Roman replied with a nod.

Lavelle flashed them all an encouraging smile, then climbed down into the tunnels followed by Ren and Napoleon. Natalia, afraid she would never see them again, tried to memorize their faces as Aurum closed the door. Roman, Natalia, Aurum, and Fraiser then slid the boulder back into place and turned back into the woods as soon as the searchlights began to reappear. The battle would soon begin...

CHAPTER EIGHTEEN

FIGHTING FIRE WITH FIRE

The late morning sun shone above when the searchlights finally disappeared behind them. Natalia, Aurum, and Fraiser continued to follow Roman past the walls of Sector Four deep into the dense forest. A half-hour passed before he came to a stop in front of a large twisting tree. A small wooden door, one of the underground tunnels' many hidden exits, sat embedded into the bark.

"Why didn't we use this last time?" Natalia huffed as she and Roman pulled against the door. Behind them, Fraiser and Aurum glanced around nervously.

"Well, we didn't know the station was out this way, and we had to meet back at the overhang, remember?" he asked, eyes meeting hers.

She shrugged. "Well, at least we can use it now."

Natalia still couldn't believe they were making their move against Vayne. Just a month ago, they were getting Lavelle out of the sectors and trying to find the location of the next station, and now they were about to attack it. Everything was moving so quickly, she hardly had the time to process it, and what little free time she'd had was spent trying to figure out how to rescue Damien. But everything she thought of led them away from the train station, and she couldn't abandon the rebels to go look for him. They still had no idea where exactly he was or what side he was on. Secretly, she hoped she would run into him at the station. If she did, she vowed not to leave unless he came with her. She wouldn't leave him behind again. The thought of never saving him made her heart ache.

Her eyes widened as the door stubbornly lurched open, sending Natalia and Roman tumbling backward. Aurum and Fraiser ran over to them and lifted them up. Napoleon and the twins emerged minutes later, hands shading their eyes from the bright sun. Another few minutes passed, and the entirety of the rebel army was back in one organized piece and ready to move out. Roman appeared next to Natalia, who scanned the forest. It would take them a while to get to the station, especially with this many people.

"Are you all right?" he asked, staring intently into her eyes. "You look a little nervous."

Natalia nodded. "I'm okay."

"Then let's get going." Roman smiled before starting into the forest once more.

~

Hours passed as the army trudged onward. The sun was beginning to set behind the canopy of tall trees when the long, metal train station identical to the first broke through the forest. Train tracks protruded from the back of the building—a new addition since Natalia and Roman's last visit. How many Araedians' memories had been lost to build that track? The station had just been brought to life, and soldiers, superior officers, and conductors entered the large doors held to the ceiling by chains. Natalia shivered. She hated these buildings. They reminded her of her failure to save those she loved—Vale *and* Damien. They reminded her of what could go wrong, and what could happen to them if things ended badly. But she couldn't afford to think about that now. It was nearly time.

"Aurum, Frasier," Roman quietly called. "Make sure everyone remains with their assigned companies and begin positioning. We don't have much longer to wait..."

Natalia glared at the station and imagined burning it to the ground as Lavelle walked up next to her, wearing her usual smile.

"Where will you be?" Natalia questioned.

"Outside with the other medics and a few rebels..." She took a deep breath. "I can't believe we're about to do this."

Natalia huffed. "Just think about our lives a few months ago compared to now. We were running around like chickens with their heads cut off, trying to figure out what to do about the testings."

"And now we're about to stop them alongside the rebels."

"Not alongside..." Natalia shook her head and smiled. It was one of the most genuine smiles of her entire life. She'd dreamt of an opportunity like this since she was a little kid. "As one of them."

Lavelle smiled. "Promise me you'll be careful, Natalia."

"I think you should be making Napoleon promise you that." She chuckled.

Lavelle's face turned bright red. "Ah, yes, the daring Napoleon. I will definitely make him promise that..."

"Did I hear my name?" Napoleon interrupted, throwing his arms around Natalia's and Lavelle's shoulders.

"Maybe." Lavelle shrugged in embarrassment.

A smile spread across Napoleon's face. He went to reply when Ren suddenly squeezed his way between Napoleon and Lavelle.

"How's it going over here?" Ren questioned with a fake grin.

Natalia bit her tongue to keep from laughing. They were only hidden within the tree line of the forest, so they had to keep quiet around the station, but Ren was making that *extremely* difficult. Lavelle cast a glance at Natalia, a silent plea for help. Natalia snickered. "We're fine. Lavelle is being her usual self and worrying about all of us."

"Promise me you two will be safe, please." She turned to Ren and Napoleon.

Napoleon threw his arm around Ren, who raised a brow. "Don't worry, Lavelle. Ren and I are in the same company, so I'll make sure he doesn't knock *too* many heads in."

The twin smirked, a hunger for violence filling his eyes. "We'll be fine, Lavelle. Don't worry about us."

Natalia smiled as Napoleon chuckled and Lavelle rolled her eyes. A shiver ran down her spine, and her body rippled with anticipation. Who knew if they would all make it out of this alive? What if something happened to one of them? What if they ran into Damien, and he hurt someone? No, that wasn't him. He would *never...* Natalia cursed herself. They would all be okay. Everything would be fine. She would make sure of it. Besides, they'd spent nearly a whole month training for this day—for this moment—and it was finally here.

~

The sun finally set, smothering the world in a heavy darkness that felt as if it could crush the air from their lungs. The rebels had split throughout the forest into three main groups consisting of two companies each. Fraiser and Aurum led the two companies of the first group that would attack the front half of the building. The second group consisted of the medics and rebels assigned to protect them and the children fleeing the station. They would stay outside while the third group, led by Roman and Napoleon would attack the back half of the building. The groups kept hidden within the dark tree line several yards from the station, awaiting Roman's signal that would begin the attack.

Natalia stood next to Roman at the edge of the forest, barely hidden within the trees. She could hear her heartbeat pounding in her ears, but the noise was suddenly drowned out by the roaring of engines. She held her breath, twisting her ring. Armored trucks began to appear, rumbling down the dirt road toward the station. The forest seemed to fall unnaturally silent and still as the rebels watched soldiers begin to drag children out of the trucks. Roman sucked in a breath.

"What's wrong?" she whispered, glancing at him, then back at the trucks. They watched the soldiers begin to walk the several dozens of children under the rising doors. A shiver ran down Natalia's spine as her memories of those doors ran through her mind. Roman shook his head in confusion.

"They're not fighting back..."

"What do you mean?"

"Every time we've interrupted or spied on the testings, the kids struggle or something...," he murmured. "They're just letting the guards take them. They're not even screaming..." Panic crept into his voice. "They *always* fight back. Why aren't they fighting back?"

Natalia laid a hand on his shoulder. Minutes passed as the children were dragged, one by one, inside the station. No one spoke or screamed the entire time—not even the soldiers. Finally, the truck doors began to close, and the engines roared to life once more. Roman quickly glanced down the tree line. His lips moved in a flash, releasing a sharp whistle. Identical whistles echoed through the forest like foreboding drums... He had given the signal to attack.

Adrenaline began to course through her veins as she watched the fire and earth Elementals of the first group sprint toward the side of the building with the rest of their companies following behind them. Eyes glowing mixtures of greens and red oranges, the earth Elementals extended their arms, sending chunks of earth flying at the wall while the fire Elementals shot whirlwinds of flames. The ground shook as the elements collided with the metal wall, exploding it. With war cries and shouts, the first group of rebels flooded inside the building. Roman whistled again, signaling for their group to follow, and together, Natalia and Roman stepped out from the trees, unscrewing their canteens of water and sprinting toward the gaping hole in the side of the station.

They leaped over metal debris, landing inside the catastrophic chaos. Knocked down from the explosion, soldiers and children began to rise from the floor. The soldiers ignited their spears and cocked their guns of crackling electricity. A few of the president's personal guards in their stark-white uniforms with blood-red bands already stood within the crowd, awaiting the ambush with glowing eyes and silver pupils. For a few moments, the world fell utterly still. Then without warning, an older boy with blonde hair jumped to his feet amongst the children and soldiers yelling, "Death to the president!"

The building sprang into action, and the battle began. A soldier with a spear of crackling electricity charged out from the crowd at Natalia. Her eyes began to glow ice-blue and silver as she formed her own spear of ice. She ducked under the soldier's first swing before rolling to her right and dodging the tip of the spear again. She lunged forward, shoving her own spear deep into the soldier's side. The electricity from his spear crackled away as he fell to the cold concrete. Behind her, Roman kicked a water fountain, sending it crashing to the ground while soldiers surrounded him. Panic filled Natalia as the soldiers grew closer to him, and in that moment, she had a single thought.

Keep him safe.

She turned, throwing her spear at the soldier closest to him. The soldier fell to the floor with the spear of ice protruding from his chest. Natalia extended her hands, calling the spewing water from the busted pipes toward her. The water curled up her arms like snakes as she ran to assist Roman, who had already slain two of the twelve soldiers that remained.

~

Aurum and Ren, having already been separated from their companies, stood back-to-back as soldiers surrounded them. Ren grunted and jumped into the air, spinning and kicking a large chunk of earth at the soldiers. He followed the strike with an uppercut motion, sending another large boulder into the crowd of black armor. It collided into two soldiers with a sickening *crunch*. Aurum conjured a wall of flames in front of her and sent it crashing into five of the soldiers. A sixth she burned and choked with a curling whip of fire. The stench of burning flesh quickly filled their noses, and a heavy, sickening pit formed in Aurum's stomach. She gagged, bile rising in her throat. She'd just brutally killed someone. She jumped when Ren's hand landed on her shoulder, pulling her out of her trance. She turned to find children running toward them with soldiers following close behind. She had to focus.

"Get out of here!" Ren pointed at the rebels near the gaping holes left by the explosions. Aurum choked down the bile in her throat, and she and Ren ran past the children to meet the soldiers. Together, they jumped into the air, their elements swirling around their hands and hungry for blood as the soldiers readied their crackling weapons.

~

Fraiser twisted her hand, snapping a soldier's neck with a current of wind while she knelt next to a young girl dressed in white—a girl from Sector One. Fraiser pulled her up from the cold concrete, glancing a few feet to the left. A soldier pushed two young boys to the ground, readying a spear. Fraiser quickly formed a shield of swirling wind in her hands and sent it flying at the soldier. It collided against the spear, knocking it from the soldier's grasp. The soldier whirled around and charged her. Fraiser set the girl down, pushing her toward the gaping hole in the wall before charging and tackling the broad man.

She drew a knife hooked to a small belt around her calf and stabbed at his throat. His hands caught hers, and both battled for control of the knife. They continued to struggle back and forth, neither gaining the advantage. He twisted his weight, sending the knife back at Fraiser's face. She barely leaned out of the way in time for it to scrape her left cheek. Using the distraction, the man flipped her onto her back, pushing the knife down on top of her. The tip of the blade had pressed against her throat when a rock suddenly smashed into the side of the man's black helmet. Fraiser jumped up, taking control of the knife, and shoved it deep into the soldier's throat. She glanced into the crowd, searching for her savior as blood slowly trickled down her left cheek. She swore she could make out the back of Napoleon's head in the distance, fighting off his own soldiers. She smiled, pride filling her as she got up and charged into the crowd.

~

Lavelle held her breath, watching the battle rage on from the edge of the forest. Tall grass grabbed at her legs in the slight wind. She couldn't stand the watching and waiting. It was eating her alive. She glanced toward the gaping holes in the building once more, and a group of children jumped through, frantically sprinting to her and the other medics and rebels. Another pair of children followed soon after them, jumping into the singed grass. The two limped forward, hanging on each other's shoulders for balance. Lavelle and two medics quickly ran to meet the two groups.

She smiled kindly and asked in a calm voice, "What happened?" She hoped they weren't too frightened.

"He was hit with an electric sword!" the young girl sobbed. "Can you help him? Please, I'm begging you, help my brother!"

"It's all right." Lavelle softly shushed the girl. "I'm going to take good care of him, don't worry."

The girl collapsed next to her brother in the grass, sobbing. Lavelle knelt next to him and inspected his leg. He flinched with a hiss as she ran her hand near the burn. The scent of burning flesh filled the air. The burn was bad—very bad.

"I have a brother, too," Lavelle said, trying to distract both the children from what she was about to do. "We're twins actually. He's in there, fighting the bad guys."

She unscrewed the cap of a glass bottle tucked into her belt, dipping her finger into the pastel-green paste. It was a cream for extreme burns she'd made with Napoleon days ago. It would hurt the boy at first, but it would take away the major pain for a few hours.

"My name is Lavelle, and my brother's name is Ren," she continued. "What's yours?"

The boy went to answer when Lavelle gently pressed the cream onto his burn. He screamed in response, and his sister grabbed his shoulder.

"I thought you were helping him!" she exclaimed.

Lavelle tried not to wince. "I am, I promise."

"Help!" a voice screamed. Lavelle faced the station to watch five soldiers clad in black jump out of the burning holes after another group of children a few yards away. The rebel guards immediately charged them.

"Come with me!" Lavelle instructed, throwing the young boy onto her back and grabbing the girl's hand. She pulled them toward the forest as the fighting raged on behind them. Suddenly, a hand grabbed Lavelle's braid, yanking her and the boy on her back to the ground. She looked up to find a soldier looming over her. She barely rolled to the side fast enough to watch the soldier stomp where her head had been. She scrambled up, sending a punch at the soldier, who ducked and swung at her. Lavelle threw up her arms, narrowly blocking the punch. She countered with a series of kicks followed by a series of jabs. Finally, a jab landed and caused the soldier to stumble backward. She then used her weight to throw a hard punch to the soldier's exposed throat. The soldier fell to the ground, gasping for air while one of the rebel guards came rushing over.

"Are you all right?" he asked.

Lavelle nodded and watched the rebel drag the soldier away. She faintly smiled to herself. All her training had paid off, and she'd actually been able to defend herself and the children long enough for the rebels to come back. She faced the children, who sat huddled together in fear. Her smile faded immediately as she helped them up and led them into the safety of the tree line.

~

Napoleon fell to the concrete, pushing and shoving at the soldier on top of him. The soldier slammed him back against the concrete, trying to wrap their hands around his neck. Napoleon gasped for air, fear replacing all feeling. He couldn't breathe and dark spots were beginning to cloud his vision. He was about to die. He was dying. He was—a whirlwind of air blasted the soldier off him, and Napoleon rolled over, inhaling deeply.

"Fraiser...," Napoleon began, only to look up and find an older boy with blonde hair and glowing light-gray irises that surrounded black pupils. The boy, who appeared around eighteen and wore the gray clothes of Sector Four, grabbed Napoleon's arm and pulled him to his feet. The soldier he'd blasted away stood, turning to face them as a second soldier ran to his aid. Napoleon glanced at the boy and nodded, and together, they exchanged a series of dodges, rocks, and whirlwinds of air with the soldiers and their crackling spears. Napoleon grunted as he lifted two rocks from the ground and sent them flying toward one of the soldier's exposed throats. He spread his hands only to quickly bring them back together, directing the rocks that slammed into each other like magnets, crushing the soldier's windpipes. Napoleon turned to find the second soldier on his knees, clutching at his throat and chest while the boy stole the air from his lungs. He fell to the cold concrete with a *thump*.

"I'm Hero!" the boy shouted over the commotion of battle.

"Napoleon!" he returned with a thankful dip of his head.

"Are you the leader of the rebels?"

"No, but you're safe now! We're here to help!"

"We know!" Hero exclaimed, gesturing out to the sea of Araedians, rebels, and soldiers and the raging battle. "We were expecting you!"

Napoleon smiled, and hope filled him. They could do this. They could *win*—not just this battle, but the war, too. He laughed to himself in awe and whispered, "Amazing..."

~

Natalia hoisted a young boy off the ground, shoving him after the other children running toward the rebels' exit.

"Go!" she exclaimed, turning to face an Elemental of Vayne's personal guard. They seemed to be targeting her, and she couldn't figure out why. She'd managed to kill two with help from Roman, whom she'd been separated from minutes ago. She had no time to think of the multiple lives she had taken, but she was sure it would haunt her later. It always did, but she couldn't stop now. The battle was far from over, and she had to keep pushing. There hadn't been any sign of Damien so far, but would he even be there? Would there be anyone that could lead her back to him after the battle was over? She'd made sure that he wasn't amongst the soldiers she had killed.

The man before her, irises glowing dark-green around silver pupils, charged her with a sword of hardened rock in his hand. Natalia dodged to the side as he swung at her face. He continued his attack with a kick to her abdomen, and she stumbled backward before shooting a large, sharp icicle toward him from the snake of water that curled up her left arm. The man twirled his sword, shattering the ice with ease. Her eyes widened. He was significantly more powerful than the two she'd faced with Roman. Or maybe she'd been relying on Roman more than she'd like to admit. Natalia rose from the ground and called more water to her arms, rotating her hands in a circle and collecting the water. She lowered her hands slightly, sending it to the floor in the form of a sphere. The sphere touched the concrete and froze, transforming into a pillar of packed ice before her.

She chopped at the top of the waist-high pillar, sending a razor-sharp disc of ice flying toward the Elemental. He paused, deflecting the disc with his sword before facing her and awaiting the next disc. Natalia punched, then jumped and kicked several more discs of ice at him. She continued until all that was left of her pillar was a pile of snow and shattered ice at the man's feet, melting into the concrete. Natalia closed her glowing eyes, feeling the release of more water from the pipes of another broken fountain as he began to stalk toward her. She extended her hands as gallons of water flew in front of her, forming an enormous second sphere that began to surround the man. He swatted at it with his sword before turning and locking eyes with her. She scowled and curled her hands into fists, allowing the water to swallow him. She then lifted the sphere into the air, refusing to release it until the man's body fell limp and began to sink.

Her hands fell to her sides, releasing the water and body to the floor. Natalia whirled around when a woman's shrill scream pierced the air. She turned to watch a rebel's burning body fall limp to the ground, and out of the chaos emerged another Elemental of the president's guard, who wore a wicked smile. Natalia stumbled back, tripping over the dead Elemental's body. She gasped as the familiar face drew closer.

"Damien…" she whispered.

~

Roman pulled his sword of ice from a soldier's body. Warm blood trickled down onto the floor as he swung his head around, frantically searching the crowd for Natalia. His eyes locked with a pair of glowing, ice-blue eyes surrounded by silver pupils, but they weren't the eyes he'd wanted to see. Instead, a woman with dirty-blonde hair and a sadistic smile, clad in Vayne's personal guard's uniform, stepped out from the raging battle and sauntered toward him. Roman frowned. He could tell she'd been with his father a long time. He knew because she was thoroughly enjoying every minute of the battle, blood, death, and chaos. He knew what kind of person she was. Everything was a game to her, and the more she hurt and killed, the more she enjoyed it.

A vicious snake of water coiled around her arm. It slid down, collecting in the palm of her hand. As she drew closer with a widening smile, it expanded and froze into her own sword of ice. Without warning, she sprinted at him, and their swords clashed with an ear-piercing scream. Roman and the woman danced with an extraordinary rhythm. Oh, yes. She'd been his father's loyal dog for a while…

They twirled, jumped, dodged, and parried for minutes. Roman swung down at the woman's calves only to find her ice sword against his. He sprung forward, continuing the attack. Every move he made, she matched and countered, and once again, their swords met, viciously pushing against the other. The woman glared into Roman's eyes before winking at him. He scowled as he studied her glowing eyes. He could see the reflection of his own, a dark-blue against the light. Roman's head slightly cocked to the side, their standstill continuing with no winner in sight. In her eyes, Roman saw what he had seen in his father all those years ago. He saw *raw evil*.

~

Natalia studied the man before her, tears of happiness filling her eyes. Hope and pure joy spread throughout her at the sight of him, regardless of his new appearance. His once shaggy brown hair had been cut short, and his hazel eyes had been replaced by orange, glowing irises that surrounded pupils of silver. Still, she couldn't stop a bright smile from spreading across her face. She was so happy to see him, and he was an Elemental, too. They could fight Vayne together now. She could teach him to love his Element if he didn't already. Everything was going to be all right because he'd found her. He'd even gone undercover as one of Vayne's personal guards to do so.

After everything that had happened, he was finally here in front of her. It felt like the weight of the world had been lifted off her shoulders. Natalia could finally save him. But her smile faltered when she glanced behind him, observing the path of chaos, destruction, death, and flames he'd left. Smoke reached in all directions, thickening the air as it attempted to claim the sets of lungs of the people in the area. Natalia slowly rose from the concrete, and Damien paused a few feet from her. She took a small step forward before immediately stopping, her smile completely dropping at the look in his fire-like eyes. She locked onto his gaze. She had never seen eyes so cold before... She then noticed the black veins that crawled toward his skin.

"Talia..." Damien whispered.

"Damien?" she questioned quietly. "Is it really you?"

He nodded, slowly taking a step forward. But something wasn't right... The way he was looking at her... His eyes were so unnaturally cold and had taken on a haze-like polish, and it... It frightened her. *He* frightened her. She felt like she was staring at a stranger.

"Damien, what happened? You don't look like yourself..."

"Why didn't you come for me, Talia?" he asked, pausing. She could've sworn she saw tears filling his eyes. "You just left me."

She ignored the pain beating against her heart. "I tried to find you, Damien, I really did." Natalia took another step forward, only two feet separating them now. Elements and bolts of electricity shot all around them from the raging battle. "There was no trace of you after the testings... I tried—"

"No, you didn't." Damien shook his head. "You gave up. You left me..."

"No...," she murmured. Why was he acting like this? She really had tried to save him, but there hadn't been anyway to find him.

"I remember. Don't you?" he jeered with a devilish smirk. "You abandoned me so that you could run off into the woods with the rebels!"

"No, Damien... That's not what happened."

"Oh, and now they've brainwashed you! The rebels kept you from me, Talia! They've been lying to you. They're evil. Can't you see? They're tearing us apart!" He roughly ran a hand through his hair as if he were fighting some internal battle. Both of his hands were shaking... Was this really her Damien? "You have to leave them and join me, Talia... You *will* join me—no, us! Together, you and I will stand alongside Vayne, and we'll destroy the rebels and save all of those they threaten!"

"What? No, Damien... What the hell did he do to you? You *hate* Vayne!" Natalia stepped back, panic rising in her throat. She watched Damien press the palm of his hand against his temple. She remembered watching him do that so many times before at the overhang when he was fighting off a migraine. Natalia suddenly paused, his words ringing throughout her mind.

They've brainwashed you...

Then everything clicked.

Damien wasn't just fighting a migraine... He was fighting himself. She could see it clear as day now. She cursed herself for not noticing sooner. All the joy and hope she'd felt shattered into a million pieces. *Damien had been brainwashed*. He'd been taken from her again.

Again. Again. Again. Again.

Natalia bit the inside of her cheek, anger flowing through her veins and spreading throughout her entire body like a wildfire. This was Vayne's doing. First, he'd taken Vale. Now he hadn't just taken Damien. He'd destroyed him. Vayne had taken her sweet and innocent Damien and turned him into some brainwashed monster. This wasn't real. It couldn't be. It had to be a nightmare.

"Talia—"

"No!" she exclaimed, her voice cracking with emotion. This couldn't be happening... He wasn't really gone. It was impossible... "You don't get to call me that...," she whispered, tears filling her eyes. She felt absolutely dejected. He had been the first to call her "Talia" after Vale. For years, he'd been her everything. She swore she could physically feel her heart breaking in two. A boy she once knew better than anyone in the world was now a complete and utter stranger...

Damien pushed his hand against his head harder. "Join me, Talia... All those dreams we had as kids... Leaving the sectors, exploring the world, running away... We could do that. If you join me, we can help Vayne defeat the rebels, then leave. He wouldn't stop us. We would have served our purposes, and we could go live the way we wanted to. Just you and me..."

Natalia released a shaky breath. She imagined the life he was describing. How she would betray Roman, her family, and the rebels... How she would betray Vale's memory. She would become Vayne's lap dog and destroy everything she believed in so she could run away with him. It would be horrible, but she would be with *him*... She clenched her fists, and her lip wobbled. No matter how much she loved Damien, she couldn't do it. She didn't want to. Natalia met Damien's gaze. It had softened, and for a moment, he looked like the little boy she'd met all those years ago. But it was all a lie. It was a dream. Damien wasn't there any more.

"I'll *never* join you," Natalia whispered.

Damien scowled, enormous flames bursting forth from his palms as water crept up her arms once more. They quickly closed the gap between them, whirlwinds of flame and water colliding. Natalia yelped when a tongue of flame burst through the water and licked her shoulder. Damien laughed sadistically.

"Do you really think you can beat me?" he sneered.

She scowled. His element fit him perfectly, and he controlled it with a deadly precision. It was a clear extension of his body, and she could tell by the way he moved that he was confident in the flames in his hands. Damien twirled a flame in his palm before extending it into a broadsword of fire. Natalia lunged forward, sending a whip of water, tipped with sharp ice, at his face. His hand flew up, catching the whip. He wrapped it around his hand and yanked it backward before she could react, and Natalia stumbled toward him and his sword of flames.

She ducked, barely dodging the fatal blow. She watched from the ground as singed hair floated down to the concrete in front of her. Her hand quickly found the end of her braid, fire still attempting to creep toward her skull. She squeezed tightly, extinguishing the flames between her fingers. Shock filled her. Damien had genuinely tried to kill her with that blow. He wasn't fighting to win. He was fighting to kill... And he was good. He was better than her.

A few tears of anger and heartbreak streamed down Natalia's cheeks as she rose to a knee. Then he charged. A shield of ice formed on the ground before her, and a shattering sound pierced the air when the shield broke into a thousand pieces. Shards of ice rained down upon Natalia's face. A single shard sliced her left cheek, and she fell onto her back once more. Damien swung his sword at her. Each blow that shattered her shields ripped a part of her heart out. How could she save him? Was there even anyone to save at this point? Natalia rolled to the side and sent a jet of water flying at him. He leaned to his right, watching the jet collide against the metal ceiling with a *thud*. Thousands of droplets rained down upon them as a ring of fire slowly encased them, evaporating the few puddles that remained on the floor.

New waves of anger and adrenaline began to shoot throughout her veins, which burned as if they had been set on fire. Vayne had taken Damien from her. He had taken one of the brightest lights in her dark life and destroyed it. He had destroyed the person who had kept her from giving up for years—her lifeline. She didn't hate Vayne any more. Natalia absolutely and utterly despised him. She'd never wanted Vayne to die more in her life than in this moment now. Natalia pushed up off the ground only for Damien to kick her back down. She slammed into the concrete, gasping for the air that was knocked from her lungs. Damien stood over her, looking down on her as if she were nothing. How had Vayne's brainwashing done this? How had it picked apart and rewired the boy before her so viciously? She returned a glare, defiantly staring directly into his cold eyes. She wanted her face to haunt him after he killed her.

~

The woman and Roman continued to thrash about, their swords chipping away at each other. Sweat covered every inch of them, and their breathing was heavy. Without warning, the woman followed up the swing of her sword with a punch that landed against Roman's temple. He fell to one knee, vision blurring as she swung her sword at his head. He barely lifted his sword in time to meet her sword above his head, the collision of the blades raining shards of ice down upon him. She countered with another swift kick that grazed his face, sending him back into the concrete.

He lifted his head from the ground, blood slowly trickling from his nose. The cold tip of her sword sat gently against his throat, and he looked up into the woman's eyes as she paused, turning her head toward the fighting around them. Roman knocked the sword away, leaping up to land a punch across her face. She stumbled backward with a hand on her cheek. She glanced at him, then back at the crowd. What was she doing? Had she gotten bored with their game?

Roman formed another sword of ice in his hands, which the woman eyed carefully. She then shrank back inside the chaos as swiftly as she'd appeared. His eyes followed the direction of her glance. He squinted, attempting to make out the two people encased in a ring of fire the woman was nearing. His eyes widened as they landed upon the girl lying on the floor...

~

Damien raised his sword above his head, the hungry flames whipping around furiously. This was it. Her everything was about to kill her. And one of the worst things about it was that a part of her thought she deserved it, too. She should've tried harder to save him. He would've done anything to rescue her if the roles had been reversed. He wouldn't have stopped until she was safe. He would've sacrificed everything, but Natalia hadn't done that. Besides, he was fighting to kill her, and she was fighting to save him, which meant there was no way for her to win. She knew Damien wouldn't stop, so maybe it would be better if he killed her. Then she wouldn't have to hurt him. But the thought still made her chest ache...

The burning in Natalia's veins grew hotter, suddenly invading her eyes. She squinted and molten hot tears dripped onto her cheeks. She hissed in excruciating pain. What was happening to her? Was this her body reacting to the fact that she was about to die? She imagined the twins, Napoleon, and Aurum. She hated that she would have to leave them. And Roman... She couldn't bear to even think about him. It hurt worse than the thought of Damien being her killer.

Natalia watched as Damien's sword fell. She instinctively threw her arm up, feeling the burning sensation crawl across her skin. Suddenly, a shield of fire shot from her hand and wrapped around her arm. The sword collided against the shield of fire, shattering into pieces that dissipated before reaching the ground. Damien's eyes widened, returning to their normal hazel in shock. Natalia rose from the ground, studying the reflection of her glowing eyes against his. Her irises had been divided in two: one half a flame-like combination of red and orange, the other half their regular ice-blue. A line of electric purple separated the halves while her pupils remained their pure silver.

"Natalia!" Roman called, pushing his way through the chaotic mess of the battle. Natalia focused on nothing but Damien as he backed away from her. His eyes darted around frantically like a wild, caged animal. Flames licked up Natalia's right arm, and snakes of water curled up her left. The raw energy and power surged throughout her body, overtaking all her senses. Her body felt ten times stronger. Fire erupted in Damien's palms, his eyes glowing once again. He lunged, launching jets of flames at Natalia, who met the flames with her own. The jets collided, sending bursts of fire swirling into the air. She slung her left arm, sending icicles flying toward him. She immediately followed the strike with a column of flames. Damien swung his arms across his body and formed a large shield before him. The icicles and column of flames collided against his shield, the impact sending Damien flying backward.

A woman with glowing ice-blue eyes and silver pupils suddenly appeared next to him and yanked him to his feet. Her eyes widened in shock as she glared at Natalia.

"Talia!" Roman's voice finally pierced her ears. She glanced to the side to find the rebels beginning their retreat into the forest. She turned back to Damien and the woman. Her body seemed to move on its own when she lifted her arms, throwing a ten-foot wall of fire followed by a wall of ice that encased them. She took a step forward when Roman appeared next to her. He gently grabbed her arm and whispered her name. Natalia looked back at Damien and the woman. Sharp spikes of fire and ice shot at them from the walls of their cage, but they blocked and parried, and soon, the woman was beginning to break through the first layer.

"Hey." Roman grabbed Natalia's shoulders, turning her so that she faced him. His hands traveled up to her cheeks. "Come on. We need to go."

She could feel the energy leaving her body, and her eyes returned to their normal blue-gray. The lull of power was loosening its grip on her. She nodded slightly and followed Roman toward the gaping holes in the side of the station, stumbling every step of the way. The world was spinning, and everything felt slow and wobbly as she watched the rebels close off three of the four holes. Aurum, Napoleon, Fraiser, and Ren stood near the last one, defending it with whirlwinds of their elements. Natalia stumbled once more, collapsing to the floor. Sweat covered her body, and she panted against the cool concrete, lying there as energy continued to drain from her.

She tried to rise, but her arms were shaking so badly that she couldn't. She collapsed again. The edges of her vision were darkening when Roman scooped her up into his arms. Aurum, Napoleon, Fraiser, and Ren turned their elements toward the soldiers who'd begun to chase after Roman and Natalia, stalling them long enough for Roman to leap through the exit. They followed quickly behind, earth Elementals blocking up the hole as soon as they were through. Then the rebels turned and sprinted into the forest along with their army. Natalia uselessly fought the heavy darkness tempting her to close her eyes and leaned back against Roman's chest. It vibrated as he spoke, but his words didn't reach her ears. She sighed and finally gave in, allowing the darkness to take her...

CHAPTER NINETEEN

THE ELEMENTAL

Natalia woke in Roman's arms and watched the canopy of trees above break into a blue sky dotted with dozens of clouds. She glanced around to find that they had just entered the rebels' camp. A column of rebels walked ahead of them, carrying on into the heart of the camp as Roman, Fraiser, Aurum, and the twins veered off toward their encirclement of tents. Roman ducked inside Natalia's tent and gently set her down on the blanketed floor. The others quickly entered, gathering around them. She could tell by the sweat covering every inch of them and the bags under their eyes that it had been a nonstop trek from the station to the camp. A solid day and a half without rest. She must have slept the whole journey back... Had Roman carried her the entire way?

"Roman, what about the new recruits?" Fraiser questioned eagerly. "They have no idea what's going on. They need our help!"

"So does Natalia!" he returned with a glare.

Natalia winced as they yelled. Her head was killing her. "No, I promise I'm—"

"We've been over this." Frasier scowled, completely ignoring her. "She's fine."

Natalia didn't even have the energy to roll her eyes.

"There's no need," Napoleon said, entering the tent with Hero. "They all know what's going on."

"What?" a plethora of voices exclaimed.

"Everyone, this is Hero Ellisaire," Napoleon said and gestured to the now brown-eyed boy.

"Hero?" Lavelle gasped. "By the Aether..."

"I recognize that voice...," Hero smiled brightly, pulling Lavelle into a hug. "It's so good to finally meet you, Lavelle."

"I can't believe you're here," she whispered.

Hero nodded. "I am, and we have a lot to discuss."

Natalia glanced at Roman, who had been watching her. He straightened and faced the others. "We can discuss this outside. Natalia needs to rest."

"It's all right," she countered again, attempting to push herself up. She gritted her teeth. Her muscles were weak and entirely drained. "I'm fine."

"No, you're not. Stay here," Roman ordered with authority.

Natalia scowled. "No, Roman. I told you I'm fi—"

"You're fine? Really, Natalia, are you? I mean, it's not like I just witnessed you almost dying because you can control more than one element!"

A smothering silence filled the air as all eyes widened and turned to her. She stared down at the blankets on the floor, confusion, anger, and fear filling her. And... tears. Why was Roman acting like this, and how was it possible that she *had* controlled more than one element? By the Aether, her head was spinning again.

"The prophecy....," Aurum whispered.

The room fell completely and utterly silent.

What prophecy? Natalia couldn't remember. She looked at Roman, who stared at her apologetically. He hadn't meant for it to come out. He was clearly stressed, and, if Natalia was being perfectly honest, he was freaking out. She could see the slight tremors wracking his hands. Was he afraid of her?

"Aurum and I will stay with Natalia," Lavelle announced, shattering the silence as she knelt next to her on the floor. "The rebels need all of you right now, and we all have a lot to discuss. *Later.* Right now, what's important is resting and helping those who need us."

"I hate to say this, but she's right," Fraiser agreed.

"You come straight to me if you need *anything.* Got it?" Roman questioned, standing.

Lavelle nodded with a smile. Roman sighed as he exited the tent along with Fraiser and Hero. Napoleon and Ren both paused at the flap of the tent, internally debating whether they should leave. Natalia nodded toward them, and they left to join the others. She then sighed, falling back onto the pillows and blankets while Lavelle and Aurum burst into non-stop questions. Natalia slowly and discreetly moved her hand across her body, her fingers pausing over her gray ring and the lavender, light-blue, and carmine gemstones around her finger. She hesitated before slowly sliding the ring off her finger and into her pocket...

~

Roman stared straight ahead, attempting to process everything that had happened. Natalia had wielded another element, and he was freaking out. Was Aurum right about what she'd implied? Was it possible that Natalia was the Aether? Had he made the right choice by leaving her in the tent? He didn't want to leave her, but he knew he had to. His head was muddled, and he could feel the beginnings of a headache. He was exhausted and confused like everyone else, but he couldn't rest yet. He still had work to do. Fraiser marched next to him, her angry footfalls the only sound besides the soft flow of the river currents. Roman glanced ahead at Hero and Napoleon. They seemed to be in deep conversation when Fraiser cut in front of him, stopping him dead in his tracks.

"Must I remind you who you are?" she questioned angrily.

Roman's eyes narrowed. "What are you talking about?"

"You are our leader, Roman. You can't afford to be distracted any more. I was willing to let it slide before, but not now. You have people to look after and—"

"And she is one of them," he spat, anger filling him. Out of all the days, today was *not* the day for Fraiser to get all self-righteous. He was allowed to care about whoever he wanted, and he wasn't about to let her stop him.

Fraiser scoffed. "I'm trying to protect you and our people. You acted like you were ready to abandon them to go take care of *her*. You risked your life back there for *her*. Do you really care about Natalia that much that you would abandon us?"

"What are you talking about? I'm not abandoning anybody! I'm here, aren't I?" Roman exclaimed. "What is it exactly that you think you're protecting me from? Natalia is no threat!"

"She is! I don't want you to get hurt chasing after some girl who's not one of us!"

"The only one hurting me right now is you!" Roman clenched his fists as his eyes began to glow their dark-blue and silver in rage. He hadn't lost control like this since he was sixteen... "And if you *ever* say she's not one of us again, Fraiser..." He was inches away from her face now. "...I'll fight you myself."

"Are you really choosing her over me?" Fraiser held her hand to her chest, then gestured to the camp. "Over everything that we've built?"

"She is a part of what we've built, and I'm not choosing anyone! You're the one who keeps making people choose. You talk about how you don't want to be alone, but you're driving everyone who cares about you away! Why? Are you jealous?"

"You think I'm *jealous*?" Fraiser asked, appalled.

Roman threw his hands up. "I don't know what you are! I don't even recognize you sometimes."

"Roman, I just don't want to lose you!"

"The only way you could lose me is by what you're doing right now! Even in death, I'd still be with you, Fraiser, but this..." Roman continued, gesturing between them. "...this is how you lose me. You think you're protecting me, but you're not. You're trying to push me away from someone I love!"

Her face dropped. "You...love her?"

"Yes." He inhaled deeply. "I do... I love her."

By the Aether, he'd finally admitted it out loud. And to Fraiser of all people—not the person he actually wanted to tell. He didn't know where or when exactly he'd fallen in love with Natalia—maybe it had been that rainy day in the forest, or when he'd told her about his mother in Four—but she'd been like a magnet from the start, constantly drawing him in whether she tried to or not. At first, he'd thought he'd taken a liking to her because she didn't automatically get along with him—because she didn't listen to every single thing he said. Then he'd realized that he couldn't read her at all, and she'd gotten a little annoying. And scary, but in a good way. The slight fear and annoyance had turned into something so much more than he could've ever imagined. He'd realized that they could trust each other with anything and everything, and there would be no judgment.

"Roman...," Fraiser whispered. She reached toward him with a sadness in her eyes. He waved her hand away, stepping back.

"This conversation is over," he said, lowering his head and crossing the river.

~

"I'm going to go get some bandages and food." Lavelle smiled as she stood. "I'll be right back."

"All right...," Natalia mumbled. She was physically and emotionally exhausted. Her entire body ached, and chills ran up and down her spine constantly. She hugged the blankets around her tighter, fighting back the tears pooling in her eyes. Damien was gone, and she feared there was no possible way of saving him. What could anyone do to reverse brainwashing?

She didn't know what kind of torture Vayne had subjected him to, but she did know this: The Damien she knew and loved died the night of the testings.

But why? Why did it have to be him? Why did any of this have to happen to them? Tears of anger spilled onto her cheeks. She didn't want to cry, but she couldn't fight it any more. Her whole world felt like it was collapsing. Then there was the matter of what the hell had happened to her. She had wielded water *and* fire... Natalia exhaled shakily as she rubbed her temples. Her head was pounding, and a cold sweat was beginning to break out on her forehead. She couldn't be the Aether... It was impossible. She wasn't the ultimate Elemental... She was just Natalia... Right? The old woman's prophecy rang through her head like a bell.

The prophecy states that the Aether will be born in one of the four sectors of Araedia, and they will be the one to save us.

"Natalia?" Aurum questioned, gently nudging her shoulder.

"What?" she said, breaking from her trance. She looked at Aurum, whose brown eyes widened with concern.

"Roman told us what happened while you were out... He told us you fought Damien...," Aurum whispered, studying her face.

"No, that wasn't Damien," Natalia choked through the tears.

"But—"

She shook her head, pushing the aching and stabbing inside her chest deep down. "That wasn't our Damien. Our Damien is dead."

"What do you mean?" Aurum's voice broke with emotion, and tears filled her eyes.

"You know what I mean, Aurum." Natalia's head dropped. "Physically, it was Damien, but mentally... He's been brainwashed. It's the only answer."

Aurum bit her lip, and tears began to fall, her face contorting in pain. "No..."

Natalia leaned forward, pulling Aurum into a hug and squeezing her tight. "He's gone..."

She jerked back and grabbed Natalia's shoulders, hope suddenly filling her eyes. "But, Natalia, maybe you can save him!"

"What?" Natalia shook her head, confused. "What do you mean?"

"The prophecy!" She ran a shaking hand through her dark-brown hair. "You wielded more than one element... That means you're *the* Elemental that can wield *all* of the elements."

"No, Aurum... It's not possible."

"Yes, it is. You can save him..." Aurum inhaled, wiping away her tears. She took Natalia's hands in hers. "You can save all of us... Natalia, you're the Aether."

CHAPTER TWENTY

OVERCHARGED BATTERY

With every second that passed, it felt like a sledgehammer came down on his head. Everything hurt. His eyes, his hands, his legs... He felt limp and weak. While his body ached and throbbed, his mind was completely numb. His eyes opened, and he searched the darkness of his bedroom. Moonlight slid through the crack between the curtains, painting a silver line across the floor and halfway up the opposite wall. Damien sat up from under the soft covers of his bed. The blankets were warm, as was the spot where he lay, yet he felt colder than ice. Something was wrong, but he wasn't alarmed. In fact, he didn't feel anything.

Damien got out of the bed and set his feet on the cold, tile floor. He glanced down. He knew the tile was cold, but it didn't feel cold. He had no reaction to it as he walked to his bathroom and flicked on the light. The black veins that had crawled toward his eyes had grown even darker, and his skin appeared paler, too. What had happened? He didn't remember coming back to his room. All he remembered was his vision of Natalia in the forest outside of the mansion, going to see Vayne in his office, and being in tremendous pain, then nothing...

Wait, Zyra had been there. Hadn't she? Damien walked to his door and stepped out into the dark hall. The golden halls usually shined in glory, but tonight, they were cold and dead, just like Damien. Taking a right and heading to the next door down, he softly knocked on Zyra's golden door. A few seconds passed before she opened it, raising a brow at Damien.

"What do you want?"

"The day I came back from the forest... What happened in Vayne's office?" Damien asked emotionlessly.

The corner of Zyra's mouth drooped into the beginnings of a frown. She poked her head out into the hall and glanced back and forth, checking to see if anyone else was around. She then grabbed Damien and pulled him inside. Unlike his dark room of blacks, grays, and maroons, Zyra's was light and airy. Silvers and shades of gray covered the plain room. There *were no personal items anywhere. One would think no one inhabited the room unless they knew it was hers. Her windows were open. A breeze blew her white curtains, and a small candle flickered on her bedside table.*

"Why are you asking?" Zyra crossed her arms over her chest.

Damien studied her carefully, trying to find any indication of what she was thinking. "I woke up in my room, but the last thing I remember was being in Vayne's office... And you clearly know something, so spit it out."

Zyra's brows narrowed as she flicked her blonde hair back over her shoulder. "What's in it for me?"

"Just tell me," Damien growled, towering over her.

"Oh, come on, Damien. Think really, really hard. You know what happened. Use what little of a brain you have."

He frowned and closed his eyes. He remembered... pain. He winced and his eyes shot open. "I remember my head hurting."

"But your head wasn't just hurting, was it?"

"No," Damien winced. He could feel it now. That a part of him was gone. A part of him was...dead. "It felt like a thousand swords were piercing it because...I was fighting something."

"What were you fighting?"

"A...feeling?" His pounding headache returned as he concentrated. He walked over to the open window, gripping the sill until his knuckles turned white.

"What kind of feeling was it? Love, hate, anger...? Come on, Damien, what was it?" Zyra placed her hands on the sides of his head, and she whispered into his ear, "What did you feel?"

Damien's voice ran cold as he whispered venomously, "Hatred."

"For who?"

"Natalia..."

~

"You both had a simple task!" Vayne exclaimed, slamming his fists down on his wooden desk. He angrily ran his hands through his dark hair, revealing a small crack in the wood. "How could you let them get away?"

Damien snapped out of his stupor and glanced between Zyra and Vayne. Though he had hardly any emotions left, he could feel the shock of seeing Natalia hours ago deep down inside him. It was like treasure that had been buried under thousands of pounds of sand. He knew it was there, yet it was still hidden. But he could feel his hatred for her. It was far from buried. It was the only thing he felt, and it was consuming him. Damien wished he'd been able to kill her, though he'd done his best to capture her alive as Vayne wished. He'd been so close to just killing her, but Natalia had revealed herself as the Aether by controlling fire.

He watched Vayne rise from his chair and march toward Zyra. His white eyes burned with anger, and he wrapped his fist around her throat, lifting her off the ground. Vayne's head snapped to Damien as he swiftly flicked his opposite hand. A dark-gray—nearly black—whirlwind of air slammed Damien back against the wall of the office with a loud *thud*. The wind swirled around his limbs, locking him in place like chains. He watched Vayne turn and throw Zyra across the room. She landed on the cold, marble floor, knocking into one of the high-backed leather chairs around the desk. It screeched, skidding backward. A small cut appeared above her right eyebrow, and blood slowly began to trickle down her face.

"You know what happens when you fail me, Zyra!"

"But, sir, we could've never anticipated what happened!" she whimpered, terror filling her voice.

Damien cocked his head to the side. Zyra was the most terrible person—besides Vayne and himself—that he knew, and she was terrified. He knew he should be afraid, too, but he wasn't. He could feel his fear deep down, but it was muted to the point that he had no reaction to it. It was as if the fear wasn't there at all.

"I'm sorry!" she exclaimed, scrambling away from the dark air that began to circle around her neck. "No! No, no! I won't fail you again, sir, please!"

"No, Zyra, you won't," Vayne spat out, a sadistic smile appearing on his face. He turned to Damien. "You weren't even the one fighting her, Zyra. I apologize. Now, go patch yourself up, dear..."

Zyra quickly rose, desperately hurrying to the door. She placed a hand on the handle before pausing to glance back at Damien. Their eyes locked, and he nodded at her. She returned a short nod, then disappeared behind the door. Damien watched Vayne slowly make his way over to the wall that he was still pinned against.

"Why didn't you capture her or my son like I asked?" Vayne snarled.

"Zyra was the one fighting Roman. I tried to trick Natalia into joining us, but—"

"I don't want your pathetic excuses, Damien! What was Zyra talking about? What didn't you anticipate?"

"She controlled more than one element!"

The wind holding Damien to the wall immediately dissipated, and Vayne's eyes widened. He stood in silence for a few long moments before he spoke. "You and Zyra will gather my personal guard..."

"After the battle, I sent three of them into the woods to follow the rebels," Damien said, his voice void of any emotion. "If they weren't caught, they should be back with the location of the rebels' camp soon."

Vayne chuckled deeply. "I underestimated you, Damien. You're more clever than I gave you credit for..." Vayne turned away from him and walked to one of the many large windows in his office, pausing and staring out over the mansion grounds and the rest of Sector One in the distance. The stark-white buildings and houses stuck out against the early morning fog. "You will capture the Aether *alive* and bring her to me. My son is no longer of use to me alive now that we've found her. Kill him on sight."

"Yes, sir." Damien nodded, straightening. Anger stirred within him. He couldn't kill Natalia now, but at least he could kill Roman.

"Once the Aether is finally in my grasp, the sectors will fall down on their knees and worship me for saving them from the horrors that have yet to come..." Vayne smiled.

Damien's brows knitted together, deeply intrigued by his words. "What horrors, sir?"

He turned to face him, still wearing that wicked smile. "There are many things about this world that you don't know. After we capture the Aether, kill my son, and destroy the rebels, I'll tell you. Until then, all you need to know is that *everything* relies on the Aether's powers becoming my own."

"Of course, sir. I will prepare the army to move out. As soon as the Elementals return, we'll destroy the rebels and bring you the Aether." Damien dipped his head before disappearing out into the hall. He had so many questions. What were the horrors Vayne was talking about? Why did he need the Aether's powers so badly? Then he imagined what he could do if he took the Aether's powers for himself. Deep down inside him, Damien felt a voice screaming at him.

No, don't do it. Betray Vayne, and you will die. He saved you, and you owe him.

Damien shook his head. No, he didn't owe him. He didn't owe anyone, so why was the voice trying to convince him that he did? It only filled him with more questions, and he knew there was only one person who could answer them.

He marched down the golden hallways shining in the sunlight that peeked through the many windows. Old pictures of the construction of the sectors' walls hung throughout the halls, along with a painting of Vayne, his wife, and a young Roman. Damien remembered watching Roman and Natalia as they fled the train station. He felt the burning hatred beginning to form inside him at the mere thought of them, but he kept his focus and stared straight ahead until he turned down one of the many branching hallways. He followed it down past his room and stopped in front of a familiar golden door. He didn't bother knocking and pushed it open, stepping into Zyra's room.

"I didn't just feel hatred," he said, locking onto her yellow-green eyes.

Zyra met his gaze, taking a bloody towel away from her eye and setting it down on her bedside table. "What do you mean?"

"You brainwashed me...*twice*," Damien hissed. "The first time, you gave me a burning hatred for Natalia and undying loyalty to Vayne. The second time, you tried to amplify them. Well, now I don't feel *anything*. I feel no loyalty, and I hate Natalia so much, I can't even comprehend it sometimes. I know I didn't always feel this way, but I don't care enough to seek revenge. Not on you."

"You're like a battery...," she whispered. "We overcharged you..."

He nodded. "You did."

"Why are you telling me this?"

Damien scoffed. "Because you and I are the same. Vayne simply sees us as his pawns, and I'm tired of it. I'm tired of being his little bitch, and I know you are, too... Aren't you?"

Zyra's eyes fell to the floor, and for a few moments, the room went silent. She lifted her head and met Damien's gaze. "I've been serving him since I was fourteen. I'm beyond tired of it."

"He plans on taking the Aether's powers as his own. He said that the sectors would fall at his feet and worship him for saving them from the horrors yet to come... We can't let those powers fall into his hands. We need to be able to fight whatever he's talking about on our own."

"So what are you suggesting, Damien?"

"We capture the Aether and let Vayne take her powers. While he's vulnerable doing that, we kill him and take the powers for ourselves." Damien smiled wickedly. With more planning, his scheme could work, but he needed to get rid of one thing first. He was still brainwashed to serve Vayne, so what if he physically couldn't force himself to turn against Vayne and kill him? He had to figure out how to reprogram his brainwashing. He had to find a new anchor... The voice once again returned.

No! it screamed. *Don't do this. You cannot do this!*

Damien smirked. He knew reprogramming his anchor would work. The voice had just confirmed that. It had given itself away by trying to stop him. The only question left was who would be his new anchor? Damien stared at Zyra, an idea unfolding. He closed the distance between them, gently cupping the side of her face. He softly ran his finger under her cut. "Are you all right?"

She nodded, staring up at him.

"What? Are you suddenly at a loss for words, Zyra? That's not like you."

"No, I'm just imagining how good it's going to feel to see the look on Vayne's face when we kill him." She smiled.

He returned her smile, staring deeply into her eyes where he could see the gears turning in her head. She knew how to reprogram him and herself. She'd figured it out, and she knew that he had, too. Damien watched her eyes trail over his lips. His plan would work. He knew it would. He pulled Zyra up to his face, their lips crashing into each other feverishly. She slowly began to pull him back toward her bed. Damien smirked beneath their kiss. Their plan was already in motion...

~

Natalia, Aurum, and Lavelle walked throughout the growing number of square tents in the direction of the hospital. Several of the rebels had been injured during the previous night's events, and Napoleon had sent for Lavelle as backup. Natalia and Aurum refused to let her go alone. They'd been resting for hours and couldn't stand to sit still any longer. Other than being a little fatigued, Natalia felt perfectly fine. In fact, she felt a renewed power flowing through her veins, heightening her senses more than ever. However, mentally, she wasn't fine.

Damien was truly gone, and even if they somehow managed to get him back, how would they fix him? Natalia's stomach began to twist in knots, and she could feel the beginnings of a headache looming over her. She had to keep busy and distract herself from him and the fact that she was the Aether. She couldn't accept either fact, especially not at the same time, so she kept her eyes on the grass below her feet while they continued between the tents. All eyes were glued to her, and rebels even parted for her, Aurum, and Lavelle to pass. Word traveled fast inside the camp, and the news of Natalia's second element had spread like a *wildfire*—ironic.

Natalia watched Aurum nod at Lavelle, and together, they stepped in front of her, trying their best to save her from the peering eyes. She smiled, eternally grateful for them. She quickened her steps and threw her arms around their shoulders, nudging between them with a smile. The three girls laughed softly and continued on to the hospital, their bodies interlaced.

Natalia expected to find Roman somewhere inside when they entered, but all they found were cots full of the injured and an overwhelmed staff. Every cot had been occupied, and a few rebels even stood, clutching their injured limbs. Napoleon jumped up from beside a young girl's cot at the sight of them, a weary yet relieved smile on his face. He was always smiling.

"Good," he said. "My backup's finally here."

"How is everything?" Lavelle questioned, placing a gentle hand on his arm.

"No one's in critical condition, but we need your help. We just don't have enough hands to help everyone." Napoleon sighed, and Natalia noticed how dark the bags under his eyes had gotten.

"Put us to work, boss man!" Aurum grinned, adopting Napoleon's nickname for Roman.

He laughed. "All right, follow me."

For hours, Natalia and the others ran back and forth between cots, delivering bandages and other supplies to the medics. At one point, she assisted Napoleon and Lavelle with someone's stitches, which still turned her stomach. She and Aurum also made runs around the room delivering meals. Finally, they decided to take a five-minute break—well, everyone except Lavelle. She refused to break until she'd finished a particularly tricky splint with another medic. Napoleon had offered to do it, but Lavelle was relentless. She refused to leave until it was done and insisted that she was more than glad to help.

A few minutes later, Natalia, Aurum, and Napoleon sat in the tall grass near the main dirt road that stretched through the camp, leaning against the side of the hospital while they ate loaves of brown bread. Natalia watched Aurum nudge Napoleon as he glanced back at the hospital doors.

"If you look over there one more time, Napoleon, I might puke." Aurum shook her head with a smile. "How are things anyway?"

Heat flooded Napoleon's cheeks. "Uh, things are good... I mean, we did just complete our most successful run yet with minimal casualties."

Aurum rolled her eyes. "You know that's not what I'm talking about."

"I'm not saying anything," he said, his face reddening even more.

"Oh, come on! Tell me, please?"

"Hey, Napoleon, I think I hear someone calling for you," Natalia said, standing and yanking him up. She pushed him toward the hospital doors with a wink.

"Thank you," he mouthed.

"Really, Natalia? Why do you always have to go and spoil my fun?" Aurum pouted and grabbed the rest of Napoleon's loaf of bread.

Natalia chuckled, tossing Aurum her loaf, too. "Here, this should compensate for your loss of entertainment."

She shrugged, tearing into the bread. "It's a start."

~

Another hour passed before Roman walked through the hospital door, sweat dripping from his messy black hair. He squinted, searching the room for Natalia. His whole body seemed to relax when his eyes landed on her. She was bent over a young boy, trying to hold two small metal rods on either side of his straightened knees to make a splint. She looked up to call for help when her eyes met his. Damn, he loved her eyes. His chest bloomed with warmth, and he immediately headed over to her, kneeling down beside her.

"What do you need me to do?" he asked.

"Hold the metal here," she said, placing her hands over his until he held the metal in the right spot. "Perfect. Now take this one."

Roman nodded, never taking his eyes off her as she grabbed bandages and began to secure them around the metal. He smiled when she scrunched her nose in concentration. Natalia quickly finished the splint and stood. He gently patted the boy's shoulder before joining her.

"Can I steal you away for a little bit?" he asked.

"Yeah." Natalia nodded with a smile. "Our shifts are over anyway."

"Great, because there are some things we all need to discuss," Roman said, leading Natalia to the nearby cots where Lavelle, Aurum, and Napoleon worked. "Are you guys almost done by any chance?"

"Yes, we are!" Lavelle beamed cheerily.

Roman returned her smile. "Follow me."

He turned, leading them out of the hospital and into the maze of tents and small wooden shacks. Rebels buzzed around everywhere, but they all paused to watch the group, mainly Natalia, pass. Roman quickened his pace. He knew she'd hate the attention that came with being the Aether. She probably hadn't even accepted the fact that she was the Aether yet. He hadn't. It was still mind-boggling to him.

After passing through most of the tents and shacks, Roman slowed his pace and allowed Aurum, Lavelle, and Napoleon to walk ahead of him. He glanced at Natalia, who still held her head down. He frowned.

"How are you feeling?"

"I'm all right," she said.

Roman immediately stopped, gently grabbing her wrist. She faced him, finally meeting his gaze. "You know I don't believe you, but I won't pry. Just please, know you can talk to me if you need to."

"I know." She gave him a small smile and intertwined their fingers.

Roman swore he could feel electricity where their skin touched. Could she feel it, too? He'd never entertained the idea of being with anyone because of his position, and he'd simply never found anyone interesting. But Natalia, she had swooped in and taken him completely by surprise from the very beginning. He loved her, and he thought there was a possibility that she could love him, too. He hoped she could because, for him, there was no turning back now. It was far too late for that.

They came upon the river, and together, eyes glowing, they parted the waters and crossed.

"Whoa...," Roman whispered, studying her new eyes. They were so vibrant. It was almost as if their glow had grown brighter. The ice-blue and red-orange was stunning, but the electric purple splitting them was what really stole the show.

"What is it?" Natalia asked, worry filling her voice.

Roman watched her eyes return to their normal blue-gray. "I've always thought your eyes were beautiful, but with the new colors... They're mesmerizing."

"Thank you." She grinned as if the words meant the world to her. As if he'd just erased every doubt she had. He knew she'd been waiting for someone to berate her—to scream and yell at her for her new powers—but he wouldn't allow that. He hoped she knew that, too.

They quickly joined Aurum, Fraiser, the twins, Napoleon, and Hero in the soft grass around the fire pit, and Roman ran his hands through the blades of tall grass that whipped around in the cool breeze. He closed his eyes, inhaling deeply. The sweet scent of fresh, running water pierced his nose. It was comforting, and he wished he could stay in this moment forever. A moment where they were all safe and happy together. Especially with what was going to come next now that Vayne had discovered that Natalia was the Aether... There was no doubt in his mind that the first thing that woman and Damien had done was tell him.

"I hate to skip pleasantries, but I've asked you all here to discuss our next move, which is to take over the sectors and destroy everything that Vayne has built. It's urgent that we act soon, and, Hero, I'd like your help since you're the one who has been in the sectors most recently. You've also managed to make contact with most of the people inside of them, which is extremely useful."

"I'm more than happy to help any way I can, but unfortunately, I only know so much," Hero said.

"That's all right. I mainly wanted to ask about the status of security in the sectors. How bad is it?" Roman asked.

Hero sighed. "In most sectors, it increases daily. Whenever Vayne can get more soldiers out there, he does, but now that we've disrupted another one of his testings, I guarantee, security will increase tenfold."

Roman's brows narrowed. "Even in Four?"

"Yes." Hero nodded. "If we're going to make a move, we need to do it by the end of the week."

"I agree. We need to strike while he's weak. He'd never expect an attack this quickly after a fight." Aurum crossed her arms.

Napoleon frowned. "Four is our best shot at getting into the sectors, though. If we can't get into Four... Then I don't know what we'll do."

"If there were a way to communicate with the sectors, we could get the people to help us get inside," Fraiser said with her resting scowl.

"But how would we do that?" Aurum questioned. "There's no way for us to communicate with them."

"We could try searching deeper into the tunnels," Napoleon murmured. "There are corridors that lead in toward the other sectors. We could find a way to send in spies to spread the word."

Fraiser's scowl deepened. "I think you forget we're not the only ones with access to the tunnels. They're too dangerous. There's too much uncharted territory. What if you stumble upon a secret lab or something worse? What would you do then, Napoleon? Vayne would block off all the tunnel entrances and exits after he tortured the information out of you."

"She's right." Aurum ran a hand through her dark hair. "There's too much uncharted territory. We don't know what could be down there."

"I agree," Ren said. "If we can find an easier, more concealed way in, then we could take Vayne down from the inside."

"If only it were that easy...," Roman murmured, silently cursing his father. "The sectors are basically impenetrable now. Our only way in would be over the walls, or possibly under if Napoleon's onto something with the tunnels. The crack in Sector Four's wall is useless, too. We can't sneak a whole army in like that. Besides, I bet it's been plugged up again."

"Roman, are you sure our army's even big enough for this yet?" Fraiser inquired, doubt spreading across her face. "What are we going to do even if we do somehow manage to beat him?"

Roman frowned in frustration. Fraiser had never doubted him before. Why would she start now? Was this about their fight earlier? "Fraiser—"

"I think we should just attack...," Natalia interrupted, all eyes glued to her. "We start at Four and work our way inside, whether that be through the tunnels or attacking the walls themselves or both. The people inside the sectors will fight with us. I know they will. We take over each sector until we get to Vayne's mansion in One, so, Fraiser, add a couple thousand or so to our army. Is that big enough for you?" Fraiser shot daggers at Natalia, who stared right back. "And *when* we win, we open up the sectors to each other and the forest. We let the people elect a new leader... We make it fair and just like it always should've been."

Roman glanced between Natalia and Fraiser. Fraiser's scowl deepened more than he'd ever seen, and she dug her fists into the earth. He needed to draw her attention away from Natalia. He would not have them fighting *again*. Besides, everything Natalia had said had been right. It had been the plan since the very beginning. Freedom for everyone. "Hero, if I could get you another projector, could you use it to communicate with those inside the sectors and let them know we're coming?"

"I could," Hero said.

"I think we have an old projector tucked away somewhere in the camp. It'll need some major fixing, but it's a start. I'll find it for you," Roman promised. He was confident in their plan. It was simple, but it would work. They were going to stop his father for good...

CHAPTER TWENTY-ONE

FEAST

Small, decorative lights had been strung between the stands that created the square, and a long row of wooden tables sat in front of a set of stands, piled high with meats, soups, vegetables, fruits, drinks, and even some warm cocoa cakes. Small circular tables and chairs were also scattered throughout the square. It hadn't taken long to set up for the feast. Lavelle was the one who'd come up with the idea. Why not celebrate the rebels' success and hard work before they take off into battle again? Besides, everyone needed a break even if it was just for the night.

Natalia watched Roman as he stood on top of one of the many tables. Every able-bodied rebel was gathered around him, listening intently as he spoke. He explained their plan and that the rebels would march on the sectors in two days' time to end Vayne's reign of terror. Natalia was awed by Roman's speaking abilities. The way he could turn strangers struggling for survival into an army capable of taking down governments sent shivers down her spine. She could feel the atmosphere shifting around his words. Tired faces were brightened with energy and hope, and a few eyes even began to glow with emotion within the crowd.

Roman paused to turn back and glance at Natalia. She nodded with a small smile, then he continued. "We've worked toward this day for so long. So many people have sacrificed so many things. We've lost brothers, sisters, mothers, fathers, friends, lovers... Victory doesn't always happen in an immediate burst of glory. Sometimes small triumphs and large hearts change the course of history. We've had our small triumphs and our large hearts, and now in two days, we will have our change in history."

The rebels erupted into cheers as did the twins, Ren, Aurum, Napoleon, and Hero. Even Fraiser gave a short yell. Natalia simply smiled, proud of Roman, her friends, the rebels, and everything they'd been able to accomplish... And everything they *will* accomplish.

Napoleon suddenly leaped up, joining Roman on the table. "Now, let's enjoy our feast!"

The rebels, smiles on their faces, dispersed amongst the square, and music suddenly began to fill the air. Natalia grinned. It had been a long time since she'd heard music, especially music so happy. At the orphanage in Sector Four, Vale would sometimes sing to her, but they were never very happy songs. They were always full of sorrow, which was all he'd ever really known. Singing and dancing weren't encouraged in the sectors either, but far away from the sectors in the rebel camp, they could sing and dance for hours and no one would be able to stop them. Rebels in their mismatched clothes played wooden instruments on top of wooden boxes while others laughed, ate, sang, and danced. Napoleon, the twins, Aurum, Fraiser, Hero, and Roman joined Natalia, who turned in circles at the wonder before her.

"I didn't know we had musicians, or instruments for that matter," she said to Roman.

"I bet you also didn't know that we throw some rowdy parties every now and then." He winked.

Napoleon gasped, eyes widening. "They have cocoa cakes!"

And with that, he disappeared into the crowd in the direction of the tables of food, dragging Lavelle behind him. Natalia laughed. She was surprised it had taken him this long to sniff them out.

"Hey, wait on us!" Aurum called, grabbing Natalia and Roman.

"I'm going to go get some Brennivan," Fraiser announced, walking in the opposite direction.

"Me too. Come on, Hero," Ren said, and together, they followed after her.

Natalia rolled her eyes with a smirk while she imagined Fraiser stumbling through their small encirclement of tents, shouting who knew what later tonight. But she had let Ren and Hero go with Fraiser, which probably wasn't the best idea, but... She shook her head. They would all be in for a treat tonight.

"Natalia, they have soup!" Aurum exclaimed as they neared the food. They hurried over to the table of bowls, surveying their options carefully. There was a cream soup full of potatoes, cheese, and small slices of venison, a broth with chunks of vegetables, and several more. Natalia grabbed the cream soup while Aurum settled with the broth. Both smelled absolutely divine, and saliva pooled in her mouth. Natalia glanced down at the end of the table to watch Fraiser, Ren, and Hero, with cups of Brennivan in their hands, join Roman near the rest of the drinks.

Suddenly, the music changed, and the rebels began to strum their wooden instruments with an even more joyous tune than before. Dozens of rebels partnered before running out to the middle of the square where they danced. Natalia set her half-eaten bowl down on the nearest table.

"Look!" Aurum pointed, stuffing a spoonful of soup into her mouth.

Natalia followed her finger to watch Lavelle drag Napoleon by hand to the middle of the square. They laughed and locked hands, jumping around amongst the crowd. Natalia took Aurum's hand.

"Shall we?" she asked in a manly voice.

Aurum laughed, and they joined the growing number of dancers. They twirled in circles and clapping began, drumming along with the beat. Natalia grinned from ear to ear. She was grateful for all the distractions she'd had today. The hospital, debating strategies, the feast... It had kept the demons at bay for the day. It had kept Damien from plaguing her every thought for hours, and Aurum was happy. Lavelle and Napoleon were happy. Roman, Ren, and Hero seemed to be enjoying themselves as well. Even Fraiser wasn't very irritable with the bottle of Brennivan by her side. It was nice to simply be able to enjoy one night without any worry—to let go.

Natalia caught glances of Lavelle and Napoleon twirling as she spun Aurum. Ren had somehow convinced Fraiser to join the dance, though Natalia suspected it had something to do with the new bottle of Brennivan in Fraiser's hand. She caught glimpses of Hero within the crowd, too, when Aurum stopped and spun Natalia in return. She came to an abrupt halt when she knocked into someone's firm chest. She turned to find Roman bursting with laughter. She smiled as they locked hands and jumped and danced. Roman wrapped his arm around her waist, hoisting her up and spinning her around in the air. Her eyes locked onto his, their noses almost touching.

His eyes were so warm and happy, and his smile was so bright and genuine. And in that moment, it was as if they were the only two people in the world. The crowd, the lights, the tables, and the square fell away, and it was just them... Natalia had never felt so safe and at peace in her life, and she couldn't stop the word from bubbling up in her head. *Home.* She felt like she was finally home after traveling for her entire life. If she could pause this moment and live in it forever, she would.

Song after song, they danced until their feet ached. Hours of drinking, eating, smiling, dancing, and laughing passed before Napoleon and Lavelle led Roman, Natalia, Aurum, Ren, Fraiser, and Hero back to their tents, unable to pry the Brennivan from their hands. They sloshed through the river, plopping down to the grass around their fire pit, and watched wide-eyed as Aurum shot flames from her fingertips into the sticks and twigs.

Napoleon sighed, leaning back into the soft grass with his hands behind his head. "I could get used to this."

"A toast!" Fraiser rose from the ground on wobbly legs and lifted her cup high into the air. "To friends! And acquaintances...," she added, glancing at Natalia.

Natalia smirked and raised her cup in return. The feast had been a great idea. It was nice to live in the moment and enjoy each other's company while they could. They all knew the darkness was coming. And soon. Too soon... "To friends and family... And acquaintances."

They repeated her words before drinking and bursting into another round of laughter as Fraiser fell backward.

"I like you better drunk, Fraiser." Natalia chuckled.

"That's because you're more tolerable when I'm drunk."

~

For hours, they continued to talk and laugh amongst themselves. It was long past midnight when Hero helped Roman carry an unconscious Fraiser back to her tent, and Lavelle and Napoleon rose from the fire, walking toward the river and continuing downstream. Ren stared after them while they disappeared into the night.

"Don't worry, little twin," Aurum teased, elbowing him.

Ren rolled his eyes, standing. "I'm going to go see if there's any food left. Want to come?"

"Of course!" Aurum smiled and stood. "I can't believe you had to ask. You know how much I love food."

"Hey, I'm coming, too!" Hero said, ducking out of Fraiser's tent with a bright smile.

Natalia chuckled and watched them walk away, playfully punching and fighting each other as they went.

"On a scale of one to ten," Roman began, walking back into the firelight and sitting down next to her. "How drunk are you?"

She leaned back into the grass, gazing at the bright stars above. "Not as drunk as you."

"What?" Roman raised a brow and mimicked her motions, staring up into the sky. "I'd say I'm a solid two, but you've got to be at least a four."

"Eh, two and a half, maybe three," Natalia said, her smile widening. "You know, I used to do this all the time back home. You could always see the stars in Four. Vale and I would name them sometimes."

"You could hardly ever see the stars in One... When I first came out here, at night, this is all I would do. It was so comforting. So peaceful..."

"How did you get out here, Roman?"

He gave her a small smile. "It's a very long story."

"I have plenty of time...," Natalia said, turning to face him through the tall grass between them. He did the same and explained the story of how he met his mother and Fraiser and discovered his powers.

"Why did your mother leave in the first place?" Natalia asked. She couldn't imagine Roman's mother leaving him, so why did she?

"My father had grown power-hungry. He desired all the elements, not the one he was given."

Natalia's eyes widened. "Vayne is an Elemental?"

"Yes." Roman nodded. "He began subjecting himself to experiments to try to obtain them all. He always said if he had all four elements, then he'd be ready when the time came. I don't know what he was talking about, or if he ever succeeded, but he craved water the most. He always spoke of its power, especially the transferring energy ability. Other Elementals can do it, too, but it's very rare. My mother found out about the experiments and tried to stop him but was instead rewarded with the knowledge of his insanity. She tried to escape with me... But my father had other plans, so she promised to come back for me, escaped over the walls, and wandered until she found a few broken-down shacks. Then the rebels were born."

"Wow...," Natalia murmured. The way Roman talked about his mother, she knew there were no hard feelings. He didn't blame her for leaving. In fact, she could tell he thought it was best that she did, but Natalia still couldn't stop herself from being a little angry at her. "Thank you for telling me."

Roman gave her a small smile, hesitating before continuing. "How are you dealing? With the events of the other night, I mean..."

"I'm fine." Natalia bit the inside of her cheek. She was lying. She knew it. He did, too, so she took another quick swig of her bottle of Brennivan. "I'm not near drunk enough for that conversation, though..."

CHAPTER TWENTY-TWO

FIRE AND ICE

Another hour passed before everyone finally retired to their tents. Natalia and Roman walked side-by-side over to their two tents. Roman paused at the flap of his and watched Natalia disappear behind her own. She lay down amongst the blankets and pillows, staring at the gray fabric above her. She didn't want to fall asleep. The upcoming battle would arrive sooner if she did, and she didn't want to return to the world of nightmares either. Would it be bad if she went and woke Roman? He would stay up with her. She knew he would...

Or maybe she should get Aurum? No, Aurum would sleep until the afternoon tomorrow after all the Brennivan she'd had. At least she had until the end of the week to get it all out of her system. A sudden wave of guilt washed over Natalia. While they were dancing and drinking, Damien was under the control of Vayne. The thought was enough to make her wish for sleep. At least in her nightmares, she could see him. She could try to save him and tell him how sorry she was. Dealing with the nightmares was better than drowning in her own thoughts... So she closed her eyes and fell into the world of dreams.

A young Natalia slowly opened her eyes to the forest beyond the walls. She stood at the edge of the overhang, gazing out over the rolling hills and forest. Tree branches swayed and danced in the breeze. Suddenly, arms wrapped around her waist, lifting her into the air. She smiled brightly as the arms spun her before gently setting her down on the soft grass. Natalia turned to gaze into Damien's bright, hazel eyes. He smiled an enormous, happy smile, and they began to talk. However, no audible words seemed to leave their mouths. It was as if they had been muted.

Natalia blinked and found herself somewhere else. She stood hidden amongst the trees, watching the young Damien and Natalia laugh and joke. She smiled to herself. She recognized this memory. She studied the happy boy in the clearing. The dimples he only showed around her were deep that day from smiling so much. They'd had so much fun together that day... Then a dark figure stepped out into the clearing behind the oblivious children. It was the Damien she'd faced only two days before.

"No, Damien!" Natalia exclaimed, bursting forth from the tree line as he drew closer to the memory. "Leave them out of this!"

Damien grinned and raised his hand high, a sword of fire erupting into his palm. Natalia lunged toward him, but she was too late. The sword slashed through the memory, tearing it at the seams. The whole world around her erupted into flames, and the scene changed again. Natalia and Damien stood in a forest now, and the flames quickly subsided, Damien's sword dissipating into the air.

"You will all die," he whispered.

Images of death flashed before her. She saw Lavelle and Ren lying on the ground with blood dripping from their mouths. Napoleon and even Fraiser, sitting against each other with spears of electricity impaling their bodies. Aurum was running through the forest, spears of deadly ice chasing after her like hungry wolves. One spear struck her left hamstring, sending her crashing to the ground. She cried out in pain as another spear struck her back. The remaining pack of spears struck the rest of her body before the image changed once more.

Natalia saw the old Damien. He screamed as a spear of electricity impaled his throat, sending him crashing to the ground. Then the image changed a final time. It was Roman. He walked through a meadow full of wildflowers, humming a melody when the evil Damien appeared behind him with his damned sword of fire. With an upward stroke, he slashed the sword along Roman's back. He fell to the ground, and a scream of agony pierced the air. Natalia could only watch through her fingers as Damien lifted Roman's head by his dark hair and slit his throat.

She awoke with a gasp. Instantly, the darkness of the tent crashed around her, enveloping her in a suffocating wave of panic. She whipped her head around, frantically trying to claw her way back to reality and out of the world of dreams. Natalia lunged for the flap of her tent, stumbling out onto the ground as the images continued to play over and over again through her head. She lay in the tall, dew-covered grass. Her body and mind were exhausted. She closed her eyes, attempting to calm her rapid breathing. The early morning sky painted the gray tents in a pastel-blue, and birds chirped in the distance. A shiver ran down Natalia's spine when a cool breeze swept over her. Her entire body was covered in a cold sweat and her head ached. It felt as if all her energy had been completely drained from her body, so she simply sat there and tried to slow her thundering heart.

After a few minutes, she dug her nails into the earth, pushing herself up from the ground and running into the forest. She knew she couldn't run from the nightmares... But that didn't mean she wouldn't try. Besides, she couldn't sit there any longer. She had to start moving. Her head was pounding, whether it be from the mental and emotional exhaustion or the aftereffects of the Brennivan, she didn't know. She hadn't even tried to really process the events of the past two days. All she knew was that Damien was gone, and everyone expected her to be the Aether. Everyone expected her to save them and be the hero, but how could she do that when she couldn't even save Damien?

She wasn't a hero, and even with the powers of water and fire, she didn't feel like the Aether. The name was foreign on her tongue and felt everything but right. How was she supposed to do this? How was she supposed to become something she wasn't? Natalia suddenly paused, observing her surroundings. Other than the occasional birdsong, the forest was quiet and covered in morning dew. The same small pool of freshwater sat a few yards away from her, reminding her of the last time she'd been here with Roman. Rustling suddenly came from the edge of the forest, and Natalia turned to watch Roman step into the clearing, the morning sky and shadows painting him gray and blue. Of course, he'd heard and followed her.

"Natalia...," His voice broke the silence of the forest into a thousand pieces.

She sighed to herself. "Don't," she whispered.

"Don't what?"

"Don't ask if I'm okay, or if I want to talk about it."

Roman took a step forward. "I think you need to. It's eating you alive."

"I can't face it." She shook her head. He stepped closer with every word she spoke, studying her face intently. Only a foot separated them now. "I just can't. It hurts too much. I—"

"You can do it," Roman said, his eyes never leaving hers. His gaze was soul-piercing, and Natalia feared if she kept her eyes locked with his much longer, she might lose herself completely. He closed the space between them, cupping her face with his hands. He ran his thumb across her cheek. "Don't stop talking. It's just you and me. Let it all out."

Natalia bit the inside of her bottom lip. "Everyone expects me to be some kind of hero that saves us all, but I'm not the hero. I can't be."

"Why not?"

"Because I didn't save Damien. We always said we'd protect each other, and I couldn't protect him when he needed me to." Natalia broke away, turning her back to Roman. "I don't deserve these powers I have. I don't deserve my friends or the rebels or anyone... I don't deserve you. It should've been you or Damien or Vale who was the Aether... Not me. And we're about to head right back into battle, and all I can think about is how afraid I am to lose someone else."

"Natalia..." Roman gently grabbed her arm and stepped around to face her again. Sadness filled his brown eyes. "It's not your fault. You could've never anticipated what was going to happen—"

"No, stop making excuses for me!" she exclaimed angrily. Natalia ran her hands through her hair. She was so tired of everyone trying to tell her that it was okay. That it wasn't her fault that Damien had been captured and brainwashed into some kind of mindless puppet. It may not have been her fault that it happened, but it was her fault for not trying hard enough to get him back. She should've never left the sectors—no, the train station—until Damien had been rescued.

"Talia, you have to let all of this go. You're not sleeping...," Roman said, taking her hands in his. "Whether it's your fault or not, it's all in the past. There's nothing we can do about it now. The only thing we can do is fight for a better future for our friends, the rebels, the sectors, Damien... Ourselves... We all deserve to be happy. Don't try to convince yourself that you don't."

Natalia gave Roman a sad smile. He was right. The past was the past, and no matter how badly she wanted to change it, she couldn't. No one could, but they could change their futures. And she swore to never let Damien's fate befall anyone else. She threw her arms around Roman, hugging him tightly. Once again, he had taken the weight off her shoulders, and he was currently the only thing holding her together.

They stood in silence in the small clearing for a few minutes when Roman pulled away slightly, keeping his arms locked around Natalia's waist. Their eyes met, and electricity shot throughout her veins. They slowly began to lean toward each other when suddenly, a twig snapped in the distance. Roman took a step in front of her, facing the direction of the noise. His eyes were glowing dark-blue and silver, and a spear of water formed in his hands. Natalia's own eyes began to sting slightly as she willed a snake of water to curl around her arm. A line of electric purple split her red-orange and ice-blue irises, and the two of them stood like statues, staring into the forest. It was unnaturally still and silent.

Without warning, a soldier clad in midnight black armor jumped from the bushes with a spear of electricity in hand, which he launched at Roman. Natalia rotated her hands around before extending them toward Roman. The two snakes of water she created circled each other and collected into a shield of ice before him. The electric spear collided against the shield with an ear-piercing screech and fell to the ground. Roman threw his own spear, the tip hardened with ice, impaling the soldier with a soft *thump*. A second soldier stepped into the clearing only to be met with two sharp icicles to the chest—one from each of them. Natalia turned to Roman, wide-eyed. Vayne's army was here. They had somehow found the rebels and their camp.

Natalia cursed. "Roman—"

"Wait." Roman took a step to meet her, holding a finger to her lips. The two of them listened intently to the surrounding forest. The early morning birds had resumed their songs, and tree branches swayed in the breeze. There were no signs of additional soldiers, but they were out in the forest somewhere.

"We have to go," Natalia whispered, turning to face him. They paused and stared at each other for a moment. Fear and adrenaline pumped through her veins. Vayne was bringing the battle to them, and he was doing it *now*. The little amount of time that they'd had was being ripped away from them. Vayne had even ripped away their moment... She was so tired of him taking everything, so before she sentenced herself to all the upcoming death and destruction, Natalia decided to take something back. She stepped forward, grabbing Roman's shirt and closing the space between them. Roman cupped her face with his hands, placing his lips on hers. Her arms moved around his neck as their kiss deepened. His lips were soft and hungry, yet gentle. Natalia seemed to release a breath she hadn't known she'd been holding. All the tension throughout her muscles released, and for the first time in a long time, she felt complete. After a few seconds, he pulled away, running his thumb over her cheek.

"I know...," he whispered.

"We have to warn them," she said softly but not weakly.

He nodded. "Come on."

Together, they sprinted through the forest, leaping over rocks, logs, and fallen branches littered across the ground. Footfalls crashing in the brush chased after them like a vicious pack of wolves, multiplying by the second.

"Soldiers!" Natalia yelled at the top of her lungs as she and Roman burst through the tree line. Her voice rang loud and clear throughout the camp, shattering the peaceful morning. Fraiser, Napoleon, the twins, Aurum, and Hero all stumbled out of their tents.

"What's happening?" Aurum asked, shoving a second boot onto her foot. In the distance, rebels scrambled out of their tents and wooden shacks. Natalia and Roman slid to a stop before turning to face the forest.

"They're here," Roman said. "I don't know how, but they're here. He found us..."

Fraiser's eyes narrowed with anger, and she walked up next to Roman with venom in her voice. "*Who* found us?"

Roman's face hardened. "My father."

Suddenly, a jet of flames shot out of the forest straight toward them. Natalia ran a few steps forward, jumped, and flipped as she kicked a column of water from the river at the flames. They collided with a *crash* and *sizzle* before dissipating into the air. War cries from upriver echoed throughout the camp. Vayne had them surrounded... Natalia faced her friends, her expression mirroring their own—shock, worry, anger, confusion.

Fraiser scowled. "Napoleon, Hero, with me!"

Soldiers clad in black had begun to pour out from the depths of the forest, charging at the camp with their weapons and elements at the ready. There were hundreds of them. The fire of electric guns roared louder while Natalia watched Fraiser lead Napoleon and Hero toward the battle. Lavelle placed her hand on Natalia's shoulder. "I'm going to protect the hospital."

She nodded. "Be careful."

"I'm coming, too," Ren said, turning to follow her.

Lavelle shoved against her brother's chest. "No, stay here."

"Lavelle, I'm not leaving you—"

"They need you here, Ren. I'll be fine. Just don't do anything stupid," she said, sprinting toward the hospital.

Four Elementals clad in stark-white armor with red bands sauntered out of the forest—two boys and two girls appearing around the age of seventeen. Both boys were fire Elementals with glowing orange and red eyes, while one girl's eyes glowed light-green for earth, and the other girl's glowed light-gray for air. Silver pupils accompanied each pair of cold eyes. They were members of Vayne's personal guard, and for a few moments, everything was still and silent. Aurum, Ren, Roman, and Natalia simply met the soldiers' icy stares, the tension in the air thickening to the point of suffocation.

Then a piercing scream carried over from upriver. A sadistic smirk lit up one of the boy's faces, and the four charged. Aurum's, Ren's, Roman's, and Natalia's eyes all began to glow a plethora of colors, and they lunged forward, sending whirlwinds of elements at Vayne's guard. The earth Elemental knelt to the ground, and as she stood, a wall of earth stood with her. The flames, chunks of earth, water, and ice collided against the girl's wall with a *crash*, and another hundred soldiers began to pour out of the forest. The wall quickly sunk back into the ground followed by columns of flames heading straight for Natalia, Roman, Ren, and Aurum. Natalia stopped dead in her tracks, and for a moment, all she felt was fear. She was terrified. What if Damien made an appearance? Did she want him to? What if one of them died? Or even worse...what if Damien killed one of them? But as the vicious flames grew closer, her entire body seemed to ignite with energy.

She extended her arms and closed her glowing eyes, reaching out to the flames. She could feel the power surging throughout the column of fire. It was...comforting... Natalia rotated her wrists, and one of the columns wobbled on its path to Ren before diving into the ground and scorching the grass. She opened her eyes and watched Aurum jump in front of her and clap her hands together, splitting the second column around them. The fire harmlessly ricocheted off her fingers and slammed into the earth. Roman and Ren countered with spears of ice and rock, which Vayne's guard deflected into their own crowd of soldiers. And just like that, Natalia's fleeting moments of fear were gone, replaced by power and a determination to protect those she loved.

"We have to fall back!" Roman exclaimed, casually thwarting a bolt of electricity with a sphere of water.

Natalia glared at the army closing in. They were highly outnumbered, and by the sounds of the battle upriver, so were the rebels there. Everyone was spread too thin. Their only hope was to fall back and fight together as one. She cursed, turning to Roman, Ren, and Aurum, who all wore grim expressions. More soldiers continued to pour out of the forest. She scowled at the thoughts running through her head. She tried to convince herself that she was wrong, but every soldier that stepped out of the forest trampled every reason that gave her hope... They were going to lose...

Roman blocked a column of air with another sphere of water. They collided, spraying mist into the air. "Get to the hospital, now!"

So they turned and ran, fleeing past their tents and running through the river. Water splashed against them, soaking their bodies. Natalia glanced to her left to find the rebels from upriver sprinting through the tents and shacks littered throughout the camp toward the hospital. They were falling back, too. She clenched her fists until her knuckles turned white, and anger burned up her throat. She didn't think her hatred for Vayne could grow any more, yet it had. He was destroying her home, and she was *running*. Planting her front foot in the dirt, Natalia jumped into the air, spun around to face Vayne's army, and extended both fists. Pure adrenaline coursed throughout her as water from the river and fire from her fists shot forth into the mass of soldiers. The flames hungrily crawled through the chinks of the armor, eating their wearers alive. The water split into a thousand shards that hardened into razor-sharp icicles that struck into the soldiers with deadly precision. The girl with glowing light-gray eyes from Vayne's personal guard gave a yelp when one of the shards embedded itself in her throat.

"Natalia, come on!" Ren yelled, grabbing her arm and pulling her back in the direction of the hospital. She spared a glance back at the sea of black, searching every visible face within. She bit the inside of her cheek. Still no Damien in sight...

~

Fraiser released a cry as she leaped over a rebel's body and twisted a soldier's neck with a thrust of air. She then swung her arms to the side, sending another soldier flying into the remains of a burning tent. The rebels had begun to retreat toward the hospital minutes ago, leaving only Fraiser and a few others to hold together what remained of their frontline. She'd ordered Hero and Napoleon to retreat with them. She hoped they had made it. Lavelle would have her head if they didn't. Fraiser continued to push forward, and bodies piled all around her. Tents and shacks blazed widely, sending thick tendrils of black smoke reaching high into the air.

Suddenly, a whip of water struck Fraiser from behind, sending her skidding across the grass. She shot back up, ignoring the blood now leaking down her back and forming swirling discs of air in her hands. Her glowing gray and silver eyes locked onto ice-blue and silver. Fraiser scowled. Those eyes reminded her of Natalia's, which only added to her anger. A woman with dirty blonde hair stalked toward her, and her whip of water formed into a spear that hardened into ice. Blood and dirt covered the woman's face. She smiled wickedly. Fraiser rolled her eyes and then charged. The woman jabbed her spear at Fraiser, who quickly sidestepped and countered by sending a disc flying at the woman's head. She ducked to watch the disc slice through the ends of her hair and dissipate as it carried on into the crowd. The woman scowled.

"Zyra? Where are you?" a voice called from within the battle surrounding them.

Zyra scoffed. "Hold on. This won't take long."

"No, it won't." Fraiser smirked.

Zyra twirled her spear in her hands, the bottom half sharpening into a blade identical to the head of the spear. She swung the blades at Fraiser, who replaced the disc she'd thrown and blocked. Without warning, one of the ends of the spear bounced off Fraiser's disc, slicing into her left shoulder. She yelped in pain before letting the disc in her right hand dissipate and grabbing the spear with a scowl. Her left hand joined Zyra's hands on the length of the spear, and they pulled and twirled as each attempted to gain control. Fraiser yanked hard against Zyra, causing cold, sharp pains to shoot across her shoulder. It felt like shards of ice were embedded in the wound. Zyra stumbled forward into the kick Fraiser sent into her stomach, but Zyra pulled Fraiser to the ground with her, shattering the spear. For minutes, they rolled around and exchanged blows, their stalemate continuing on with the bloody battle raging around them.

~

Aurum and Ren stood back-to-back as they blocked the entourage of soldiers firing bolts of electricity at them. On their side of the battle, the rebels were very slowly beginning to gain the upper hand. Vayne's army had caught the rebels by surprise and had spread them thin, but it was the soldiers clad in black who were spread thin now. They didn't know the terrain like the rebels did, and their guns and spears of electricity were no match for the elements. Aurum and Ren twirled around, each step extraordinarily in sync with the others. Ren knelt, allowing Aurum to roll off his back and send a strong jet of flames at one of the boys from Vayne's personal guard. Ren stomped on the earth, dislodging a sharp, angled rock that he sent following after the vicious flames. The boy extended his arms in defense, creating a small shield of fire. Aurum's flames attacked his, countering them easily, while the sharp rock flew through the cascade of fire and pierced the boy's chest. He fell to the hard ground with a *thump* and did not rise again...

~

"Here we are again!" Hero shouted to Napoleon.

Napoleon glanced back at Hero to watch him lift a soldier from the ground with a torrent of winds and send the soldier flying into the mass of rebels and soldiers. Hero was adapting to his powers nicely.

"Yeah, we really need a new hobby!" Napoleon returned, using shackles of rock from the earth to trap a soldier's feet. Stuck in place, the soldier could only watch as he sent two large rocks hurtling at the soldier's chest. The rocks collided against the dark armor viciously, and the soldier fell to the ground along with shards of broken rocks. Napoleon turned and stood as Hero sucked the wind from a soldier's throat before turning to face him, too. Napoleon had no idea where anyone else was. Fraiser had disappeared minutes ago, and he could only hope that Lavelle and the others were safe. He didn't like being separated from them.

"We need to find Fraiser!" Napoleon exclaimed. The battle was becoming more chaotic by the second, and he didn't want her out in it all alone. No one needed to be in this alone. He promised himself that he and Hero would find Fraiser, then reunite with the others. The only chance they had of winning was if they were all fighting together.

Hero nodded. "Let's go!"

Napoleon took off into the crowd with Hero behind him, dodging stray elements, bolts of electricity, and the electric tips of spears and swords. Bodies lay all around them—rebels and soldiers. He ducked behind a burning shack and glanced around. Everything was on fire... Despair filled him as the smoke of his burning home stung his eyes, nostrils, and lungs. He shivered before running out from behind the shack and back into the chaos of battle. His glowing light-green irises and black pupils suddenly narrowed as they landed upon a familiar face...

~

Fraiser and Zyra panted and circled each other slowly. Blood, dirt, and sweat covered every inch of their bodies. Blood from Zyra's nose dripped onto the ground, mixing with the mud. She lunged forward, and her spear shattered when it collided against Fraiser's discs of swirling air. Fraiser countered with a right uppercut to Zyra's jaw. She stumbled backward, sending sharp blades of ice at Fraiser, who swung her arms about and redirected the blades into the ground.

"Zyra!" the same voice growled, even closer than before. "You've had your fun, but playtime's over!"

Zyra charged Fraiser, who sent her discs flying at Zyra's head. She ducked under the first disc and then the second before jumping and sharply kicking Fraiser's side. She tumbled to the ground, quickly pushing herself back up only to be knocked back down by Zyra's fist, which was hardened with a layer of ice. Warm blood dripped from Fraiser's mouth, and she sat up, head spinning. A knife of ice formed in Zyra's hands as Fraiser rose to a knee. She gasped, eyes widening when the cold ice pierced her lower abdomen. Fraiser continued to gasp, falling to the ground and grasping at the knife.

"This was fun." Zyra smiled sadistically. "Let's do it again sometime."

And with that, she disappeared into the crowd. Fraiser cursed and curled her fingers around the ice handle of the knife. She slowly pulled against it, the knife sliding a couple of inches out of her flesh before she let go with a strangled cry. The knife dug back into her stomach, causing more blood to soak through her shirt. A metallic taste filled the air.

"Fraiser!" Napoleon exclaimed, hurtling over a body. "Do *not* pull that knife out!"

She frowned. "I thought you left, Napoleon."

"Oh, come on," he said, scooping her into his arms. "Have some faith in me now, Fraiser. I'd never leave you behind."

Fraiser chuckled, causing an abundance of blood to pour out of her wound and soak Napoleon's shirt as well. A sudden, bitter coldness began to creep throughout her body. Shivers ran down her spine, and her teeth began to chatter. She clung to Napoleon's bloodied shirt, reciting every curse she knew. She could only watch as Napoleon trudged on behind Hero, who cleared a path through the fighting to the hospital.

~

Natalia's spear of ice struck through a soldier's black armor, pinning the lifeless body to the ground. A man, his black helmet shattered to pieces, ran at her, but a whip of fire curled around his throat, yanking him back. Natalia whirled around to watch Aurum fling the man off into the remnants of a burning shack. Splinters and embers flew high into the air.

"Fraiser!" Roman's voice suddenly pierced the air.

Aurum's glowing eyes widened with panic, mirroring Natalia's. A new spurt of adrenaline filled her as she and Aurum sprinted to the hospital where Roman, Hero, Napoleon, and Lavelle knelt next to Fraiser.

"What happened?" Ren exclaimed, running up behind them.

"This blonde..." Fraiser strained breathlessly. She tried to sit up only to collapse back to the ground. "She stabbed me with a knife of ice."

"Fraiser, don't move," Roman ordered.

"Shut up, Roman." She rolled her eyes. "Ow, Napoleon!"

"I'm sorry! I'm sorry!" he exclaimed, sweat dripping from his dark hair. He looked to Lavelle, and his terror was crystal-clear. "I can't get the bleeding to stop."

"Here." She held out more bandages and cloths.

"I swear to the Aether, when I get my hands on that little—" Fraiser screamed in pain when Napoleon wiped away at the continuously flowing blood. She dug her fingers into the soft grass. "I'm going to kill her! By the Aether, I am going to *kill* her."

"Was she one of Vayne's personal guards?" Roman asked urgently.

"She had to have been." Fraiser shook her head with a wince. Her head lulled to the side, and her eyelids looked like they weighed tons. Her adrenaline had run its course, and she was fading quickly. "She was too skilled with her element... Roman, you have to be careful with her."

"I fought her at the train station. She was with—"

"Damien!" Aurum exclaimed.

Everyone whirled around and watched Damien, eyes glowing ferociously, ignite a sword of flames in his hands. The world seemed to move in slow motion as he swung his sword of fire at the person closest to him... Hero.

CHAPTER TWENTY-THREE

BURN

Waves of heat distorted the air around the sword of flames arching through the air, its tongues of fire reaching out hungrily. The world seemed to move in slow motion as Natalia watched Hero stumble backward, attempting to avoid the blow, but he couldn't stop the tip of the sword from falling down and scorching the left side of his face. His deafening scream filled the air. If it wasn't for the ball of fire Aurum sent flying at Damien to knock him off balance, Hero would be dead. If it wasn't for Aurum, *Damien would've killed Hero.*

A sharp pain struck through Natalia's stomach, and she could feel the bile rising in her throat. She couldn't make sense of all the emotions clouding her mind. Anger, shock, horror, sadness, hurt... Suddenly, the world rushed back into its normal pace. Aurum's flames had barely been enough to throw the sword off course. Hero fell back into Napoleon's arms, and Damien quickly turned and sprinted for the forest. Natalia, Roman, Aurum, and Ren immediately shot after him, leaving Lavelle and Napoleon behind with Fraiser and Hero. The only sound Natalia could hear was the pounding of her heart in her ears. Everything else was silent while the anger and adrenaline coursed through her veins, but her heart ached. Damien had tried to kill Hero and was most likely leading the attack on the rebels for Vayne. He was hurting and killing so many, and she knew he was too far gone for saving now. *They would have to kill him.*

The thought nearly brought her to her knees. No matter how hard she tried to hate Damien for his actions, she couldn't. As they neared the edge of the forest, the sound of rushing footsteps filled the air. Natalia glanced behind her to watch a fresh wave of soldiers clad in black burst forth from the forest toward the heart of the camp. Roman and Ren, a few steps behind Aurum and Natalia, both paused. Soldiers immediately ran at them, but that was the last thing Natalia saw before she and Aurum disappeared into the woods. They swept their arms about, knocking tree branches aside. An uneasy feeling began to settle in the air, and the hair on the back of Natalia's neck stood up. Damien had always been fast, but he wasn't running as fast as he could. He was several yards ahead of them but remained at an easily followable distance. If he really wanted to lose them in the forest, he was very capable of doing so...

~

Ren, eyes glowing forest-green and black, watched Roman impale the last soldier with a spear of ice, blood splattering both of their faces. They had slain the majority of the second wave, but some had still made it past them into the heart of the camp. Ren prayed to the Aether that Lavelle and the others would be all right, but they couldn't turn back and leave Aurum and Natalia.

"We need to catch up with the girls. *Now*," Roman said with an expression as hard as stone.

Ren nodded, and they sprinted into the brush, following the paths of broken branches and trampled grass. For a few minutes, they ran on with no sign of anyone, and a sinking feeling hit Ren like a sledgehammer. Something was wrong. He could feel it in the air—in his bones. He turned and glanced back over his shoulder as they ran, observing the thick surrounding trees and brush. He slowed and strained his ears to pick out a soft set of footfalls chasing after them. Who was that? Had Lavelle or Napoleon followed them?

He then faced forward, and watched Roman gain speed in a nearly inhuman-like way. He knew that Roman cared for everyone, and he knew that he cared for Natalia... But the way Roman was pushing himself now... He looked like a dying man desperately chasing after his one and only chance of survival. A realization hit Ren like a brick wall. Roman didn't just care for Natalia. He was in love with her, and he wouldn't stop pushing until he knew she was safe again. Ren grunted and pushed his legs farther, attempting to catch up and ignore the stinging in his lungs. Suddenly, a force rammed into his side, sending him flying off the trail into the depths of the forest.

"Ren!" Roman's voice exclaimed.

"Go! I've got this!" Ren returned as he started to wrestle a boy clad in white armor. The boy's eyes glowed a red-orange around silver. He was from Vayne's personal guard. The two tumbled around amongst the foliage, clawing and scratching. The boy's fist landed against Ren's cheek, knocking him to the dirt. Ren rolled and barely avoided the flames that crashed into the ground where he'd been seconds before. The boy shot a ball of fire at Ren, who swung his arms from his sides to above his head. A small wall of earth formed in front of him. The flames crashed against it harmlessly. As the wall sunk back into the ground, the boy charged him, leaping over the top of the wall and tackling him back to the forest floor. The boy wrapped his hands around Ren's throat with a vicious smile. Ren gagged and clawed at the boy's hands, panic seeping through him.

Keeping a single hand against his throat, the boy reached back and formed a knife of hungry flames, raising it high. Ren blinked furiously as his eyes began to burn ferociously. Was this what dying felt like? The stinging increased until it was unbearable, and he fought back screams of pain. Without warning, the whole world seemed to shift around him, and his senses exploded.

Ren's black pupils began to glow the purest of silver as tendrils of gold began to creep around his irises. He could feel *everything*. He could feel the pounding of the five sets of footsteps—Damien's and those chasing after Damien in the dirt: Natalia, Aurum, Roman, and...*someone else...* They were close... He could feel the river flowing throughout the rebel's camp, its currents swirling and strong. He could even feel the resistance of the fish swimming through it. He could feel the wind whipping around the tents and the ravaging fires that burned on with no signs of slowing. Each sensation was different yet flowed together in a perfect symphony. He felt the raw, untamed power flowing through his veins as his eyes locked onto the knife of fire flying at his face. He didn't so much as flinch when the fire halted, hovering less than an inch above his forehead. The boy jerked back in shock while the fire swirled out of his palm and curled around Ren's wrists. He stumbled backward, and Ren rose to his feet.

Rock from the ground followed him, circling around the flames that constantly twisted around his wrists. The rock and flames suddenly leaked away from his arms, forming a rotating sphere of rock and fire in front of him. Currents of wind quickly joined them, and Ren watched the sweat and water from his forehead and surrounding plants join the other three elements. The sphere of water, earth, fire, and air formed into a long spear, and Ren's irises glowed a striking pure gold around silver pupils. Lighter yellow highlights struck throughout the gold, causing his eyes to appear nearly fluorescent.

The spear flew toward the boy, striking through his chest. His body fell to the hard ground with a thump, and Ren paused, staring down at his hands. They hummed with energy and power. What did this mean? Was he able to control more than one element like Natalia? Was it possible that he was the...? No, he didn't have time to think about it now, not when his friends needed him. Ren took a deep breath before turning and sprinting after the others, his entire body tingling with his new power.

~

Natalia forced herself to push farther. She and Aurum had been chasing Damien for a few minutes now and had barely gained a step toward him. Suddenly, he turned to the left and disappeared into a cluster of dense trees and brush. Aurum and Natalia came to an abrupt halt, their panting the only sound.

"Do we follow him?" Aurum whispered between breaths, never taking her eyes from the brush.

Natalia nodded. "We have to. We can't just let him get away..."

"There could be dozens of soldiers waiting for us on the other side of those trees," Aurum said, finally tearing her eyes away.

"We can *not* let him get away." She took a step forward. "I don't care what's waiting on the other side even if it's Vayne himself. Now are you coming with me or not?"

"Of course." Aurum smirked. "I can't let you have all the fun."

The girls faced the trees and burst through after Damien. Natalia cleared the thick brush into a small clearing scattered with trees and rotting, fallen logs only to be met with a force that knocked into her, sending her flying into a nearby tree. Her vision blurred, and the stench of burning clothes and flesh filled her nose. She looked down to find flames grabbing at the edge of her shirt and her side. She fumbled with the canteen hooked to her belt, dousing her burning waist in cool water.

Natalia turned her blurred sight to Aurum, who swung at Damien with fiery fists. He ducked and countered with his sword of fire that she blocked with a shield of flames. Natalia pushed against the ground and rose to one knee. She faltered, falling back against the tree once more as a soft ringing filled her ears. Squeezing her eyes shut and taking a deep breath, she rose with glowing, multi-colored eyes. Damien's sword crashed against Aurum's flame-encased hands, and the two shoved against each other. Natalia felt a slight ache in her heart as she watched them—family turning on family. She clenched her fists and pushed the aching deep down. She wouldn't feel it any more.

Footfalls suddenly pierced her ears as someone sprinted through the forest. Natalia whirled around to watch Zyra, eyes glowing ice-blue and silver, emerge from the brush. Natalia scowled and sent a ball of flames flying toward her. Zyra easily somersaulted over them and countered with a razor-sharp disc of ice. Natalia extended her arms, clapping them together. The ice shattered harmlessly at her feet. Finally breaking their stalemate, Aurum and Damien stumbled backward. Natalia ran forward and grabbed Aurum's arm to steady her. Zyra did the same with Damien, and the four faced each other in the small clearing. A snake of water curled up Natalia's arm while fire circled around her right knuckles, and Aurum produced her whip of fire and a small shield of restless flames. Damien tightened his grip on his sword when Zyra leaned over and whispered into his ear. His eyes widened and his nose scrunched as he shot her a look of confusion.

Something hadn't gone according to their plan... But what? For a few heartbeats, he merely stood there. He was in shock, Natalia realized. *Damien* was in *shock*.

"What now?" Aurum whispered. "They have some kind of plan, it's obvious, but—"

Natalia held up a hand, a plan of her own forming. "What's wrong, Damien? You look confused. Did someone screw up your evil, mastermind plan?" Natalia asked, venom filling her voice. Damien always seemed to be one step ahead of them, but what if she could turn the tables? After all, he'd been fighting to kill all along, and she'd been fighting to save him. She knew him just as well as he knew her, so what would he do if she played dirty? What if she got under his skin instead? Natalia let out an emotionless laugh. "Oh, seriously, Damien, what happened? You look like someone just killed your father again!"

Aurum gasped beside her, and Zyra simply smirked, clearly itching to spill blood. Damien's lips hardened, and his glowing red-orange and silver eyes narrowed. "I'll admit, I'm a little disappointed... Our plan will still work, but I was just taken aback by how useless you are. Without even knowing it, you failed me again... You're not who you think you are."

Natalia shrugged. "Neither are you."

The four charged each other. Zyra launched a series of sharp icicles at them, which Natalia dodged while Aurum stopped to block them with her shield. She flung her whip out from behind the shield, catching Zyra's wrist. Zyra screamed in pain as the whip scorched her skin. Natalia extended her arms and charged Damien, shaping her elements into a sword of swirling water and fire. The sword clashed against his sword of flames, and they danced around each other in a complicated symphony of strikes and parries. Shivers ran down Natalia's spine when Aurum's scream pierced the air. Natalia kicked Damien away, sending him to the forest floor, and turned to face Aurum and Zyra, who held a blade of deadly ice against Aurum's neck. Natalia's eyes widened, and she dropped her sword. The elements dissipated on the ground and panic swept through her. She could feel the slight shake in her hands. No, no, no.

"Don't you dare...," Natalia whispered.

Zyra smiled. "Not so tough now, are you?"

Damien kicked the back of Natalia's leg, sending her to her knees. "Do it."

"No!" Natalia yelled hoarsely. She watched Zyra flip the ice around in her palm and slam the handle into the side of Aurum's head, knocking her out cold. Confusion filled Natalia. Why didn't they just kill them both and be done with it?

"I'll admit, I'm a little disappointed... Our plan will still work. I was just taken aback by how useless you are. Without even knowing it, you failed me again... You're not who you think you are." Damien's words replayed in her head. *"You're not who you think you are..."* Natalia said to herself. Her eyes widened. They weren't after her or Aurum—they were the bait. Damien and Zyra were after someone else... But who? Roman? Who did Vayne really want?

"Unfortunately, *Talia*," Damien whispered in her ear, slowly letting her name roll off his tongue. "We can only take one prisoner, and since you're the most powerful Elemental besides the Aether, we have to kill you."

Natalia's mouth fell open. What did he just say? But she could control water *and* fire... That was unheard of... Her blood froze. If she wasn't the Aether, then who was?

"Move, and I slit your throat," Roman's steady voice said. Damien stiffened behind her, and Natalia risked a glance over her shoulder. Roman stood with the tip of a blade of ice against Damien's neck, and relief flooded through her at the sight of him.

Damien allowed his sword of flames to dissipate. With a chuckle, he whispered one last thing to Natalia before he stood. "I know you so well because you and I are the *same*. You'll destroy what you love most. You'll destroy what you have with him. He's too good for you... And we both know it."

Natalia bit her lip angrily as he turned to Roman with his hands raised nonchalantly. She rose and took a few steps back, eyeing Damien and Zyra carefully. Damien's eyes darted between Roman and Natalia. He lingered on her for a few moments before he returned his gaze to Roman. She knew what the look meant. *Mark my words, don't say I didn't warn you. We both know I'm right...*

"Your father wants you dead," he said to Roman with a smile. "I guess we both have daddy issues."

"Zyra, let Aurum go," Roman commanded, never breaking eye contact with Damien. Zyra and Damien both laughed, and Roman pressed his blade of ice harder against Damien's neck, causing a small stream of blood to trickle down into his white armor. "Tell her to let her go."

"Zyra?" Damien grinned. "Now!"

Damien ducked as a knife of ice flew right where his head had been and dug itself into Roman's shoulder. He ran a few steps away before turning back, extending his arms, and sending a huge wave of flames at Roman and Natalia. She jumped in front of Roman and encased them in a shield of her own flames. The cascades of fire swirling around them roared viciously, and when they dissipated, they were met with nothing but scorched grass and trees. Damien and Zyra were gone and so was Aurum...

~

Ren knelt at the edge of the tree line and watched Damien's flames curl around Natalia's shield, scorching everything around them. He could feel the earth dying beneath the heat, the power surging through the fire, the moisture leaving the surrounding air, and the currents of wind weaving the smoke amongst the trees. The sensations were so foreign, yet he'd never felt so alive. It was like finding a piece of himself that he didn't know had been missing. Ren watched Natalia's and Damien's flames dissipate into the air. *Natalia's* flames... She could control water and fire, but so could Ren... He could control water, earth, fire, and air. Was it possible that he was the Aether, too? Could there be two, or were they both some form of the Aether? The idea of it made his head hurt.

Ren then watched Damien pick up Aurum and disappear into the forest with Zyra following behind. He glanced back at Roman and Natalia and the direction of the remains of the rebel camp. Lavelle would kill him. No one would know where he had gone. They might even think him dead, but they wouldn't find his body. That would leave them with enough hope, wouldn't it? There was no time to go back and explain what he was about to do. He couldn't just let them take Aurum... Whether he was the Aether or not, he had the power to make a difference now. A surge of that power flowed through Ren's veins. If anyone could save Aurum, it was him.

Sorry, Lavelle, he thought, turning back and taking one last look at the black smoke billowing into the air that marked the location of their camp. *I'm about to do something stupid.*

Ren's eyes began to glow gold and silver as he reached out to the earth with his mind. He could feel the indents of Zyra's and Damien's footprints in the ground,

He stood and quietly made his way around the clearing, avoiding a shocked and defeated Natalia and Roman. He then followed Zyra's and Damien's paths of footprints into the depths of the forest back toward the four sectors of Araedia.

CHAPTER TWENTY-FOUR

ASHES

Natalia and Roman tore through the brush, racing toward the black smoke rising high into the sky. Nothing seemed real. She prayed that it wasn't. This was all just another one of her nightmares... She'd wake up soon, right? She'd wake up, and the camp would be fine. Fraiser and Hero would be fine. Aurum and Ren would still be there...

They hadn't been able to find Ren after the battle with Damien. They had searched the forest until screams from the camp pierced the air, and new columns of smoke billowed. Natalia couldn't let herself think about how Lavelle would react when she found out that Aurum and Ren—especially Ren—were both missing. She was barely keeping herself together. Though, at least they knew Aurum was alive... For now... But no one had any idea what had happened to Ren. He'd simply vanished.

Natalia and Roman raced past the blur of the forest around them and burst out of the tree line into the large clearing that made up the rebel camp—or what was left of it. The entirety of it was in ruins. All the air left Natalia's lungs, and a sickening pit formed in her stomach, along with a wave of nausea. Beside her, Roman went eerily still for a few moments. The majority of the tents and shacks were on fire or sprawled on the ground in trampled piles. Even the square was burning, sending black smoke billowing into the sky that darkened with storm clouds. Vayne's army was gone, but the damage they had done would last forever. Natalia's blood ran cold when her eyes landed on the hospital. It had been set on fire... Piercing screams came from the wounded still trapped inside. Roman noticed the hospital as soon as Natalia did, and they took off toward the flames growing higher and higher.

Lavelle knelt near a cluster of ruined tents next to an unconscious Fraiser. "Help them!" she exclaimed, tears streaming down her cheeks as she put pressure on Fraiser's wound. The knife of ice had been removed and lay on the ground beside them. A few feet away, Napoleon knelt next to Hero, holding a blood-covered rag to his face. Roman and Natalia ran up to the hospital doors, frantically trying to tear them open. As soon as he moved his arm, Roman released the door handle with a painful hiss, clutching his left shoulder that Zyra had hit with her knife of ice. More blood drenched Roman's dark shirt.

Natalia's eyes widened, fear shooting through her entire body at the sight of the blood—*his* blood. "Roman—"

"I'm fine," he snapped.

She pulled against the doors again. They didn't budge... Something was barring the other side. Natalia caught movement out of the corner of her eye and glanced back. Some of the remaining rebels had begun to gather around, hopelessly staring at the building as it burned. She felt a tear roll down her cheek and quickly wiped it away, yanking against the doors once more.

"Are there any fire Elementals?" Natalia yelled, turning to the empty faces watching her. No one answered. There were fire Elementals in the crowd, but what could they do? She could feel what they felt. She could feel how hungry, violent, and defiant the flames were. They were too wild and out of control. No fire Elemental would be able to stop them—and it was a good thing she wasn't *just* a fire Elemental. Her eyes met Roman's, and he blinked back tears. "Roman, the river!"

His eyes widened with hope. "Check the back door!" he commanded at the rebels gathered around them. He turned to face Natalia and the river that flowed through the camp behind her. Together, their eyes began to glow red-orange, purple, and ice-blue and dark-blue around silver pupils. They sprinted a few yards past charred tents, smoke, and small, flickering fires until the river came into view. Natalia slid to a stop, kicking ashes and dirt into the air. She and Roman extended their arms to the river and slowly lifted their hands. A large snake of water several feet wide began to weave its way out of the flowing currents and in the direction of the burning building.

"Faster," Natalia panted, fear causing her throat to close. She and Roman twisted and thrust their arms forward as the snake whipped by them, shooting at the hospital and rebels surrounding it. They watched the snake collide and burst against the building, raining drops of water everywhere. She ran back through the rubble with spheres of circling water in her palms. Roman followed behind her with a circling sphere in one hand and a snake of water climbing up and supporting his shoulder in the other. Natalia lunged forward, throwing her spheres at the flames clawing their way back to life. Roman did the same, extinguishing most of the flames at the front doors.

Maybe the fire had died enough that Natalia could wield them now. She prayed to the Aether that she could and once again extended her arms. She closed her eyes, frowning at how heavy and tired they felt. She pushed away the exhaustion creeping upon her and narrowed her focus on the flames. She imagined them receding and dying to nothing but smoke and embers. With a steadying breath, she reached out at the flames. They flickered against her will as her mind touched them, and she gritted her teeth.

Natalia grabbed at the fire again as sobs echoed throughout the camp. This time, the fire pushed back, ripping the door off its handles and sending flames flying out of the doorway. Roman lunged in front of her and used the water supporting his arm to shield them. Suddenly, a wooden beam fell from the ceiling of the hospital, causing half of the roof to collapse inward. The surrounding rebels jumped back with gasps and shrieks of terror. Natalia clenched her fists. It was no use. No matter how hard she tried, the fire couldn't be tamed. It was too wild and destructive. She dropped to her knees, sobs racking her body as the rebels who'd run to the back door returned. They held two additional rebels between them, but no one else. And then, the remainder of the roof groaned and collapsed. Sparks flew high into the dawn. Cries rang out, and rebels scrambled away. Roman pulled Natalia back toward Lavelle, Fraiser, Napoleon, and Hero. She turned to face them to find Lavelle staring directly at her. There had to have been at least fifty rebels in the hospital... *Fifty* lives gone just like that.

"Natalia...," she whispered hoarsely. "Where's Ren and Aurum?"

Natalia felt the tears stream down her face. "Damien... He took Aurum... Someone attacked Ren while he and Roman were following us—" Her voice broke. "He was there one minute, then gone the next. We couldn't find any trace of him... Lavelle, I'm so, so sorry."

Lavelle moved away from Fraiser's side, her hands shaking. Napoleon rose and walked to her as a young girl took Lavelle's place by Fraiser, keeping pressure on her wound. Napoleon wiped at the tears streaming down her cheeks, but she pushed his hand away. Natalia could feel the anger rolling off her in waves. She had never seen Lavelle so angry in her entire life—she didn't even know she *could* be that angry. Lavelle squeezed her eyes shut, dropping her head into her hands. Her shaking fingers clawed desperately at her blonde hair. She suddenly released a painful cry, grabbing at her eyes.

"Lavelle?" Natalia and Napoleon exclaimed, rushing over to her.

She backed away with an extended arm and cried out, covering her eyes once more. Her next cry turned into a sob as she dropped to the ground. Napoleon took another step forward. Natalia felt her throat closing again as fear gripped her along with an overwhelming sense of...defeat... Failure. The rebels had lost. She had failed them. They had all failed. Ren was *missing* with absolutely no trace of him anywhere... Aurum was *taken*. She'd let Damien take her. The utter despair hit her like a wave, dragging her under and drowning her. She couldn't begin to imagine how Lavelle felt. Her brother—her twin—was just...gone.

"Wait, Napoleon," Roman ordered, grabbing his arm.

Lavelle released a vicious cry of mental and physical pain. Currents of strong air shot from her fingertips, blowing them all to the ground before her eyes flashed open. Her irises glowed dark-gray around her pupils as black as the smoke surrounding them. Natalia felt her heart sink. Everything was happening so fast. Their new home had been destroyed. Rebels were dead. Ren, Aurum, and Damien had disappeared. Damien had also alluded to the fact that he didn't think Natalia was the Aether... And now Lavelle was an Elemental. It made sense why she would turn now. Everything that they knew and loved was gone—obliterated. Lavelle's emotions were eating her alive... Just like everyone else.

Napoleon shot up from the ground. "Lavelle, let me help you, please..."

Lavelle looked down at the currents of wind weaving between her fingers. They accelerated before dissipating into the air. "We have to find him," she whispered, tears continuing to roll down her face. "We have to find him. He's still alive. I *know* he is."

He knelt next to her, taking her face in his hands. "We will. I promise we will."

"He has to die," Lavelle rasped.

"What?" Napoleon's face dropped.

"Who?" Natalia whispered.

"*Vayne*," she said. "Vayne has to die. He has to pay for this..." She gestured at the camp. "...for everything that's happened. We need to move out now—"

"Look around you, Lavelle!" Roman shouted. "We can't move out! There's nothing left to move!"

"Roman—" Natalia began.

"No!" He ran a shaking hand through his hair, muttering. "This is all my fault..."

"You know that's not true, Roman." Natalia shook her head. "You know it's not."

Roman turned away from her and walked over to a still-unconscious Fraiser. Natalia watched him struggle to lift her off the ground with his shoulder, but he did so, regardless of the pain it would cause him. He turned to the young medic beside him. "Set up as many salvageable tents as possible. We need to regroup and help our wounded. Natalia, stay here with Napoleon and Lavelle. Help set up the tents and make sure Hero gets to one. Everyone else, search the area for survivors. No one goes too far into the forest, and no one goes anywhere alone. Save whatever supplies you can and pile it in the square... And take care of each other." Roman dropped his head before heading to one of the only tents left standing near the square.

All around Natalia, the rebels wailed and sobbed. Smoke thickened the air, threatening to smother them all. She wiped at the tears on her cheeks. This was not the time to break down. The rebels needed her. Lavelle needed her... Aurum and Ren needed her, too, and so did Roman. No, she would not break. She would let Roman distract himself with Fraiser. That would be better for him anyway. He didn't need to keep staring at what Damien and his father had done to them.

She took a shaky breath before turning to face Napoleon, who held Lavelle tightly to his chest. He glanced up at Natalia with red eyes rimmed with tears. His face crumbled before he leaned his head into Lavelle's hair. Natalia took another deep breath and knelt next to them, wrapping her arms around them. "We're going to make Vayne pay."

"He has to die," Lavelle said, her eyes beginning to glow again. The wind around them began to howl.

"Hey, relax... He will die, but not today. It's not time... Not yet..." Natalia turned to Napoleon. "Take her to the square. Do what Roman said and save whatever supplies you can find. Help the others and set up every tent that we have left. We're going to make it through this."

"What will you do?" he asked, rising with Lavelle.

Natalia stood. "I'm going to put out the fires and help everyone get back to the square. After that, I'll put together as many able-bodied rebels as possible and set up a perimeter. When the perimeters are set, I'm taking a census. We need to know how many people we lost today..."

Napoleon stood eerily still. "Why?"

"Because Lavelle is right. Vayne needs to die, and he needs to die soon. We'll move forward with our plan for taking the sectors. We have no reason to stay out here. There's nothing left for us any more." She bit the inside of her cheek. "He's destroyed it all...so now we destroy him. We regroup, march to Sector Four, increase our army when we take it, and move on to Three, then Two and One. Once all four sectors are behind us, we take the mansion and kill Vayne..."

"Talia," Napoleon hesitated. She watched him clench and unclench his fists. Finally, he asked, "What will you do about Damien?"

Natalia's stare hardened. It seemed as if the world around her had gone still and ice-cold. She watched a shiver wrack down Napoleon's spine. Yes, it had gotten colder, and she knew why. She closed her eyes, which she hadn't even noticed were glowing, and focused on trying to breathe and reign her power back in. "If he gets in my way, I'll kill him."

"And if he doesn't?" Lavelle asked. Natalia could see the question looming in her eyes.

Are you still trying to save him?

"Then we capture him..." She ran a hand through her hair, squeezing her eyes shut. "I don't know. I doubt he'll stay out of this. When it comes down to it, though, I'll kill him if I have to."

"Okay..." Napoleon nodded. "I'll get started with the square... Be careful."

Natalia nodded in return. "You too."

~

Roman paced back and forth outside the flap of the gray tent. He clenched his fists shut to keep them from shaking, but even his closed fists shook in rage, fear, and so many more emotions. The rebels had begun to carry the wounded over to the square and the few tents remaining around it. They needed more tents... A lot more... Before the attack, their numbers had climbed to well over a thousand. He could now only estimate seven hundred, yet he knew there must be survivors spread throughout the forest. There had to be.

The medic who had ducked inside with Fraiser and ushered him out minutes ago was still in her tent. Waiting was excruciating, and so was the sight before him. He observed the camp they had spent years creating and watched as most of it continued to burn. Everything that the rebels had worked for had been reduced to ashes. Even some of the rebels themselves had been reduced to ashes, too. They were dead because of him. It was his fault. He should've known better than to wait. He should've attacked the sectors as soon as they'd taken the train station... But would they have had enough manpower or stamina to do so after? None of the new rebels would've had any idea what was going on, but... No, he'd been right to wait... Right?

Roman shook his head, attempting to escape his own mind. He was tearing himself apart, thought by thought. But the crushing weight hit him like a freight train.

He stood unnaturally still while the deaths and losses of his people threatened to crush him. He knew he was strong in many ways, but seeing his people in pain was unbearable for him. He gasped helplessly and tears filled his eyes. Roman wiped his face with his dirty, bloody hands. The people around him looked to him for guidance, tears streaming down their own faces. He could not cry. He wouldn't.

His jaw hardened, and he scanned their distraught faces. He could feel himself falling apart, but he would not show it. He would be strong for them. It didn't matter that one side of him screamed and cursed himself while the other took pity and told him everything was going to be okay—that it wasn't his fault... He didn't know which side to believe. All he knew was that he couldn't break...

A few moments later, the medic stepped out of the tent, and Roman immediately ducked inside, not bothering to wait to hear what the woman had to say.

Fraiser's eyes blinked heavily as she smirked at him. "What are you looking at?"

Roman knelt next to her and the piles of blankets she lay on. He grabbed her hand, enclosing it in both of his. "I'm so sorry..."

"Why are you sorry? You're not the one who stabbed me."

"How are you feeling?"

She rolled her eyes. "Like someone just pulled a knife of ice out of my gut."

"Fraiser, I'm serious!" Roman clutched her hands tighter, tears welling in his eyes. He could feel the waves of emotions hitting him like a tsunami. Sooner or later, he'd be pulled under and drowned.

"Roman?" Fraiser narrowed her eyes, clearly sensing something awful had happened. He could see the question in her green eyes before she spoke it aloud. "What did they do?"

He dropped his head, a few tears sliding down his cheeks. He shook it before raising his chin to meet her eyes. His own glowing, dark blue and silver eyes reflected back at him in hers. "Vayne sent Damien and the girl you fought—Zyra—after us. They destroyed *everything*. They burned down the hospital, they killed hundreds of us... Damien burnt half of Hero's face... Natalia and Aurum chased after him. Ren and I followed but got separated. He just disappeared. There's been no trace of him whatsoever, and we searched the entire area. We don't know if he's dead or captured. And Aurum... Damien and Zyra took her. We don't know why... The entire battle was a set-up."

"That doesn't make any sense..." She stared at him. After a few moments of blinking back tears, she cleared her throat. "Anything else?"

"Lavelle is an air Elemental."

"What?" Fraiser exclaimed. "Now I know you're making all of this up."

Roman's eyes widened. "By the Aether, *Lavelle* is an *air Elemental*!"

"I don't believe a word you're—"

"Fraiser, what if she could heal you like Natalia healed me back in the forest when we were traveling to Four? It's rare, but it's possible for Elementals of the same element to heal each other, and that's what Lavelle does in the first place! She's a healer!"

"Roman, if what you're saying is true, then Lavelle hasn't even been an Elemental for an hour. How in the Aether's name could she heal me?"

"There's no harm in trying."

"For you, there's no harm!" Fraiser rolled her eyes with a scoff. "You really are one of the dumbest people I've ever met."

"It's not like you're much smarter." He laughed lightly between the few tears that continued to streak down his cheeks. He already felt lighter just having her awake next to him. "I'm serious, though, Fraiser. We should give her a chance."

"I'm going to assume that the emotional weight of the battle on top of losing her twin brother is what caused Lavelle's transformation, which means we should give her some time before we ask."

"Are you being considerate? I think I need to go ask her now, because you *must* be dying."

Fraiser chuckled with a wince. "Screw you."

Roman smiled, but it quickly faded.

She looked up at him. "Roman, I'm sorry about fighting with you the other day... About Natalia... I know that you love her, and even if I don't like her, I'm not going to get in the way. I won't fight with you about her any more. It's not worth it—though I wish you could've fallen in love with someone else..." She gave him a sad smile. "But sometimes, we just can't help who we love."

"I'm sorry, too." Roman's smile returned, growing brighter as his thoughts clung to the kiss he and Natalia had shared in the woods. The memory of her lips was the only anchor keeping him from losing himself in the raging sea threatening to devour him. A shiver ran down his spine, and he knew he would sacrifice anything and everything he had for those lips.

"Stop smiling like an idiot." Fraiser crossed her arms, and Roman opened his mouth to explain but ended up biting back another laugh when she rolled her eyes again. "I don't want to know."

He chuckled. "Thank you, Fraiser."

"You're welcome." She nodded. "Now, please tell me they didn't destroy all the food. I'm starving."

"I'll go find you something," he said, rising. "I need to check on the others as well."

"Hurry up," Fraiser called as he walked out of the tent.

~

The sun had disappeared within the dense canopy of the forest hours ago. The cold night breeze wove through the trees, blowing strands of Ren's blond hair in his face. He leaned against the low-hanging branches of a nearby tree. Sweat covered every inch of him, and a dull headache stretched across his forehead and behind his blue eyes. His entire body ached and shivered. He was exhausted, and whatever powers he had discovered merely hours ago had drained his energy completely. But he had to keep trailing Vayne's army. He couldn't let Damien or Aurum out of his sight. He *had* to keep going. He was the Aether now, and no one could stop Vayne except him.

Ren wiped the sweat from his brow and watched the army trudge along through the forest, scanning faces for Aurum, Damien, and the woman Damien called Zyra. His eyes narrowed as he took in Damien's face toward the back of the army. He saw Aurum next. Her arms were bound behind her back with shackles of hardened ice, and a cloth gag sat between her teeth. Zyra walked behind her, twirling a knife of ice along her fingers.

"How many casualties?" Damien asked Zyra as they walked.

Ren's eyes widened. He was yards away, yet he could hear every word they said as if he were right next to them.

"We lost nearly every human soldier, but we're still over nine hundred strong as of now. Vayne will have more soldiers for us when we return."

Damien nodded and turned to Aurum with a smug smirk. "I wonder how many of your people died... You know, your friends actually managed to take out most of Vayne's personal guard. I only had one come back."

"Ah, yes." Zyra smiled sadistically. "That's why I put a knife through that one girl. What *was* her name again?"

"Fraiser, I believe," Damien answered, eyeing Aurum. "You can unmuzzle the dog, Zyra dearest."

"Let's hope her bark is worse than her bite," she said, ripping the gag from Aurum's mouth. "Because her bite wasn't much."

"Who are you?" Aurum demanded, meeting Damien's gaze. Ren could see the fire blazing in her eyes from here. Anger and heartbreak filled her voice. "What happened to the boy I could always count on to argue and laugh with—who I could count on to be there?"

Damien frowned. "He died, and he's dead because of your friend."

"No, he's not dead." She shook her head. "He's still in there. I know the real you is in there, Damien, because you would've killed me by now if he wasn't."

"You don't know what you're talking about." Zyra laughed. "I like this one, Damien, she's funny."

"None of this is Natalia's fault. It's not yours, either. Vayne did this to you." Aurum nodded at Zyra. "*She* did this to you."

Damien paused, roughly grabbing Aurum's chin and forcing her to face him. Their noses were centimeters apart. "The only reason I haven't gutted you is because I need you for my plan. After you've served your purpose, I'll brainwash you myself... And *that* is a fate worse than death."

"What did you do to him?" Aurum said to Zyra.

"We fixed him," she said coolly.

"No, you *broke* him!" Aurum jumped and kicked her unbound feet. They collided with Zyra's stomach, sending them both to the dirt. The reverberations in the ground tickled up Ren's arms, causing the hairs on the back of his neck to stand as he watched with clenched fists. Damien chuckled and lifted Aurum to her feet. She struggled against his grip, but it was no use.

Zyra then rose and wrapped the gag back around Aurum's mouth. She smiled at Aurum before punching her in the face. She tumbled to the ground, blood seeping through the cloth in her mouth. Enraged, Ren bit his bottom lip so hard that the metallic sting of blood met his tongue. He would kill Vayne and Zyra for turning Damien into this monster, then he would kill Damien himself. It would be a mercy to kill him—a mercy that some would argue that Damien didn't deserve—and spare him from the consequences of his actions. It didn't matter that he had been brainwashed... Ren would kill him.

"Enough." Damien waved Zyra away. "Tell the men to keep marching. We aren't stopping until we're back in Sector One."

Zyra nodded and disappeared into the crowd of soldiers, her white armor stark against the black sea. Damien turned to Aurum and lifted her off the ground once again. He brushed a loose strand of her brown hair from her face, then, with one hand placed on her back, they began to walk again, the army continuing on into the darkening forest.

CHAPTER TWENTY-FIVE

STATIC

The morning sun slowly began to ascend behind the trees of the forest, casting shadows over the burnt rubble of the rebel camp. Most of the dead had been rounded up and burned or buried. They had lost over three hundred rebels… Natalia knelt next to a group of rebels pitching one of the few salvageable tents that they could find. She stood with a yawn, rubbing the sleep from her eyes. No one in the camp had slept last night. The cries of the wounded and mourners and the filthy stench of smoke and death made sure of that. The remaining food and water had been distributed last night along with a census. Roman had been right about survivors in the forest, and the rebels' final number amounted to 772. Ren and Aurum, however, hadn't been counted…

Natalia rose from beside the now-pitched tent and began walking through the camp, helping out wherever she could. Minutes passed before she saw Roman heading toward her. She turned and watched as he splashed through the river that wound through the camp and paused a few feet away from her. The last time she'd seen him was when the hospital had collapsed. He looked so tired—and sad. Pain squeezed her chest. She wouldn't show her weariness now. She had to be strong for him and their people… And herself.

For a few moments, they simply stared at each other, then Natalia ran to Roman and threw her arms around him. He slipped his arms around her waist, pulling her closer to him.

"Are you all right?" she whispered.

"As all right as I can be…," Roman said, keeping one arm around her waist as he cupped her cheek. "Are you all right?"

She nodded, feeling a little lightheaded. Touching Roman as she was now— she'd have to get used to it. It was thrilling, and her entire being seemed to hum to life wherever their skin met. But she couldn't stop herself from feeling a little guilty. How was she allowed to touch him when others had just had their own lovers ripped away by the clutches of death that still loomed heavy over everything around them? How was that fair to them? Was that what she and Roman were now? Lovers? She wanted that with him, and it was certainly a conversation to be had but not now. It wasn't the time. "Where have you been?"

"Searching the forest..."

"For survivors?" Natalia raised a brow. All the survivors had been found and brought back to what remained of the camp yesterday. She still couldn't believe it had only been a day since Damien had attacked. The entirety of the camp was still in shock.

"No." Roman shook his head. "I was trying to see if I could find any sign of Aurum or Ren... And I just couldn't stand being here with everything like this."

She followed Roman's gaze at the surrounding rubble. She gently grabbed both sides of his face and turned him to face her. The sunlight hit his eyes, illuminating their golden highlights. She could get lost in his eyes forever. She leaned her brow against his chest and closed her eyes as he placed a soft kiss on the top of her head— definitely something she would have to get used to in the future. If they had one... She prayed to the Aether that they would. She wanted to learn his touch. She'd fight even harder to make sure that she could.

"I have a plan...," she whispered.

~

Lavelle watched Napoleon wrinkle his nose at the stench of smoke as he opened another door of a ruined shack. She stood, mindlessly staring into the gloom of ashes and smoke while he brought his shirt up over his nose and mouth, shielding his lungs from the smoke tumbling out. Its tendrils snaked through the slight breeze and curled around her like dark fingers of death. A part of her wished she was dead. She and Ren had gone through so much to find each other only to be ripped apart again, and she didn't even know what had taken him from her. There was no sign of him anywhere. He had vanished completely, which most had tried to convince her was a good thing. There was no body to recover; therefore, he was still alive... Lavelle cursed the fools who believed that. If there were no body, it meant he had to have been captured, which was a fate worse than death. What if Vayne tortured and brainwashed Ren like Damien? She would rather find his body than face that...

Napoleon turned to face Lavelle with a weary smile. His face and hair—like hers—were covered in soot and dirt. For the past hour, she and Napoleon had been searching for supplies in the few shacks that had somehow survived the assault on the camp. She knew he was trying to distract her, keep her thoughts away from the brother she now thought of. He knew it would consume her, and it was. Without Ren, she was lost. Without her other half, she was nothing.

Dirt and soot covered every inch of the building and the singed wooden crates inside. Napoleon eased inside, his boots causing tendrils of smoke to rise from the wooden planks below him. Sunlight shone through a hole in the crumbling roof, illuminating the dust swirling in the air. He backed outside.

"Hey." He smiled at her. "I need your help with this one."

She shook her head. His alternative distraction involved him trying to coax her into using her element. She hadn't been able to summon a single gust of wind so far. Her voice was hoarse as she spoke. "I couldn't help you with the last one. I can't help you with this one, either."

Napoleon took her hands in his. "Lavelle, I know you want to get Aurum and your brother back. Believe me, I do, too, but we can't just leave the camp with nothing. We'll never make it to the walls—we'll never make it to Ren and Aurum without supplies... And you need to try to use your Element. It could save your life."

"Or destroy it. That's what this whole war is about." She took a few steps toward him, anger and pain hitting her so hard, her chest hurt. "Who's the strongest Elemental? Well, we supposedly have the strongest Elemental, but we're still losing! All we're doing is destroying and killing each other!"

"No, Lavelle, we're protecting each other, too." He wiped the soot from her cheek. "And Natalia was able to heal Roman with her element once. Yes, there's a lot of death and destruction, but would you rather go back to your old life of being controlled by Vayne? I know I wouldn't. I'd rather be here with you and the others."

Lavelle crossed her arms, and Napoleon smiled at her. "Come on. Just try this last one."

She leaned her head on his chest with a sigh, fear shooting through her. "It's not going to work."

"When Ren first started to use his element, he was terrified. So was I when I first discovered it."

"How did you discover your element, Napoleon?"

Napoleon smiled sadly. "It's a very long story... And maybe after all of this is over, I'll have the time to tell you... But do you know why Ren insisted on figuring out his element despite how terrified he was?"

"Why?"

"Because he wanted to be strong enough to save you when the time came, and he was. You don't have time to train like he did, but you have time to become used to it. You don't have to use your element to fight, but if you're familiar with it, sometimes it'll fight for you."

She bit her bottom lip. Ren had done everything to get her back—to save her—so she would do the same. She met Napoleon's gaze. "What do you need me to do?"

"Can you get all of the dirt and soot out?"

Lavelle walked over to the door of the shack and stepped inside. She coughed as the dirt, soot, and dust filled her lungs and stung her eyes. She closed them and stood as still as possible. She scowled. How was she supposed to focus on *this* while Aurum and Ren were gone? How would they find them? What if there wasn't anyone to find? What if they were...dead? *What if Ren is dead?*

Tears welled in Lavelle's eyes as they began to glow dark-gray around pupils as black as night. No, her brother was not dead. She could barely feel it, but it was as if a string of wind connected her soul to his—a line stretching across the lands that separated them. No, Ren wasn't dead. He was out there, and one way or another, she was going to find him. She opened her eyes, and tendrils of wind began to swirl around her palms, blowing her hair around her face. Soot, dirt, dust, and smoke rose and collected in a small funnel in front of her. Lavelle extended her hands outward, straining to keep the funnel from wobbling. The funnel began to grow, collecting splinters of wood. She pushed up, tearing off the remains of the roof as the funnel shot high into the air and dispersed. She turned to find Napoleon grinning at her, and she couldn't help but smile back before turning and opening the nearest crate. Her eyes widened at the sight before her.

"Napoleon," she said breathlessly. "Is that what I think it is?"

Napoleon was next to her in an instant, eyes wide as well. "Yeah, it is..."

~

Natalia and Roman stood amongst the encirclement of remaining tents near the square. The rebels had been able to save more than she'd originally thought. Around sixty tents had been pitched, and piles of electric weapons and black armor—taken from the remains of Vayne's soldiers that had fallen in battle—sat in a pile near three dozen crates of food.

The two of them paused outside a tent a few rows down by where Fraiser was resting. Natalia bit her lower lip nervously. Hero had woken up a few hours after the attack but had refused to see anyone. How bad was the burn? She remembered watching Damien slash his sword of fire down Hero's face. She couldn't imagine that kind of pain. A shiver ran down her spine, and Roman, seeming to sense her discomfort, slipped his hand into hers. She smiled softly at him. This is how they would beat Vayne—together. No matter how many times Roman's father beat them down, they would always get back up because they all had each other.

"Natalia! Roman!" Napoleon's voice rang throughout the camp.

The two whirled around to watch Napoleon and Lavelle hurriedly dipping in and out of the crowd toward them, their hands also intertwined.

"What's wrong?" Roman called, rushing to meet them. "Are you all right?"

"We're better than all right!" Napoleon grinned.

Natalia felt a flutter in her chest. All the rebels had known in the past twenty-four hours was pain, suffering, and heartbreak, but what she heard in Napoleon's voice now was... *Hope.* It was hope, and the sight of it nearly brought her to her knees.

"You'll never believe what we found," Lavelle said with a slight smile.

"What did you find?" Natalia asked breathlessly.

"We were searching through the last of the shacks, and Lavelle used her element to clear away all the soot. We found a ton of boxes and crates—"

"Napoleon! What did you find?" Roman exclaimed.

"A projector!" Lavelle's smile turned to a grin wide enough to match Napoleon's. "We found a projector."

Napoleon shook his head. "Not just any projector, though. We tried it out, and it *works.*"

"Well, it turned on, but we know someone who can easily fix it," Lavelle said, nodding at the tents behind Natalia and Roman.

"Hero...," Roman whispered. "By the Aether... Natalia, if we can get Hero to fix the projector, then—"

"The plan will work," Natalia finished. "We can contact the sectors and let them know we're coming and to be ready."

"There's one more thing," Lavelle said.

Roman turned to her, a smile forming on his lips. "What?"

"I'm going to try to heal Fraiser like Natalia did with you in the woods."

"Lavelle." Natalia took a step forward. "Are you sure you want to try that? It's not that I don't have faith in you, but you've barely had your element for a day."

Lavelle frowned, and Natalia could see the determination on her face. "I know that, but I have to at least try. Fraiser can refuse if she wants, but element or no element, I'm going to help her. It's my job."

Natalia nodded. "Okay, you and Napoleon go see Fraiser. Roman and I are going to go talk to Hero. If we can get him to agree to fix the projector, we can begin step one of the plan."

Napoleon raised a brow. "What plan are we enacting exactly?"

She grabbed Roman's hand again, leading him to Hero's tent. She glanced back over her shoulder with a smirk. "Our plan to take back the sectors and kick Vayne's ass."

"If Hero can fix the projector and make contact with the sectors," Roman whispered against Natalia's ear, "we need to tell the people immediately. They need it. They need a reason to move on, and so do we. There's nothing left for us here. It's all been destroyed."

Natalia watched the solemn faces of the other rebels as they drew closer to Hero's tent. Roman was right. There was nothing left for them here any more. They had to fix the projector. It would give the rebels hope, and hope was exactly what they needed... Along with some justice. They would make Vayne, Zyra, and Damien all pay for what they had done here.

"Our spirits may be broken, but we're still alive. When there's life, there's hope," Natalia said, ducking inside the tent with Roman following behind her. Darkness enveloped them. The only source of light was the sun battling to shine through the thick fabric of the tent. In the darkest corner, a hunched figure sat, facing away from them. His blond hair appeared nearly black in the depths of the shadows.

Natalia inched toward him. "Hero?"

"I'm sorry, I can't see you right now," Hero said, his voice strained.

"Hero, I'm so sorry about what happened, but...we need you. Napoleon and Lavelle found a projector. It works, but it needs some fixing. We have a plan to march on the sectors. If we can let them know we're coming—"

Hero stood, whirling around to face them. She bit the inside of her cheek, fighting back a gasp. Roman stiffened next to her. A sickening burn peeked out from under the bandages around his face. The beginning of the injury ran from two inches above the end of Hero's left eyebrow—or what was left of his eyebrow—down to his collarbone. Peeling, red skin could be seen around the edges of the bandages.

"What's the point?" Hero shrugged. "Vayne's already won."

"No, he hasn't," Natalia whispered. "Don't say that. Don't give up, Hero."

"Vayne hasn't won until every last one of us is dead," Roman said, clenching his fists at his sides. "The fight continues as long as a single rebel breathes."

"He'll kill us all if we march on the sectors." Hero released a humorless laugh. "He'll kill us all if we do anything. We should run now while we still can. Leave the sectors behind and find a new land to keep our people alive."

"Our people are still inside those damned walls," she hissed. "Or have you forgotten, Hero? Have you forgotten those messages you used to send out over the projectors? Have you forgotten the hope you gave people—gave *me*?"

"There is no hope now! Look what they did to us!" he exclaimed, arms raised to encompass the remains of the camp outside of his tent. He pointed to his face. "Look what they did to me... They destroyed hope. There is none left here..."

"*Yes, there is.*" Roman stepped toward him, but Hero retreated a step back into the shadows. "Napoleon found a *projector*, Hero. If you can fix it, we can prepare the sectors to fight with us. You know they'll fight with us. You said so yourself. Hope is not destroyed, not yet... You have to help us save it."

The remainder of Hero's brows knit together, and he began pacing the width of the tent. Natalia could only watch the gears turn in his head as he brought a hand to his chin, thinking through everything they'd said. She took a small step forward to stand beside Roman. Hero was scared. They all were, but they couldn't just let Vayne win. They had to do something. With or without Hero's help, she was marching on the sectors. She didn't care if she had to do it by herself.

He paused to meet their gaze. "Where's the projector?"

Natalia could see a small spark of life returning to his brown eyes. "It's in one of the shacks, but—"

Hero shook his head with a wince. "I don't need to know the specifics of the plan right now. Whatever it is... I'm in. I'll find the projector and fix it, then get in touch with my contacts inside. You can fill me in on the plan later."

"Thank you." Roman nodded.

"Don't thank me," Hero murmured. He shivered, rubbing his arms. "When do we march?"

"Tomorrow morning," Natalia answered, glancing at Roman. His eyes found hers, and the hair on the back of her neck stood. Just the way he looked at her was electric. "We'll address the people after we run the plan over with Fraiser, Napoleon, and Lavelle."

"Are you going to talk to them now?"

"Yes." She nodded.

"I'm going to go find the projector and get started. It could take a few hours," Hero said, walking out of the tent.

Roman ducked out after him, placing a hand on his shoulder. "We'll make them pay for what they did to you...to us."

Hero's eyes darkened and a devilish smirk appeared on his lips, that spark of light turning to a spark of revenge. "Yes, we will."

Natalia watched him disappear into the ruins of the camp, worry filling her. She had never seen Hero so...dark. But she couldn't blame him after everything that they had been through. *One way or another, it will all be over soon,* she told herself.

"Come on," Roman said, walking to Fraiser's tent.

Suddenly, a yelp of pain from the tent pierced the air. Roman's eyes widened, and he hurriedly ducked inside. Natalia followed behind him. She knew letting Lavelle try to heal Fraiser was a mistake. Yes, Lavelle was a great medic, but dabbling with healing and the elements after only having her element for a day was dangerously stupid.

Natalia nearly bumped into Roman's back as he stopped to watch the sight before him. Fraiser was clutching Lavelle's and Napoleon's hands while Lavelle knelt next to her, eyes glowing dark-gray and black. Fraiser's own eyes glowed gray and silver, and a current of wind circled around her lower stomach where the knife of ice had been. Fraiser and Lavelle both winced, and the wind began to dissipate.

A shiver ran down Natalia's spine, and the urge hit her like a tsunami. She didn't know why, but something inside her *begged* her to join them. It was as if her life—Fraiser's and the others' lives—depended on it. She recognized the instincts. They were the same instincts that had guided her in the forest when she'd helped heal Roman. So Natalia grabbed Roman's hand, dragged him over to the cot, and placed their hands on Lavelle's shoulder. Natalia felt her own eyes begin to glow and watched as Roman's and Napoleon's did the same. All five of their eyes shone a cascade of colors, and the dissipating wind grew back stronger than it had been before. She could feel the transfer of her energy running through her veins, leaving her body, and flowing through the bond that they all shared as Elementals. It was as if a strong, bright light knitted them all together.

Fraiser's wound was greater than they had expected. She was taking a lot of energy... Natalia could feel her eyes growing heavy, and it felt as if her muscles were shrinking. They needed to let go before Fraiser took too much of their energy. Natalia focused on her hand, slowly forcing it to Roman's. She grunted, prying his fingers from Lavelle's shoulder. The energy transferring was dangerous for all of them, but it seemed nearly impossible to let go. But they had to. She struggled to turn her head and lift her opposite hand, the other still pulling against Roman's hand on Lavelle's shoulder. She slowly placed her free hand on Roman's chest and pushed with all her might. He stumbled backward, grabbing Natalia's hand and pulling her with him. It was clear that he knew how important it was for them to let go, too.

As soon as they were free, they turned to Napoleon and Lavelle. Natalia quickly pried Lavelle's hand away from Fraiser's, and Roman repeated the action with Napoleon. The four stumbled back, all panting as sweat dripped down their bodies. Fraiser gasped on the cot, bags forming under her normal, green eyes. She slowly sat up with a wince. She lifted her shirt and tore away the bandages around her waist to reveal a large scab where the knife had been. Natalia was right. Fraiser's wound had been a lot worse than expected.

"Is everyone all right?" Roman asked between breaths.

Napoleon nodded, and Lavelle gave a thumbs-up. Natalia returned a nod as well, thanking the Aether that it had worked. They were lucky... "We're never doing this again. Not unless someone's dying. It's too dangerous," she said.

"Agreed," Napoleon panted.

Fraiser rolled her eyes. "It takes too long anyway."

"Shut up, Fraiser," Natalia said, fighting back a grin. She still didn't like Fraiser very much, but they needed her. It was good to have her back, too, even if she wasn't completely healed.

"So what's this plan we've all heard so much about?" Fraiser rose and extended her hands to Lavelle, who still sat on the floor. Lavelle grabbed them, and Fraiser pulled her to her feet. "Napoleon said they found a projector."

"Is Hero going to fix it?" he asked, hope sparkling in his blue eyes.

"Yes." Roman nodded. "He's doing it now."

Fraiser's brows furrowed. "We're going to contact the sectors?"

"We are," Natalia said. "After he makes contact, Hero is going to tell them that the rebels are beginning the march to Four tomorrow morning, so they'll be ready when we get there. Rebel support has been growing for months, and when we call out to them to let them know we're coming... We could have this war finished within the week."

"What if he can't make contact?" Fraiser frowned.

"It doesn't matter. There's no use in us staying here. There's nothing left," she replied.

"Either way," Roman began, glancing between the two girls, "we're marching tomorrow morning. Vayne won't expect us to retaliate so soon. We'll take Sector Four, then work our way over until we get to One. With the sectors behind us, we'll bring the fight to him, and he won't have anywhere to run or hide."

Fraiser ran a hand through her dark hair. "Every one of us will have to fight for this to work."

"I can't imagine why anyone wouldn't want to fight." Napoleon shook his head. "We've always had support within the walls."

"Even those who didn't support us didn't get in our way," Roman said. "They just stayed out of it. But they're waiting for us. They've always been waiting for us to do something big—something big enough that makes them disregard the consequences of outwardly supporting us. Vayne can't target them if everyone's revolting."

Napoleon nodded. "Vayne's taken everything from everyone. We all have reasons to fight, and they will fight with us—both the rebels and those in the sectors alike."

"What do we do about Sector Four's wall?" Lavelle questioned. "We all know security has increased since the testings."

Roman's eyes narrowed with determination. "We use the grappling hooks, our elements, the crack if it's still there... We hit them with everything we have and give them hell. We'll get over that wall."

"Okay." Fraiser shrugged. "Let's do it."

"Fraiser, Lavelle." Roman pointed between them. "You two stay here and rest. Natalia, I need you to begin gathering people in the square. Napoleon, you come with me. We're going to go check on Hero before we confirm the plan."

Everyone nodded, and Natalia gave Roman a soft smile. He returned her smile with a wink before ducking out of the tent with Napoleon in tow behind him.

Fraiser shuddered, looking at Natalia and the flap of the tent still swinging shut. "*That* was *disgusting*."

Natalia faced her with a glare, fighting back another smile. Lavelle snickered, and all three of them burst into laughter...

~

Roman walked in the direction of the shack Napoleon had pointed at. He couldn't believe what had happened in the tent. Through Lavelle, they had somehow all managed to transfer energy over to Fraiser. He didn't know that it was even possible to do so. The book he'd stolen from his father all those years ago had never mentioned any Elemental capable of *that*.

Roman gritted his teeth. His father had beaten him for taking that book... To this day, Vayne was still haunting him, but it would end soon. He was ready for the war between them to be over. It had lasted too long... Had cost too many lives... And now there were new lives—new people—he didn't want anywhere near his father. Natalia... If Vayne ever got his hands on her... Roman would die before he let that happen. That sole thought was what kept the regret at bay. He'd regretted the path his father had fallen down—wished he could've gone back and changed it. Fraiser had asked him before if he'd be able to kill his father when the time came. He'd never been able to give her an answer...

Until now.

A part of him had always thought that he'd somehow be able to take the chance to convince his father to change, but not now. He'd never take that chance with Natalia around. So if Fraiser asked him again, Roman would tell her yes. He'd be able to kill his father when the time came to protect Natalia from him.

Roman and Napoleon poked their heads inside the shack to find Hero sitting on one of the many crates inside, twisting the knobs on the projector. A steady stream of static filled the air.

Roman knocked on the wood twice. "How's it going?"

"Well, it works," Hero hissed, wincing as ear-piercing static screamed. He twisted a few buttons, and the steady hum returned. "That's all I've been able to get so far. It's actually in very good condition considering the circumstances..." He glanced at them. "How's Fraiser?"

"Mostly healed," he answered, watching Hero twist the biggest knob on the projector to the right. "Natalia's gathering everyone in the square. We're going to announce the plan soon—"

"By the Aether!" Napoleon yelled, covering his ears as static pierced the air. Roman did the same, and Hero quickly flipped the knob back to the left.

"You've got to be kidding!" He scowled, striking the projector. Small metal parts clanged against the floor, and the steady flow of static began to hiss choppily. A short screeching filled the shack for a few moments before the static turned to the silence of an empty channel. Hero's eyes widened, and he slowly leaned closer to the projector. "Hello?"

Nothing.

Hero frowned. "Hello?"

Roman sighed. "It's all right, Hero—"

"Hello?" a clear, masculine voice exclaimed through the speaker. "Did you just say Hero?"

"Spenser?" Hero grinned. "Spenser, is that you?"

"Hero? Hero, you made it! Are you with the rebels?"

"Yes, he is," Roman said, clapping Hero's shoulder. Napoleon rose to the tips of his toes and peaked over their shoulders with a grin.

Hero turned the volume up. "Spenser, you're talking to Vayne's son and leader of the rebels, Roman. Roman, this is Spenser Barron. He lives in Sector Four."

"Perfect," Roman said. "Spenser, I need your help."

"What do you need?" the voice crackled.

"The rebels are beginning the march to Sector Four tomorrow morning. We're going to liberate Four, then Two, Three, and One. Is there any way you can prepare Sector Four?"

"All of the sectors have been on a twenty-four-hour curfew for three days straight. I've been able to keep in touch with all our contacts in each sector so far, but our correspondents in Sector One stopped responding a few hours ago."

Hero's brows furrowed. "All of them?"

"Every single one..." Spenser sighed. "Something's going on in One, and the poor people here in Sector Four won't last much longer under this curfew... So when you get to the walls of Four, we'll be waiting on the other side. I'll find a way to spread the word. We'll back you and the rebels, Roman. We're tired of living like this. It's not really living at all... We'll gather as much supplies as we can. We'll be ready."

Roman nodded, adrenaline pumping through his veins. "Good."

"What do you think happened to the people in One?" Hero asked.

"My father's army is weak right now," Roman responded. "Because of our elements, we were able to take a good number of them down with us when they attacked. My bet is that he's integrated citizens into the army."

"All of them?" Napoleon questioned.

Roman shook his head. "No, he'll have taken all the able-bodied men and women and brought them to his mansion. The rest of the sector will remain on curfew, and if you can't contact them at all, then that means he's probably cut all forms of communication within the sector as well."

"Can that many people even fit in the mansion?" Spenser asked, static hissing at the end of his words.

Roman ran a hand through his hair. "No, he can't fit that many people in there even with all the underground basement cells."

"That's it!" Napoleon exclaimed. "*Underground!* Could he have taken them down into the tunnels?"

"It's possible." Roman shrugged. "There are sections of the tunnels that we've never been able to access because they've been blocked off. Maybe they're hidden behind those blocks."

"There's nowhere else they could be, Roman!" Napoleon ran a hand through his light brown hair. "That's where they are!"

Roman nodded, running through everything in his head. Their plan could still work, but they needed those civilians... They needed every single person they could get. "All right, change of plans. Spenser, can you still hear me?"

"Loud and clear."

"Prepare as many civilians in Four as you can. Expect the rebels at the walls the day after tomorrow—around sunset—but you *have* to be there for this to work."

Napoleon's brows furrowed. "Roman, what are you up to?"

"Napoleon, you're going to lead an underground team to search the tunnels for the people of One while we attack Four. You free the people in the tunnels and join us when we attack One."

"It's risky," Spenser hummed. "But it's now or never. I'll spread the word. We'll be there at sunset."

"Thank you, Spenser," Roman responded before turning and leaving the shack, Napoleon trailing behind him. "Hero, join us in the square when you're done."

"I will," Hero called. "Be careful, Spenser."

"You as well, Hero. Spenser, over and out."

"Hero, over and out."

CHAPTER TWENTY-SIX

FIGHT WITH ME

Roman walked over to Natalia, who was staring out into the depths of the forest illuminated by the morning sun. The breeze weaving throughout the forest blew small strands of black hair across her face. She had gathered the rebels in the square as he'd asked minutes ago, and it was time for his speech before they declared war. The nerves that had wracked his body instantly eased at the sight of her. He was so thankful for her. Natalia turned to face him, her lips a grim line and her brows slightly knit together. He bit back a smile. She was making his favorite face, and for a moment, it seemed as if nothing had ever changed. They weren't about to march off to their possible deaths and fight his father. For a moment, they were just two kids out in the forest on a sunny day... But dark clouds loomed in the distance. The days ahead would be dark, rainy, and cold.

"What are you thinking about?" he asked softly, brushing a knuckle along her cheek.

She took a deep breath, shaking her head slightly. "I just can't get what Damien said in the forest out of my head."

Roman frowned. "What did he say?"

"It was right after Zyra made her appearance and whispered something to him. He told me that I'm not who I think I am. I could tell by the look on his face that some factor in his plan had changed... Then he said that I wasn't the Aether."

"What?" Roman jerked back. That was *impossible*. He had witnessed Natalia wielding both fire and ice. "Why would he lie about that? You have to be the Aether. You're the only one of us who can wield multiple elements."

"I know, but..." She pinched the bridge of her nose. "He wasn't lying. I know he wasn't. He believed every word that he said."

"Then he was brainwashed to say that," he said. Damien was a liar, and every word he said was poison straight from Vayne's mouth. He was nothing more than another puppet.

"No, he wasn't."

It was Roman's turn to shake his head. "Are you saying that you believe him? You actually believe you're not the Aether?"

"Yes," Natalia whispered. "He wasn't going to take me prisoner, Roman. He was going to kill me and just take Aurum..." Her eyes suddenly widened as if she had pieced together one of the biggest puzzles in the sectors, and maybe she had.

"What?" Roman urged, fear flooding his veins.

"He was going to just take Aurum and kill me because I was the most powerful Elemental besides the Aether... He said so himself."

Roman simply stood there, dumbfounded. If Damien was right, and Natalia wasn't the Aether, then why take Aurum? She was a powerful Elemental, but she wasn't the Aether or Natalia. She could be handled—used as bait. So who was Damien trying to set a trap for? It couldn't be any of the rebels because Damien didn't know who was close with who... It could be Roman himself, but if he'd wanted to set a trap for him, he would have taken Natalia alive... So the trap had to be for someone he knew before, which left the twins. All of Roman's air suddenly left his lungs. The trap wasn't for Lavelle because she didn't have her powers then, and only one of the twins was missing. Ren wasn't dead. He was *missing*. "Son of a..."

"What?" Natalia questioned, panic creeping into her voice. "You figured it out, didn't you?"

"No, it's impossible...," he murmured.

"Roman, what is it?" She grabbed the sides of his face, fear etched all over her own.

"It's Ren," he whispered. "It was all a trap for Ren."

Natalia's face dropped, and she stumbled back as if she'd been struck. "What?" she repeated.

"It was obviously a trap to lure someone back to the sectors, but he doesn't know me or any of the rebels, which means the trap was for someone he already knew. It wasn't for you or Aurum, and Lavelle didn't have her powers then. That only leaves one person, who conveniently happens to be missing."

"You and Ren got separated, and Zyra came late to the battle..." Natalia ran a hand through her hair, pacing. "What if she saw Ren somehow wield more than one element and told Damien? It would explain his reaction, and—by the Aether. *By Ren!* You're right, Roman! The trap was for Ren!"

He shook his head. "I can't believe it."

"It makes sense," she said, peering over his shoulder at the square—at their people—then returning her slate eyes to him. "If they knew that the Aether was on our side..."

"We can't tell them yet." Roman shook his head. "Not until we find out where he is or if he's been captured."

"I bet he went after Aurum," Natalia murmured. Fear filled her eyes, sending pain through him. He hated the fear surrounding her now. He'd kill it if he could. "If Vayne or Damien get their clutches on him—"

"They won't," he said, grabbing her hand. Roman flashed her a wicked grin. "They'll be too busy dealing with us to notice anything or anyone else."

Natalia rolled her eyes with a crooked smile. The mischievous gleam in her eyes told him that she agreed. "Stop stalling your speech. We'll never reach the sectors at this rate."

Roman smirked. "Come on, then."

~

Natalia watched Roman climb on top of the stacked crates in the center of the square, the entirety of the rebels crowding around him. Silence fell over the square as he stood, towering above them all. Even the early morning wind rustling the leaves on the trees paused to listen.

After healing Fraiser last night, Roman had left to check on Hero and the projector. When he'd returned, eyes full of hope, and told her that they'd made contact with Sector Four, her knees had nearly buckled with relief. He'd then gathered the rebels and explained their plan to march on the sectors—one team would search the tunnels beneath the sectors with Napoleon and the other would fight in Four. He'd told them to prepare for battle... And prepared they had.

Natalia again stood amongst rebels clad in black armor and equipped with guns and spears of electricity taken from Vayne's own army. Roman, Napoleon, Lavelle, Hero, and Fraiser had all donned armor as well. Natalia ran a hand over the raised red and blue swirls of paint she and the others had painted on their armor last night to distinguish them from Vayne's soldiers. Her chest swelled with pride as Roman's gaze met hers amongst the crowd. Anywhere she went his eyes followed her. She was so proud of him. After everything he'd been through, he was still fighting. He smiled softly at her before turning to the rebels, his face returning to the cool mask it had been a few moments before. That smile would always take her breath away—ease her racing heart as it had minutes ago. Ren and Aurum would be all right. The rebels would get to the sectors before Vayne could brainwash or harm either of them...

They'll be okay. We'll all be okay..., she told herself, willing the words to be true. She wouldn't let the fear fighting its way up take hold. She'd fight it tooth and nail just like she'd fight tooth and nail for those around her. She'd block out the fear of losing them all and replace it with a burning desire to protect and...*win.*

"I know what I'm asking of you all today," Roman said, his voice ringing out over the square. "I wish I didn't have to ask it... But tomorrow I will fight. I will fight for every single one of you until my last breath leaves my body." Natalia shuddered at those words. That fear she could never fight against—the fear of losing him. But she wouldn't allow that to happen. She wouldn't let Roman die, but if he somehow did, she'd go with him. "I don't deserve to ask you to fight alongside me because of all the pain my father—Vayne—has caused, but he will stand no longer. I ask you to remember the things you'd rather forget... The way Vayne sent his army to hunt us down and slaughter us, the brainwashing and murdering of the innocent children in our sectors, the destruction of Araedia's freedom and morals—*our* freedom and morals.

I ask you to remember the loved ones he's taken from us... I ask you all to fight with me for them. For our future and our children's futures. If you fight with me tomorrow, a whole new world will begin whether we live or die. The people in the sectors will fight with us!" A round of cheers erupted through the remains of the camp. The wind picked up as if it cheered with them. "So I ask you, rebels of Araedia... Will you help me destroy my father and bring peace to our home? Will you fight with me?"

A chorus of cheers, whoops, and war cries encased the square. Natalia glanced to her right where Napoleon, Lavelle, and Fraiser stood. They roared with the rebels, determination shining in their eyes. Hero, a bandage still wrapped around his face, released his own vicious cry to Natalia's left. Chills snaked their way down her spine, and adrenaline shot along her veins. She was so thankful for every unique, beautiful life around her. She was proud of her friends and the people they would lead. A warmth bloomed in her chest when her eyes once again met Roman's. She read the silent question in his gaze.

Will you fight with me?

"Always," she mouthed.

"*Rebels,*" he exclaimed with a raised fist, never breaking from her gaze. "*To war!*"

A new wave of war cries emerged, and Natalia, Fraiser, Napoleon, and Hero met Roman by the crates as he descended. Roman interlaced his fingers with hers, and together, they led the entirety of the rebels to the edge of the forest... Toward the sectors... Toward home. Multitudes of eyes began to glow a cascade of colors, electricity filling the air. Everything she and the rebels had worked for and accomplished had led to this moment—to *him.* And Natalia knew as she and Roman took their first steps into the forest that this moment would change their world forever...

~

Ren watched from the branches of a large oak tree as Damien and Zyra—Aurum between them in her shackles of ice—led Vayne's army toward the walls of Sector One, a black snake writhing from the edge of the forest through the tall grass swaying in the wind. Ren was surprised to find that he didn't have to squint from the distance to watch Damien walk up to the wall and shout a command to the soldiers stationed above. His sight must've been enhanced after becoming the Aether, which he still couldn't quite wrap his head around, but he didn't have time to consider why he'd been chosen. He had to figure out how he was going to get inside the walls.

Ren inhaled a sharp breath as a section of the concrete wall around twelve feet wide sunk into the ground, a door for Vayne's army to march right through. He tightened his grip around a branch of the oak when Damien pushed Aurum forward and began leading them inside. White, hot rage flooded his vision. The Damien he'd known was gone. He'd been gone for some time now, so Ren didn't feel sorry as he plotted Damien's death for everything he'd done—all the pain he'd caused Aurum, Natalia, and the rebels. And his twin...

Armored trucks greeted the army at the tree line. He had to get on one of those trucks. Suddenly, a twig snapped beneath Ren. He looked down and watched a soldier stumble through the brush with a curse. Ren glanced between the trucks and the black armor shining in the few rays of sun that peeked through the canopy above. His eyes stung, and they began to glow gold around the purest silver pupils. Power flowed through every inch of him, coating him with strength. Everything sharpened. His sight became even more clear, and he could smell the salt of the soldier's sweat below as it dripped down his back. Even the bark against his fingers seemed to have more texture than before. He could feel each groove and tremble through the wood when he let go and jumped.

Ren rotated his wrist, sending shackles of earth climbing around the soldier's ankles. The young man didn't have time to scream as he landed soundlessly in front of him and punched, sending the black helmet he wore flying off his head. The man fell to the ground, out cold. Ren quickly stripped the young man of his armor and slid it on over his mismatched clothes. He put the man's helmet on before leaning him against a tree and binding his hands and feet in shackles of earth. Ren then turned to face the sea of black snaking toward the opening in the wall and began to walk.

CHAPTER TWENTY-SEVEN

POISON

Damien strode down the golden hallway with his chin high. His plan was working, though Zyra informing him that *Ren* was the Aether, not Natalia, had thrown a slight kink into things. She'd seen Ren's confrontation with one of Vayne's personal guards from the thick brush of the forest. *She had seen Ren wield all four elements...* Damien remembered the shock that had frozen his entire body as she'd whispered the truth in his ear. She had just entered the clearing to find him fighting Aurum and Natalia. He still couldn't quite believe it himself. Damien had what he thought were faint memories, blurred by the scrambling of his mind, of Ren cowering when a twig snapped near the clearing atop the overhang. The only time Ren had ever shown any signs of courage or violence had been when Lavelle's safety was threatened. Other than those rare occasions, there wasn't a cruel bone in Ren's body.

Regardless of the surprise, Damien's plan *was* working. He could feel the anchor of his brainwashing changing every day. The constant battle raging through his head had slightly quieted, and the swords didn't pierce his mind as frequently or sharply as they had before. His head felt a little clearer, and he could finally begin to make his way through the thick fog that clouded his mind and guided his every decision. However, his hatred for Natalia and the rebels still burned, but now it burned alongside his desire to steal the powers of the Aether and overthrow Vayne for good.

Behind him, Zyra—who was the reason for the change—and a soldier clad in black dragged Aurum between them. Damien didn't have feelings for Zyra. He was simply using her to alter his anchor. She wasn't his enemy, though he wasn't sure he could call her his friend either. All Damien and Zyra knew was that they couldn't escape Vayne without the other, and an unspoken agreement between them kept them from leaving each other behind—kept them both alive.

Damien risked a glance back at Aurum, and a familiar numbness spread over him. Not only had Vayne brainwashed him to hate Natalia and faithfully serve him, but he had stripped Damien of all feelings for anyone or anything else. Aurum had been right. They had broken him, but Damien couldn't find it in himself to care. All he wanted was to be free of Vayne and take the Aether's power. That way, no one could ever hurt him again. He could leave the sectors behind to rot and fade away, and Zyra would go with him. They'd leave Araedia and try to find civilization beyond the walls. Those civilizations were out there. Zyra had said so herself. She'd heard Vayne murmuring about them behind the doors of his office along with the greater evil that he whispered was out there. Zyra had also mentioned some kind of map hidden and locked away within the depths of Vayne's office. If only Damien could get his hands on it...

Damien rolled his eyes, turning to the two guards who stood outside of Vayne's office with guns of electricity in their hands and spears strapped to their backs. He wasn't scared of the greater evil. With the Aether's powers, he'd have nothing to worry about. Besides, there was no way of telling if what *Vayne* thought was evil was *actually* evil. It was all about perspective.

"Ready to meet your president?" Zyra smiled sweetly at Aurum.

Aurum lifted her head to meet Zyra's gaze, her eyes flashing red and silver. "He is *not* my president."

"I'd watch my tongue if I were you." Zyra shrugged, dragging her along. "Or he might scramble your brain and make it his own."

Damien smirked when Aurum's face paled. Her brown eyes flicked to his, and his smirk widened into a grin. She would find no mercy in him. He didn't particularly care what happened to her. He just needed her for bait—Ren's bait. Damien knew Ren had followed them after he'd taken Aurum. The scouts they'd placed in the surrounding trees had confirmed it, and the guard Damien had sent to the backlines hadn't returned to him, meaning that Ren had taken that bait, too. The Aether was somewhere in the mansion. Damien just had to find him.

Damien opened the door to the office and walked inside, pausing a foot away from Vayne's grand wooden desk. Zyra and the soldier holding Aurum halted beside him. He couldn't stop the shiver that ravaged his spine as Vayne's eery white eyes with black veins raked over him then Zyra and Aurum, who studied the marble flooring like her life depended on it. Zyra shoved her onto her knees before the desk.

"*This* is the Aether?" Vayne's black brow rose.

Damien turned to Aurum to find her staring at his hands—the hands he couldn't stop from shaking. "No sir, but—"

Vayne's chair screeched as it slid back and collided against the wall with an ear-piercing *bang*. Damien flinched, and Vayne marched around his desk, whipping a strand of dark air across his face. Damien stumbled backward, barely regaining his balance in enough time to watch Vayne send a column of those wicked winds into his chest. He flew back into a framed picture of the walls in early construction days, sending it crashing to the ground. Shards of glass pierced his skin and blood began to trickle down a cut under his right eye.

"I warned you what would happen if you failed me again, *boy*," Vayne spat. The dark wind swirled around Damien's ankles and wrists, chaining him to the floor. A phantom touch of darkness lifted his head to meet Vayne's gaze. Utter rage burned in those horrific eyes, and the president slowly slipped a hand of darkness around Damien's throat. Damien silently cursed himself when untamed fear shot throughout his entire being.

No, no, no, no, no. I'm sorry, I'm sorry, I'm sorry, the voice in the back of Damien's head begged. *I am worthless without you. Forgive me, please. I'm yours to command forever, and I am sorry—*

No. That wasn't Damien. That wasn't him—it was the brainwashing. He gasped for a deep breath to calm himself. He had to fight the voice. He couldn't let it drag him back underwater and drown him. The dark hand around Damien's throat tightened, and his gasp for breath became a sharp, hoarse intake that resulted in nothing.

"Natalia Rhys isn't the Aether!" Zyra exclaimed—just as Damien had instructed her to. Both Aurum's and the president's eyes widened. Vayne slowly turned to Zyra.

"What did you say?" he growled.

The dark wind remained tight around Damien's throat, but he could endure it for a few minutes at least. Zyra's timing had been perfect. His instructions to her had been simple: let Vayne rough him up a bit, let Vayne believe he was still in control, then tell him the truth.

"She wielded both fire and water, so we thought that she was the Aether," Zyra said, her yellow-green eyes sliding to Damien. He barely glimpsed the concern in her gaze before it disappeared in a flash. "Until I witnessed the actual Aether discovering his powers in the forest. It was a young boy from the sectors—Ren Dalnum. We couldn't capture him because of Natalia, your son, and her." Zyra nodded at Aurum, tightening her grip around her arms. "So we changed our plans and set a trap for him instead. The Aether is on his way here as we speak. He is currently inside Sector One searching for her."

Damien couldn't stop himself from glancing at Aurum. Her face was paler than freshly fallen snow, and he wasn't quite sure she was breathing. Vayne smiled wickedly, releasing his grip on Damien, who collapsed to the floor and gasped for precious air. A dark chuckle filled the room as Vayne prowled over to Aurum. She finally sucked in a shuddering breath and met the president's stare. Her eyes began to glow red and silver.

"Oh, please," Vayne purred, rolling his eyes. His hand slid under her chin, then gripped the sides of her jaw. "We'll have none of that."

"Where would you like us to keep her?" Damien asked, rising from the marble floor. "In the dungeons or in the tunnels with the others?"

Vayne gave Aurum a smile colder than death. "Take her to the lab."

"You want us to brainwash her." Zyra smirked sadistically, excitement filling her voice. Damien's veins turned to ice at the excitement—it was real. Zyra wasn't playing the role any more. Her desire to harm was real, and he found himself wishing that it wasn't. This was why they couldn't call each other friends. They were both using each other to get what they wanted, but what Zyra wanted was to hurt others. Damien just needed to be free again—to be free of Vayne and the sectors forever.

"What?" Aurum exclaimed, eyes widening in insurmountable fear. A bit of hardened ice appeared in her mouth a moment later, cutting off whatever she had been about to say next. Zyra's glowing ice-blue and silver eyes returned to their normal green beside her.

"I want Damien to do it," Vayne said, turning to face him. "As a reward for setting a trap for the Aether."

Damien forced his own grin, the mask of the brainwashed dog he'd once been sliding into place just like the bead of cold sweat that slid down his back. He'd have to go back to that hellhole... The lab... Images—memories, he realized—of walls and a ceiling so black that he couldn't tell where they began or ended flashed through his head, along with a headache. It was still so hard to remember things... He knew that they'd brainwashed him there. He knew the lab was full of a suffocating darkness and excruciating pain, and he never wanted to step foot into that room again.

Damien nodded. "Thank you, sir. I apologize for the confusion with the Aether. I will present myself better next time."

"There will be no confusion next time, Damien," Vayne snapped, "because it will be my son and that imposter, Rhys, kneeling before me. Once the Aether is in my grasp and I take his powers, we will destroy the rebels slowly... One Elemental at a time."

"And we'll make Roman and his precious imposter watch while we do so," Zyra cooed.

"Indeed we will." Vayne nodded, turning back to his desk. He threw a dismissive wave over his shoulder. "Damien, take her to the lab and begin immediately. I want the Aether's gift to be prepared for his arrival. Zyra, fortify the mansion and make sure the guards in the tunnels are alert as well. I don't want any surprises."

"Where would you like her kept after the brainwashing?" Damien asked, pulling Aurum up from the floor and walking to the red curtains that hid the door leading to the dungeons and lab.

"Wherever you feel like keeping her, Damien. I don't particularly care. Just make sure she hates her rebels and serves me by the time you're finished." Vayne returned to his desk chair, grinning widely. "And do make sure you take quite a while with the process. *Enjoy it.* You're all dismissed."

He nodded to Vayne, then met Zyra's gaze. She bit her bottom lip, hiding her smile, and sauntered from the office along with the guard that had been holding Aurum. Damien brushed away the curtains and entered the four-digit code to unlock the metal door behind the red velvet. He found himself frowning as he yanked Aurum through and slammed the door shut behind them. It locked with a deep *click*...

Yes, his plan was working perfectly, and soon, he'd be able to leave. He couldn't wait to get his hands on Ren and watch Vayne take his powers. However, he couldn't stop the slight throb that pulsed against his heart and stomach. Regret—he realized. That was regret... He wouldn't wish the pain and torture of brainwashing upon anyone... But if he had to sacrifice Aurum to survive, then he would... So he could finally kill the president and leave the pain behind.

~

Ren glanced around the solid white, unnaturally clean hall. Black doors with four-digit code locks flanked the walls. On the opposite side of those doors lay pure darkness. The dungeons were an utterly horrifying and disorienting—yet ingenious—maze of cells. He blinked away the headache threatening him from the blanching walls. It hadn't been difficult for Ren to secure a rotation down in the depths of the dungeons. Every soldier had grumbled when one of the commanders announced vacant positions that needed filling after their return from the destruction of the rebel camp. Ren had made sure not to seem too eager to fill the spot, but he knew he'd run into Aurum or Damien down here eventually. He straightened the dark helmet that had tilted on his head.

His plan was simple. He'd patrol the dungeons until he found Aurum, break her out with the four-digit code—after he figured out what it was—then escape down into the tunnels that connected all four sectors. If they were lucky, maybe they'd run into the rebels if they chose to invade through the underground labyrinth.

Without warning, the white door at the end of the hall leading to the dome-like room of branching doorways flung open. In marched Damien, dragging Aurum along with a bit of ice in her mouth. Ren, stationed at the intersection of the hall, straightened as they passed. Aurum was alive and seemed to be unharmed. Relief flooded through him, but the relief was short-lived when Damien led her to the dark armored door that sat at the end of the hall. Fear sluiced through Ren, and he had to squeeze his eyes shut to keep them from glowing through his helmet's visor. Damien paused in front of the door and turned back to Ren, who opened his eyes after the stinging glow had subsided.

"Keep all of the other guards out of this branch of the dungeon," he said, opening the door to reveal utter darkness and a chair darker than night itself. "I only want one of you on this hall."

Ren nodded and headed toward one of the branching halls of the intersection. He rounded the corner and halted, listening to the closing *boom* of that heavy door. He swore he could feel the vibrations rattling his bones—his very soul. What was Damien about to do to Aurum? That room wasn't like the others. It wasn't a cell... Ren was halfway to the next guarded intersection of the dungeons when the screaming began. Ice slid along his veins. *Aurum's* screaming.

~

Thirty minutes passed before Damien shoved the cart of syringes into the ebony walls, the glasses and vials atop it rattling viciously. He ran shaky hands through his dark sweaty hair as he paced before the nearly invisible black chair Aurum lay on. Beads of sweat rolled down his neck and back, drenching his shirt. He couldn't stand it—the torturing. He couldn't take one more minute of it.

Tears continued to pour down Aurum's cheeks, and her brown eyes met his. They were glazed and heavy. He immediately averted his gaze, finding the surrounding darkness a lot more interesting. Those brown eyes had once been full of such joy and light. Now, they were utterly lifeless. Because of *him*. Damien winced, shaking his head. He blinked furiously at the images that flashed before him. He saw the room they were in now, but he was the one on the table. He saw the hateful face of the skinny man—Remus—who had stuck the syringes in his body all those months ago. He felt the tremors of pain and fear that had wracked his body. He remembered the claws that tore his brain apart, and he remembered how Remus had smiled when he'd forced Damien to give him everything Vayne wanted. Damien would never forget that face. Remus would be next after he killed Vayne—two lives that he would thoroughly enjoy taking with no remorse whatsoever.

But he couldn't do this any more. He couldn't torture Aurum. It wasn't that he still cared for her. No, he still felt nothing for everyone around him. Even his hatred for Natalia had dulled and become a secondary thought. But he couldn't put Aurum through what he had endured. He couldn't put *anyone* through it. Death would be kinder than that.

Damien took a steadying breath and walked over to the chair. He met Aurum's gaze once again. Her face was pallid, causing her scattered freckles to stick out, and her lips were nearly white. Sweat covered every inch of her, plastering her brown hair to her neck. He unlocked the bands around her wrists and ankles, then moved to the thick band around her abdomen. His eyes began to glow red-orange and silver as he ripped it off the hinges connecting it to the table. Finally, he removed the band surrounding her head.

Aurum whimpered and more tears began to flow from her eyes as he carefully lifted her out of the chair and stalked to the armored door. He froze dead in his tracks at the thin black veins beginning to crawl toward her irises. Memories of punching his mirror to spare himself from the view of his own dark veins blinded him.

Damien cursed and cursed and cursed himself.

He had brought this unbearable pain down upon someone else. He shook his head, willing numbness into it—his heart. All this pain and suffering was because of Vayne. All he had to do was survive this act to ensure his plan succeeded and kill Vayne; then he could be free.

Only a little while longer, Damien promised himself. *You can make it a little while longer… Then you can leave forever and* never *look back.*

"Where…" Aurum gasped, struggling to keep her head upright. "Where are you…taking me…now?"

"Just close your eyes," Damien said before nudging the armored door open to reveal the blinding white hallway.

Aurum hissed and squeezed her eyes shut as she turned into Damien's chest, shielding her eyes. Damien continued down the hallway past the dozens of black cell doors. The guard at the intersection straightened at the sight of them. Damien quickly passed the guard and the intersection before pausing at a cell door on the right side of the main hall.

"Open it," he commanded.

The guard froze before stealing a quick glance at the cell door. He remained utterly silent, dropping his shaking head.

"Do they not teach you newbies the codes any more?" Damien rolled his eyes, dumping Aurum into the guard's arms. Damien found he was too exhausted to even be angry at the guard. He simply didn't care any more—unless it involved his plan. He quickly punched in the four-digit code on the keypad and opened the silent door. A man lying on the dark floor of the cell lifted his unnaturally pale face. His dark-blue eyes, full of hatred and disgust, met Damien's. Damien gave the black-haired man a crooked smile and turned back to the guard. "Get *all* the cell codes from your superior officer. Remember, they change every hour."

The guard nodded, striding inside and gently leaning Aurum up against the wall. He mumbled a quick apology to Damien as he exited. Damien closed and locked the door behind him with a soft *thud*.

"Make sure this cell isn't disturbed," Damien said, turning down the hallway toward the white door that led to the domed room. It was time for him to begin his hunt for the Aether. "I'll be back within the hour."

~

Ren clenched his fists to keep them from shaking. Rage and fear coursed through him like a vicious disease, and his stomach turned. How was he supposed to get Aurum out if the codes changed every hour? He didn't even know what superior officer to ask for the codes...

He glared at the back of Damien's head until he disappeared behind the white door. What in the Aether's name had he done to Aurum? She had looked so... broken... He had to get her out. Soon. He cursed himself colorfully. The last half-hour had been a different form of torture for Ren. Every fiber of his being had been screaming at him to burst through that door and save Aurum. But he didn't have the codes to that door either, and there was no breaking through the armor encasing it. He'd had no choice but to wait.

Ren rushed over to Aurum's cell door, leaning his ear against it. Nothing. He heard nothing. He bit the inside of his cheek until the metallic tang of blood filled his mouth. Ren then closed his eyes as his irises began to glow gold around the purest of silver pupils and focused every fiber of his being on listening through the door into the cell. A few moments of silence passed. Suddenly, the sound of fabric and bare feet scraping against the floor filled Ren's senses.

"It's all right," the man inside Aurum's cell whispered. "You can lay down. Here..." More rustling of fabric. "Take my jacket. I know it's not much, but it'll help with the tremors."

"Thank you," Aurum rasped.

"Don't worry about it." Ren could hear the man's gentle smile in his voice. "What's your name?"

"Aurum Everrett."

"It's nice to meet you, Aurum, though I wish it were under better circumstances."

A vicious cough wracked through Aurum. "Why are you in here?" she asked.

"Vayne didn't approve of a trick I liked to play with his projectors, so he sent his dogs to hunt me down... Again, might I add."

"What trick?"

"I helped a group of rebel sympathizers communicate between the sectors. We were trying to rally the people together."

"So you know Hero Ellisaire," Aurum whispered, her voice growing soft enough that Ren had to strain his ears to listen.

"Yes—wait, do you know him?"

"He's with the rebels...or..." Aurum's voice broke. "He *was*. I don't know if he survived the attack on our camp."

Ren heard a sigh from the man, then a *thump*. He must've dropped to the floor... Ren couldn't believe what he was hearing. This man had helped Hero with the projectors. He supported the rebels, too. It took every ounce of Ren's will not to try to tear through the door. He had to get them out.

"Are they coming?" the man asked. "Are the rebels coming?"

There was no verbal reply.

"I see...," the man murmured, feigning disappointment.

Aurum and the man were smart. They knew who might be listening.

"What's your..." Aurum cleared her throat, fighting against the hoarseness. "What's your name?"

"Vale. My name is Vale Ashlocke."

CHAPTER TWENTY-EIGHT

A DIFFERENT WORLD

Not a sliver of the late morning sun remained as the walls of Sector Four finally began to peek through the small gaps in the thick canopy of trees. Dark storm clouds raged and roiled above the mass of rebels creeping through the forest. The rain collided against their painted armor with soft *thumps*, and Natalia scowled at the small streams of blue and red paint sliding down her arm. She glanced up at the sky. She had never seen it so dark before.

Glowing eyes filled the forest around her, casting rainbows of colors upon passing plants, bushes, and trees. Soon, they'd push aside the boulder guarding one of the many entrances into the tunnels snaking beneath the sectors. Their army would split, and Napoleon and Lavelle would lead the underground team through the mazes of tunnels in search of the Araedians of Sector One. The thought of being separated sent shivers down Natalia's spine and fear flooding through her soul.

She came to a halt beside Roman at the edge of the tree line. His golden-brown eyes squinted against the rain and narrowed as they met with the wall. A few guards walked along the length of it, oblivious to the obscured army lurking yards and yards away. Natalia's crack in the wall seemed to beckon to her even with the distance. She caught movement in the corner of her eye and turned to find Fraiser beside her. She glanced between Roman and Natalia.

"We need to move now," Fraiser whispered. "If we want to meet with Spenser and the army inside on time, we have to split now."

Roman nodded. "Is Napoleon and his team ready?"

"They await your orders,"

"All right," Roman said, standing and walking deeper into the forest toward the seventeen rebels—including Napoleon and Lavelle—waiting beside the boulder. "Let's send them in."

Natalia released a shaky breath and followed Roman and Fraiser to the boulder. Lavelle's usually happy and smiling face was colder than the wind and rain pounding against them. Nothing but raw hatred shone behind those blue eyes. Four Elementals quickly pushed away the boulder and opened the trapdoor. One by one, the rebels began to lower themselves down into the smothering darkness of the tunnels. The darkness reminded her of the threat they faced—reminded her of Vayne and everything he stood for. But as more rebels climbed down, small flames flickered to life in the sea of darkness, along with an assortment of glowing red and orange irises and a few sets of silver pupils. Natalia forced a small smile on her face. The rebels were the light. They were the only light that could counter that darkness, and she would make sure those lights kept burning even if it killed her.

A few minutes passed before Lavelle and Napoleon were the only two left standing above the door. Roman pulled Napoleon into a hug, squeezing him tightly. Natalia fought back the burning in her eyes as she watched the two brothers. They weren't brothers by blood, but they were brothers in every other way that counted. Fraiser stalked over to them, and they pulled away.

She punched Napoleon's shoulder. "You give them hell down there."

"I will." Napoleon nodded, his face grim—brother to sister. He furiously blinked back the silver lining his eyes.

"Don't you *dare* get yourself killed. That goes for you too, blondie," Fraiser said with a pointed look at Lavelle.

"We'll be careful." Lavelle managed a small smile.

Natalia pulled both Napoleon and Lavelle into the tightest hug she'd ever given. "I love you two *so much*."

"When we see you again, Natalia, it'll be a different world," Napoleon murmured.

They pulled away, and Natalia watched with dread coiled in her stomach as Napoleon helped Lavelle down onto the ladder leading below. She told herself over and over that this wouldn't be the last time she saw them. Roman slipped his hand into hers.

"Come back to us," he said.

"We will." Napoleon flashed them all a reassuring smile before pulling the door above him shut and disappearing into the depths below. The boulder was immediately pushed back, locking the team underground.

Natalia and Roman turned to Fraiser and an approaching Hero. A clean bandage adorned his head.

"The rebels are ready," Hero said, squinting through the rain. "Noon will be upon us soon."

"Get to your positions. It's time." Roman glanced between Fraiser and Hero. He offered them both a small smile before locking eyes with Fraiser. "Be careful."

Fraiser shot him a wicked smirk, Hero nodding beside her. The two then disappeared into the mass of rebels at the edge of the forest. Everyone knew what to look for—the signal to trigger the rebels' attack on Sector Four. Natalia grasped Roman's hand so hard, she was surprised he hadn't said anything. But Roman simply faced her and placed his hands on her cheeks, cupping her face.

"I love you," he said, planting a gentle kiss on her lips. "I will always love you. In this life and the next."

Pure joy flooded Natalia's soul. She felt as if she had been launched into the heavens above, soaring above the thunderous dark clouds and dancing in the rays of sunlight hidden behind them. The high was short-lived, however, and she came crashing back down to the cold and damp forest floor. Though they were the most precious words she'd ever heard in her life, she couldn't help but feel that they were a farewell.

"You sound like you're saying goodbye..." Natalia shook her head. "This is *not* goodbye, Roman."

"I know." He gave her a crooked smile, tucking a loose strand of hair behind her ear. "But I just had to tell you... I've never smiled the way I smile when I'm around you in my entire life."

Natalia squeezed her eyes shut to keep her tears from spilling over and laid her head on his armored chest. Over his heart. Roman wrapped his arms around her waist, holding her tight.

Throughout her entire life, one of the only things Natalia had ever wanted was to find love—to find family. She thanked the Aether every night that she'd been able to find one of them. She thanked the Aether for Vale—her old family—and she thanked the Aether for the family that surrounded her now. But she had never believed that she could ever find a love like this. And now that she had it, she would do everything in her power to keep it.

She tipped her head up and kissed Roman as if it were the last time she ever would. *"You're my heart, and I love you."*

~

Natalia and Roman, eyes glowing dark-blue around silver, stepped out from the cover of the tree line, pausing halfway between the forest and the wall. Natalia's own eyes began to glow red-orange and ice-blue, split by that electric line of purple. Her pupils burned such a pure silver that they were nearly white amongst the darkness of the world around them. She smirked at the guards along the wall that pointed and shouted at them. Before their orders could reach any ears, Natalia and Roman planted their right feet in unison. The rain began to pound harder and harder as if the heavens above were urging them on, bellowing their support. They extended their arms to their sides, upturned fingertips nearly touching as water began to swirl around them.

Natalia glanced to the sky, watching the rain shoot toward them and into the swirl of currents. The belt of water encasing Roman and Natalia drifted higher as it grew and grew, lifting above their chests. By the time it passed their heads, the band of currents was several feet thick. Slowly, they began to shift their hands out in front of them, tucking their arms in close. The water mimicked the movements and began to cave in on itself and create a giant swirling sphere over half the height of the thirty-foot wall.

Shouts of alarm from the top of the wall filled the air, and soldiers clad in black pointed from the towering mass of concrete. Moments later, bolts of electricity arced over the sphere of water through the dark sky, hurtling straight toward Roman and Natalia. Suddenly, an enormous blast of vicious winds collided with the bolts, knocking them into each other and sending them plummeting to the ground with a thunderous *boom*. Natalia didn't have to turn back to know that it was Fraiser's winds that had protected them—the winds that would continue to protect them.

Together, Roman and Natalia half-turned, drawing their hands back to their right shoulders before lunging forward with their left feet and sending the sphere— now a large battering ram—flying right at the crack in the wall. The battering ram hardened into an impenetrable ice as it flew and collided against the concrete with an ear-shattering *crash*.

The earth around them quaked, and for a few moments, only dust and rain could be seen. The dust finally cleared to reveal a gaping hole through the wall of Sec- tor Four. A hole large enough for an entire army to fit through, debris of ice and concrete surrounding it. The world seemed to slow as the rebels stepped out from within the depths of the forest. On top of the sloping hill inside the wall, Vayne's army of soldiers clad in the darkest black waited. They outnumbered the rebels two to one, but that had been expected, and the rebels were not afraid.

Time slammed back into place, and Roman, Natalia, and the rebels charged Vayne's army, war cries sounding from both sides while they sprinted at each other through the rain.

Natalia leaped into the air, drawing back her fists as water collected around them. She came crashing to the ground, slamming her fists when she collided with the wet soil and grass. Spikes of ice shot forth and impaled a dozen charging soldiers. They collapsed with defeating *thuds*. She rose, and swords of water began to form in her palms before hardening into deadly, glistening ice. She lunged into the fray of battle, swinging, slicing, and stabbing. Blood and mud splattered across her face as her swords found a home in the abdomen of a soldier. She barely had enough time to rip the swords free and cross them above her head to meet a spear of electricity. Her arms shook, straining against the strength of the soldier towering over her.

Without warning, a bolt of electricity cleaved through the air, slamming into their locked weapons. Ice and sparks rained down as the swords and spear shattered, sending Natalia and the soldier flying. She grunted when she collided against a fellow rebel, knocking them both to the ground to tumble through the gore and mud already gathering. They slid to a stop, and Natalia lifted her head to meet Fraiser's burning gaze. She watched as Fraiser rose, clutching at her side. Through the bloody frenzy of battle clouding her mind, concern shot through Natalia. Had Fraiser still not completely recovered from her wound during the attack on their camp? She didn't have time to ask as Fraiser grabbed her arm and pulled her to her feet before turning to face the soldier who had fired the bolt of electricity. The soldier with the spear, having replaced the broken one, stood beside him. Natalia smirked as she and Fraiser formed long knives of swirling wind and ice and charged the soldiers. Together, they were death incarnate.

~

Roman flicked his wrist, sending a slender, razor-sharp icicle through the helmet of a soldier. He didn't bother to watch the body fall, instead risking a glance at the sloping hill. Vayne's army continued to pour down, a rushing river of poisonous black amongst the grass blowing sideways in the wind and rain. His glowing eyes widened in surprise at the sight of Fraiser and Natalia, fighting side-by-side. Together, they tore a hole through Vayne's forces and scattered soldiers left and right. If he could join them and have all three of them push up the hill, the rebels could easily win the battle. However, if the battle continued on as it was doing now, Roman feared they might never make their way up the onslaught of soldiers piling down. They needed the high ground and soon, before their numbers diminished too greatly.

Roman's spear of ice cracked as it collided with a spear of electricity. He parried the soldier's next strike and spun, the tip of his spear catching against two black plates of armor on the soldier's side. He tightened his grip on his spear before sending it through the soldier's chest and turning to face his next opponent.

Out of the corner of his eye, he glimpsed Hero fighting further down the hill to his left. Eyes—or eye, as one was still hidden beneath the dirty bandages surrounding his head—glowing gray around pitch-black pupils, Hero sent a torrent of wind into a soldier, flinging them far back into the throng of battle. Roman wondered how he could manage with the limited vision. Roman whirled, spear shooting toward the closest set of black armor. The spear struck home with a *thud*, and the soldier didn't rise again.

"Roman!"

A cry rang out across the field, barely audible.

He turned back to Hero to find him shouting and pointing at the peak of the hill. Roman's heart seemed to stop at the sight of the four cannons looming over them, vultures ready to swoop down and annihilate them. The words of warning Roman tried to scream caught in his throat, and he could only watch as devastatingly large bolts of crackling electricity fired from all four cannons—straight into the mass of rebels. The earth shook at the impact, and bodies—rebels and Vayne's scum alike—flew, scattering gore and even a few limbs. Roman himself was knocked to the ground as electricity licked between bodies and stretched out in blue-purple veins along the trampled grass and soil. Panic filled his being.

Natalia, Fraiser...

Hero was by his side a moment later, hauling him up.

"I have an idea!" Hero shouted over the chaos.

Roman turned back to the cannons smoking atop the hill. They sparked every few heartbeats, recharging. He quickly scanned the slope for any sign of Natalia or Fraiser. They were nowhere in sight. Fear began to creep its way up Roman's spine. He needed to find them. "I don't care what it is. Do it. I'm going to go find Natalia and Fraiser."

"Tell the rebels to fall back while you're at it. We give Vayne the hill." He wiped at the sweat sticking his blond hair to his forehead. "I need every earth and air Elemental we have to meet me at the hill's base in five minutes."

"Will the cannons be recharged by then?"

"They might be," Hero panted. "But with ammunition that large and with that amount of power... It'll take a few minutes before they're ready to fire again, but you and I both know it's a risk we have to take. We can't take any more hits like that."

Roman nodded. "I'll give the order to retreat and send as many Elementals your way as I can. Be careful, Hero."

"Make sure you're all off that hill before the five minutes are up, Roman."

Hero then disappeared into the chaos surrounding them, shouting orders as he went. Roman scanned the expanse of the hill before him once again. Where were they? Where were they? He knew they weren't dead. They couldn't be. Fraiser and Natalia had been yards and yards ahead of him—higher up the hill. A new kind of fear spread over Roman as his eyes narrowed, landing on the two Elementals still fighting their way up toward the cannons. The battle around him seemed to fall quiet and slow, and every fiber of his being honed in on Fraiser and Natalia. Roman had only one singular thought in his head as he threw himself into the maelstrom of clashing weapons and elements, carving a path to Natalia and Fraiser: *Get them out.*

~

Natalia slashed her knife of ice across a soldier's throat, blood once again splattering across her face. Beside her, Fraiser sucked the air from one and sent her knife of swirling air hurtling for another. It found its mark in the side of a neck clad in black. They had made good progress up the hill, killing their way through Vayne's ranks, but they still had several yards between them and those deadly cannons they'd narrowly avoided. If Natalia and Fraiser had been a few extra yards uphill, they would've been blown to bits.

Natalia had lost sight of Roman ages ago. In fact, she felt as if she hadn't seen him in hours—days. If this was what a small battle felt like, she had no interest in experiencing full-out war, lined up on an open battlefield. The bloodshed was horrendous, but she knew it was necessary to save Araedia and the rebels—to save those she loved. Natalia prayed to the Aether that Hero's friend Spenser and the people of Four would show. Soon. The rebels needed quick battles, and they needed the numbers even more, especially after those cannons. She and Fraiser had shared one look after they'd fired and agreed that they would *not* allow them to fire again.

A guttural cry pierced the air, and Natalia whirled to watch a soldier charge her. She planted her feet in the mud, readying to lunge with her long knives of ice when a gust of wind slammed the soldier down to the ground. With a twist of her wrists,

Fraiser snapped the soldier's neck with a deafening *crack* that sent shivers wracking down Natalia's spine. Like Natalia, a mixture of sweat, blood, and dirt dripped down Fraiser's dark face.

"Something's wrong," she said, lifting her remaining blade and pointing at the base of the hill. Rebels had begun to gather, abandoning the hill. Had their numbers dwindled that badly already?

"It's the cannons," Natalia murmured. "It has to be..."

"They're retreating." Fraiser tilted her blade, rain deflecting from the swirling symphonies of air. "Why in the Aether's name are we retreating?"

"Talia!"

She barely heard the scream. Natalia jerked her head to survey the slope leading to the gathering rebels. All she found was Vayne's cronies giving chase to the rebels as they fled. Anger burned within her like a wildfire. She glanced at the knife of ice in her hand to find it gone—melted. It had been replaced by a long knife of wicked flames.

"Talia! Fraiser!"

Natalia's eyes widened as the voice neared. "Roman?"

Behind her, Fraiser blasted a column of wind into the fray of black armor, holding them back. Natalia watched Roman cut through a soldier with a single slice of his spear of ice before sprinting to them, sweat dripping from the tips of his nose and dark hair. Gore covered his face and painted armor.

"Are you all right?" she asked, panic flooding her voice as he reached them. She ran her eyes over every inch of him. He seemed fine other than a few cuts and bruises.

"Yes." He grabbed her hand. "But we have to go. *Now.*"

"Roman, what's happening?" Fraiser snarled, stalking over.

He shook his head, grabbing her hand, too. "There's no time to explain. We have to get off this hill."

Natalia's brows rose. "But the cannons—"

"Leave them!" he exclaimed and began leading them down the slope.

Natalia threw a glance over her shoulder at the cannons and army surrounding them. The sparking grew brighter, and tendrils of soldiers broke off from the bulk of the army, chasing after them and the rebels below. Fraiser chucked her knife of air into the fray behind them, not bothering to look back. A groan of pain followed a second later. Natalia let go of her flaming knife, tossing it backward and allowing the flames to spread and expand into a wall of fire to meet their pursuers. Some soldiers screamed, some scrambled around it, and others even dared to jump through the flames.

Together, the three raced down the hill, sliding and tripping in the mud and mass of dead bodies. Natalia didn't have the courage within her to dare to search for familiar faces among them. A deadly rumbling sounded behind them, building up with each passing heartbeat. She didn't have to look to know that the cannons had finished recharging. Suddenly, two bolts of electricity shook the earth as they fired. She could only watch in horror as one of the bolts flew past into the throng of fleeing rebels. The second, however, landed a few yards to their left, flinging everyone to the ground. Small tendrils of electricity licked and pinched Natalia's skin, and for a few moments, everything was black, and a ringing filled her ears. She couldn't feel her arms or legs as she forced herself onto her stomach, hands digging into the mud when she pushed herself up. She wobbled but managed to stay upright to survey her surroundings.

Fraiser, who struggled to rise to her knees, had been launched farther down the hill, and Roman lay on his back a few feet away, twitching as a web of electricity wracked his body. Natalia stumbled over to him before quickly pulling him to his feet. He winced with a groan.

"I know, I know." Natalia grabbed his hand and led him into a limping run. "Come on. Just a little farther, Roman."

They were halfway down the hill, but only two of the four cannons had fired. Natalia watched Fraiser trip and tumble down the few remaining yards of the slope. She collapsed at the bottom with a *thud* before scrambling back to her feet and throwing herself over a waist-high wall of earth and air surrounding the rebels at the base. Dozens of shades of gray and green eyes glowed—a few silver pupils shining amongst them.

"Hurry!" Hero's voice rang out.

The earth rumbled beneath them once again, and Natalia jolted into a sprint, dragging Roman along behind her. They weren't going to make it. They were too slow. Cries erupted from the rebels, begging them to run, run, run. Even the wind at their backs seemed to scream, urging them to push farther—*faster*. They had to be faster. Natalia's eyes were stinging as they began to glow once more. She focused on the rain falling from the sky and colliding against the dirt. She felt the water flowing through the mud.

She extended her arm as they ran, and a runway of ice appeared before them. She tightened her grip on Roman's hand and launched herself at the ice. Natalia and Roman collided against it, the reverberations of their impact rattling her bones, and together, they slid down the remainder of the slope in a flash. The ice runway ended at the base of the earthen wall, and Natalia barely threw her arms up in enough time to stop herself from colliding against it face-first. Several pairs of hands reached over the wall, grabbed her and Roman, and quickly pulled them over.

Natalia lifted her head over the wall to watch the entire hill collapse and tear the cannons apart as they fired their last two shots down into Vayne's pursuing army. A rockslide followed, wiping away the majority of black armor on the slope. A few moments later, the rush of mud, rock, grass, and bodies collided against the rebels' wall. Dust once again clouded her vision. Half a minute passed before it finally cleared to reveal the remains of the hill. It was as if someone had taken a knife and sliced off half of the slope leading up into Sector Four. The battlefield grew eerily quiet, and Vayne's remaining soldiers became utterly still. Then, Hero, eye glowing, leaped over the wall and charged up the remnants of the hill with a vicious cry. The rebels immediately followed, racing toward their victory with war cries of their own.

"What. The. Hell." Fraiser panted, leaning against the earthen wall. "Was. That?"

"*That*," Roman said, chuckling breathlessly. "Was Hero's big idea."

Fraiser shook her head. "He's *insane*."

"Well, if *you* think he's insane, Fraiser..." Natalia smiled, running a hand through the sweaty mess of her braid. Mud and blood had begun to dry amongst the black strands. "...then he must be."

Roman laughed at the glare Fraiser threw her way. The sound was music to Natalia's ears. He stood with a wince, extending a hand to Natalia. "Come on. We're not done yet."

Natalia took his hand and rose, wiping her muddy hands on her pants as he extended a hand to Fraiser, too. Fraiser rolled her eyes and wiped her own hands through the mud before accepting his. Roman elbowed her with a smirk, and together, the three trudged back up the remains of the hill.

CHAPTER TWENTY-NINE

SURVIVE

The darkness of the tunnels thrashed against the flames held high in the air, casting dancing shadows along the dirt floor and walls. Napoleon glanced back at Lavelle and the fifteen rebels—some with glowing orange and red eyes—behind her as he led them deeper into the depths of the tunnels. Nearly two hours had passed since they'd entered the tunnels, and the steady thrum of rain could still be heard above. A cold breeze slithered over his skin, sending a shiver down the column of his spine.

"Are you all right?" Lavelle's soft voice whispered.

He gave her a nod, taking her hand in his. "I am now."

She smiled, knocking the breath from Napoleon's lungs. If only Lavelle knew how much she affected him. The Aether knew he was wrapped around her finger. Napoleon cursed himself. He should've told her how he felt before they'd entered the tunnels—hell, before they'd left the camp. What if he never got the chance to tell her that he loved her? That he had loved her the moment he had laid eyes on her. Napoleon didn't know what he'd do if something happened to Lavelle and—no, he couldn't think like that. He wouldn't let anything happen to her. They'd both survive this, then he'd tell her. He would tell her everything—that she was everything. He'd tell her how every smile, laugh, and blush had sent his pulse catapulting. How every time their eyes had met, he'd felt like they were the only two people left in the world. He turned left, beginning another long trek down the straight tunnel path. He'd tell her how he wished to laugh with her for eternity.

"How do you know where to go?" Lavelle asked. "I'm so turned around in here. I don't understand how you do it."

"Before Roman and Fraiser rescued me from the testings, I worked in the sewer tunnels of Four. They're built the same in each sector, so I know which tunnels lead underneath the sector itself and which tunnels lead out for drainage."

"That doesn't sound like it was a fun job." Lavelle crinkled her nose.

Napoleon chuckled softly. "No, it wasn't. It was very smelly, too."

They walked on in eery silence for a few minutes until they rounded a corner to meet a crossroad of three tunnels. The rebels halted, muttering, and Napoleon tilted his head to the side, studying each opening carefully. As far as he could see, the middle tunnel was a straight shot. The right tunnel ran vertically before smoothing out into a rounded corner that led farther right, and the left tunnel continued straight for a few yards before sharply cutting back to the right into a dark abyss.

"Which one?" Lavelle questioned.

"The middle tunnel leads farther into Two...," he murmured with a glance at the right tunnel. The structure was a little different than the usual drainage tunnel, but there was no way it led into One. The walls were too narrow. "It's the left tunnel. That one will take us to One."

She raised a brow. "Are you sure?"

"Positive," he said, taking the left tunnel.

"You guessed, didn't you?"

"Eh, a little bit." He winked at her.

Lavelle gaped, lightly smacking his shoulder. "Are you serious?"

"No." Napoleon laughed. "The right tunnel is a drainage tunnel."

"You're unbelievable," she muttered, clearly fighting the smile pulling at the corners of her mouth. Behind her, one of the rebels snickered.

Hand-in-hand, Napoleon and Lavelle continued down the left tunnel, finally crossing over into Sector One...

~

Aurum lifted her aching head from the cell floor. Her entire body was stiff and sore and—*by the Aether*, her head *hurt*. The cell was pitch-black. She could barely see the hand she lifted in front of her face, but even the darkness couldn't hide the new film that seemed to cover everything. Her sight—hell, her entire body—felt alien. It was as if her eyes and brain had been scrubbed clean too many times, and she was peering through a glass of crystal. Everything felt...foggy.

Aurum groaned, pushing herself up into a sitting position. A few feet away, Vale stirred. Anger began to spread through her—a fire kindling to life through the fog. She hated Vayne. She hated him more than anything in all of Araedia. He'd destroyed nearly every good part of Damien that had ever existed. And the power Vayne held over him... It made her stomach churn. Vayne had ordered Damien to brainwash her as a gift. But was it really a gift to Damien? After all, he hadn't gone through with it. Not completely.

The raging fire within her suddenly flickered out. Damien had never returned to the cell after last night—never fulfilled his orders. He'd simply dumped her here and left. Why? Was a part of the old Damien still trapped somewhere in that hollow shell of a person he'd become? Was there someone in there to save?

Aurum shook her head. She didn't care if the old Damien was still in there or not. All she knew was that for whatever reason, Damien had decided to halt her brainwashing, and she couldn't help but feel a little thankful. A mere half hour of that torture had been the worst pain she'd ever experienced in her life. She had no words to describe it. The only explanation she could come up with was that it had felt like her mind was being torn apart. *Slowly.* Brick by brick.

Her stomach growled, hunger gnawing at her being. She had never been this hungry. Aurum smiled to herself as she imagined Fraiser, her usual scowl on her face, snapping at her to "Suck it up and deal with it." She then replayed the day that she'd stolen Natalia's bowl of soup from where it cooked on the fire in the rebel's camp. Oh, what she'd give to steal Natalia's soup one more time.

Aurum's smile quickly faded. She didn't know if any of her friends—her family—were even still alive. Had they survived the attack on their camp? Surely, they had, or else Damien and Zyra would've thrown it in her face. *Zyra.* The memory of her words in Vayne's office slammed into Aurum like an armored truck. Zyra had claimed that Natalia wasn't the Aether. She'd claimed *Ren* was the Aether, and that they hadn't captured him because of Natalia and Roman—and herself. Aurum's headache worsened as she ran her hands through her dirty hair.

"So we changed our plans and set a trap for him instead. The Aether is on his way here as we speak. He is currently inside Sector One searching for her."

Aurum cursed colorfully. They'd set a trap for Ren. Ren was the Aether—not Natalia, but Ren. She couldn't believe it. Her heartbeat was feral in her chest and ears. What in the Aether's name was going on? She took a deep breath. She had no way to prove if what Zyra had claimed was true. She didn't know why Zyra would lie, but until she saw Ren with her own eyes, she wouldn't believe it. At least she knew that Natalia, Roman, and Ren were alive. The others... They had to be alive, too. She wouldn't allow herself to think anything different.

"Finally awake?" Vale asked, standing from the cell floor to stretch. Aurum was surprised by how tall he was. Even through the darkness of the cell that smothered every detail about him, she could see that his head nearly touched the ceiling. She shivered, trying to imagine how he'd survived in here without going crazy. Aurum rubbed her temples. She'd been in and out for the past few hours.

She nodded. "I think so."

"How are you feeling?"

"Like my brain was almost ripped from my skull." She frowned. "How long was I out?"

"A day and a half, give or take." Vale shrugged, kneeling next to the jacket she'd returned to him at some point and tossing something to her. "Here, eat this. It's stale, but it's the best we prisoners get."

Aurum caught the small loaf of bread. It was hard as a rock, but that didn't stop her from tearing into it eagerly. She couldn't stop the small moan that escaped her lips. "Thank you so much."

"Don't thank me," Vale said and offered her a soft smile.

She didn't bother to stop eating to offer one back. The bread was gone within the next minute, and she leaned her head back against the cool brick wall with a wince. "So, what now?"

He chuckled humorlessly. "Now, we survive."

"You mean to tell me you've never tried to escape?" Panic filled Aurum. She was Vayne's bait for Ren's trap. She couldn't just sit here and wait for him and the others to come to her rescue—to trigger that trap. Her panic began to slow. They'd been preparing plans for an attack on the sectors the night before the ambush on the rebel camp. Fraiser wouldn't let them just abandon that plan. Neither would Roman. If they were going to try to get her back, they'd bring whatever was left of the rebels with them. They weren't stupid enough to abandon the plan for *her*... Were they? She prayed they weren't.

"I didn't say *that*." Vale's expression grew grim. "But let's just say there's no point in trying. In the six months I've been here, I've learned that attempting escape isn't worth the consequence."

"But you have an Elemental helping you this time," Aurum said, willing flames to her fingertips... But they never came. Only pitiful sparks erupted, and even the familiar sting of her glowing eyes was absent.

"You have no energy to spare," he offered, clearly noticing the alarm on her face. "And you're still starving. They give us just enough food to stay alive, and that's it. There's never enough to summon the elements."

Aurum raised a brow. "Are you an Elemental?"

"No." He shook his head. "No, I'm not, but one of my cellmates a few months back was."

"What happened to them?"

"He passed in his sleep. He was old and had been in here for *years*," Vale said. "He used to be a history teacher in Two during the construction of the walls, but he was caught teaching the forbidden side of history to his students. Vayne had all the class's memories wiped but imprisoned him. He was one of the first to disobey Vayne's history ban, which he was very proud of."

"Did he tell you what he'd been teaching the kids?"

Vale nodded. "He talked about how Araedia had been one of the most populated civilizations on the continent in the beginning, but war ended up splitting the people in two. One half left Araedia to explore the rest of the land while the other half stayed. He talked about the other civilizations that are out there and the construction of the walls under a very young Vayne. He talked about how Vayne eradicated our history, burned our books, murdered scholars and teachers, and threatened anyone who dared to speak about our past."

"He was there when Vayne destroyed our history?" Aurum asked.

"He was sixteen when the walls went up."

"Wow." Aurum ran a hand through her knotted hair, processing his words. "So how'd you end up in here six months ago?"

"It's a long story," Vale said.

She shrugged. "I've got nothing but time."

"You sure you won't fall asleep on me?"

"Promise I won't." Aurum rolled her eyes as he let out a low chuckle.

"I'm originally from Sector Four. I grew up on the streets there with my little sister. We were constantly in and out of the orphanage, doing whatever we could to survive."

Aurum's thoughts drifted to Natalia. She'd grown up in Four's orphanage, too. Maybe he'd spoken to her or seen her once or twice... But Vale was a few years older than both of them, so he might not have seen her at all.

He sighed, and even though she couldn't see him, she could feel the weight of his memories pulling him down. After all these years, they still clung to him like chains. "Believe it or not, my sister and I had been attending history lessons at the orphanage. *Forbidden* history lessons. One day, Vayne's cronies came busting through the doors. Everyone scattered, but they gave chase. I made sure my sister got away, but I was captured in the process. I was sixteen at the time."

Shock rooted Aurum to the cell floor. Natalia had never mentioned any event like that at the orphanage. There was only one orphanage in Four, and Natalia would've been there when the attack took place. Where had she been during all of this? She shook her head, regaining her composure. "Wait, you said you've only been here for six months, but you were captured at sixteen?"

Vale's shadow nodded. "After they captured me, I was loaded into one of those armored trucks. We were halfway through Sector Two when the rebels attacked. Well, it wasn't exactly an attack… The rebels had merely been on a supply run, but during their escape, they ran into my truck on the road. The truck ended up flipping…" Aurum's mouth dropped. She could hear the smile in Vale's voice as he continued. "To this day I still haven't figured out how the hell it flipped, but it did. I got out and booked it. It was well into the night, so—thank the Aether—no one saw me get away. I ran for what felt like *hours* until I reached the outskirts of Two.

From there, I stole some beige clothes from a clothesline, stuck to the alleys, and dedicated myself to causing as much trouble for Vayne's soldiers as I could. From petty pranks to throwing apples at the backs of their heads, I rebelled in every little way that I could until I stumbled upon a group of underground rebel sympathizers. With no way to get back to Four and a *very* personal vendetta against Vayne, I officially joined the cause. For the next four years, I aided the rebels in whatever way I could. I even helped establish the hidden channel on the projectors to communicate between the sectors."

Aurum nodded. "With Hero."

"That kid's brilliant," Vale said with pride. "About seven months ago, Hero and I decided it was time to rally the people together. If we could unite, then there was a chance we could fight back and stop Vayne, so we started airing recordings to every channel we could. We encouraged the rebels' agenda and tried to spread hope, but our luck didn't last long. Vayne heard the recordings and began hunting us. We had to move the recordings to air only on the secret channel. It cut our listeners, but the people had heard our messages. Some even searched for them and found the channel, but we'd brought a lot of attention to the projectors. Vayne ended up wiping out as many channels as he could, hence why there's so little now."

"I'd always wondered why the other channels had disappeared all those months ago. Vayne got rid of my favorite music channel because of you."

Vale laughed. "Yeah, sorry about that."

"I have a question, though. Why didn't you just join the rebels in the forest?" Aurum asked. "It sounds like you had every opportunity to."

"As far as I know, my sister's still in Four. I'm not leaving without her. Everything I've ever done has been for her."

"Did you ever ask Hero to look for her in Four?"

"I did." A great sadness filled his voice. "He searched, but he never found her. I think I taught her to hide too well..." A few moments of heavy silence passed, and Vale took a deep breath. "Anyway, Vayne upped security in the sectors—especially One and Two—after our messages. I was aiding the rebels one night when his soldiers intercepted us. I was captured again and brought here. They tried to torture any information they could out of me, but I never broke. Not once. Because I knew if I broke, then the better world I want for my sister would break, too... She needed the rebels. I needed them. We all need them... But everything I've done and endured has been for her. *All of it.*"

A shiver wracked Aurum's spine. She couldn't imagine the pain that he must've gone through... But the love in his heart... It was incredible. Overwhelming. Endless. "What was your sister's name?"

"Her name was—"

Without warning, the cell door swung open, flooding the smothering darkness with the disorienting, bright white lights of the hall. Aurum and Vale hissed and shielded their eyes. A guard stood in the doorway, carrying a tray of food. The helmet of a second guard appeared over the guard's shoulder. It happened fast. One moment the guard was standing there with the tray, then the man beneath the helmet was sprawled on the cell floor, two loaves of bread and two cups of water clattering to the ground along with the tray. The second guard stepped into the cell, gently pulling Aurum to her feet.

She snatched one of the loaves of bread and allowed herself to be hauled up. "Who are you?"

"Of course, you'd grab the bread first." The guard chuckled and removed his helmet.

Aurum didn't bother to silence the sob clawing up her throat. "Ren!"

She threw her arms around him, squeezing him tight. Her brows narrowed together. Something about him felt different. The energy around him seemed to crackle with power, and his body felt more muscular. Had Zyra spoken truthfully in Vayne's office? Was Ren *actually* the Aether? If it weren't for Vale's presence, she'd ask, but it was too dangerous of a question. She trusted Vale in a sense, but she didn't trust him enough for that.

"Who?" Vale questioned, confusion clear in his tone.

"You didn't really think I'd let Damien just take you, right?" Ren said, wrapping his arms around her waist. "Come on, let's get out of here. You too, pretty boy."

Vale smirked before stepping out of the cell. Aurum followed after him while Ren shut the door behind them. She blinked furiously at the blinding hall, spinning in a quick circle. Where were they supposed to go? Everything looked the same.

"I assume you know the way." Vale looked at Ren before throwing a nervous glance at Aurum.

She looked Vale up and down. It was the first time she'd truly seen him. He couldn't have been much older than Roman. His hair was as pitch-black as their cell, and his eyes were the darkest cerulean blue. He had a strong nose, and his skin was paler than moonlight from being locked away in the dark for so long. She ran her eyes over him once more. She found herself wondering if he'd remain pale or if the color would ever find his skin again. Her cheeks heated when he raised a dark brow at her. He was handsome.

Ren nodded. "Follow me. We're going to the tunnels."

"Are the others here?" Aurum turned to Ren, ripping off a chunk of bread. She was still *starving*.

"No, it's just me. I..." He bit his lip. "I don't know if the others made it. I never went back to the camp."

Dread pooled in Aurum's stomach, and she stuffed her loaf of bread into the pocket of her pants. She was no longer hungry.

"Hey, rebels, we need to leave. *Now*," Vale urged.

He was right. They needed to move before they were caught. Aurum could worry about the others later. But they were alive. She knew they were. She wouldn't allow herself to consider the alternative.

"Come on," Ren said, leading them to the white door at the end of the hall. He swung it open to reveal a domed room full of branching hallways. They turned right, following him down dim, spiraling stairs.

"How in the Aether's name did you even manage all of this?" Vale asked.

Ren threw a smirk over his shoulder, amusement dancing in his blue eyes. "It was quite simple, really. I couldn't figure out any of the cell codes to rescue you guys earlier, so I just waited until someone came along with a food tray. Then I pulled the rookie card and waited for them to unlock the door. The rest you know."

"Unbelievable," Vale murmured.

Aurum reined in her laugh. She didn't care how Ren had done it—how he'd followed Damien and snuck into Vayne's mansion without springing the trap. It had to have been the armor, though. Still, she didn't care about how lucky he'd been. All she knew was that she and Vale were out, and she was with Ren again. As long as they were together, it didn't matter. They'd get through whatever was thrown against them. They'd reunite with the others, and they'd all be safe and alive. She wouldn't believe anything else.

The stairs leveled out into a large, blindingly white-tiled room with slanted tile ceilings—not a room Aurum realized, but a hangar. The hangar was completely empty, and an enormous, armored black door sat across from them. A control panel shined in the light on the wall beside it, and halfway down either wall toward the black door, two archways gaped, leading into additional hangars.

"*This* is the entrance to the tunnels?" Vale breathed. His eyes were wild as they surveyed the room like an animal about to be caged.

Ren cursed, and Aurum whirled to watch three soldiers clad in that hateful black emerge from the archway to the left. Everyone froze, and for a few moments, they simply stared at each other.

"What are you standing there for, soldier?" one of the guards spat, shattering the sudden silence. "Hurry up and get them back inside!"

"Yeah, we don't need Vayne hearing about their little prison break," a second muttered with a sigh. "We're going to have to tell Vayne the ones we shot just starved."

Confusion flooded Aurum. What were the guards talking about? *Who* were they talking about was the better question. She hadn't seen any sign of a prison break throughout the halls of the dungeon. Now that she thought about it, she hadn't seen any guards either. Was it because they were all down here stopping whatever had happened?

The third guard shrugged. "At least none of them escaped."

Ren grabbed Aurum and Vale's arms, slowly leading them to the black door that the third soldier marched over to. The soldier passed the door and walked to the control panel, entering a code before pressing a large blue button. The mighty black doors began to slide apart, revealing another large white room full of people—civilians—dressed in varying shades of beige, cream, and white. They all sat chained to the floor. The sharp reek of unwashed bodies slammed into Aurum like a tsunami. The air was hot and humid, and coughing and murmurs spread through the crowd of Araedians piled on top of each other. There were *hundreds* of them.

It was Vale's turn to mumble a curse. "Why are civilians down here?"

"They're from One and Two...," Aurum whispered. "Ren, what's going on?"

Ren didn't answer. He had no answer, she realized as he led them closer to the door. In the back of the white room of civilians, a dark metal gate guarded the entrance to the tunnels. Aurum had no doubt that the other hangars were the same as this one, full of people from the sectors—or One and Two at least. Not one shade of brown or gray was visible... Vayne had converted his hangars into additional dungeons, but why? And why only capture civilians from One and Two?

"Lock them up, then come with us," the first soldier ordered. "We need to search the corridors one last time... Just in case any of the others broke out."

"Yes, sir." Ren nodded, leading Aurum and Vale past the black doors.

Aurum glanced at the faces around her as she and Vale allowed Ren to push them to the ground over the nearest set of unoccupied chains. Some of the faces around her were full of fear and dread while others were stoic and hateful. Additional guards stood in the corners of the room, watching carefully with their guns of electricity. What had happened to these people? Why were they here?

"Don't worry," Ren said, clicking the chains shut around Aurum and Vale's wrists. "I'll get us out of this. I promise."

Aurum and Vale watched Ren rise and retreat behind the closing black doors. They shut and locked with a thunderous *click*. Murmurs rippled through the throng of Araedians around them. She bit the inside of her cheek. She hadn't been out of her cell for more than five minutes before returning to captivity. A sudden wave of exhaustion slammed into her. Her body and her mind still ached and throbbed. At least she and Vale had Ren. He'd find a way to get them out of this. Hope was not lost.

Vale sighed before leaning over to a young boy with coppery hair beside them. "Hey, what's going on?"

"Are you rebels?" the boy asked, surveying Vale's and Aurum's mismatched clothing with raised brows and awe shining in his eyes.

"Yes." Aurum nodded. "But we're a little out of sorts. Can you tell us what happened? How did everyone get in here?"

The boy frowned. "No one knows why, but Vayne started rounding up as many people as he could from Sector Two. His soldiers forced us into these big trucks that took us through the wall into Sector One. They brought us down here and locked us up alongside Araedians from One."

"What were those guards talking about before?" Vale asked with a nod toward the black doors. "They said others had broken out."

"Apparently a few people from Two who dealt in electrical wiring managed to fry their locks and hack through the doors in the second hangar. They didn't get very far though, and now they have soldiers stationed in here with us." The boy motioned with his chained wrists to the corners of the large room and the two soldiers who stood in each corner. "But we heard the people shouting down the halls before the guards killed them. They said that the rebels were coming—that they'd already begun liberating Sector Four."

"Pipe down!" one of the soldiers shouted into the sea of murmuring white and beige. The room grew eerily quiet.

"That's all I know," the boy whispered.

Aurum's heart was pounding, and her hands shook slightly, but she offered the boy a soft smile, dipping her head. "Thank you."

"Spenser must've warned our contacts in Two that the rebels were coming," Vale muttered.

"But how would he know what the rebels were planning?" Aurum shook her head. There were so many missing pieces to the puzzle—so many things they didn't know. Had the rebels figured out how to contact the sectors? Had enough of them survived to attack Four?

"Maybe the rebels snuck into Four or found some way to communicate through the hidden channels on the projectors." Vale shrugged. "I don't know, but something's happening. Something big. Vayne wouldn't pull all these people down here for nothing."

"If the rebels truly have attacked and liberated Four..." Aurum ran through the beginnings of the plan they'd been forming before the attack on the rebel camp. Roman had wanted to strike at Four by the end of the week, but there was no doubt that the rebels' numbers had dropped. Even with aid from the Araedians within the walls, would they still risk attacking the sectors? But Roman had also mentioned hunting for an old projector to try to make contact with Four... Could they have found it in the aftermath of the battle? Could they have fixed it? "They might actually be coming...," she whispered to herself, not quite believing it.

Beside her, Vale had gone completely silent. Aurum glanced at him as he stared at the chains around his wrists with dull and vacant cerulean eyes. She frowned, a pit forming in her stomach. Vale had been in that cell a lot longer than she had. She couldn't imagine finally having hope of escape—tasting freedom—only to be immediately shackled again.

But the rebels were coming. They had to be. It would explain why Vayne had trapped so many civilians down here. It would explain the attempted prison break in the hangars and those dangerous and inspiring words that had echoed down these halls. Vayne was trying to take away their numbers—trying to separate the sectors even further. He was trying to break them. But they couldn't break. *They would not break*. Help was on the way. If Ren didn't save them first, the rebels would. After all, Napoleon had mentioned using the underground tunnels during their planning. If the rebels went through with that part of the plan, it would lead the underground team right to the hangars... And Aurum would make sure she was ready—that everyone in the hangar was ready. She'd have them organized and prepared to escape... When the rebels came, they would fight for their freedom.

Hope was not lost. Aurum grabbed Vale's hand, offering him a reassuring squeeze. His eyes met hers, and she prayed he could read the message in her eyes.

Hope is not lost.

Vale squeezed back, and she could've sworn a little bit of light filled his eyes again. Aurum looked through the gaps between the Araedians to the dark metal gate at the back of the room—the tunnel entrance. A large lock sat below the metal handle, the darkness beyond it as still and silent as a tomb. She just prayed to the Aether that it wouldn't become one.

~

Natalia, Roman, and Fraiser crested the remnants of the hill to find Hero and the rebels surrounding the survivors of Vayne's army, the rain still pounding overhead, and beyond...

"By the Aether," Natalia whispered, halting at what lay before her.

Tears welled in her eyes at the sight of the entirety of Sector Four. There were hundreds of them. Araedians young and old had come. Some wore armor—most likely stolen—while others wore their simple, gray clothes. Guns and spears of electricity were scattered throughout the crowd, and even a few eyes glowed—though none, however, surrounded silver pupils.

Fraiser snorted. "They're just a tad bit late."

"Apologies," a young man with blood and dirt splattered across his sun-kissed skin said, stepping forward from the crowd. He couldn't have been more than a year or two older than Roman. "We were too busy holding off the other half of the army you just faced."

"Spenser!" Hero blurted, sprinting over from where he stood amongst a circle of Vayne's soldiers, who were being bound by metal cuffs from the newly arrived army. He threw his arms around Spenser, enveloping him in a tight embrace.

A small smile graced Spenser's lips. His hair was a dark brown, and his blue eyes sparkled like the clearest river. A brusque energy seemed to smolder behind those river eyes—still battle-hungry. Dark stubble surrounded his chin, and a small scar split his right brow. Natalia assumed that Spenser wasn't one to smile often.

"You made it," Spenser breathed, ruffling Hero's hair. "What happened to your face?"

"Vayne attacked our camp a few days ago," he said, pulling away. Shadows dimmed his brown eyes. "One of his mutts burned me."

Spenser hummed. "Should leave a wicked scar by the looks of it." Hero rolled his eyes. Spenser then turned to face Natalia, Roman, and Fraiser, surveying them carefully. "You're Roman, I presume."

Roman nodded, stepping forward and extending his hand. "Thank you for coming."

"Again, apologies for the delay," he said with a pointed look at Fraiser as he accepted Roman's hand. It only earned him one of Fraiser's signature scowls.

"That scowling ball of sunshine is Fraiser Hale, and this is Natalia Rhys," Roman introduced.

Natalia dipped her head in greeting. "How much of Four came?"

"The majority." Spenser turned back to face the civilians with a grateful glance. "Add around one thousand or so to your army."

"I'm from Four as well, so thank you." Natalia smiled, surveying the faces in the crowd. She could've sworn she met the familiar eyes of fellow orphans, and she even saw the round old man who owned Four's bakery. He used to trade with her and Vale for leftover cookies. "This means more than you know."

Spenser's irises began to glow a deep, dark blue surrounding black pupils. *He was a water Elemental.* How had he made it past the testings? "You don't need to thank me for this. It's about time someone handed Vayne's ass to him."

"Now there's something we can agree on," Fraiser murmured.

"We're ready to move on your command." Spenser looked at Roman. "But you should know that we lost contact with our correspondents in Two while you were marching here. I fear Vayne's taken them as well as the people of One."

"We've got an underground team on it," Natalia said, trying to mask her panic at the news. She cursed Vayne. How would this impact their numbers? There was no way Vayne could fit all of One and Two in the tunnels. He could hide maybe a thousand or so down there, but any more than that was impossible. Unless he'd somehow expanded his tunnels... No, she wouldn't think like that. Napoleon and Lavelle would find the people and get them out. The rebels could still win.

Roman's face had gone expressionless, and she could see the guilt of his father's actions weighing on him. It seemed to push his shoulders down, smothering every sense of hope he'd had. She took a step toward him and subtly nudged his elbow.

Roman met her gaze and straightened. He didn't break his eyes away from hers as he spoke. "Begin moving everyone to the gates. We march on Three immediately."

Spenser nodded, and he and Hero disappeared into the crowd of rebels, shouting orders to prepare to march. Frasier turned to Roman, her scowl never lightening. "What do we do with the prisoners?"

"Leave them here with the injured and those who will remain in Four," Roman said, grabbing Natalia's hand and beginning the walk toward the inner wall that connected Three and Four—the gate. "We're not senseless killers."

CHAPTER THIRTY

THE GATES

The rain had lightened to a slight drizzle after the rebels had broken through the large iron gates in the center of the wall separating Sector Three and Four nearly half an hour ago. Not a single one of Vayne's soldiers had been there to stop them from marching through. Roman suspected his father had pulled them all back to protect One.

Natalia recalled the glorious sight of those gates crumbling to the ground under the weight of the maelstrom of elements they'd thrown at it. Air, water, earth, and fire had all joined to form a singular blast to knock them down. The elements had come together and combined just as the sectors would. She couldn't wait for those gates to be Vayne's—the gates to his mansion where they'd hopefully find Aurum and Ren. If they weren't there, she didn't know what she'd do. If Damien had killed them...

"Are you all right?" Roman asked, his brows narrowing. His wet hair stuck to his forehead, and dirt and blood still covered his face as he walked through the dense forest of Sector Three beside her. Fraiser, Hero, and Spenser trailed a few steps behind them, along with the bulk of the rebels' army.

Natalia nodded, grateful that he'd pulled her from her thoughts. "I'm ready to end this."

"Aren't we all?" Spenser flounced, walking between them with a smile that didn't quite reach his river eyes. The scar on his brow was painted red in the few rays of the setting sun that managed to peek through the smothering dark gray clouds. Those few rays bathed the looming trees and tall grass in small patches of orange, red, and pink. The landscape of Three was lush and flat—nowhere near as hilly as Sector Four.

"Has anyone ever told you how much of a pleasure it is to be in your presence?" Fraiser said to Spenser with mock kindness.

Hero rolled his eyes. "And that's why *I* led the rebels inside the walls."

Natalia, Fraiser, and Hero chuckled while Spenser threw them all a glare.

Roman halted at the edge of the tree line. "We're here."

Natalia walked up beside him, peering through the branches and leaves. A large expanse of clustered wooden and brick houses lay before them. Bright wooden lampposts illuminated the dirt streets woven between them, connecting every house to a rounded intersection at the center of Three where four large dirt roads branched out in each direction.

Natalia knew this was the heart of Sector Three. Damien had described it to her several times in the past—the mixtures of shops and homes that housed the majority of their population and kept the entirety of Three alive. She knew that one of the old mills he used to work at to provide for his mother and brothers was a ten-minute walk south. She pushed thoughts of that old Damien away—the memories of the mischievous gleam in his hazel eyes when he'd tease one of them or the dimples that graced his cheeks when he laughed. That Damien was gone and had been gone for some time now... But being in his old home was stirring memories. Memories that Natalia liked to pretend had never happened.

"So what's the plan?" Fraiser whispered, squinting through the brush. "I don't see any guards."

"Or civilians." Hero frowned.

Natalia scanned the streets. They were right. Three was completely empty. The only sign of inhabitance was the lights shining within the windows of the shops and houses and the smoke rising from a few chimneys. The people were there, but why wasn't a single soul outside? Where was Vayne's army? His soldiers? Surely he wouldn't allow the rebels to simply take Three without a fight. Panic began to claw its way through her. Something wasn't right.

"They must be under curfew," Spenser said. "Vayne's been extremely fond of those recently."

Fraiser scowled. "That doesn't explain the lack of guards."

"It's a trap," Roman murmured. "It has to be."

"So let's spring it." Spenser shrugged.

Natalia's eyes narrowed. "We can't just send our people in there to die."

"Well, we can't just sit here either," Spenser said. "People are going to die in this war. Some already have. Everyone knows the risks. I say, we march through and spring the trap."

"Roman, what if we send in a small team first?" Hero pointed toward the nearest wooden house. "If we can get inside, the people in Three might be able to tell us what the trap is and help us get around it. Once we have more information and know what we're up against, the rest of the army can come through, and we can spring the trap."

Roman nodded. "I'll go."

"I'm coming with you," Natalia said, meeting his gaze. She refused to take no for an answer, and she knew that he could see that in her eyes. "Don't even bother arguing about it."

"Fine." He frowned. "But the rest of you are staying here."

Anger flashed across Fraiser's face, her ever-present scowl deepening. "Like hell—"

"That's an *order*," Roman commanded, turning to face her.

Natalia bit the inside of her cheek. She couldn't recall a time Roman had ever pulled rank. Even Fraiser seemed at a loss for words.

No one dared argue after that. Fraiser, Hero, and Spenser would remain with the army while Natalia and Roman snuck into Three. If they didn't return from the cluster of houses within the hour, the rebels would charge into the heart of Sector Three, regardless of the trap that lay before them.

Natalia and Roman crept out from the edge of the forest, carefully making their way through the tall, swaying grass. The windows of the first few houses were dark and desolate, so they carried on deeper into the streets. The last visible rays of light began to sink behind the tops of the trees, and they quickly found themselves cast in the shadows of the maze of alleys between the buildings.

A slight breeze threaded through the alley, blowing strands of Roman's dark hair in his face. Natalia studied him carefully for a few moments—his cheeks, the soft curve of his lips, his eyes, the slight stubble running across his chin. She rolled her eyes with a small smile. He'd forgotten to shave again. She turned back to face the bend in the alley ahead. She had more than one mission tonight. Not only was she going to uncover what Vayne's trap for the rebels was, but she was also going to protect his son with her life. She would not allow a single hair on his head to be harmed. But if somehow, something happened to Roman, the entire world would pay for it through fire and ice.

Roman took the bend, veering to the right alongside a storefront with a covered wooden porch and railing. Across the street, lights set the small dirt path connecting the street to one of the four main roads branching off the rounded intersection blazing. Natalia reached toward the railing, ready to hop over when Roman grabbed her and pulled her back into the cover of the dark alley. They watched as a patrol of four guards marched down the street before disappearing down a large side road. She let out a breath she hadn't known she'd been holding. They waited two minutes and glanced down either side of the street three times before finally hopping the railing and crouching down in the shadows. They then lifted their heads and peered into one of the shop's windows.

Six soldiers clad in the black armor of Vayne's army stood around a long table where a map of the sectors lay. An array of axes, leather gloves, rope, and other lumber supplies lined the walls of the store. A wooden counter sat a few feet behind the table where a young man and woman stood, fear clear on their pale faces. One of the soldiers lifted a hand toward the woman and snapped twice. Beside her, the man's eyes filled with anger and hatred as she hurried into a back room and reappeared a few moments later with a wooden plate of bread that she set before the soldiers.

"They've commandeered the shop," Natalia whispered. "They're waiting for us..."

Roman nodded, angling his head higher. "Can you see what's on the map?"

"No." She cursed. "The bucket heads are in the way."

Suddenly, the woman's brown eyes lifted to meet Natalia's through the window and widened. Natalia froze. Roman stiffened beside her, and the entire world seemed to slow. She could hear her heart pounding in her ears as she prayed to the Aether that the woman wouldn't cry out and give them away to the soldiers. They'd have nowhere to hide if she did. It'd be a chase through the alleys. So Natalia did the only thing she could think of. Slowly, she reached down to the canteen strapped to her belt and opened it as her eyes began to glow ice blue, purple, and red-orange around silver pupils. She lifted her hands out in front of her and molded the globe of water into one word: *rebels.*

The woman's eyes widened even further. Natalia didn't think the woman was breathing, but then she stilled herself, took a deep breath, and mouthed two words.

Help us.

Natalia couldn't stop the sigh of relief that left her parted lips. Even Roman loosed a shaky breath. She pointed at the soldiers and map, fingertips pressing against the glass, and whispered, "*Where are they?*"

The woman turned and walked behind the counter, joining the young man once again. She clutched onto his arm, squeezing tight. Her eyes were full of fear and dread.

Everywhere.

"Get down," Roman said, grabbing Natalia's waist and pulling her toward the railing. She quickly hopped over the rail back into the shadows of the dark alleyway,

Roman following behind her. Huddled together, they watched as another group of six soldiers exited the house next door and piled into the lumber shop.

Everywhere, Natalia repeated to herself. Vayne must have deployed his soldiers here while the rebels were taking Four. Her gaze slid to the houses across the dirt road. Were those homes infested with Vayne's soldiers, too? Had every home and shop been overrun? She turned to Roman, who seemed to be lost in the same thoughts. A frown dragged at his mouth. Was their only option to simply march on Three and hope that the people could get out and fight with them? Would they take the people as hostages and use them against the rebels? If the rest of the sector was anything like that shop, the people of Three were terrified and in terrible danger.

"I don't know what to do," she whispered.

"Come on." Roman grabbed her hand. "We can't give up. Let's try one more house and see if we can talk to someone who knows what's going on. If it's the same, we'll go back and figure something out with Fraiser and the others."

Natalia nodded, allowing him to help her to her feet. She glanced around the corner of the store to find the street empty. They cut left, steering clear of the lumber shop, and turned down a large alleyway on the opposite side of the road. Wooden barrels and crates spotted their path, and they passed two houses—hiding in the shadows of the second as more guards strolled by, patrolling the branching streets—before veering to the right toward the rounded intersection at the center of Three. Natalia and Roman continued straight before cutting left again to enter a large marketplace lined with wooden stalls and branching side streets.

And dozens and dozens of soldiers, who turned to face them.

Natalia's blood ran cold, and for a few moments, everyone simply stared at each other. She knew the soldiers were taking in their mismatched clothes and painted armor—the blood and dirt covering their faces. She knew everything had clicked when the nearest soldier lifted a finger and pointed. But she didn't hear what the soldier said. All she heard was Roman exclaiming one word over and over: *run, run, run.*

Natalia and Roman tore back down the alleyway, shouts of alarm and pounding footsteps racing after them like a pack of starving wolves. Bolts of electricity fired from the soldiers' guns crackled after them. They rounded a corner to watch the bolts crash into the side of a brick house where they'd been moments before, sending sparks and tendrils of electricity scattering. Natalia's eyes began to sting with the familiar glow of red-orange, purple, and ice-blue irises surrounding molten silver pupils. She half-turned, slashing her arm at the soldiers as they pursued them around the corner. A roaring tsunami of flames erupted from her palm, viciously colliding with the first five soldiers. The flames whipped about, singeing through the black armor and the surrounding wooden walls of buildings. The flames quickly crawled up the walls and across the alley, spreading to the thatched roofs like a beacon.

Well, if Vayne's army hadn't known Roman and Natalia were there before, they certainly did now. She pumped her arms faster—pushed her legs harder into the ground. The soldiers would get through the flames eventually, but now was their time to lose them in the maze of alleyways.

"We're almost there!" Roman shouted as they darted back across the street that housed the lumber shop.

The woman had been right. Soldiers were everywhere. They poured out of commandeered houses and stores and side streets, polluting the roads like a smothering poison. But the soldiers weren't the only ones crowding the streets. The people of Three had begun to open their doors and windows to peer out into the darkness of the early night. A few had even braved their porches to search for the stench of smoke and flames building in the air.

Natalia glanced over her shoulder to find several soldiers still pursuing them. She turned and followed Roman down a narrow branching alley. He slowed, allowing her to pass him before he shoved against two towering stacks of barrels and crates, sending them crashing to the ground. Natalia didn't dare look back at the hollering soldiers as they broke free of the houses into the tall grass. They made it five steps when the crackle of more bolts of electricity raced after them.

"Look out!" Natalia tackled Roman to the ground as a bolt landed and exploded into the ground where he'd been only a moment before. Mud and grass flew high into the air, showering over them.

Roman wiped at his eyes with a curse and jumped to his feet, barely forming a sphere of water in enough time to swallow the second bolt that fired toward them. He grunted, stumbling backward from the force of the electricity. Flashing blue-purple shades of light from the crackling streaks of electricity danced across his face. Roman regained his footing and, with a leap and extension of his arms, sent the sphere hurtling back at the throng of black armor gathering at the outskirts of the sector.

"Rebels!" a voice shouted from the tree line of the forest. Natalia whipped around as Fraiser appeared a moment later, eyes glowing gray and silver. A wicked grin lightened her face. Hero and Spenser stood behind her, eyes glowing gray and dark blue around the darkest black pupils. "Attack!"

War cries pierced the air as the entirety of the rebel army burst forth from the trees and charged Sector Three. Roman and Natalia whirled, once again facing the growing mass of Vayne's army. With the new additions from Four, the rebels had doubled in size. They were well over one thousand strong and would be a fair match against the force that barreled at them. But the rebels had something Vayne's army didn't—an advantage that tipped the scales in their favor. The elements.

Natalia offered him a wink before launching into a sprint. As she ran, a swirling sphere of water formed in her left hand while a hungry globe of flames formed in her right. She leaped into the air, blasting her elements forward. They collided against armor with a deafening *crash*. Cries went up from the soldiers as they met the rebels. Natalia formed a long spear of hardened ice in her hands, twirling and slicing every soldier within reach. She had just slit a soldier's throat when a second round of cries filled the air. The hair on the back of her neck rose, and she risked a glance at the expanse of Sector Three. Her heart felt as if it would crush under the weight of the awe filling it. Throughout every street and between every house and shop, the people of Three were there. And they were fighting, too.

~

Roman finally let his spear of ice fall to the ground and shatter into pieces as he panted. Sweat and mud coated every inch of his skin, and a trickle of blood ran from the corner of his mouth. The remains of the outskirts of Three was nothing but bodies, trampled grass, blood and gore, and a few piles of cinders where small houses had once stood. He took a few shaky steps forward. Several rebels and citizens of Three and Four scurried across the battlefield, searching for the injured and binding the few of Vayne's soldiers that had survived. He adjusted his left shoulder—still sore from the attack on the rebels' camp all those days ago.

He was alone, having stayed to pick off the last of Vayne's soldiers who wouldn't give up, while the others regrouped in the city center. Natalia had wanted to stay with him, but he'd needed a minute alone to work through what he was feeling...

The battle hadn't lasted long. Vayne's soldiers succumbed to the elements and the growing rebel forces almost immediately. The people of Three had fought viciously alongside them, truly turning the tide of the battle, though it had left dozens of rebels and Araedians dead and even more injured. Fraiser had insisted they'd gained more than they'd lost—even if the majority of their new recruits were untrained civilians. She'd reminded him that his father's army was made up of nearly five thousand men and claimed the Araedians would put up a good fight in the coming battle like they had today.

But it didn't feel that way to Roman. Their army had increased to over three thousand, yet all he saw were the deaths that stained his hands crimson—the soldiers of his father's army that he'd killed himself and the rebels and Araedians he'd ordered into battle. They were all his fault. Even his father's victims were his fault. He should've stopped Vayne years ago—should've killed him the day he'd killed Roman's mother. He could never forget that day. It still haunted his dreams even now.

Roman shook his head. He didn't have time to wallow in his self-pity. If he refused to acknowledge the weight bearing down on his shoulders, it'd go away. At least for a little while... He knew Natalia had seen through it before, though, and she would see through it now. She'd see right through every wall he'd put up to hide it, but he didn't want to hide it—not from her. The others couldn't know, but Natalia could. He could live with that.

"Roman," Fraiser said, emerging from within the depths of the alleys behind him.

He faced her. Blood and mud were smeared across every inch of her face and body, and despite the sweat dripping down her temple, she held her chin and shoulders high as if the battle had been nothing for her... As if she could do it all again at a moment's notice.

"Are you all right?" he asked, willing strength into his voice to keep it from shaking.

She nodded, eyeing him closely. "You, on the other hand..."

"I'm fine." Roman frowned. "Have you seen the others?"

"They're all waiting for you," Fraiser said flatly. She turned and started back into the alley. "So get moving."

Roman sighed and followed Fraiser through the winding streets, dodging piles of singed wood and crumbling bricks. Smoke billowed in the air, scorching his lungs and causing his eyes to water. They rounded a corner onto one of the main avenues leading to the intersection at the center of the sector. Bodies clad in black armor and regular brown clothes lined the street along with even more smoking debris. Corpses were being dragged to the sides, clearing a path through the rubble. A few women carrying bandages darted out from one of the allies and dispersed. Some ran into houses full of the wailing injured, while others tended to those on the streets.

Roman couldn't stop the shiver that rolled down his spine. Fraiser glanced over her shoulder at him before quickening her pace and cutting across the avenue to a small wooden building. The lights inside shone through the many holes in the light-gray curtains, illuminating the crumbling wooden porch and stairs. She paused before the door and met his gaze with a scowl.

"I know when you're in your own head." She rolled her eyes. "Don't shut me out."

"You shut me out all the time," he said.

"That's different, Roman."

"Is it?" he asked, tilting his head.

Fraiser scoffed. "Don't try to take up my self-destructive tendencies."

"Are you saying that because you care, Fraiser, or are you regretting not sharing your own feelings?"

She shrugged. "Maybe a bit of both."

They held each other's stare for a few long, silent moments, neither willing to look away. Roman smirked. They were both way too hardheaded for their own good. He could read Fraiser like an open book, just as she could read him.

"I saw you throw that spear of ice at that guy coming at me," she said. "I only lead our game by two points now."

His smirk widened into a grin. "Let's keep it that way. I really get tired of having to save your..."

"Ah, Roman, don't get soft on me." Disgust crossed her face. "That's gross... But in all seriousness... When you're ready to talk, you can talk to me. Just know that."

"Look who's getting soft now." He crossed his arms. "But the same goes for you, too."

Fraiser reached behind her to grab the knob of the door. She still had yet to break eye contact with him. "The others are in here with the self-proclaimed leaders of Three. They're the ones who kept the civilians organized, and they want to discuss our next move."

"All right." Roman nodded. "Open the door."

Fraiser's scowl deepened, and she turned, finally breaking his gaze to open the door. Roman chuckled softly as he followed her into the warm light of the room and closed the door behind them. A worn red rug occupied most of the front room. At the center of the rug, Natalia, Hero, and Spenser all stood over a large wooden table with an older burly man and a tall, fierce-looking woman with auburn hair who appeared to be in her late twenties. They both immediately stepped forward to introduce themselves as Darri Haas and Feura Fletcher. Roman recognized Darri's name. He'd always been involved in the governing of Three but had been forced to step down years ago when his opinion had clashed with one of Vayne's commanders in the Circle. One thing about Darri was clear: He was highly respected by the civilians of Three.

Behind them, a branching hallway led deeper into the few additional rooms of the house. Roman quickly mumbled his own introduction, stepping past them to stand in front of Natalia. The weight finally lifted off his shoulders when her eyes met his. The Aether save him—her eyes alone were enough to send his heart galloping. He gave her a small smile, lifting his hand to wipe at the mud smeared across her cheek. She returned his smile and grabbed his hand, interlacing their fingers. Watching her fight earlier had been equally terrifying and enchanting. Terrifying because of the danger she was putting herself in... Enchanting because of the way she moved and flowed with her elements like she was lost in some elaborate dance to music that only she could hear...

Roman turned to Hero and Spenser and dipped his head in greeting as Fraiser, Feura, and Darri joined them at the table, spreading a map of the sectors across the rough wooden surface.

Feura cleared her throat, her auburn hair shining in the dim light. "We were all discussing how we're going to transport the rebels and the army to the gates of One while you were out," she said, respectfully dipping her head toward Roman. "I have it on good authority that Vayne's emptied all of One and most of Two of the Araedians that lived there. We might find a few able-bodied stragglers on our way through, but this looks like our final numbers for now."

Roman bit his tongue to keep from cursing. His father definitely had the numbers... But they had the elements... Could the Elementals make up for their disadvantage? He ran his free hand through his dark hair. They did have a second advantage, though. One that Vayne could never match. The rebels and Araedians had heart—a true cause and loved ones to fight for. His father was just fighting for his deranged dream of becoming the Aether, and his soldiers' loyalty was brainwashed into them. Those factors would make a difference, and if Natalia was right about Ren being the Aether...then they'd have him, too. If he was still alive.

"Napoleon was right," Natalia murmured. Roman and the others faced her, drawing their eyes away from the markings of the map. She met each of their gazes one by one. "Vayne can't keep that many people in his mansion, so they must be in the tunnels like Napoleon said. He'll find them, and he'll bring them back. We just have to give him *time*."

Hero nodded. "If he succeeds, our numbers would match Vayne's—maybe even surpass his."

"But if he doesn't, we're still outnumbered," Spenser said, crossing his arms and leaning against the table.

"And time is one thing we cannot give him," Darri added gruffly. "We cannot allow him to brainwash more troops."

Spenser shook his head. "Or give him the opportunity to fortify himself even farther. He had those cannons in Four... There's no telling what he has in One."

"We have no other option," Natalia declared incredulously. "We can fight now and go down swinging, or we can roll over and let Vayne stomp out this rebellion—everything we've all been working toward. The time to fight is now, regardless of our numbers. This is our shot."

"So let's make it count," Fraiser said with a wicked smirk.

"I agree," Feura said. "Vayne abandoned fifteen armored trucks here in Three—it's impossible that he didn't abandon some in Two as well. We can take the fifteen we have now into Sector Two and leave one truck behind to look for more trucks to transport the army, which will travel toward Two on foot. The other fourteen trucks can continue on to the gates of One while those left behind send the additional trucks found in Two back to meet the army on the road. Then they can rendezvous with the previous fourteen at One's gate."

"It might take a few trips to get everyone there, but it'll work." Roman nodded, his hand tightening around Natalia's as adrenaline began to course through his veins. She squeezed back. Everything was starting to fall into place.

Spenser pushed off the table. "But we need to prioritize Elementals in the trucks that head to One first."

"Well, would you look at that?" Fraiser grinned in mock kindness. "You actually had a halfway decent idea, Spenser."

Spenser's brows knit together, and he uncrossed his arms to flash her a vulgar gesture. Roman rolled his eyes as Darri frowned. Natalia, Hero, and Feura merely exchanged amused glances.

"Elementals will be prioritized," Darri said, his voice coarse and rough. "After all, they're the ones who can bust down the gate with a good chance of survival."

"I'll have the trucks brought to the intersection immediately." Feura quickly crossed the room to the door and disappeared out into the night.

Darri walked to the door, pausing with his hand on the knob. He turned to meet Roman's gaze. "Prepare the people. You'll be at the gates of One within the hour."

He then opened the door and left, following after Feura.

"Come on," Roman said, glancing at Natalia, Fraiser, Hero, and Spenser before finally allowing his eyes to roam over the map and settle on the circle of wall surrounding Vayne's mansion in the heart of One.

Within the hour...

He lifted his head. "We've got work to do."

Fraiser rolled her eyes, passing them all with a dramatic sigh. "We *always* have work to do."

Roman smiled, grateful to have each and every one of them by his side as they exited the house. He couldn't have asked for a more loyal group of friends, and he couldn't imagine his future without any of them, especially the girl holding his hand now. Roman just prayed to the Aether that he would indeed have a future, and that they'd all be in it.

~

Napoleon halted before the dark looming bend in the tunnel an hour later. A slight breeze wafted from the bend, blowing strands of his light brown hair across his forehead. It was exactly what he'd been waiting for—the breeze. It meant his suspicions were right. Napoleon, Lavelle, and the rebels were deep into Sector One by now, and it was only a matter of time until they were under Vayne's mansion. But as Napoleon had suspected, they already were. Whatever room lay around that bend was a part of Vayne's underground network. He turned to face Lavelle and the rebels. His eyes lingered on the blonde hair and bright blue eyes that reflected the flickering flames in the palms of the fire Elementals.

"Lights out," Napoleon said, gently pulling his fingers from Lavelle's. The flames immediately guttered out, nearly smothering them in the darkness.

"What are you doing?" Lavelle asked, a slight panic lacing her words. Even through the dark, he knew her brows were knit together.

"I'm going to scout ahead." He took a few steps toward the bend. "I need you all to stay here and wait until I get back."

"No, I'm coming with you."

"Lavelle, the one thing I know about what's around this corner is that it belongs to Vayne. It could be anything down there, and I'm not taking you or any of the others through until I know it's safe." Napoleon felt more than saw the glare she threw at him. He sighed. "Please, just stay here. I'll be back soon. I promise."

"You have five minutes before I come marching down that tunnel, Napoleon. *Five minutes.*"

He smiled, then disappeared around the bend to meet another turn—and another. The tunnel zig-zagged for several yards before opening into a cross-road and forking in two directions. At the end of the tunnel in front of him, the faint glow of bright white lights illuminated the earthen floor and walls and the thick metal gate set before him. A large lock hung below the metal handle. To his right, the second tunnel—much larger and wider than the tunnels he'd come from—shot diagonally farther into the gloom. Red and blue wires ran along its earthen walls.

The hairs on the back of Napoleon's neck stood as he knelt in front of the lock and scooped up a handful of dirt. He held his palm to the small keyhole, closing his eyes against the stinging and glowing of his light green irises and pupils darker than the night. A shiver wracked down his spine as he molded the dirt into a perfect key. He quickly unlocked the gate and stepped through. He needed to hurry. Lavelle's five minutes were nearly up, and he didn't want her anywhere remotely close to anything that belonged to Vayne.

Napoleon took five steps before rounding the final corner. His breath caught in his throat as the bright lights of a stark white hangar appeared before him. He couldn't believe his own eyes. He blinked furiously, adjusting to the light and trying to convince himself he wasn't having a nightmare. A second gate guarded the entrance to the blinding hangar, but behind that gate, *hundreds* of Araedians dressed in whites, beiges, and creams knelt, chained to the floor. Guards stood in the corners of the room with guns and spears of electricity in their hands. The stale stench of hundreds—maybe even a thousand—of unwashed bodies crammed together hit him like a crashing wave, causing his eyes to water. Excrement stained the floor of the left corner of the hangar; however, a few puddles could be seen in the tiny, near-invisible gaps between the Araedians. A chorus of hoarse coughs and murmurs filled the air, echoing through the chamber.

Napoleon had been right. Vayne had captured the people of One and Two and hidden them away in the depths of his mansion to keep the rebels from growing their army. He cursed. He had to get these people out. But how? He scanned the crowd for any familiar faces but found none. There were too many people piled on top of each other to tell any of them apart—too many to tell if Aurum or Ren were there.

Suddenly, deafening alarms blared to life, screaming horridly as the lights began to flash between red and white. Napoleon covered his ears and squinted through the thick gate barring him from the hangar. The large black doors slid open, and a soldier sprinted in.

"All soldiers to the courtyard *immediately*! The rebels have been spotted near the gates of One!"

Murmurs spread through the room like wildfire, and some Araedians began to tug at their chains. Heads swung from side to side as the soldiers quickly began to file out of the hangar, abandoning their posts.

"You two stay here," the soldier who'd given the announcement ordered, pointing at the last two guards heading toward the doors. "Make sure they don't cause any trouble."

"What in the Aether's name is going on?" Lavelle shouted over the alarms.

Napoleon jumped, rocking back into the gate with a small *crash* as he turned to face her. The entirety of the tunnel team stood behind her, confusion and panic marking all of their expressions. "Roman and the others are near the gates. Vayne must've called all his soldiers up to the surface. Lavelle, we were right. He's got the people of One *and* Two down here."

"What about Ren?" Lavelle's eyes widened. "Did you see Ren or Aurum?"

"No." Napoleon shook his head. "I'm sorry... Maybe there's more hangars? If we can get these people out, then we might have time to check—"

"Napoleon, unlock the gate." Lavelle's usual vibrant blue eyes were cold and distant, and her voice was unnaturally steady. He opened his mouth to say more, but she merely repeated herself. "Unlock the gate."

So Napoleon knelt and grabbed another handful of dirt, holding it up to the keyhole of the lock. He bit the inside of his cheek. They'd need to take out the two soldiers as quickly as possible. If they triggered an alarm, the rebels would never be able to get all the civilians out. He waited as the earth again molded into a perfect key.

Then he unlocked the gate.

CHAPTER THIRTY-ONE

THE AETHER

It had been hours since Ren had left Aurum and her cellmate in the hangars far below Vayne's mansion. He'd left them in chains to spend the next hour pretending to comb through the maze of dungeons and cells with the other guards. They'd needed to confirm that no other Araedians had escaped in their little prison break, which of course, no one else had. Ren managed to piece enough information together from the guards to learn that a few of the civilians of Two who'd worked with wires had short-circuited their handcuffs to try to escape, but they hadn't made it far. The guards had shot and killed them on sight.

Ren had felt so sick after that, it'd taken all of his willpower to keep from hurling in his helmet—and from pummeling the guards into the ground with rage. It hurt his heart that his people from Two had been murdered, but he couldn't help feeling a little pride, too. They were the only ones who'd had the guts and courage to fight back. They were the true heroes here today—the true rebels—and he promised himself he wouldn't let their sacrifices be in vain.

Ren followed the guards through the stark-white halls into the barracks, passing rows and rows of metal bed frames and mattresses. He nearly sighed at the sight of the beds. Keeping up his disguise as a guard was proving to be extremely painful and taxing, and he didn't know how much more of it he could take. He just wished he could lie down and close his eyes for a few minutes, but he couldn't. Every guard and soldier in the mansion had been ordered to report to the armory on the west wing of the ground floor *immediately*. With a yawn, Ren rolled his shoulders and began to follow the guards piling out of the barracks and into the golden halls.

He passed hundreds and hundreds of murmuring soldiers clad in midnight armor as he made his way toward the armory. A slight panic began to creep through his veins. Vayne was readying his troops for something big... Something must have happened in the sectors. It was the only explanation... The mansion grew eerily and utterly quiet as Ren rounded a corner and entered the large, armored door of the armory. The hairs on the back of his neck stood at the sight of the multitude of weapons lining the long, black walls stretching before him. The room was enormous, and the number of weapons inside was sufficient to supply an army of several thousand. His heart dropped into his stomach. How were the rebels supposed to defeat this?

A slight shove in Ren's back had him moving to the racks of weapons. He hadn't even noticed he'd paused to gawk in the middle of the doorway. Ren cursed himself. He had to get his act together—pretend he'd been here before. He steered away from the guns of electricity and headed toward the rows and rows of deadly spears. He had absolutely no idea how to use the guns and would expose himself immediately if he tried. His hand closed around the cold, slippery steel. It was surprisingly heavy as Ren lifted it off the rack and followed the sea of black soldiers to the open doors at the opposite end of the armory. Everything about this felt wrong, and he found himself longing for the rebel camp miles deep into the forest... And the people within it.

The doors led out into one of the many large courtyards within the walls of the mansion. Storm clouds darkened the sky overhead, and grass peeked between the cobblestone beneath his feet. Rainwater drizzled down the pillars supporting the mezzanine and balconies above, and the air in the courtyard felt charged despite the rain—as if the tiniest spark would have the world around Ren and the soldiers piling into the courtyard erupting like a volcano. He walked over to one of the raised stone slabs and sat, scanning every black helmet in sight. The thousands of guns and spears in the armory flashed through his mind, and Ren allowed his shoulders to slump as he leaned his helmeted head against the shaft of his spear.

Thousands and thousands...

∼

Ren shivered against the cold drops of rain that pelted his armor and the cobblestones beneath his feet nearly two hours later. Though the sun was hidden behind the storm clouds, he knew it would set within minutes. The waiting was killing him. Every fiber of his being was screaming at him to abandon his cover and storm back down into the dungeons. He could free Aurum and save the hangars full of hundreds and hundreds of Araedians, but superior officers—marked by the white band around the right arm of their armor—surrounded every exit within the courtyard. How could he get through them? They'd see right through every excuse and lie he spun, and Ren had a feeling they didn't take insubordination lightly. Not a single complaint had been uttered the entire time. Not a soul had even tried to avoid the rain. The army had been told to wait, so they had waited, and he knew they'd wait until they were told otherwise. It was an inhuman sort of obedience that had him questioning if every man and woman under the black helmets had been brainwashed.

But soldiers had been talking in the barracks. He'd even overheard a few conversations in the dungeons. These people still had their personalities. They weren't completely lost and hollow like Damien was. They'd been allowed to keep more of themselves than he had. So why were they still so loyal to Vayne? Was it because this job protected their families and secured a better quality of life? Or had they all been brainwashed to simply *obey*?

"Attention!" A feminine voice rang throughout the courtyard. Every soldier stood, their weapons sheathed at their sides or across their backs. Ren followed suit, straightening to his full height, but compared to those around him, he was not very tall. He glanced up at one of the balconies overlooking the courtyard. The woman—Zyra—who had accompanied Damien in the forest during the attack on the rebels stood there, a sadistic smirk pulling at the corners of her mouth. A strong wind blew at her long, blonde hair. "The wall patrol has spotted the remains of the rebels in Sector Two. The entirety of sectors Three and Four are with them."

The world seemed to slow as Zyra's words hit Ren. They had survived—the rebels had survived, and they were coming. And the people of Araedia were with them. Shivers that had nothing to do with the cold rain wracked his spine. Ren was thankful for the visor of the helmet that shielded his eyes as they began to sting and glow with emotion. He still squeezed them shut, though. He couldn't be caught, especially not now. He *had* to get down to the dungeons, no matter the cost. The rebels still needed numbers—the people who Vayne had tried to take away from them.

Ren opened his eyes. Zyra half-turned to face the glass doors to the balcony as a familiar face flung them open and walked to the metal railing. Damien's face was stone-cold. The gaze he swept over the courtyard was even colder. Ren's heart ached at the sight of him. The Damien he'd grown up with was completely and utterly gone—devoid of the playful challenge and mischief that used to warm his eyes. Damien crossed his arms over his armored chest, nodding at Zyra to continue.

"The rebels have commandeered armored trucks left in Two and Three," she said. "They are transporting their army to the gates of One as we speak. We expect them to arrive within the hour. Prepare to march. We leave for the gates immediately."

Ren's hands began to sweat inside his black leather gloves. Panic rooted him to the spot, and he found he was unable to tear his eyes away from Damien, who stared into the sea of black below. The sea surged forward, and the soldiers began marching through the courtyard toward the fifteen-foot walls and gate that surrounded Vayne's mansion. Soldiers jostled Ren from side to side, threatening to carry him with them. He pushed against the unfazed drones, attempting to claw his way back toward the doors into the halls of the mansion. Superior officers be damned. He couldn't sit and wait for a chance to escape any more. He had to get to Aurum *now*.

Ren broke into a run, barely squeezing between the armored bodies. He rounded one of the pillars supporting the mezzanine above only to slam into a soldier, causing him to slip on the wet cobblestone and tumble to the ground. Ren bit back a cry as his bare head collided against the stone, his helmet skidding across the rough stone. Not a single soldier turned their head when he pushed himself back to his feet, fighting his blurring vision, and glanced at the balcony across the courtyard. Zyra was gone. Damien, however, remained at the railing.

And he was looking right at Ren.

Their eyes locked, and the entire world went still—even the rain seemed to pause. But time came slamming back into place as Damien's eyes began to glow, and he leaped over the railing. Ren turned and sprinted to the nearest door, his eyes glowing gold and silver. He didn't spare the superior officer a glance, nor did he dare to look back at Damien, when he sent a column of cobblestones—ripped from the earth beneath him—slamming into the officer. Ren yanked the door open and tore down the golden hallway.

Glorious pictures and paintings flashed by as he ran toward the branching intersection at the end of the hall. He cut right, his wet boots slipping on the tile floor and nearly sending him careening into an ornate red couch. He steadied himself before continuing down the hall to the door he knew would take him to the barracks. From there, he'd be able to find his way to the dungeons.

"Ren!" Damien's voice beckoned.

Ren threw the barrack door open, sprinting through the rows and rows of bunked beds. He disappeared behind the next door a split second after Damien entered the barracks, racing down the blindingly white hall toward the black dungeon door. The only sound was his feet colliding against the white tiles until two pairs of footfalls suddenly echoed through the hall. Ren jumped and whirled, slashing his arm across his body. A column of air sprung forth from his arm, slicing at Damien, who jumped and flipped, easily dodging the column.

"Where are you off to? You're going to miss the big family reunion, Ren," Damien said with a smirk promising pain and death.

"Sorry, you're actually not invited," he snarled, slowly backing toward the door.

Damien huffed, stalking after him. "So did you find Aurum yet?"

"I was the guard who helped you lock her up." It was Ren's turn to smirk. He was almost to the door. He just needed to keep Damien talking. "It was actually pretty easy to sneak her out after you left. No one even noticed."

"Ah..." He nodded. "I must admit, I was focused on more important matters that day, but if Aurum's long gone, then why are you still here?"

Ren clenched his fists, pausing before the door. "Why are you doing this, Damien?"

"You didn't get her out." Damien halted, too, and his smirk grew into a feral grin. "Where is she? Down in the hangars with the rest of the potential traitors?"

"Go to hell!"

Damien lifted his hands. "Shall we take the fight to her, brother?"

"You're not my brother...," Ren said softly but not weakly. He shifted his hand behind his back, grabbing the handle. "Not any more."

Damien lunged forward, shooting cascades of swirling flames from his hands. They hissed at Ren as he opened the dungeon door and slammed it shut behind him. A moment later, the flames crashed against the metal with a *boom*. Ren didn't falter and continued straight down the dungeon hall past Aurum's old cell. He rounded a few familiar corners before descending the steps to the hangars. He was halfway to the dark doors at the end when Damien appeared at the foot of the stairs.

"You can't run from this," he said, closing the distance between them.

Ren whirled to face him. Damien was right—he couldn't run. It was futile to run. Damien paused, his eyes darting behind Ren, but Ren didn't turn. He wouldn't dare take his eyes off Damien not even as the black doors slid open.

Damien's mouth curled into a wicked grin. *"Well, this day just keeps getting better and better."*

~

Napoleon, Lavelle, and the rebels of the tunnel team, eyes glowing, burst through the gate into the blindingly white hangar. Cries of shock filled the air over the flashing alarms as Napoleon sent a javelin of rock soaring high over the heads of the civilians at the first soldier stationed by the doors. One of the fire Elementals among the rebels sent his own spear of flames toward the second, and the javelin and spear found their marks against the soldiers' helmets, knocking them out cold. Screams of terror echoed through the hangar while the bodies slumped to the floor.

Napoleon's eyes immediately returned to their normal blue. The last thing he wanted to do was scare the people even more than they already were. He still couldn't believe the number of Araedians Vayne had shoved into the cramped space. The stench of unwashed bodies and excrement hit him again, stinging his eyes and nose profusely, and for a few moments, everyone simply stared at them through disheveled hair and frightened eyes. The alarms finally fell silent, though the lights continued to flash, then a voice filled the air—a familiar voice, heavy with emotion.

"Do not fear! The rebels have come," a young woman announced yards away at the back of the hangar near the large, armored doors. She lifted her chin high above the hundreds of heads surrounding her and stood as tall as her chains would allow, which was a mere crouch. Napoleon's breath caught in his throat at the sight of her dark brown hair and the defiance in her brown eyes. *Aurum.* Shock rooted him to the tile floor.

"They are here to save us!" Aurum's shout bounced off the stark-white walls. Napoleon could tell this was not her first time speaking to them collectively. Nearly every head had turned to watch her, and the trust in their eyes was unmistakable. She sucked away their fear, and their backs straightened while their chins lifted. "People of Araedia, do not be afraid. Our freedom and the time to fight is finally upon us!"

Aurum was alive, and they had found her... A shiver wracked Napoleon's body. Sobs and cheers of delight and determination erupted through the hangar, and people began to pull against their chains vigorously. The air seemed to spark with energy and electricity as the reality of their rescue dawned upon the civilians. He could feel his own adrenaline beginning to snake through his veins. They'd done it. They'd found the people Vayne had tried to take from them—found the numbers and spirit they needed to win this war.

"Aurum!" Lavelle exclaimed, rushing between the crowd of Araedians. She collapsed to her knees, enveloping Aurum in the biggest hug. Aurum rocked back, but the cuffs pulling against her wrists held her upright. Napoleon couldn't tell if she was laughing or sobbing as she squeezed Lavelle back.

"We'll start unlocking the chains," a young man—one of the rebels from the tunnel team known as Alec—said from behind.

Napoleon faced him and nodded before carefully making his way through the civilians. Hands reached up to him along with words of gratitude. He held as many hands as he could, promising them all that they'd be out soon. His heart was broken for the people—that they'd sat here, chained to the floor like animals for hours and hours. But the rebels would right this wrong. They would do it together with the Araedians from all the sectors by their side. If Vayne were smart, he'd be terrified of the storm brewing underneath his home—because he'd just given them another reason to unite.

Napoleon's heavy heart began to lighten with happiness at the sight of Aurum through the crowd. He feared it might beat out of his chest as he stopped before her and Lavelle. Aurum's dark eyes lifted to meet his, and he didn't care that they were welling with tears or that a few of those tears were falling down his face as he grinned at her.

"You'll have to unlock us from the control panel," Aurum said, nodding toward the gleaming buttons near the towering black doors. Her grip around Lavelle tightened as if she were the only thing anchoring Aurum to the ground—not the chains. "There are no keys."

Napoleon turned to the rebels spread throughout the hangar behind him, struggling with the cuffs. "Did you guys catch that?"

"We're on it." Alec nodded. He and two others quickly made their way to the panel, mumbling over the different switches and buttons.

"Did everyone survive the attack on the camp?" Aurum questioned, panic flashing across her face.

"Yes," Napoleon answered, glancing at the dark-haired man beside her. The man dipped his head in greeting. "You and Ren were the only ones unaccounted for."

"*He's alive.*" Aurum looked to Lavelle, who straightened.

Lavelle stumbled back into Napoleon's chest. "What?"

"Ren's here. He tried to rescue Vale and I, but we didn't make it past these damned hangars," she said. Cheers erupted from the Araedians as their chains fell to the floor with echoing *clicks*, and Aurum and the man—Vale—stood, rubbing their red wrists. The people around them stood as well, hugging and checking their loved ones. Napoleon didn't think it was possible for the hangar to become more cramped than it already was, but he was wrong. *Very* wrong. They needed to move—start getting the people out.

"Where is he now?" Lavelle asked, grabbing Aurum's shoulders. "Where's my brother?"

"We don't know," Vale said. "He was disguised as a guard, so—"

"The courtyard...," Napoleon mumbled. "Vayne's called all the guards to the courtyard."

Lavelle whirled to face him. "Napoleon, we have to get him out of there."

"We can't." He shook his head. "I don't even know where the courtyard is, and our mission is to get these people to safety."

"Not all of them want safety," Vale said, facing Aurum. "We've talked with them. The majority want to fight with us—with the rebels."

"But Ren—" Lavelle started.

Aurum gently took Lavelle's hands from her shoulders. "We can't get to Ren right now, Lavelle. It's too dangerous and there are two more hangars full of Araedians who need us. Would Ren abandon them if he were here?"

Napoleon felt his heart break again as tears slid down Lavelle's cheeks. "No," she whispered. "No, he wouldn't."

"Napoleon," Alec called from within the depths of the crowd. He appeared at Napoleon's side a moment later. "Everyone's unlocked. We await your orders."

"Well done," Napoleon said, not used to the authority ringing in his own voice.

Without warning, the crowd began to grow restless behind them, pushing and shoving toward the tunnel exit as shouts and calls of panic rang out. An older man knocked into Napoleon, causing him to stumble backward through a puddle of urine. He hissed a curse and lifted his head, desperately trying to force his way back to Lavelle and the others through the roiling crowd.

"*Stop!*" Aurum shouted, shooting a column of flames high into the air with glowing eyes. Everyone in the hangar froze, their heads lifting to watch the flames collide against the ceiling and dissipate into tendrils of smoke. "We can't all run to the exit, or we'll trample each other! Everyone, just stay calm and don't move. We'll start leading you out in a moment!"

Murmurs shot throughout the hangar, and several Araedians shifted about nervously but they stayed still. Napoleon sighed, nodding his thanks to Aurum. They had to get moving. The people wouldn't remain like this for long. He shoved his way back to the others and faced Alec.

"Begin leading them into the tunnels. *Calmly,*" Napoleon said, pointing at the gaping mouth of the dark gate. "Go back to the crossroads and take a left down the large tunnel with the red and blue wires. It will lead you out but be careful. We're in Vayne's domain. Act like there's a trap around every corner."

Vale snorted, smoothing back his disheveled hair. "There very well might be."

"Don't even speak that into existence." Aurum elbowed him with a glare.

"What about you?" Alec raised his brows. "Aren't you coming?"

"There's two more hangars left to clear." Napoleon glanced at the control panel by the doors. "Once we free everyone there, we'll be right behind you. Now go. We don't have any time to spare."

Alec nodded and disappeared into the restless crowd, shouting orders to the people and the rebels alike. Painfully slow, the Araedians of One and Two began to line up and follow him and the rebels into the dark abyss of the tunnels as calmly as they could. Napoleon frowned. It would take *minutes* to lead everyone through the small winding tunnel. He prayed to the Aether that they'd reach the large tunnel quickly—they'd move a lot faster in there.

"Where are the others?" Aurum asked.

"Natalia and Roman are leading the army through the sectors as we speak," Napoleon said. He began making his way to the panel and the looming black door. "From what I've heard, they've reached the gates of One, which means we need to hurry up and get the rest of the people out. Those who can't fight can find somewhere to hide while everyone else marches to the gates. We need all the numbers we can get."

Vale was at Napoleon's side in an instant. He jumped as Vale grabbed his arm. His dark blue eyes flashed with a whirlwind of different emotions—fear, hope... denial. "Did you just say Natalia?" he breathed, his words barely more than a rush of air. "Natalia Rhys?"

"That's one of our friends." Aurum joined them where they'd paused in front of the panel, Lavelle trailing behind her. Aurum clicked a large blue button, but nothing happened. She cursed colorfully.

"You know her?" Lavelle asked, studying Vale carefully.

Confusion flooded through Napoleon. How could he know Natalia? He ran his eyes over Vale and his dingy, mismatched clothes. If he were from Four, he might have known her before the testings, but there was no way to indicate what sector he was from.

Vale released Napoleon and clamped his lips together, clearly fighting hard to keep the tears in his eyes from spilling over. "She's my little sister."

"What?" Aurum and Lavelle exclaimed simultaneously, whirling to face Napoleon and Vale as the large black door slid open on silent hinges behind them. Two archways halfway down either side of the walls gaped, leading to the additional hangars they needed to get to.

Napoleon's mouth dropped. Natalia was Vale's sister... He was her brother. Napoleon shook his head. Natalia had never mentioned having an older brother, and from the looks on Aurum's and Lavelle's faces, she'd never mentioned it to them, either. He wondered if anyone knew at all.

"Well, this day just keeps getting better and better," a masculine voice echoed.

Napoleon and the others faced the open doorway and the two figures standing across from each other in the yards of the empty, white-tiled hangar that stretched before them. Napoleon squinted at the two figures—both clearly male and very familiar. The closest figure, sweaty blond hair clinging to his head, had his back turned and stood between the first figure and the door to the hangar as if he were protecting them. Napoleon's gaze traveled to the second figure—the brown hair and glowing red-orange and silver eyes. Lavelle gasped beside him, and Aurum straightened. Vale simply stood there, never breaking the deadly stare he threw at the second figure.

"Damien...," Aurum whispered.

"It turns out we'll get our family reunion after all, Ren," Damien mused.

Shock rooted Napoleon to the spot as Ren glanced over his shoulder with golden irises glowing so bright, Napoleon had to squint. Ren's pupils glowed the purest silver he'd ever seen. What had happened to him? How had he gotten here? *How was he alive?*

"Go!" Ren yelled, facing Damien once more. "I'll hold him off!"

"Ren—" Lavelle began, but her twin cut her off.

"Go, Lavelle! *Now!*"

"No!" she exclaimed, emotion thick in her voice. Napoleon glanced at her to find tears in her eyes and her fists clenched and shaking.

Aurum shook her head. "I can't believe it... I thought they were lying, but it's true. It's all true."

"What's true?" Lavelle exclaimed, never breaking her gaze away from Ren.

"Didn't you know, Lavelle?" Damien called across the hangar with a sickening smile. The sound of Lavelle's name rolling off Damien's tongue had Napoleon seething with rage. The mere look he was giving her made him want to tear Vayne's mansion apart. Brick by brick. "Your little brother has a big secret he's been keeping. Should you tell them, Ren, or should I?"

"Enough!" Ren lunged and thrust his arms forward. A roaring wave of flames shot from his hands. A shield of flames appeared before Damien as he knit his hands together, splitting the whipping flames around him. They collided with the tiles, bouncing and ricocheting like deadly flaming ribbons. The shield and wave then dissipated high into the air, causing a stifling heat to spread. Shrieks of terror filled the hangar behind Napoleon and the others as the people began to shove and push again, desperately trying to claw their way into the tunnels.

"Fine." Damien shrugged. "I'll tell them."

Napoleon's pulse was racing. Lavelle didn't even seem to be breathing beside him, and a loaded quiet fell over them—a gun of electricity about to fire. Ren had just... He'd just wielded *fire*. But he was an *earth* Elemental—with *black* pupils, not silver! It was impossible. It couldn't be true. There couldn't be *two* Aethers... Natalia had wielded fire and water... But her eyes weren't gold, and the silver in her eyes didn't shine nearly as brightly as Ren's. So if she wasn't the Aether, what was she? Was Ren...

The air around them crackled with energy, and Damien's glowing eyes gleamed with a thrilling power. The corners of his mouth curled higher. He was enjoying this—the truth hanging over all their heads. Damien scanned each of their faces before his gaze returned to Ren, and he uttered the words that rang through the hangars with a weight heavier than the entirety of Araedia.

"Ren is the Aether."

~

Lavelle clenched her fists so hard they shook, and a heavy silence smothered the hangar before them as Damien's words rang through the air. Ren—her twin—was the Aether. He could wield all four elements... He was the ultimate Elemental. She tried to sort through the web of emotions clouding her thoughts—fear, anger, shock, relief. Ren was the Aether, but he was alive. That was all that mattered.

Now what mattered was clearing the additional hangars—one to the left and the other to the right—and getting everyone out, themselves included. They had to free the Araedians and meet Natalia, Roman, and the others at the gate. Behind them, people were dashing into the tunnels, nearly trampling over each other. They needed more time... But Damien was here. Regardless of whether Ren was the Aether or not, he couldn't face him alone. She wouldn't let him. Lavelle's gaze slid over Damien. His smile was horrid, and the gleam of his eyes turned her stomach. He thought he'd surprised them—gained power and an advantage over them. Oh, how wrong he was...

Lavelle unfurled her fists, taking a step forward as her eyes began to glow dark gray around black pupils. "You're not the only one with a surprise, Damien."

She leaped forward and swung, sending fists of air flying toward him. Damien rolled, dodging them easily, but by the time he rose, she was at Ren's side. The glare he shot at her was that of a feral animal. Lavelle ignored him and looked at her twin, who smiled at her. She knew that smile—the same as the one on her own lips. Home. They were both finally home.

Ren turned back to Napoleon, Vale, and Aurum. "Go free the others. We'll hold him off."

Napoleon opened his mouth to argue, but Lavelle cut him off with a curt nod as if to say *I trust you. Now trust me.* He nodded in return before sprinting to the left hangar. Lavelle met Aurum's glowing eyes as she took a hesitant step toward the hangar to the right.

"We'll be right back," she said before following Vale down the hall.

The twins faced Damien once more. A wicked, curved blade of air appeared in Lavelle's hands as the tiles beneath Ren began to split apart with ear-piercing *clinks*. Chunks of earth broke through the floor, floating up to meet in his hands and form two earthen swords. Damien rolled his shoulders before forming his own swords of flame, and together, the twins charged.

Damien was quick—too quick. He feigned to his left as if to strike Ren, but dropped his right shoulder, slashing his two swords at Lavelle. She stumbled backward, narrowly avoiding the deadly tips and falling to the floor. Her eyes widened at the burning ends of her hair and the burning stench that filled her nose. She pawed at the strands furiously until nothing but singed edges remained. Her hair, instead of falling at her upper back, now fell at her shoulders. He'd burned off *inches*. Lavelle watched as Damien's and Ren's swords arced through the air and slammed into each other to form an "X" of sputtering flames and flakes of rock.

With a grunt, Ren knocked their swords apart and threw his shoulder into Damien's chest, separating them. Ren was at Lavelle's side in an instant, grabbing her arm and pulling her to her feet. The twins turned to find Damien charging them. They leaped apart as he swung his swords between them. One of Damien's swords collided against Lavelle's curved blade above her head, the other catching Ren's near his abdomen. The impact sent reverberations shooting through her arms. Tightening her grip on the handle of swirling air currents, Lavelle rotated the blade down toward the tiles and yanked. Damien's sword hurtled through the hangar and dissipated before it could strike the floor. Damien pushed harder against Ren's blades before sending a kick to his stomach and extending his free hand at Lavelle, blasting a maelstrom of flames at her. She dropped her blade and brought her arms up. A shield of air appeared before her, barely swallowing the flames in time. Lavelle shoved the whirlwind of air and flames back at Damien, who sent them careening into the hangar wall with a wave of fire.

He didn't have time to turn and block the small, sharp rocks Ren flung at his back. The rocks embedded into Damien's armor, and he released a cry, tumbling to his knees. Lavelle met her brother's gaze as she ran to stand beside him. Ren released another wave of sharp rocks. Damien stood, battering them away with his newly formed sword. Behind the twins, Araedians dressed in white, beige, and cream began to flood into the main hangar from the branching archways. Lavelle couldn't stop the sigh of relief that slipped through her lips. Napoleon and the others had unlocked the additional hangers.

Her relief was short-lived. Screams of panic echoed through the room behind them as the civilians witnessed Damien and Ren exchanging round after round of rocks and flame. They began to shove and push, herding each other into a big cluster before the gaping doorway. It would take *several minutes* to get everyone into the tunnels if they were calm, but at the rate they were beginning to panic, they'd never make it through. More and more people began piling into the room—hundreds of them—and they were pushing Ren toward Damien, causing the space between Ren and Damien and themselves to grow smaller and smaller.

Lavelle pointed at the tunnel entrance behind them. "The tunnels! Hurry! Go into the tunnels!"

"Lavelle!" Ren exclaimed.

She whirled to watch Damien, who'd spread a shield of fire before himself, send a massive column of flames flying—but not at her and Ren. The flames soared over their heads, arcing at the civilians. Cries of fear erupted all around as Lavelle sprinted back at the people. She raised her arms high and strained with every ounce of energy she had. Wind shot forth from her palms, creating a swirling dome of currents over the people. The flames came slamming down with such force, the impact knocked Lavelle to her knees, but the dome held.

Vale suddenly appeared behind them in the archway to the right. His eyes danced between Damien, Ren, and Lavelle before focusing on the Araedians. He waved his arms in the air as he made his way through the crowd toward the open doorway. "Follow me!" he shouted, hurrying in the direction of the tunnel entrance. "Into the tunnels!"

As one, the people turned and followed, seeming to finally grasp that those tunnels were their only way out. Regardless of how scared they were, it was the only option they had. Aurum and Napoleon appeared through the archways moments later, herding the last of the civilians toward Vale and the others and lifting up those who had fallen. Lavelle cursed. There were at least a thousand of them. Her brows narrowed at the women and children that made up the majority. Where were all the men? Aurum and Vale's hangar had included everyone... What had Vayne done to those in the other two hangars? Aurum and Napoleon were at Lavelle's side in an instant, pulling her to her feet. Behind them, Damien had finally halted his bombardment and was exchanging blow after blow with Ren, and their newly formed swords clashing against each other. She let her arms and the dome drop.

"They're all women and children..." Lavelle muttered. "The hangar you and Vale were in wasn't like that."

Aurum nodded. "All of the men from the additional hangars were taken hours ago. I think Vayne's integrated them into his army."

"What?" Lavelle couldn't stop the tremors that began to wrack her hands. Not only was she scared, but her body was tiring. The dome had taken nearly all the energy she'd had left.

"He can't brainwash that many people at once," Napoleon said, shaking his head. "Why would they fight for him?"

"He has their families and probably threatened to kill them if they didn't join him. What other choice did they have?" Aurum glanced at the tunnels. "But if they knew they were safe, I bet they'd switch sides again and fight with us."

"All we'd have to do is let those who want to fight do exactly that. If they stood with us on the battlefield, it'd show the men that they got out," Napoleon added.

They were right. The soldiers would see the clothes of their sectors and know they'd been freed, and if Vayne's own soldiers turned against him, he'd stand no chance. The numbers would finally be on the rebels' side. They'd have all of Three and Four and the majority of One and Two. Vayne would never win against that.

Suddenly, a cry of pain filled the air. Lavelle, Aurum, and Napoleon turned and watched Ren stumble backward, clutching at his arm. The Araedians only needed a few more minutes, and Damien would be severely outnumbered. Lavelle's heart began to race. They could end him right here and right now if they wanted to... Ren slashed his sword at Damien before blasting a column of air that knocked him to the floor, sending him sliding along the tiles. Her twin retreated back to their side as Damien collided against the wall beside the stairs with a *thump*.

Regardless of the distance now separating them, Lavelle could easily see the heavy rising and falling of Damien's chest. He wouldn't last long against all of them. He knew it, too. Panic flooded through her veins at the gleam in Damien's eyes. She'd seen that gleam before when she and Ren had gone with Aurum and first met him and Natalia out in the woods. It was the gleam of a cornered, wild animal preparing for its last stand—utterly dangerous and unpredictable. And in that moment, the terrifying truth slammed into her. If Damien was going down, he would do everything in his power to make sure they went down with him. She couldn't let him do that. She had to keep him distracted long enough for the civilians to get out, then she could worry about herself and the others. But was she capable of killing him—the boy she'd once considered her other brother? Was there any last chance at all that the old Damien was still in there?

"Why, Damien?" Lavelle's voice echoed. "Why are you doing this? Is all this hate actually in your heart, or are you just that far gone? What did Vayne do to you?"

"You're a smart girl, Lavelle," he spat, rising from the tiles. "You read the people around you as fast as you and Talia used to read those stolen books. You already know the answers to your questions, and *I* know that you're *stalling*."

She shrugged, her lips a hard line. "I figured I'd save you the embarrassment of getting your ass kicked again."

"Well," Damien chuckled. "Look who finally decided to show their fire. Did you get tired of others making decisions for you?" He shook his head, grinning wickedly. "I remember all of you thought Aurum and I had the biggest tempers, but I always knew it was really you—especially if your beloved twin was involved. I wonder how angry you'll be when I kill him and your friends, or will you just fall apart instead?"

"Enough!" Napoleon snapped, and his eyes began to glow light green and a black darker than night itself. He took a step in front of Lavelle, with Ren following suit on her opposite side.

Aurum's eyes began to glow red and silver beside her. Lavelle watched Aurum throw one last glance over her shoulder at the tunnels behind them. Vale and the last of the civilians had finally vanished into the darkness beyond. The stalling was over.

"It's the end of the line for you, Damien," Aurum said, facing him once more.

Damien's grin grew. "It might look that way to you, but who's to say I wasn't doing some stalling of my own?" Absolute silence. Lavelle wondered if the others could hear her thundering heart—if any of them were even breathing. "Did you know that we rigged explosions through the tunnels days ago? That the right push of a button on that panel..." He nodded and pointed with his flaming sword to the one beside the grand black doors behind them. "...detonates the bombs, snuffing out every life in those tunnels within ninety seconds."

Lavelle clenched her fists to keep them from shaking. That sentence alone had decided Damien's fate. They'd have to kill him to keep him from detonating those explosives, but fighting in the same room as the panel was risky. All it would take was one stray shot, a deflection—anything—to hit one of those buttons, and it'd be over. Lavelle wished with every ounce of her being that she'd been able to train with her element before this. She didn't know how far luck and determination would take her in this battle, but she prayed to the Aether—to Ren?—that it would be enough, because Damien was going to turn this into a dogfight.

And he did.

Damien lunged forward, pushing off the wall and sending a massive wave of head-high flames curling at them with the swipe of an arm. Lavelle's eyes widened. He was so *powerful*—not as powerful as Ren, but Ren also wasn't used to his new elements... Had Damien merely been toying with them earlier? Aurum and Ren leaped toward the wave, extending their arms in unison. Their own wave of fire roared up and combined before hurtling to meet Damien's. Flame met flame in a blindingly bright whirlwind. The flames blasted off each other, ricocheting onto the walls and floor, but they didn't stop Damien from charging through with spears of fire in hand. In the blink of an eye, he had both spears flying at Lavelle and Napoleon before sending two more at Aurum and Ren. Lavelle's eyes began to glow dark gray and black again as she attempted to form a shield of air before her. She was too slow—her energy already spent. Without warning, Napoleon tackled her, sending them sprawling across the floor. They could only watch as the spears aimed at them flew by and molded into long fingers of flame headed straight for the panel.

A scream of pain shattered through the hangar as the fire collided against a small white button and red numbers appeared above the doorway. One minute and thirty seconds... One minute and twenty-nine seconds. Twenty-eight. Twenty-seven.

"Run!" Ren exclaimed, pulling Aurum up from the floor and tearing toward the tunnels. Lavelle winced at the sight of the long burn down Aurum's right arm as they passed. Napoleon rose and helped Lavelle to her feet, taking off after Ren and Aurum. At the opposite end of the hangar, Damien sprinted to the foot of the stairs and paused. He turned and smirked at them before disappearing up the steps.

Napoleon grabbed Lavelle's hand. "Lavelle, we have to go. *Now!*"

One minute and sixteen seconds. Fifteen. Fourteen.

Ren and Aurum disappeared into the gaping darkness of the tunnel, with Napoleon and Lavelle following several steps behind. Ren and Aurum's collective shouts echoed against the walls: run, run, run. Far ahead, the quickening reverberations of footfalls filed down the tunnel—the last of the Araedians fleeing the tunnel system... Lavelle's eyes began to glow as a vicious wind shot forth from her hand, flying down the sides of the walls to urge them on faster.

One minute and nine seconds.

They cut left down the large earthen tunnel with red and blue wires lining the walls. The explosives. How hadn't she noticed them before? Her heart raced faster than she thought was possible, and sweat covered every inch of her, plastering her hair to her neck. The tunnel was so dark, she could barely make out Aurum and Ren's shadows a few yards ahead.

Fifty seconds.

She pumped her arms faster—pushed her legs harder against the earth. Napoleon panted frantically beside her.

Forty seconds.

Aurum and Ren disappeared around a corner ahead.

Thirty seconds. Twenty-nine. Twenty-eight.

Napoleon and Lavelle rounded the corner. Several yards down the straight tunnel, a dark blue light greeted them. The night sky.

Twenty seconds.

The heads of shadows holding flames with glowing orange and red eyes appeared in the gaping mouth of the tunnel's exit as the last of the Araedians jumped out.

Ten seconds.

The shadows cleared out of the way as Aurum and Ren burst through the tunnel, dropping down onto the grass below.

Five seconds.

Napoleon's hand tightened around Lavelle's. Only a few more yards.

Four.

Three.

Lavelle's lungs burned. They weren't going to make it. Tears flooded her eyes, blurring her vision.

Two.

One.

The ground began to shake and rumble as the explosives were set off inside the hangars, following the snaking blue and red wires down the tunnel. Napoleon and Lavelle barely kept their footing as they stumbled toward the night. She turned her head to watch vicious flames lick after them, followed by the collapsing earthen ceiling.

She faced the night sky, catching a glimpse of the few stars that managed to peek through the dark clouds above. Only a few more feet. By the Aether—

They weren't going to make it...

Napoleon squeezed her hand one last time—as if to say goodbye—and in her final moments, Lavelle wished that she'd had the courage to tell him how much she adored him.

But then Napoleon lunged, flinging them at the gaping hole. Together, they fell through the air, passing out of the shadows and heat of the tunnel and into the cool, rainy night. They collided against the hard ground and tall grass as the fire and tunnel ceiling collapsed and engulfed their previous footing. Flames burst forth from the tunnel, singeing and distorting the air above. Napoleon grabbed Lavelle by the waist and scrambled back from the falling debris that chased after them. Ren's and Aurum's arms met them a moment later, pulling them farther away. A sob escaped Aurum's lips as she and Ren enveloped Napoleon and Lavelle.

A few yards behind them, Vale stood amongst the surrounding trees with the rebels and the mass of civilians. There were at least fifteen hundred of them. In the distance, the concrete walls that surrounded Vayne's mansion loomed above the forest canopy. Aurum and Ren finally released them, taking a few steps back. All four of them were panting. Aurum's panting turned to a soft, near-hysterical laughter, and she hugged Ren. Lavelle looked at the tunnel and the fire that burned through the cracks in the debris.

Napoleon's hand gently grabbed her chin, turning her head to meet his gaze. His shining blue eyes bore into hers, and she smiled faintly. It was like looking into the starry sky above. Then both of his hands slid to cup her cheeks as he brought his lips down to hers and kissed her. The kiss was eager—passionate—yet gentle, and his lips were soft and warm. Lavelle wrapped her arms around his neck, and he pulled her in tighter.

Ren cleared his throat.

Napoleon and Lavelle parted instantly, both blushing vigorously. She bit her bottom lip, glancing between her brother and Napoleon, who rubbed the back of his neck with a nervous smile. The glare Ren was giving him was absolutely terrifying. Aurum elbowed Ren in the gut, causing him to double over, and Vale chuckled behind them.

"Enough, little twin," she said. "You can be an overprotective brother later." Aurum winked at the two of them before turning to Vale and the rebels. "We've still got work to do."

CHAPTER THIRTY-TWO

FINALE

Natalia tapped her leg furiously against the metal floor of the armored truck as it rumbled toward the gates of Sector One. Feura had been right about Vayne abandoning more trucks in Two. He'd left enough so that the rebels aboard the truck that had stayed behind would each drive a truck back to meet the army on the road. From there, it wouldn't take the rebels long to join the other fourteen trucks that continued down the long winding road through Two.

She tugged at the tight, claustrophobic belts strapping her to her seat. A shiver ran down her spine as the belt merely tightened. There were no windows in the truck—though if there had been, they wouldn't have been visible through the twenty people crammed together shoulder-to-shoulder. A row of filled seats lined three of the four walls, and the only source of light inside were the faint strips underneath the chairs that illuminated the walkway.

All these trucks reminded her of was the night of the testings—the night she'd lost Damien... But also the night she'd found Roman. She turned to her left, where he sat beside her. It was the other way around, really. He was the one who had found her—saved her in ways she hadn't thought possible. When the world had seemed so dark and hopeless and absolutely drained of color, he'd been the one to throw back the curtains and let the light in. And instead of bringing back the colors that had faded away, he'd created an entirely new and different palette of the brightest shades she'd ever seen. She'd never stop loving him for that.

Fraiser sat on his other side, wiping at the sweat beading down her face with a scowl. The truck was unbearably hot and muggy. Hero and Spenser sat along the opposite wall, their murmuring voices filling the air through the throng of Elementals standing between them. The few non-Elemental rebels who had volunteered to join the front lines at the gates sat at the back of the truck. Overall, there were around 280 Elementals and rebels spread throughout the fourteen trucks.

Natalia's hands began to shake as they drew closer and closer to the gates of One. She hated to admit it, but she was afraid—not for herself, but for those around her. And Napoleon and Lavelle down in the tunnels... She prayed to the Aether they were all right—Ren and Aurum, too. She couldn't bear to imagine a future without them, and she knew she'd fight until her dying breath to protect and preserve a future where they were all safe and alive. The battle that lay ahead loomed over her like the smothering, pitch-black storm clouds outside, and she felt as if each step toward One was another step closer to falling off the edge of a depthless abyss. But all she could do was hope that they'd all survive when they fell.

Roman slid a hand across their seats, resting it on her bouncing knee as the truck began to slow. Natalia met his gaze, and he offered her a small smile.

The truck finally stopped, and the back doors flung open. The standing rebels and Elementals quickly exited the vehicle, some armed with stolen guns, spears, and mismatched armor. Everyone seated quickly clicked free of their straps and poured out onto the grass that whipped furiously in the wind and rain. Thunder rolled loud above them, and the slight drizzle had once again turned and begun its violent assault on the earth. Lightning veins scattered and flashed across the sky with loud *cracks*. Natalia and Roman both shielded their eyes from the rain as they hurried around the truck with Fraiser, Hero, and Spenser only a few steps behind. They paused several feet past the hood, and Natalia's breath caught in her throat. Fifty yards ahead, the thick metal gates of Sector One stood before them, hundreds of figures in black armor waiting at the top.

She glanced behind them. The fourteen armored trucks were lined up in the grass, and the rebels and Elementals stood in a row, readying themselves for battle. She faced the wall and soldiers atop it once more, running through every and any kind of strategy she could think of. Anything that could help them break through with the lowest number of casualties. Beside her, Roman, Fraiser, Hero, and Spenser seemed to be doing the same, all their faces serious and contemplative. They were outnumbered, but that was no surprise. It had been expected.

"We're going to split into two teams," Roman said, shattering the heavy silence that had fallen over them. "Twelve Elementals can head for the gates while everyone else provides cover fire. The twelve will go in and out as quickly as possible. They'll hit the gates with all they have and hightail it back to the trucks, where we'll regroup once they're down. The majority of the army should hopefully be here by then, and we can all storm One together."

"And we'll have preserved our numbers opening the gates so that we can hit Vayne's army with full force," Hero said, staring at the gates with disdain.

Fraiser stepped forward, gaze flicking between Natalia and Roman. "The twelve need to be strictly silver-eyed Elementals. The more power, the better."

"Agreed," Natalia stated.

"I'll ask around and see how many I can scrounge up," Hero said before starting toward the trucks and the crowd of Elementals.

Roman turned to Spenser. "Will you lead the cover fire team with Hero?"

"Yes." He nodded. "Just don't get yourselves killed down there."

"It takes a lot more than some gates and a couple of soldiers to kill me." Fraiser smirked wickedly.

"At this point, love," Spenser drawled. "I don't think anything can kill you."

Fraiser's smirk turned into a feral grin. "Damn right."

Natalia rolled her eyes before glancing over her shoulder to find Hero with nine Elementals in tow. There were four women and five men dressed in the mismatched clothes and stolen armor of the rebels. The youngest of them couldn't have been much older than Natalia herself, and the oldest wasn't a day over forty.

"I've explained the basics of the plan," Hero said. "This lot's ready and willing to fight. In fact, everyone's ready. We await your orders, Roman."

Roman wiped his wet hair from his forehead. "You and Spenser are leading the cover fire team. Go ahead and line everyone up to march... We're about to begin."

~

Ten minutes later, Natalia stood at the crest of a small hill overlooking the thirty yards remaining between her and the gates of Sector One. The trucks still sat parked yards behind them, and below her, Hero and Spenser began to march the 268 rebels and Elementals toward the walls. Once the remainder of the army arrived, their numbers would amass to over three thousand—against Vayne's five thousand...

They were a multitude of glowing eyes of all shades of gray, green, red, and orange. The few humans within the crowd cocked their guns of electricity, their spears crackling to life. The soldiers atop the wall ran about, readying their own guns. Natalia was very grateful that not one of those dreaded cannons from Four was in sight... But would they be inside the sector? She shuddered at the thought. Just four of those cannons had nearly shattered through their ranks. If Vayne had more inside... The Aether help them.

Suddenly, Fraiser appeared at her side, a hunger for destruction burning in her glowing gray and silver eyes. "I can't wait to watch these gates fall."

"It will certainly be a sight to see," Natalia murmured. "I'm a little worried about what's waiting for us on the other side, though. Those cannons in Four—"

"We dealt with them then, and we'll deal with them if and when they come next." Fraiser flashed her a quick, genuine smile. Natalia swore that the battle had already begun, and she was dead. She'd never seen Fraiser *actually* smile—or offer kind reassurance.

Hero, Spenser, and the rebels broke out into a run before them, quickly closing the distance between them and the soldiers on the walls. A maelstrom of elements and electricity exploded from the Elementals, and shields of swirling air, earth, and fire appeared above their heads, barring the answering shots from Vayne's soldiers.

"It's time," Fraiser said. "Are you ready?"

Natalia nodded, and Roman, dark blue and silver eyes glowing, stepped away from the nine other Elementals he'd been briefing on the fine details of their plan. Get in, knock the gates down, get out... and don't die. He glanced at Fraiser—his sister in everything but blood—and Natalia could see the lifetime of memories with her flashing through his eyes. He smiled softly, and his eyes met Natalia's own, studying her entirely as if it were the last time he'd ever see her. The pure love that filled his eyes made her want to cry out of joy, but before she could say anything, Roman turned and uttered one word: *Now*!

The twelve silver-eyed Elementals launched into a sprint down the small hill, heading straight toward the chaos of battle before them. Elements shot high in the night air as they collided with bolts of electricity and soldiers, knocking some of them off the other side of the wall. Already a few rebels' bodies lay at the feet of the cover fire team before the gates, Vayne's soldiers having found the gaps between their shields. The all too familiar stab of anger and pain filled Natalia's chest at the sight of her people's deaths. She'd make Vayne pay for every single one of them. Starting with ripping down his damned gates.

A line of electric purple split Natalia's red-orange and ice-blue irises as her eyes began to glow. They reached the rebels within seconds, slipping through them as quickly as they could. Natalia's foot caught against the outstretched arm of a downed rebel, causing her to stumble forward. She regained her footing only to watch a bolt of electricity collide with the young man in front of her, sending him flying. He was thrown to the mud with a vicious *thump*, the shadows of the swirling shields of fire above casting odd shadows on his writhing body. Nausea pooled in her stomach, but she leaped over him and continued on.

A few yards of unmarred grass stretched before her and the gate, and the rebels began to move forward, extending their shields as far as they could over her and the other eleven silver-eyed Elementals breaking through the ranks. Natalia extended her arms behind her as she sprinted at the gates, one gathering a large column of rainwater as she ran, and the other summoning a large column of flames. Roman did the same a few feet to her left, and Fraiser and the other nine followed a few steps behind with their own elements. They were a formidable force of amassing power. Without warning, something crackled above Natalia, and she glanced up to watch a spear of electricity hurtle toward her only to be met with a large chunk of earth. She glanced back at the nearest earth Elemental—a younger woman with glowing dark green eyes that were already focused on her. Natalia was about to dip her head in thanks when a spear of flames cut through the air, quicker than she'd ever seen before, and struck the woman in the chest, staking her to the muddy ground.

Blindingly hot anger flooded through her as she lifted her eyes to the walls above to find two sets of glowing green and red irises around silver pupils. The young boy's and girl's stark-white armor and blood-red bands around their right biceps gleamed in the rain against the dark night sky... The last two surviving members of Vayne's personal guard—other than Damien and Zyra—had graced the rebels with their presence. Natalia cursed, launching herself into the air and firing her columns of water and flames at the gates. The water froze into hardened ice before it slammed into the thick metal with a groan. A tumult of elements followed suit, crashing into the gates so hard the wall trembled. But when all the dust and smoke disappeared, all that was there to greet them was a mere dent.

"Keep firing!" Roman shouted, sending a spear of ice up at the two Elementals. "Don't let up!"

Natalia grunted as she threw punch after punch of fire and ice at the gates. Fraiser, who had shifted up beside her, did the same, sending battering ram after battering ram of vicious winds at the dreaded metal.

"Look out!" Natalia exclaimed, lunging for Fraiser. The two collided, falling and rolling through the mud just as a spear of rock embedded itself into the ground where Fraiser had stood a moment before. They immediately shot to their feet, both scowling at Vayne's lapdogs atop the wall. Natalia scowled. She remembered seeing them when Vayne had attacked the rebel camp.

"We need to take them out *now*," Fraiser growled. "Or we'll never get this damned gate down."

Suddenly, two javelins of ice cut through the air, each hurtling toward the young boy and girl. The boy leaped aside, dodging the javelin with ease. The girl—having been focused on Fraiser and Natalia—jumped a second too late, the ice striking her side and sending her tumbling back over the other side of the wall. Natalia winced and watched Roman, eyes glowing furiously, send another series of spears and javelins at the boy. He dodged all of them and sent his own flames hurtling down. They collided against the shield of ice Roman had spread before himself.

Natalia looked at the dent in the gates, then at Fraiser. "At this rate, it'll take us hours to get through that metal—if we can get through it at all. We have to try something else."

"I have an idea," Fraiser said, glancing behind them at the hill where they'd parked the trucks. She chewed her bottom lip. "A brilliantly *stupid* idea, but..."

Natalia nodded. "Let's do it."

Fraiser flashed her a grin before tearing back across the battlefield through the throng of rebels with Natalia close behind. They quickly broke out through the backside of the rebels' ranks and sprinted across the trampled yards of grass that stood between them and the beginning of the slope that led up the hill. Natalia dropped and slid across the wet mud, narrowly dodging a stray bolt of electricity that flew over her head. She popped up and continued on. Her calves began to burn as she and Fraiser hit the hill. Fraiser's idea had to have something to do with the trucks. Why else would they make the trek back during all the fighting? Natalia didn't care how "brilliantly stupid" her idea was. She just hoped it would work.

They paused at the top of the hill, the sounds of their heavy panting filling the air. Natalia turned to the battle below. Bodies were beginning to pile up, and the dent in the gates hadn't budged. She spotted Roman still firing at the last of his father's personal guard while the cover fire team continued to shield everyone as best as they could. The rumbling of an engine awakening filled the air, and she whirled to find Fraiser in the driver's seat of one of the armored trucks. She poked her head out of the rolled-down window.

"Well, are you just going to stand there?" she asked incredulously. "Get in!"

Natalia's brows rose in surprise, but she quickly ran over to the passenger door and flung it open before climbing inside. She reached across her shoulder for the belt to strap herself into the seat, but Fraiser scoffed.

"What?" Natalia scowled as Fraiser floored the truck, nearly knocking her out of her seat.

Fraiser shook her head. "You won't need it."

Natalia opened her mouth to respond, but a flicker of movement had her turning her head toward one of the small mirrors extending from each side of the truck. She was squinting at the shadows disappearing rapidly behind them when headlights suddenly set the reflection in the mirror ablaze. She gasped, twisting around to look out the window through the hair blowing across her face. A shiver wracked down her spine at the sight of armored trucks pulling up beside the ones already parked on the hill. The rebel army was beginning to arrive. They had to take care of the gates. *Now.* They couldn't afford to bunch up their entire army at the foot of the wall to wait to be fired upon.

She whirled back around to face Fraiser and the path before them. They'd already cleared the slope and were heading straight for the mass of the cover fire team and the silver-eyed Elementals bombarding the gates right in front of them.

"Do you trust me?" Fraiser shouted over the wind as she increased the speed of the truck.

"It's a little late to be asking that now!"

Natalia watched as Fraiser chuckled and then slammed the butt of her palm against the middle of the steering wheel, causing the deep horn of the truck to blare. The rebels in front of them whirled to find the truck once again increasing its speed—straight at them. Cries of panic met Natalia's ears over the roaring wind, and the cover team scattered. Moments later, Roman and the other silver-eyed Elementals did the same, leaping out of the truck's path.

"Get ready to jump!" Fraiser exclaimed, her left hand feeling along the driver's door for the handle while she steered with her right.

Natalia cursed at the sight of the nearing gates. They'd collide with it in mere seconds. Fraiser's idea wasn't just stupid. It was suicide. Natalia quickly found the small handle on her door, and she opened it, flinging herself out into the freezing rain. She collided against the mud with a hard *smack*, barely lifting her head in time to watch the armored truck ram into the gates. The truck exploded, shaking the earth around them. Vayne's soldiers atop the wall fell to their knees—some even wobbling off the wall completely and falling to their deaths with sickening *crunches*. Natalia ducked her head down and covered it with her hands, shrieking as debris and shards of sharp metal embedded into the mud around her and her left arm.

Smoke billowed high into the night sky, and the flames, nearly as tall as the wall of One itself, burned high.

Suddenly, a battering ram of winds shot forth and collided against the debris, clearing the earth of flames and smoke long enough for Natalia to release an uneven breath at the sight before her. The truck's explosion had ripped the dent in the gate *wide open*. The ground beneath the fiery rubble of the car began to shift as an earth Elemental slid the car to the side. A clear path into Sector One loomed before her and the rebels. Natalia glanced a few yards to her left to find Fraiser grinning wickedly as her glowing gray and silver eyes returned to their normal green. She then turned to the rebels and the small hill behind them, Natalia following her line of sight as she pushed herself to her feet. Atop the small hill, dozens and dozens of headlights had appeared, and more continued to zoom into view while the rebel army gathered fifty yards before the broken gates of One.

~

Roman panted as he and the remains of the cover fire team jogged up the small hill to the awaiting trucks, the rest of the silver-eyed Elementals waiting for them at the top. They had lost around thirty rebels and Elementals during their assault on the gates, but the entirety of their army was pulling in on four wheels. The rebels had made it, and now all that lay between him and his father was another wall—the inner wall that surrounded the mansion. The remaining soldiers from his father's army had retreated from the wall's edge and would most likely await him and the rebels once they marched through. A shiver wracked down his spine at the sight of their growing numbers and the gaping hole in the gates. Rebels, Araedians, and Elementals began exiting the armored trucks, calling back and forth and readying themselves. Feura was at the front of them, leading all three thousand to the edge of the hill. Roman glanced at the two figures beginning to scale it behind him. He shook his head. They'd nearly stopped his heart with that stunt.

Fraiser and Natalia were *insane*. Brilliant, but absolutely insane.

The girls trudged up the last few feet of the hill with frenzied expressions as if the adrenaline of their actions hadn't quite worn off yet. By the hungry gleam in Fraiser's eyes, Roman doubted hers would. In fact, he'd probably never hear the end of their little escapade. Natalia and Fraiser paused beside him, glancing between him, Feura, and the mass of their army.

"If you two ever do anything like that again...," Roman began.

Fraiser lifted a hand, rolling her eyes. "Please, spare me." She crossed her arms. "You should be thanking us, Ro. We just brought your father's gates down."

He frowned and met Natalia's gaze. She simply shrugged and mouthed *Sorry*. He sighed, wiping at the small trickle of blood running from a minute cut on her chin before turning to find Feura approaching them with a gun of electricity in hand.

"We're ready," she said. "All we need now is you."

Roman nodded, his eyes wandering across the expanse of people before him. Every single one of them was prepared to die fighting for their freedom. Many of them would. They were outnumbered and would likely lose if Napoleon didn't show soon. But they had no other choice. It was time to face their fates.

A breeze shifted through the night air, gently caressing Roman's cheek and blowing the hair from his forehead, and he suddenly felt as if his mother were beside him. Of course, when he looked, she wasn't there, but he knew she was still watching over him—letting him know she was proud, and that she would always be there with him, even in death. Tears welled in Roman's eyes as he took a step forward and cleared his throat.

"Tonight," he announced, his voice carrying over the silence that had befallen the hill, "the rebels and the sectors of Araedia unite as one. *We* unite as one to stop the evil that has polluted our minds, families, friends, and land for decades. History has already been made here, but we are far from done. This is our right. Our duty... Everything that's happened, all the loss we've experienced, has led us to this moment—to this battle." The hairs on Roman's arms stood as eyes within the crowd began to glow. He could feel the tension boiling in the air. "This is what we're meant to do, and by the Aether, we will prevail for ourselves, those around us, those who came before us... And for those who will come after us. Rebels and citizens of a new Araedia, our time is now!" Shouts and war cries filled the air as people shifted restlessly on their feet. "We will storm Sector One! We will defeat everything Vayne throws at us! And we will create a new Araedia!"

The cheering and shouting grew louder, echoing off the walls of One before them. More eyes began to glow, and weapons were cocked and readied; it was a cascade of glowing colors. Beside him, Natalia and Fraiser released their own vicious cries, throwing their fists high in the air.

"Rebels!" Roman shouted, adrenaline pumping through his veins and pounding in his ears. *"Attack!"*

Roman, Natalia, and Fraiser all whirled, eyes glowing as they sprinted down the hill at the hole in the gates. Feura and the entirety of the rebels followed closely behind. They quickly crossed the yards of singed and trampled grass and burst through the smoke surrounding the hole. On the other side of the wall, the deserted, blindingly white buildings with dozens of windows and multiple stories—far richer and cleaner than all of the other sectors combined—and paved streets of Sector One greeted them along with a sea of strategically scattered black armor. Roman bellowed a vicious cry and lunged, sending a large spike of ice hurtling toward the closest group of soldiers. The ice struck a soldier, shattering into hundreds of tiny shards that pierced the others. He was immediately absorbed by the bloodshed, and Roman allowed himself to enter the fray with open arms.

~

Natalia ducked as a spear of electricity flew at her head and turned to watch it imbed in a rebel a few yards behind her. The older woman in mismatched clothing hit the ground with a sickening *thump*, never to rise again. White-hot anger boiled through Natalia, renewing her body with strength and adrenaline. Eyes glowing, she thrust her arms forward, two columns of scalding flames melting the soldier who'd thrown the spear into a pile of steaming metal, bones, and burning flesh. She sprinted at the nearest soldier, whose back was turned as he fired his gun, and launched into the air to bring a razor-sharp knife of ice down into the bare flesh showing between the neck of the dark armor and helmet. Warm blood coated Natalia's hands and splattered against her face. A year ago, she could've never pictured herself fighting like this—coldly murdering those who stood in her way. But this was war, and it was their deaths or her family's.

The rebels had closed the distance between themselves and the wall and had broken through the gap in the gates within seconds. The world had immediately erupted into chaos as the stark-white buildings and apartments of One emerged. The roads paved with a smooth, light gray concrete were quickly becoming stained with crimson blood. Vayne's soldiers were everywhere. He'd been ready for them and had stationed the bulk of his army throughout the maze of streets winding through the heart of One. Natalia cursed him. This would be a dog fight all the way to his mansion.

She ripped her knife free of the soldier's neck before a raging ball of flames collided against her side, knocking her to the ground. Natalia rolled and leaped back to her feet as the world swayed around her. She met the wicked, glowing red and silver eyes of the boy from Vayne's personal guard. A vicious sneer fell over his face, and she found herself wishing he'd fallen off the other side of the wall like the other soldiers when the truck had hit. She met his gaze, forming a swirling sphere of ice and fire in each hand. She pushed her feet into the ground, readying herself to lunge, but hesitated at the strange fogginess that seemed to cloud his eyes in the reflection of her flames. They were utterly blank—as if he had no control over his mind or body.

Brainwashing...

Natalia's stomach twisted at the familiar sight, and instead of a boy with blond hair and raging red and silver eyes, she saw a boy with dark hair, normal hazel eyes, and a warm smile gracing his soft features. She saw Damien. However, the image of him quickly disappeared when the boy launched at her, brandishing a staff of flames. He slung the staff at her side, and Natalia's swirling spheres of ice and fire molded against her hands as she caught it an inch away from her painted armor. The two shoved back and forth, battling over the length of the spear when a blast of wind swept the boy's feet out from under him. He fell to the hard concrete with wide eyes and opened his mouth, but Natalia shoved the spear into his chest with a *squelch*. All that left his lips was a final, ragged breath. She stumbled backward, head whipping from side to side amongst the chaos surrounding her. A few yards to her left, Hero's one eye glowed gray and black as he and Spenser dodged the swinging spear of a soldier. His gaze met hers for a brief second, and she nodded her thanks to him for providing that blast of wind.

All around, blood, gore, and bodies littered the once beautiful and clean streets of Sector One. People screamed in rage and fear as they battled on. Through a brief break in the dense sea of black armor, mismatched clothing, and flying Elements and electricity, Natalia spotted a gap between the buildings that revealed the large, hilly field that opened out before the gates of Vayne's mansion in the distance. The field and the beginnings of the forest that spread across its left flank were the only things separating the rebel army and the mansion. Confusion flooded her, and she glanced back at the wall. Her mouth nearly dropped. They were at least two hundred yards into the sector, the wall a looming giant in the growing distance. At this rate, it wouldn't take much longer for them to reach the field... But the battle was far from over, and they had a lot of land to cover.

～

Fraiser sent her swirling disc of air hurtling toward a soldier who was charging her as she jumped and flipped, narrowly dodging the sweep of a second soldier's electric sword. She countered with a fist to the tall man's exposed throat, and he crumbled. Fraiser ripped the sword from his hands and sliced it along his neck. Warm blood splattered across her hands and sizzled along the electric blade. She sent her second disc of air hurtling into the crowd of black that was beginning to swarm around a group of civilians from Four. A satisfied smirk pulled at the corner of her lips when it embedded itself in a soldier's shoulder, and she twirled the blade as she charged forward, forming a second blade of swirling air currents in her free hand.

She leaped into the swarm, slashing and ducking then slashing again. Adrenaline pumped through her veins, pushing her further and further. The thrill of battle never ceased to amaze her. She'd been born for this. Body after body slumped to the ground in her wake, and soon, the entirety of the soldiers had dwindled down to two. She chucked her sword of air at the one closest and crushed the air pipe of the second with the flick of her wrist.

The civilians of Four nodded their thanks at Fraiser before throwing themselves back into the fray of battle. They'd made excellent progress through One, considering their numbers, but Vayne's plan was finally clear to her. He'd sent less than half of his seven thousand troops here to the heart of One, meaning to spread the rebels as thin as he could—dwindle what little numbers they had—before they reached the field and his mansion ahead. There, the rest of his army would be waiting to slaughter them. She couldn't yet see them between the gaps in the impeccably white buildings and apartments, but she knew they would be there.

Fraiser cursed at the thought and swung her blade harder and faster. She had to kill more—take out as many of his soldiers as she could. Each life she took was another life saved. She prayed to the Aether that Napoleon and Lavelle had found the captives of the sectors. Even if they had the elements on their side, they were completely outnumbered. If Napoleon didn't show, the rebels wouldn't stand a chance... They would fall, and every single one of them would die. Fraiser's grip on her blade tightened, and she charged toward another group of poisonous black armor.

～

Sweat dripped down Natalia's neck, and fatigue clawed at her like a starving beast. Her arms began to grow heavy as she launched blade after blade of ice and fire. She and the rebels had been fighting for *hours*—from the walls of Sector Four in the late morning all the way to the streets of One in the beginning of the night. It had been a long day, and the effects of it were taking its toll. And she knew if she was getting tired, so was the rest of the army. But Damien still hadn't made his appearance—*another* battle yet to take place. The rebels needed this one over. Fast.

The wind and rain increased, tearing at her armor and the hair that had been torn from her braid. She dropped to the slick concrete, sliding under a punch and slicing the back of a soldier's ankles through their black leather boots with a long knife of ice. The soldier dropped to the ground with a shrill scream, and she cut both of her knives—one of flame and one of ice—across the soldier's neck, spilling blood down the black armor and onto the street. Natalia quickly leaped back to her feet and scanned the faces around her for Roman. Fear began to course through her until she spotted him at the edge of a street corner a few yards away. She glanced between him and the nearing field. They only had one more block until they reached the tall grass whipping furiously in the wind. Natalia turned to watch him send a javelin of ice through a soldier's abdomen before turning to meet her gaze. She ducked and slashed, quickly fighting her way toward him through the frenzy of battle. He too fought his way back up the avenue, cutting the distance between them in half.

"We're too spread out!" Roman shouted over the chaos, turning and sending two knives of ice into the sea of black. Sweat and mud covered his face and neck. "We need to reform our front line if we want to make it to the field!"

Natalia formed a shield of fire before her that absorbed a bolt of electricity. She extended her hands, launching the shield at the owner of the bolt. "And how exactly do we do that?"

"Like this!" Fraiser suddenly exclaimed, bounding through the crowd with Hero and Spenser behind her. Spenser paused beside Roman and Natalia, and the three watched as Fraiser and Hero sprinted past them and into the middle of the crowded intersection of paved streets before them. Fraiser blasted a few soldiers away and faced Hero.

Spenser fired his gun of electricity at a soldier who'd neared them and turned to Roman and Natalia. "Cover them."

Natalia nodded, and together, the three of them pushed through the crowd into the intersection, firing bolts of electricity, flames, and ice toward anyone who dared to approach. Hero and Fraiser faced each other and lifted their upturned palms out in unison. Dozens and dozens of wind currents sprang forth, swirling into the air. A third Elemental—a young boy with glowing gray and silver eyes—stepped out from the throng of battle and joined them. They all extended their arms out to their sides, and the currents began to grow bigger and taller, merging and twisting together to funnel into a small twister the height of the two-story apartments on the block.

Windows shattered nearby, and the shards flew through the air along with chunks of dirt and grass and even a few weapons and scraps of armor. The chaos around them paused, and everyone stopped to watch the twister begin to move down the avenue in the direction of the field, sucking up anyone within its path. Rebels and Araedians immediately divided and sprinted to the edges of the white buildings, forming shields of elements before them and leaving Vayne's soldiers stranded, alone and dumfounded in the center of the street—directly in the path of the twister.

Shouting rose up behind them, and Natalia turned to see the fighting had begun anew, except the majority of Vayne's soldiers were crowded in the street before them. Those behind the twister were severely outnumbered and quickly succumbed to the rebels and Elementals. Her breath lodged in her throat when the twister collided with the bulk of soldiers, sucking them up into the sky and launching them out into the field. She cringed at the sight of their flailing bodies smacking against the ground.

"Rebels!" Roman shouted, wind ripping at his hair viciously. "Pull together!"

Natalia took a step closer to him, and the rebels behind them did the same, condensing into one large column of people. Slowly following after the path of the twister, over three thousand rebels began to march down the cleared street. The Elementals and rebels who'd shielded themselves against the buildings began to break off and join the throng as it passed. The last of Vayne's soldiers dealt with, Fraiser, Hero, and the young boy walked yards ahead and guided the twister out into the open field. They paused when they hit the tall grass and pushed their arms up at the dark storm clouds, dispersing the twister into whipping currents of wind.

Natalia and Roman were soon upon them, and the boy, whose face had grown pale, quickly disappeared into the ranks of the army. Fraiser and Hero bent over with their hands on their knees, panting rapidly. Fraiser's dark skin had paled, and Hero's was a sickly white with a greenish tinge. Spenser tucked his gun over his shoulder into the large holster strapped across his back and rushed to Hero. He threw Hero's arm around his neck, and Hero straightened as best as he could, leaning the entirety of his weight into Spenser's side. Roman paused next to Fraiser and put a hand on her shoulder. She gave him a shaky thumbs-up in return.

Natalia glanced between them, the expanse of the field, and the edge of the forest that jutted out to her left. Small hills rose and fell in the field like cresting waves brought to life by the swaying grass. Thunder sounded above and lightning crackled across the sky, illuminating the uphill slope that led to a small ridge halfway between them and the gray cement walls of Vayne's mansion. She frowned. The

field was around three hundred yards long—much larger than she had anticipated...
Could they make it that far?

Dark shadows flickered across the expanse of the ridge, catching her eye. Her
heart dropped into her stomach as the lightning flashed again to reveal the eight
cannons and dozens and dozens of soldiers awaiting them at the top. Fraiser cursed
vulgarly, shakily straightening. Roman's arms went slack at his sides, and Natalia
turned to watch him go rigid. Hero barely lifted his head to widen his eye, and
Spenser simply stood there. The rebels and Araedians behind them were utterly
silent. In fact, the entire world seemed utterly silent... Until the sound of marching
boots filled the air over the rain, and darkness began to sweep up and over the many
hills like a plague. Lightning flashed once more, and Natalia inhaled sharply at the
sight of Vayne's army. There had to be at least six thousand of them. Even with the
elements, the rebels wouldn't stand a chance against them and the cannons. A mere
four of those dreaded chunks of metal had nearly wiped them out completely back
in Sector Four. How in the Aether's name would they survive *eight?*

"Roman...," Fraiser whispered, slowly shaking her head. Her usual fiery green
eyes were dull and dead, and her clenched fists shook at her sides. "What do we do?"

"We fight," he said, his voice shaking with emotion. Roman blinked furiously,
clearly fighting at the tears welling in his eyes. Natalia felt her heart cracking as he
clenched his jaw. "It's the only thing we can do."

Fraiser sucked on the inside of her cheek and scrunched her nose, fighting back
her own tears. Hero's head dropped in defeat.

"I guess your friends didn't make it after all," Spenser murmured, his river eyes
never leaving the army that marched closer and closer.

Anger boiled through Natalia. Anger, despair, fear... Their impending deaths...
She felt it all, and it was utterly overwhelming and all-consuming. Her lip wobbled
at the thought of Napoleon's and Lavelle's cold bodies lying still in some random
tunnel underneath them—at the thought of Aurum and Ren being tortured, brainwashed like Damien, and eventually killed in Vayne's clutches... The thought of
Fraiser, Hero, and Spenser's bodies all covered in blood and mud out in the field
before her. Fraiser's guts spilling out of her stomach and burns covering every inch
of her. Hero's other eye gone, ripped from its socket by some sick and sadistic Elemental like Zyra, and blood spilling from his mouth and ears. Spenser blown to
pieces, directly hit by one of the cannons. Her stomach turned at the thought and
image of Roman kneeling before his father. Bile rose in her throat as the imaginary

Vayne beheaded his son, watching as his head rolled to Natalia's feet while she screamed. Then Damien appeared before her and—

No.

Natalia shook her head, squeezing her eyes shut. It wasn't real. That wasn't real. She wouldn't let that happen. They weren't going to die. Napoleon and Lavelle were coming. They had to be. She refused to give up on them, and she refused to give up on the battle before them now. She was so sick of Vayne always winning—always taking those she loved most away. It had started with Vale, then it was Damien... and Aurum... Possibly Ren...

No. She would not stand for it. She would not let him win again. Even if it took every single life behind and beside her—even if it took her own—she'd fight and fight and fight until she got to those damned mansion gates. She'd rip them down and tear Vayne's heart out herself.

She whirled to face Roman, Fraiser, Hero, and Spenser. "Don't you *dare* give up now. This is far from over."

Natalia could feel her eyes beginning to glow their multicolored shades of ice blue, purple, and red-orange around silver. She could feel the fire burning underneath her skin, which was as cold and hard as ice. She was water, ice, and flames, and she was no longer tired. She was no longer afraid. Her power swelled inside her building up and up like a volcano before eruption. Flames burst forth from her left fingertips, and shards of ice protruded from her right. Shivers rolled down her spine, and she marched forward. Roman and Frasier were beside her in an instant, brandishing their own glowing gray, dark-blue, and silver eyes along with swirling spheres of their elements. Natalia didn't have to look back to know Spenser, Hero, and the rest of their army were behind them. She could sense them—feel the reverberations of their footsteps in the earth and the energy buzzing through the air. No matter what, they would all fight, and if they died... At least they would die trying.

The rain began to pound harder, and more thunder and lightning boomed and flashed. The cannons atop the ridge began to spark as they charged and readied. Vayne's army was halfway across the field when Natalia broke into a sprint, and the rebels charged.

~

The armies met with a sickening *clash*, bodies and armor crashing together in a fury of electricity and elements. Violent screams and shouts of pain filled the air as

Natalia dodged an electric bolt and jabbed at the soldier who'd fired at her with her left hand. A torrent of flames rapidly surged around the soldier's black helmet, clawing and scraping at the visor. The protective shield shattered, and the flames entered the helmet viciously. The soldier collapsed to the ground, hoarse screams echoing out and joining the chorus of horrid shouting around her.

Natalia whirled, sensing the attack an instant before it happened. The shards of ice around her right fingertips spread down the entirety of her hand before she reached out and caught the arching sword. The electricity crackled and sizzled against the ice, melting the spots where her fingers met her palm. She punched with her left arm, sending a wave of fire at the soldier, who ducked and wrenched the sword from her hand. A snake of water and fire crept up each of her arms, twining and elongating into viper's heads that hissed six inches past her clenched fists. Natalia lunged forward, the vipers of her left hand catching the sword once more while the two on the right dove for the soldier's exposed throat. Their teeth of ice and fire sank into the soldier's skin and clamped down so hard, a stomach-churning *pop* sounded.

Blood splattered across her face as the body disappeared into the tall grass. The blood dripped down her cheeks, mixing with the mud, sweat, and rain and sliding down her back. Her drenched hair clung to her neck as she wiped the burning mixture from her eyes to glance around the field. Dread pooled in her stomach. Vayne's army was *everywhere.* There were so many of them, she could hardly see any rebels fighting within the chaos of the battle. Their bodies, however, weren't hard to spot. Corpses dressed in mismatched clothes and painted black armor lay in every spot she looked. They were losing. Badly.

Suddenly, one deafening word rang out over the battlefield in a hoarse cry: *"Cannons!"*

Natalia turned to the ridge to watch all eight cannons fire enormous bolts of crackling, deadly blue-white electricity high into the air. Her eyes widened, and fear shot through her like a disease. The bolts arched toward the rebels and Vayne's soldiers alike, falling with rapid speed. She sprinted to her right as fast as she could as a bolt came hurtling directly for her. Both rebels and soldiers ran beside her, neither bothering to fight each other now. She flung herself forward, scrambling up one of the small sloping hills covering the field.

She crested the hill as the bolt collided against the tall grass and exploded, showering the world in mud and dirt. The earth shook violently, sending everyone in a ten-yard radius crashing to the ground. Natalia bit back a cry when her face struck the earth, driving her teeth into her bottom lip. Everything was spinning, and she could hear a slight ringing in her ears. She quickly slid her hands and legs underneath her and wobbled to her feet. She had to keep moving—keep fighting. Blood dripped from Natalia's nose and mouth when she turned to survey the damage below.

The grass was singed in a jagged circle surrounded by twitching, burned bodies and body parts. Groans of pain, smoke, and the stench of burning flesh floated through the air. Bile rose in her throat, and tears stung her eyes. Natalia pivoted in a circle atop the small hill. It felt like someone had punched her in the gut at the sight of the seven other craters and rebels falling around her. Bodies were piling high, and she watched a soldier ram a spear of electricity through a young rebel while another was shot with an electric bolt. A few hills ahead, Fraiser, eyes glowing, took on an entire battalion, flinging currents of wind left and right. Back toward the outskirts of Sector One, Hero and Spenser stood back-to-back amongst a large group of rebels and Vayne's soldiers. Rebels fell all around them. Natalia cursed viciously. Where were Napoleon and Lavelle? What if something had happened, and they weren't coming? Fear cascaded through her. Wait...

Where's Roman?

Natalia spun in a circle once more, scanning the field for him. This time it felt different. She didn't know when she had stopped breathing, or when her heart had started beating so loud, she could hear it in her ears. There was no sign of him—no glowing dark blue and silver eyes or spears of water and ice. Had he been hit by the cannons? Her stomach churned at the thought. Where was he?

Where was he? Where was he? Where was he?

Without warning, three of Vayne's soldiers came charging up the small slope of the hill. Natalia whirled, sending columns of flame and water hurtling toward them. Two of the soldiers leaped to the side as the third was struck with the water and tumbled down the hill. A spear of water formed in her hands, and the tipped frosted over into razor-sharp, hardened ice. She twirled it while the soldiers slinked up the last few feet of the slope and began to circle her slowly. They unsheathed their electric swords, blue-purple sparks crackling through the rain. Her glowing eyes reflected against the visor of the black helmet before her—but then a second pair of glowing dark blue irises surrounding bright silver pupils appeared above hers in the reflection.

Natalia lunged forward with her spear, batting away the electric sword and plunging the tip of ice deep into the soldier's abdomen. She turned and watched the last soldier fall to the ground, his head cleaved from his body. Relief flooded through Natalia as her eyes scanned Roman from head to toe. He seemed to be all right besides a few scrapes and blooming bruises. She released a shaky breath and looked back up to his face, so grateful that he was alive. A sword of hardened ice dripping dark blood slackened in his hand when his eyes flitted up to meet hers.

The crackling of the eight cannons had them both facing the dreaded ridge yards in the distance. Roman was beside her in an instant, grabbing her arm and pulling her down the hill. Eight bolts rocketed into the air, heading straight for the remaining mass of rebels. Wet hair clung to Natalia's face as she glanced up and watched the bolts collide with their people. Roman tackled her to the ground, throwing his body over hers as the world shook once more. She wrapped her arms around his head and pulled him into her shoulder.

Natalia squeezed her eyes shut, an emptiness filling her. She knew that one more round from those cannons would be the end of them—*all* of them. It might not even take the full round... The blows were catastrophic, and they were so severely outnumbered... They'd finally reached it. The point of no return—no chance of victory. The last reverberations of the cannon bolts colliding against the ground shifted the mud. She and Roman waited a few moments before standing, wobbly on their feet, and holding onto each other's arms until the world finally stopped spinning. Natalia looked to the mansion and the edge of the forest reaching out into the field before it.

They'd lost... *The rebels had lost.* Why had she ever let herself hope in the first place? They should have never entered One. If they'd regrouped and waited, maybe they would've had a better chance—a better plan to deal with the cannons that were sparking and recharging before her.

Suddenly, a blast of all four elements shot through the air, hurling toward the eight cannons. The blasts collided with the cannon closest to the edge of the forest, and an explosion of electric sparks and flame burst out across the field, burning the nearby soldiers to crisps and turning the cannon into a molten hot pile of metal. Natalia's breath caught in her throat.

There, at the edge of the forest, eyes glowing the brightest gold and silver, was Ren.

CHAPTER THIRTY-THREE

CRASH AND BURN

For a few moments, Ren simply stood there. Alone. But then shadows began to move through the trees behind him, and civilians dressed in whites, beiges, and creams broke through the tree line, joining him at the edge of the forest. The entire battlefield paused to watch as Ren stepped forward.

"Citizens of Araedia, your families are free!" Ren's voice rang out loud and clear across the field. Everything had fallen quiet. It seemed as if even the rain had stilled to hear his words. "Vayne Averie holds nothing over you any longer! You do not have to fight for him! You are all free!"

Battle cries arose across the field and the forest's edge as the civilians suddenly burst forth, charging directly into the side of Vayne's dumbfounded army with nothing but sticks, rocks, and their own arms and legs. Elementals dressed in mismatched clothing—Napoleon's tunnel team—led the front lines, and the rebels smashed into the sea of black. Atop the ridge, waves of tall fire ignited the sky as it collided against the second cannon. Another whirl of all four elements followed it, wrapping around the cannon like a deadly snake. Natalia turned back to where Ren had been standing to find Aurum beside him with glowing red and silver eyes.

"They made it...," Roman whispered. "They found the lost civilians..."

"And they're all alive," Natalia said, her voice cracking with heavy emotion.

Shivers rolled down her entire body, and adrenaline rushed like great rapids through her veins. Napoleon, Aurum, the twins... They were all alive. Her voice seemed far away as she spoke hoarsely, "If we can help Ren and Aurum take down those cannons, we'll have a straight shot at the mansion."

Roman faced her, meeting her gaze. Life—no, hope—had lit up his brown eyes once again. Their chances of survival had raised along with their numbers. There had to be at least two thousand rebels joining them, raising the army to around five thousand. But they were still outnumbered by Vayne's army, and they would need to be strategic if they wanted to win. Roman nodded, and the two of them took off up the next hill. They crested it, only to stop dead in their tracks.

"What's going on?" Natalia exclaimed, shaking her head. She couldn't believe her eyes. It was impossible. Absolutely impossible...

"They've switched sides...," Roman said breathlessly. "Ren's speech... Some of Vayne's soldiers are switching sides."

He was right. *Hundreds*—no, at least a *thousand*—of Vayne's troops had begun to fire and swing their spears and swords of electricity at their fellow soldiers. With the numbers turning as they were... The rebels could match Vayne's army... They *were* matching his army. Napoleon and the tunnel team had found the lost civilians, and as Ren had said, their captured loved ones were now free. The people and those forced into Vayne's army no longer had to obey Vayne to survive. The rebels were offering them hope for a new future—a future where they didn't have to fight against the rebels. And those were the soldiers turning on Vayne now.

"Stop gawking and move your asses toward those cannons!" Fraiser shouted as she sprinted past them.

Natalia raced after her, Roman a step behind. The three of them blasted their elements in every direction as they made their way to the left side of the ridge and began the ascent up the slope. Soldiers were everywhere, but they were unorganized. The rebel reinforcements and the betrayal of their own had thrown everything and everyone into a catastrophic chaos. Natalia spotted Napoleon and Lavelle a few yards from the edge of the forest. They stood back-to-back, firing columns of rocks and wind as fast as they could. An oddly familiar man with dark hair and mismatched clothes leaped from the fray of battle to land beside them and fire a gun of electricity at the surrounding soldiers. Resisting the urge to run to them was nearly impossible.

But they were alive, and they had found Aurum and Ren. Natalia's heart was beating so fast, she feared it would explode. Her family was here. They'd come, and they'd brought the lost civilians of the sectors with them...

～

Ren's breathing was ragged as his power surged through him. His entire body was pounding with an unnatural heat that hummed over his limbs. The rebels had been losing badly when he'd burst through the tree line, but with the revelation of the reinforcements, the civilians forced into Vayne's army had turned against him. It'd taken them longer to arrive than they'd originally thought, especially when they'd stopped to leave the elderly, the women, and the children who didn't want to fight hidden within the forest.

Ren grunted as he slashed a sword of rock across a soldier's abdomen and sprinted over to Aurum, who fought near the molten second cannon. He'd managed to take out the first two with her help, but they needed to find a less tiring method to destroy them. It was taking up too much of his energy—energy that he needed to save for the wicked man hiding behind the mansion gates. And Ren knew if it was taking up his newfound power and energy, it was stealing away Aurum's, too. He watched her sling her whip of fire at a soldier's throat. The fiery cord tightened around the exposed neck, and with a swift jerk, the soldier was sprawled out in the mud, the stench of burning flesh filling the air. Her whip flew toward another soldier and snapped the soldier's helmet so hard, it went flying off into the man behind him. An idea suddenly formed in Ren's head, and he sprinted toward the third cannon a few yards away.

"What are you doing?" Aurum hollered, blasting a wave of flames into the wall of black armor forming around her. She leaped away with another blast and chased after him.

Ren sent a column of air slamming into the soldiers manning the third cannon, and they went flying into the throng of battle. He charged the cannon, ramming into the large metal barrel. It shifted to the side with a low groan.

Ren grunted as he pushed at the barrel again. "Help me turn it toward the others!"

Aurum's lips parted in surprise, but she was by him in an instant, throwing all her body weight into shifting the cannon. Slowly, it rotated to the side, facing down the row of the five other cannons. Ren darted his eyes between the row and the gates of Vayne's mansion. Aurum shoved his shoulder and mounted the cannon herself.

"Go!" she shouted.

He took a few hesitant steps forward but turned back. He couldn't just leave her...

"*Ren, go!*" Aurum hissed, shoving a hand of flames at him. He ducked, and the fire flew over his head into the battle raging around them. She fiddled with the trigger of the cannon, which crackled as it began to charge.

Ren cursed and sprinted into the crowd. He ran as fast as he could, shoving his way through the mass of bodies and armor. Araedians and Elementals alike screamed all around him, and blood, mud, and rain splattered about. He fired small bursts of all four elements into the soldiers that blocked his path, and before he knew it, he was standing before the fifteen-foot metal gates. How would he break through these?

The roaring blast of the cannons had Ren whirling to face the battlefield. His breath caught in his throat as he watched Aurum fire the bolt down the row of cannons, blowing two of them into nothing but a singed pile of red-hot metal. But instead of recharging to fire at the last three, she hopped down and began to try to rotate the barrel once again. Three figures suddenly appeared by her side—Roman, Natalia, and Fraiser. Ren squinted as they joined her and pushed. The cannon finally came to a halt, and his eyes widened at its target. He sprinted to the right as far away from the gates as he could get when the cannon began to spark again.

The bolt launched into the air, hurtling directly into the mansion gates with a deafening *crash*. Sparks, smoke, and chunks of metal and rock showered Ren as he was knocked to the grass and mud. His ears rang slightly, but he swiftly rose and staggered forward. He waited for the world to stop spinning before glancing back to the others to find Roman and Natalia holding off a horde of soldiers while Frasier and Aurum tried to push and aim the cannon back down the row. Using every ounce of will he had, Ren turned his back to them and edged around the smoking crater that had taken the gates' place.

Chunks of concrete, debris, and red-hot metal littered the freshly cut courtyard grass and the cobblestone path that led up to the covered stairs of the mansion. Two figures—Damien and Zyra—clothed in stark white armor with a blood-red band around their right biceps waited at the foot of the stairs while the third, who wore the darkest black armor with details of decorative gold, stood underneath the roofing before the large, windowed double doors.

President Vayne Averie...

Ren's eyes began to sting and glow brighter as he reached for his new power. Zyra's eyes turned a deadly ice blue and silver, and she flashed Ren a smile as claws of ice formed at her fingertips. Ren concentrated hard, returning her smile with his own fingertips of flame. The raw power nipped at his fingers, begging to be unleashed further. He glanced at Damien, who simply stood there, his normal hazel eyes blazing with an emotion he couldn't quite place. Then Ren lifted his gaze to meet Vayne's, and he couldn't stop the breath of shock and fear that escaped his lips. Roman's father's eyes were as white as snow, and black veins stretched across them. A faint gray line outlined his barely visible irises. Even his pupils were stark white, and his skin was so pale it appeared translucent. Nausea pooled in Ren's stomach as Vayne's eyes scanned him maliciously.

"There you are..." Vayne smiled wickedly. "I've been waiting for you for some time now, Ren Dalnum." Ren scowled, causing Vayne to laugh. "Are you prepared to finally hand over what's rightfully mine?"

Ren scoffed. The Aether's powers were his and his alone. He would die before he let Vayne get his clutches on them. "They're not yours."

"How foolish of you...," Vayne murmured. "My wife used to tell me the same. She prattled on and on about how if I kept messing with the balance of life that only death would follow. She was right, but it wasn't *my* death that followed. So unless you desire that same fate for yourself, your twin sister, my son, and everyone in your entire little... *army*..." He chuckled. "...I suggest you submit now, and this can all be over."

"Do you really think I came all this way to submit to you?" Ren seethed.

Zyra stepped out from under the covering into the pounding rain. "Watch your tone."

"Leash your dog, Averie," Ren said, his voice low and lethal as he allowed his fingertips to flare into larger flames. The hunger within the fire grew—a burning desire to attack. He found that each of the four elements had their own separate personality. They were all extremely different, yet when combined, they flowed with a fluidity unknown to the strongest rivers. But right now, the fire was overtaking the others. It was calling for violence. "Or I'll do it for you."

"As entertaining as that would be," Damien said, taking a step forward and joining Zyra in the rain. "I'm afraid you're quite outnumbered here, Ren, and you have nowhere to run this time."

"He doesn't need to run!" a feminine voice rang out across the courtyard.

Ren half-turned to glance at the smoking ruins of the gates behind him, never quite taking his eyes off Zyra, Damien, and Vayne. Vayne's head tilted to the side, and another sick smile tugged at the corner of his mouth as he, too, gazed at the ruins. A few moments of utter silence passed, and it seemed as if the entire world had fallen silent when Natalia, eyes glowing ice blue, red-orange, and electric purple, stepped out from the cover of the billowing smoke. Roman appeared next to her a moment later with glowing dark blue and silver eyes. Wait, where were Aurum and Fraiser? They'd been with Roman and Natalia, too.

"And he's not as outnumbered as you think, Damien," Natalia said, forming a snake of water on one arm and a snake of fire on the other.

Vayne's gaze was alight with curiosity and hunger—no, starvation—for power. "What an interesting turn of events..." His eyes flickered between Natalia and Ren before drifting over to Roman. "Hello, my son. Have you finally come to face me?"

Roman's jaw tightened in rage, his blue eyes burning with a danger that set every one of Ren's nerves on edge. A spear of water that hardened into ice formed in

Roman's hands, and sharp rocks floated up from the ground to swirl around Ren's knuckles. Zyra grinned as her claws elongated into long, razor-sharp knives. The tension was so thick in the air, Ren feared he might suffocate.

"Have you nothing to say to me after all these years of pestering me with your pathetic vagabonds?" Vayne took a step down the stairs. Then another. And another until he stood between Zyra and Damien. Ren hadn't even noticed that Roman and Natalia had moved and were now standing on either side of him.

"I can't wait to watch you fall," Roman hissed, deadly quiet.

~

Natalia's heart pounded faster than it ever had before, and her body—like Roman and Ren's—was covered in sweat, grime, and dried blood. Though she hated to admit it, she couldn't stop the fear that crept over her as Vayne's eyes began to glow entirely *black*. She glanced between him and Damien, who hadn't taken his hazel eyes off her since she'd first appeared. Only now did his eyes—eyes that had meant everything to her once—begin to glow red-orange and silver. She wouldn't be afraid. *She would not be afraid...*

Without warning, Vayne lunged forward, slicing through the air with a hand that sent a hauntingly black blade of large, vicious winds hurtling for Natalia, Roman, and Ren. Natalia brought her arms forward to block it, but it was no use. The wind slammed into all three of them, knocking and separating them in three different directions. They crashed into the ground with hard, reverberating *thumps*. Zyra was upon Natalia within seconds, and Natalia barely rolled to the side in time to watch Zyra's knife of ice embed into the thick mud where her head had been. She quickly rose to her feet, shooting her snake of fire off her arm. A viper of ice formed before Zyra and met the flames. They clashed, bursting and shattering into a shower of snow and ashes that fluttered to the ground.

Zyra smiled, tilting her head to the side. "Now that I really see you up close, I can truly say I don't get why Damien was so obsessed with you before. But it's no bother. He's all mine now."

Natalia gritted her teeth as she extinguished the snake of fire that had replaced the other on her arm. Two long knives of ice appeared in her hands, matching the ones in Zyra's. "You can have him."

Zyra charged and Natalia leaped to meet her, slicing and blocking. To Natalia's left, Ren and Damien exchanged blow after blow, dodging swords of flame and rock. A cry of pain suddenly filled the air as Natalia landed a kick to Zyra's stomach, knocking her to the ground. Natalia whirled to find Roman clutching at a gaping slice across his side from the blade of dark wind Vayne clutched. Blood poured down Roman's armor and pooled at his feet. He straightened with a wince and flung a long knife of ice toward his father. Vayne batted it away, sending his own blade plunging through the air. Overwhelming fear struck Natalia like lightning, igniting every inch of her body.

"Roman!" she screamed as an explosion from the battlefield beyond rattled the earth. Roman barely threw himself to the side in time to watch the blade pass and plunge into the shaking ground.

Natalia sensed the attack a moment before it happened, ducking to watch Zyra's knife slice through inches of her dark hair. She stumbled backward and fired a razor-sharp icicle from her hand. Zyra leaped to the side, the icicle flying past her head and landing between Ren and Damien, who paused their dance of swords for a moment to look at the two girls. Damien's eyes hardened, and he turned back to Ren once more. Zyra faced Natalia with a scowl and a cut across her right cheek. A small stream of blood trickled from the wound. Zyra was quick but not quick enough.

Vayne suddenly yelled, causing everyone to stop and watch as he jumped into the air, spun, and sent a vicious tumult of winds colliding into Roman's chest. Roman flew across the courtyard, slamming into the mansion wall with a bone-crunching *crack*. He tried to rise but cried out in pain as he fell back to the mud, clutching his side. Behind Natalia, Damien tackled Ren to the ground. They wrestled furiously, neither gaining an advantage. Panic wrapped around Natalia's throat like a noose. If she couldn't find a way to tilt the odds in their favor soon, they would lose... Roman and Ren would die, and so would she.

Natalia dropped to a knee and sunk her hands into the muddy ground. Ice shot across the mud and rainwater, forming shackles of ice around Zyra's feet and ankles. Losing her balance, Zyra fell forward and more ice trapped her hands and wrists. She screamed a long line of curses at Natalia, who merely turned to face Vayne. He smiled sadistically, forming a large spear of dark wind. Natalia charged him, a spear of ice and flames appearing in her own hands.

Their spears collided with great force. She spun and swung as Vayne blocked and countered. On they danced while Zyra continued to struggle against her shackles, and Ren and Damien leaped to their feet to fire their elements at each other. Vayne's spear arched down at Natalia, who held her own above her head to block the blow. The tip of his spear hit the ice, shattering it into a million pieces. Vayne pivoted, sending a fist of wind into her stomach. Natalia lifted her hands, but she was far too late. With a yelp, she went flying backward, colliding against the cold bite of the remnants of the metal gates with a bone-shattering *crack*. She screamed and winced as she grabbed at her head. The world wouldn't stop spinning. Her ears rang, muffling Roman's shouts from across the courtyard.

"I must admit, I've enjoyed our little bout." Vayne sauntered toward her with a sickening chuckle. "And watching everything my son loves being destroyed before his eyes is a very satisfying feat... but I wonder... What exactly are you?"

Natalia formed another flame inside her palms and blasted it at him. Vayne knelt to the ground, his spear shifting to a shield of swirling winds. The fire whipped around the shield, viciously burning and dissipating it into nothing. Natalia panted and let her arms fall to her sides. She was exhausted. Nearly every ounce of her energy was gone. Her head lulled to the side, and she spotted Roman in the grass. She sucked in a breath as tears welled in her eyes. He couldn't stand. She swore she could feel her heart shattering to pieces. He was too gravely injured, but it didn't stop him from dragging himself through the mud—crawling toward her.

"Well, the better question, is *who* are you," Vayne said, looming over her. "I've never discovered anyone in my texts able to control more than one element who's *not* the Aether... How remarkable... but such a shame that you must die." He looked over at Ren and Damien. Ren knocked Damien farther and farther back with blow after blow of rock, wind, fire, and water. Vayne's eyes suddenly met Natalia's. "I ordered Damien to use up as much of the Aether's energy as he could. Even if it cost him his life. You will not witness the death of your friends, but I assure you they will not come long after your own."

"Go to hell!" Natalia cried, attempting to push up off the ground, but Vayne slammed her back down with a column of wind that knocked the breath from her lungs. He was too strong—too enhanced by his psychotic self-experimentation. She gasped for air, tears spilling over her cheeks. Vayne lifted his arms above his head, and a razor-sharp sword of black air formed.

"Talia!" Roman's agonized voice rang out across the courtyard.

"No!" Ren screamed.

She glanced between Roman in the grass and Ren, who now threw everything he had at Damien so he could try to get to her. She gasped, pain searing across her spine, head, and side. He wasn't going to make it to her in time. She was going to die, and Roman would, too. Ren would be alone against Vayne, Zyra, and Damien, and he would lose... And the rebels would fall... They'd lost.

She. Had. Lost.

The world seemed to move in slow motion, and there was no sound that pierced Natalia's ears even though she knew Roman was screaming. She released a single short breath as the sword plummeted toward her chest. Natalia closed her eyes, and a moment later, a shadow flickered across her face. She opened her eyes to watch Fraiser fling herself in front of Natalia, taking the sword's blow to her ribs.

"*No!*" Natalia screamed hoarsely as Fraiser hit the ground.

"*Fraiser!*" Roman's voice echoed across the courtyard. He cried out in pain as he failed to lift himself once more. Ren shot Damien with a column of rock and flames, sending him flying into a burning pile of debris before turning toward them. His face fell. Natalia reached for Fraiser as Vayne chuckled above them. She pulled her body onto her lap, holding her close with tears streaming down both of their faces. Fraiser winced and panted rapidly. Where had she even come from?

The sound of ice shattering had Natalia's head whirling to watch Zyra rise and sprint at Roman, knives of ice in hand. Fear and anger unlike anything Natalia had ever felt in her life lit her entire being on fire. She didn't dare fight the rising power within her as it crested to the surface and exploded outward. Natalia screamed while scorching fire emanated from every inch of her, blasting Vayne and Zyra yards away. They landed before the gaping crater, rolling to a stop. Zyra quickly rose from the ground only to have a spear of ice pierce through her chest, and with a solid *thump*, she collapsed.

Natalia looked at Roman in the grass and the hatred in his eyes. He shot a second spear at his father. Vayne blocked it but stumbled backward. Ren was before him a moment later, firing all four elements into his chest. Vayne released a wretched cry, collapsing down into the crater. Blows of dark wind met Ren's as Vayne threw everything he had at the Aether.

"Ren needs your help," Fraiser whispered.

Natalia met her gaze. Her normal green eyes shone with tears, and her skin had already begun to pale. A sob wracked Natalia. "Why, Fraiser?"

"Because they need you." She smiled—like what she'd just done had been worth it. Like she'd do it over and over again if she had to. "*They all need you.*"

"No." Natalia shook her head. Fraiser's eyelids drooped. "No, Fraiser, you have to stay awake. Hey, look at me. Don't close your eyes!"

Fraiser chuckled with a wince. "I'm not afraid to die, Talia."

"Fraiser, I'm so sorry—"

"It's okay... Everything's okay. Just promise me..." Fraiser sucked in a breath and clutched Natalia's hand. Tears spilled down her cheeks. "Promise me that you'll take care of Roman."

"I will." Natalia's lip wobbled as she nodded. "I always will, I promise."

Fraiser smiled—truly smiled—one final time.

"They need you...," she whispered, closing her eyes. Her head lulled to the side, and a hysteric sob escaped Natalia's chest. She looked up to find Roman somehow standing next to Ren. They threw element after element at Vayne, trying to encase him in a circular cage of water, earth, fire, and wind, but it didn't matter. Vayne was fighting hard, and his darkened air was slicing through cage after cage. The black veins throughout his body seemed to pulse with an unnatural beat. His experiments had enhanced him greatly, and he was slowly climbing his way out of the crater. Fraiser was right. They needed her. Natalia set Fraiser down gently and rose.

Movement flickered in the corner of her eye. She turned to watch Damien stumble forward. He'd finally managed to crawl out from the debris Ren had thrown him in. His eyes flickered back and forth between their glowing red-orange and silver and their normal hazel. He winced, clutching at his head before meeting her gaze. Black veins stretched toward his hazel irises, and...

Natalia was rooted to the spot as she stared at *him*. At the old Damien. The usual glaze that covered his eyes was entirely gone, replaced by overwhelming emotions. His eyes were clear... As were the tears that poured down his face. Damien bit his lip, and his gaze suddenly hardened. Natalia's eyes widened, and she sprinted for Ren and Roman despite the pain ravaging her side and back. Damien sprinted for them, too. She had to get there first. She *had* to. For the first time in her entire life, she truly had no idea what he was going to do. She couldn't read him.

But she didn't get there first, and Natalia could only watch as Damien sprinted at them, and...

He passed them, leaping down into the crater. Natalia was at Roman's and Ren's sides instantly, adding fire and water to the cage surrounding Vayne and now Damien.

"What are you doing?" Vayne yelled viciously.

Damien formed a spear of fire in his hands and plunged it deep into Vayne's abdomen. Vayne screeched horridly, reaching for Damien's throat as Ren's eyes began to glow brighter than the sun on its brightest day. Natalia squinted through the light, throwing every ounce of energy she had left into the cage that was shrinking around Vayne...and Damien. What was Damien doing? He wasn't trying to save Vayne. Was it really him? Had he somehow clawed his way back to the boy that he'd once been? Vayne screamed, shouted, and cursed in protest, but he was no match for the elements now.

He was no match for all of them. United.

"Roman!" Vayne's horrid eyes met his son's. "You know you can't survive in Araedia—in this world—without me! I know *everything*! Without me, you can't protect them. You will all *die*!"

Natalia glanced at Roman to watch his eyes narrow as he pushed his element further. Whatever Vayne was talking about—whatever force they needed protection from—clearly was not cause enough to stop.

Air. Earth. Fire. Water. They all encased Vayne and Damien. Then Vayne reached into a pouch at his belt to reveal a small, round silver object with a red button. A detonator.

"No!" Roman shouted.

Natalia, Ren, and Roman pushed harder, condensing the cage even further. Damien released Vayne and backed as far away from him as he could inside the cage, encasing himself in his own flames as Vayne's finger smashed the button.

The bomb exploded inside the cage of elements, incinerating *everything* inside and deepening the crater even further. The entire world shook, and Ren, Natalia, and Roman were blasted back as the fiery explosion swam and mixed with the elements before firing and launching high into the air—a whirlwind of water, earth, fire, and wind. The sky was alight for several long seconds, illuminating everything around before the elements dissipated into the dark sky and the world fell dark once again...

And the enormous crater was utterly empty besides a single pair of dark-veined, white eyes... Vayne's eyes...

Natalia rolled onto her back with a groan, reaching for Roman, who had landed beside her. A yard away, Ren pulled himself up to his knees, his eyes returning to their normal blue as he faced them. She sat up, dragging herself over to Roman. Tears poured from his brown eyes as she pulled him into her, hugging him tightly. The rain finally slowed to a light drizzle, and the dark sky began to lighten on the horizon. It was almost morning. Roman glanced up, causing Natalia to turn to watch Ren stumble over to them and collapse into their outstretched arms.

It was over.

CHAPTER THIRTY-FOUR

AFTERMATH

A few yards from the remains of the mansion gates, Aurum watched in a tangled web of terror and awe as a monstrously beautiful whirlwind of air, water, earth, and fire exploded high into the air from behind the mansion walls, illuminating and rocking the earth to its core. She wobbled before collapsing to her knees. Those around her—Vayne's soldiers, Araedians, and rebels alike—fell, too, and the entire battlefield stopped to stare at the outburst of power.

Ever since Fraiser had left to aid Ren, Roman, and Natalia, the battle had become a living nightmare. Both sides had suffered tremendously. Over at least a thousand—possibly two thousand—bodies and dozens of smoking craters littered the entire field, and the tall grass and ground were stained with blood and guts. It was impossible to tell who exactly was winning, but the sight of elements flying through the air and black armor firing against black armor made hope bubble up in Aurum's chest. If they were losing, they would've retreated already.

The stomach-churning stench of blood, mud, spilled guts, and death was thick in the air, and she could feel the tremors wracking her body from her exertion. She was tired... So very tired... She didn't know how much longer she could last, but something about the explosion told her the war wouldn't last another five minutes. This was it. They'd either won, or they'd lost.

Suddenly, a hand grabbed Aurum's shoulder. She whirled—eyes and a ball of flames in her own hand glowing bright—to find Vale standing beside her. His stolen gun was pointed at the nearest soldier clad in black, but the battlefield was still utterly frozen, everyone focused on the glorious cascade of swirling elements as loud as a battalion of armored trucks. From the corner of her eye, Aurum could see Napoleon and Lavelle off a few yards to her left. The roaring elements finally dissipated into the rainy night sky, plunging the field into darkness once again. An eery silence settled across the ridge as everyone waited to see who would exit the gates...

To see who would be victorious... Aurum held her breath, and she clutched Vale's arm, standing shakily. She was thankful to have someone she could trust by her side.

A full minute passed before all the smoke cleared, and three shadowed figures appeared at the ruined gates of the mansion. Her heart sank. *Only three...*

But then the middle figure's eyes began to glow the purest gold and silver, and the horizon beyond began to lighten. The rain finally stopped, and a masculine voice—Ren's voice—rang across the field.

"Vayne Averie is defeated! All soldiers of his army surrender now or face the consequences of fighting against the Aether!"

Gasps, cries, and shouts of pain, disbelief, victory, and shock rang out all around. Several of the soldiers surrounding Aurum and Vale glanced at each other, blinking rapidly. Their hazy eyes seemed to clear slightly, and many of them dropped their weapons. However, further down the ridge, the sounds of fighting began anew.

"On your knees!" Vale shouted, walking forward with his gun. Additional rebels and Araedians flocked over to him and Aurum with their guns pointed toward the soldiers. "Hands on your heads! Don't move, or we won't hesitate to shoot."

Aurum turned to face Napoleon and Lavelle. The majority of the soldiers near them had dropped their weapons as well, but some were still trying to fight like those beneath the ridge. They must have known that there was no future for them now with Vayne gone... Aurum could only watch as those soldiers were quickly taken out. She faced the gates where Ren stood with Natalia and Roman, who had an arm slung across the back of Natalia's shoulder. Roman winced when they tried to step forward. Panic filled Aurum. He was hurt. There was no sign of Zyra, so she must've been... *defeated* too... But Damien... What had happened to him—and Fraiser. *Where was Fraiser?* Aurum shook the dark thoughts threatening to corrupt her mind away. She was probably searching for a medic for Roman. She'd be back any minute now. Any minute...

Some of the rebels, Araedians, and those in Vayne's army who'd turned against him continued to wrangle up the remains of Vayne's loyal soldiers. The others sprinted past Aurum to reinforce and aid the fighting below the ridge. She should do something—anything—but she found it impossible to move her feet. Shock rooted her to the spot, robbing the world of all sound. She could only watch as Vale stopped before her, and Napoleon and Lavelle made their way over. Vale shook her gently, but she still couldn't move. The only thing she could hear or focus on were the words playing in her head over and over again.

It's over. It's over. It's all over. You've won.

She couldn't believe it. None of it felt real until Ren, Roman, and Natalia began to make their way from the gates toward them. The rebels had won, and once the fighting below the ridge—which already sounded as if it were almost over—was dealt with, they could all finally rest...

~

Natalia strained to keep her balance against Roman's weight. She grunted, tightening her grip on his arm. She only had to make it a few more yards, then everything would finally be okay. They wouldn't have to fight a moment longer. Ren suddenly slipped in front of her and walked to Roman's opposite side, sliding Roman's free arm across his shoulders. Together, Ren and Natalia helped Roman down the last slope toward the only thing keeping her from breaking apart entirely: her family.

Roman's weight wasn't the sole object dragging her down. The loss of Fraiser and Damien, and all the pain of this war—this *day*—was threatening to pull her below the waves and drown her. After Vale had disappeared that night all those years ago, Damien had been the one to fill the gaping hole he'd left in her chest—in her life. Who would fill that hole now? Even through Vayne's brainwashing, she'd held onto him as tightly as she could, but he was *gone*. Truly gone... Natalia gritted her teeth. She had to push the pain down, keep it hidden far, far away, so she could finally reunite with everyone she loved.

Natalia, Roman, and Ren paused before Aurum, Lavelle, Napoleon, and...

No.

It simply wasn't possible.

A feeble whine slipped between Natalia's lips. She gently slipped out from under Roman's arm, making sure he was steady against Ren before taking a hesitant step forward. Her jaw slackened, and her entire body felt numb. This wasn't real. She was dreaming. This was all a dream, and she was about to wake up because it was impossible that her *brother*...

"Talia...," Vale whispered, tears streaming down his face, that familiar face with the same black hair and blue eyes. He took a hesitant step toward her, away from Aurum's side.

Natalia didn't know when she'd started crying, or when the violent sobs had begun to escape from her chest. Or when she'd run forward and fallen into Vale's warmth and thrown her arms around him as tightly as she could, bawling into his shoulder. She didn't see the twins embrace as they too cried, or the way Aurum's face fell when Roman explained what had happened to Damien and why Fraiser wasn't standing with them now. She didn't see the tears pouring down Napoleon's cheeks, or him throwing his arms around Aurum and Roman, whose eyes never left her. All she saw and felt was Vale. Her brother... He was *alive*, and he'd kept his promise. She was not alone.

"And Damien?" Lavelle's voice suddenly broke through the haze.

Natalia took a step back from Vale, searching him up and down for any wounds before she turned to Lavelle, Aurum, and Napoleon to do the same. They were fine. All of them appeared fine besides a lot of cuts, scrapes, and bruises. Natalia opened her mouth to respond but found that the words were lodged in her throat. No matter how hard she tried, more tears spilled over her cheeks, and she choked on the words.

He's dead.

Vale grabbed her hand, and Roman took a shaky step toward her. She faced him. His golden-brown eyes were hard and never left hers as he spoke, the words short and clipped.

"Damien, my father, Zyra, and...Frasier...are all gone." Roman pointedly shifted his gaze to Vale, then back to her. "It's just us left."

A gut-wrenching silence fell over everyone, and for a few moments, they simply stood there. In the silence, Natalia could feel the waves of grief beginning to pull her down into that deep dark abyss again. She couldn't let it take her. She had to keep going—keep pushing.

"Roman." She forced a small smile onto her face, tightening her grip on Vale's hand. "Well, *everyone*... This is my brother, Vale. We grew up in Four's orphanage together. Vale, this is everyone."

Roman's eyes softened, and he extended a hand to Vale. A real smile tugged at Natalia's lips as Vale took it, and they shook.

"I didn't know you had a brother," Ren said.

Aurum let out a solemn chuckle. "None of us did until Vale told us."

Without warning, Hero and Spenser appeared at the crest of the slope that led up the ridge. Blood, mud, cuts, and bruises covered every inch of them, and Spenser was limping on his right leg. They jogged over to everyone, slightly out of breath.

"The fighting under the ridge is under control," Spenser said, shifting his weight to rest on his left leg. "Feura, Darri, and the representatives of sectors One and Two are on their way to the mansion as we speak."

Roman straightened beside Natalia. She looked at him to find his jaw set firmly, fists clenched at his sides. She knew he needed to see a doctor, but she also knew Roman was way too stubborn to get help before they'd sorted everything out.

Napoleon stepped forward, eyebrows knitting together. "What about the representative for Four?"

"We haven't been able to locate her yet." Hero frowned. "Unfortunately, I don't think she survived the fighting."

"How long do we have until the representatives arrive?" Roman asked.

Spenser shrugged. "Fifteen minutes, give or take. Why?"

"Because we're not done yet." Roman turned and began to hobble back toward the mansion.

"Roman." Natalia ran after him, catching up easily. She still had so many things to talk about with the others, especially Vale, but it could wait a little while longer. She grabbed his arm and slipped it over her shoulder again, taking some of his weight. "What are you doing?"

He leaned into her and rested his sweaty head down on hers for a moment as they slowly made their way to the gates, the others all following and asking questions close behind. "Right now, Araedia is vulnerable, and we have no idea whose hands the government will fall into. I need to get into my father's office before people we don't know or trust go through it. There's no telling what he's hidden in there, and I want to be the one who finds whatever it is first."

Natalia and Roman entered the courtyard again, skirting around the enormous crater. They paused, and Natalia's eyes flickered back and forth between Fraiser and Zyra's cold bodies and the single pair of white eyes—Vayne's eyes—lying in the center of the crater. There were no remains of Damien—of the boy she'd literally run into in the forest. Her heart ached at the thought of his smile that day... That boy had been utterly incinerated.

The twins and Napoleon appeared beside them a moment later, followed by Aurum, Vale, and Hero and Spenser. Ren's eyes began to glow gold and silver, and he waved his hand out toward Vayne's eyes. The ground shifted and slid, swallowing the eyes up and burying them deep, deep down within the earth. Ren pivoted, waving over Zyra's body, which also sank into the ground. He swept his hand over to Fraiser and paused, glancing at Roman.

He shook his head. "No, not here. We'll..." His voice broke. "...we'll get her on the way out..." Natalia squeezed his hand that she held on her shoulder, and Roman leaned into her once more.

"I'll stay here with her." Vale's voice echoed through the courtyard.

Roman and Natalia turned to face him, as did the others. Hero and Spenser exchanged a glance before nodding.

"We will, too," Hero said.

Vale dipped his head at Roman. "No one will move her until you're ready to do so."

"Thank you," Roman whispered.

Natalia offered Vale, Hero, and Spenser a smile before she and Roman turned and walked up the mansion steps with Aurum, the twins, and Napoleon behind them. Together, they pushed open the large doors and entered the gilded hallway spotted with decorative pieces, paintings, and pictures. Natalia sucked in a breath, quickly releasing it when a shiver wracked her spine. For a hall so bright with colors, it was unnaturally cold. Mud and even small droplets of blood were left in their wake, smudging the polished marble floor as they carried on down the hall and took a right. The mansion was entirely silent, and not a single servant or soldier was visible. They were alone...

Except for the hunched, old woman standing at the end of the foyer.

Everyone fell entirely still, and she slowly hobbled toward them. Natalia's breath caught in her throat at the sight of the woman's white hair. It was as white as freshly fallen snow, and her green eyes gleamed with mischief and knowledge... They gleamed with memories.

"You," Natalia whispered.

Roman and Napoleon looked to Natalia with crinkled brows, and Aurum stepped forward, her hands shaking slightly at her sides. The twins merely stood in shock. The old woman paused a few feet away and gave them a roguish grin.

"Me," she chirped.

Natalia shook her head. It wasn't possible. This woman had been through all four sectors—had been the one to tell, Aurum, Damien, and the twins about Elementals and the world beyond the walls—but now she was here. *How?* Natalia opened her mouth to speak, but she was at a loss for words. This old woman, who'd brought them all together...

"My, look how much you've all grown!" the old woman exclaimed proudly. "And look what you've accomplished."

"How?" Ren breathed. "How did you...?"

"You rebels aren't the only ones with access to the tunnels." She winked, and Natalia knew the old woman already knew all of their questions. And she had an answer for every one of them, too. "As for why I did what I did, you should know that I have lived in Araedia for a very long time. Some might say too long, but when Vayne Averie took over the sectors, built those walls, separated everyone, and began hunting Elementals and searching for the Aether, I knew there was only one way to stop him. We had to bring everyone back together, Elementals and Araedians alike. So I began to spread the truth—the truth of Valgaris—to whoever would listen.

For years, I was ridiculed and pursued by fearful people, Vayne's soldiers, and Vayne himself. I was at my wits end—nearly ready to give up—when I met a young boy named Damien Mendax. Though he'd never admit it aloud, he was the first to believe me. Then I met a young girl named Natalia Rhys. She believed me, too." She looked at Aurum and the twins. "As did a set of twins and a girl with a golden heart."

Shock. It was the only thing Natalia could think or feel. This woman had set them on their paths. The paths that had led them to one another and the rebels. And today. Roman grabbed her hand, intertwining their fingers.

"Why us?" Aurum questioned. "Why did you choose us?"

"I didn't," the old woman said, her knowing smile never leaving her face. "*You chose yourselves...*" Everyone stepped aside as the old woman hobbled through them, pausing before the turn that would lead her to the mansion doors. She turned and pointed at Ren. "You've been trying to complete the puzzle for so long. Now, you think you've done it—that you have one final piece left, but you don't. This end is only the beginning."

And with that, she disappeared around the corner. Natalia watched Ren stutter before running after her. By the look on his face when he glanced down the hall, she knew the old woman was gone. Natalia couldn't help her slight huff of amusement. Over all these years, the woman hadn't changed a bit. She was still a talker, and once she'd finished her piece, she still disappeared without a trace. Some things never changed...

Napoleon shook his head in disbelief. "I have *so* many questions."

"Don't we all...," Lavelle murmured.

Roman's jaw tightened, and he gently let go of Natalia's hand, continuing on down the hall. "Let's keep moving."

He was right. They needed to hurry and get into Vayne's office. Besides, Natalia had the feeling it wouldn't be the last time she saw the old woman. She put the thought aside and followed after him.

She couldn't help but stare at everything they passed. She'd never seen such finery in her life, and the fact that people lived like this was nearly impossible for her to grasp. What did one do with so many things? Roman cut down another hallway with a single door at the end. They passed pictures of the construction of the walls and—Natalia's eyes narrowed on a painting of three people. A middle-aged man with black hair and happy, light brown eyes smiled with his arm around the waist of a woman with brown hair and blue eyes. Her smile was ethereal. One of her arms was tucked behind the man's back, and both of their free hands sat on the shoulders of a young boy before them. Natalia slowed, turning her head to peer closer as they passed. A mop of wild dark hair sat upon the boy's head, and his eyes were a sparkling brown with honey-amber highlights. The grin that lightened his face was unmistakable. Natalia looked at Roman, whose jaw was still set, and his gaze was trained, unblinkingly, straight ahead.

"Your mother was stunning," she murmured.

Roman flashed her a small, solemn smile. "Yes, she was."

They hobbled to the door and stopped, allowing Napoleon to step ahead and open it. She felt Roman take a deep breath before they walked inside. If the hallways of the mansion were cold, Vayne's office was a perilous blizzard. The marble floors, furniture, and desk seemed to be painted in the slate gray light that peeked in through the windows. Everything felt dry, cold, and empty, and Natalia found herself very glad that Roman, Napoleon, Ren, Lavelle, and Aurum were with her now. Vayne's office was daunting.

"Anything specific we're looking for?" Aurum asked, her voice void of all emotion.

Natalia glanced at her and reached out to touch her arm. Aurum met her gaze, and Natalia could've sworn her heart cracked a little. The utter despair and exhaustion in her eyes were so…sad… And she looked so tired. They all did. The rebels had won the war, but Natalia couldn't help but feel that they'd lost miserably. By the look on Napoleon and the twins' faces, they felt the same. They needed to search through Vayne's office quickly so they could finish this and finally rest. But a part of Natalia didn't want to rest—was afraid to. Who would piece their society back together? Feura and Darri? They couldn't bare the weight of all four sectors by themselves… What about the sector representatives that Vayne had appointed? What would they do? And her mind—the thing that scared her the most… What would her mind do once everyone stopped working and everything fell quiet? What demons would haunt her then?

Roman shook his head. "No, but whatever it is, it won't be out in plain sight. My father is—was—fond of secret compartments and such…"

Aurum nodded before walking to one of the many bookcases lining the walls. Napoleon and Lavelle, walking closely together, began to draw back the red curtains over the windows. Ren shuffled over to peer outside, while Roman and Natalia hobbled over to his father's desk. They rounded it, and Natalia pulled the chair back along the floor, helping Roman down into it.

"How are you feeling?" she asked.

"Better now that I know that that guy was Vale."

Natalia let out a quiet chuckle, but she knew that the humor was a mask for him. He was clearly fighting hard to keep his pain locked away—the mental and physical pain. She didn't blame him. After all, she was doing the same. The cuts in her left arm from the metal shards that had embedded in her skin after she and Fraiser had rammed One's gates were throbbing, and she was quite positive that one of her ribs was broken. Roman opened the first of many drawers built into the right side of the desk, while she knelt next to him and began searching through the drawers on the left.

For several minutes, the office was silent, and both Natalia and Roman found nothing but useless documents and paperwork. Aurum and Ren, who had joined her at the bookshelves, came up empty-handed as well.

"What is this?" Napoleon suddenly asked.

Everyone turned to face him and Lavelle and the golden door behind the velvet curtain they'd drawn back.

"My father's entrance into the dungeons and labs," Roman answered, his mouth a hard line.

"Close it," Lavelle whispered. "I never want to go back down there again."

"We can have others search it later if need be," Ren said as Napoleon let the curtain fall back into place.

The sound of Roman opening the bottom right drawer had Natalia turning to face him. Other than a few thin stacks of papers, it was empty. Roman cursed, slamming his fist down against the drawer with a hollow *thump*. Everyone froze, and Natalia could feel her heartbeat quickening in her chest. Roman ripped the papers out, tapping against the bottom again. Another hollow *thump*. Aurum, Napoleon, and the twins ran over, gathering around Natalia and Roman.

"Does anyone have a knife?" Roman asked.

"Here," Ren said, weaving around the chair. His eyes began to glow, and a knife of ice appeared in his hand. He held it out to Roman.

Roman grabbed it hesitantly, brows raised.

"Did you just form that without a water source?" Natalia whispered, shock flooding through her. Water Elementals had to have sources to use their element... But Ren wasn't just any Elemental any more.

"Yeah, I guess I did...," he murmured.

Napoleon shrugged. "Must be an Aether perk."

"Enough talk," Aurum said. "Open the damn drawer."

Natalia bit the inside of her cheek. She didn't know what exactly Roman was looking for—or what he'd just found—but she understood why he was doing it. If his father had left sensitive documents, weapons, plans, or something of the sort that didn't need to fall into another set of dangerous hands, they needed to get rid of it.

Roman slammed the blade down between the bottom of the drawer and its wall, pushing against the hilt. The sound of wood creaking and splitting filled the air. He gave another hard push. The bottom of the drawer popped up a moment later. Roman was right. His father really had loved secret compartments. Natalia leaned over the arm of the chair to watch as he quickly pulled up the rest of the bottom and set it on the floor. Her brows knit together at the sight of an old, large leather-bound book. Carefully, Roman grabbed the book and softly placed it on his father's desk. A silence loomed over everyone as they stared at the worn leather and thick, yellowing pages. Natalia's head whirled. There was no telling what was inked on those pages, but if Vayne had kept it hidden, it had to be important. Or dangerous.

Suddenly, Lavelle reached out, flipping it open to the first page. She gasped. Aurum's and Ren's mouths dropped, and Napoleon's eyes didn't leave the page. Roman was scarily still, but Natalia...

Natalia smiled.

Because before her, etched in pitch black ink were four walls—the sectors. Around them, trees and hills rolled over the southern span of the continent, Valgaris, stretching up half of the western coastline until they reached the dark second half that led up into lands of ice far on the northern tip of the land. To the east, the hills flattened out into a plain that led into a large forest, spanning across the entire eastern coast. Lakes and rivers spotted the map, and several islands scattered around the edges of the continent. But at the very center, there was nothing but a circular wall. A wall encasing buildings...

Another city...

The End of Book One

ABOUT THE AUTHOR

A.J. Wolfe is a native Mississippian who'd rather spend her time with books than people. When not writing or re-reading *Throne of Glass* or *Pride and Prejudice*, she can be found harassing her two dogs, Lila and Lulu, scrounging around the house for morsels of chocolate, listening to an unhealthy amount of music, and playing video games.

A.J. has been writing ever since she could form coherent sentences, but she didn't realize how badly she wanted to write a complete book until she read the Inheritance Cycle by Christopher Paolini.

A.J.'s favorite things include being a fantasy nerd, exquisite sarcasm, Manchester City, traveling, and her family.

You can connect with her at
AJ-Wolfe.com
@ajwolfewrites